"Invite me in, Mia."

And then his lips were on hers again, taking her in another mind-numbing kiss. Her soul was seared, branded by a man she hardly knew. Yet it felt right. So very right. How could she be so attracted to the same man her sister had slept with? Conceived a baby with? This wasn't going to happen. It couldn't.

Her little plan was backfiring.

Because as much as the battle raged inside her head with all those thoughts, she couldn't stop kissing Adam. She couldn't stop wanting him. She hadn't yet said yes or no and his kisses kept coming, delving and probing her mouth, his lips teasing and tempting hers. A strangled sound rose from her throat. "Adam."

She was breathless, out of oxygen and falling fast.

He was an amazing kisser.

He was probably an amazing lover.

How long had it been since she'd been flipped inside out like this?

Maybe never.

She slipped a hand into her beaded purse, grabbed for her key and pressed it into his hand. "You're invited in," she said, her voice a raspy whisper.

***

The Billi

is pa   ies,

THE BILLIONAIRE'S DADDY TEST

BY
CHARLENE SANDS

Charlene Sands is a *USA TODAY* bestselling author of more than thirty-five romance novels, writing sensual contemporary romances and stories of the Old West. Her books have been honored with a National Readers' Choice Award, a CataRomance Reviewers' Choice Award, and she's a double recipient of the Booksellers' Best Award. She belongs to the Orange County chapter and the Los Angeles chapter of RWA.

Charlene writes "hunky heroes with heart." She knows a little something about true romance—she married her high school sweetheart! When not writing, Charlene enjoys sunny Pacific beaches, great coffee, reading books from her favorite authors and spending time with her family. You can find her on Facebook and Twitter. Charlene loves to hear from her readers! You can write her at PO Box 4883, West Hills, CA 91308, USA, or sign up for her newsletter for fun blogs and ongoing contests at www.charlenesands.com.

To the two new babies in my life!
You are welcomed and loved so much.
With four "princesses" now, you and your sisters have
made my "baby" research so much fun!
I am truly blessed.

One

Adam Chase had a right to know his baby daughter.

Mia couldn't deny that, but her heart still bled as if a dozen knives were piercing her. Darn her conscience for leading her to Moonlight Beach this morning. Her toes sifted through sand as she walked along the shoreline, flip-flops in hand. It was cooler than she'd expected; the fog flowing in from the sea coated the bright beach with a layer of gloom. Was it an omen? Had she made the wrong choice in coming here today? The image of Rose's innocent little face popped into her mind. Sweet Cheeks, she called her, because she had the rosiest cheeks of any baby Mia had ever seen. Her lips were perfectly pink, and when she'd smiled her first little baby smile, Mia had melted.

Rose was all Mia had left of her sister, Anna.

Mia shifted her gaze to the ocean. Just as she'd hoped, she spotted a male figure swimming way beyond the breaking waves hitting the shore. He was doing laps as if there were roped-off columns keeping him on point. If the scant research she'd found was anything to go by, it was surely him. Adam Chase, world-class architect, lived at the beach, was a recluse by nature and an avid swimmer. It only made sense he'd do his daily laps early, before the beach was populated.

A breeze lifted her hair, and goose bumps erupted on her arms. She shivered, partly from the cold, but also because what she came here to do was monumental. She'd have to be made of stone not to be frightened right now.

She didn't know what she'd say to him. She'd rehearsed a thousand and one lines, but never once had she practiced the truth.

With another glance at the water, she spotted him swimming in. Her throat tightened. It was time for the show, whatever that was. Mia was good at thinking on her feet. She calculated her steps carefully, so she'd intersect with him on the sand. Her hair lifted in the breeze, and another shiver racked her body. He stopped swimming and rose up from the shallow water, his shoulders broad as a Viking's. Her heart thumped a little faster. He came forward in long smooth strides. She scanned his iron chest, rippled with muscle—all that grace and power. The few pictures she'd found in her research hadn't done him justice. He was out-and-out beautiful in a godly way and so very tall.

He shook his head, and the sun-streaked tendrils of his hair rained droplets down along his shoulders.

"Ow!" Something pricked her foot from underneath. Pain slashed the soft pad and a sharp sting burned. She grabbed her foot and plunked down in the sand. Blood spurted out instantly. Gently, she brushed the sticky sand away and gasped when she saw the damage. Her foot was cut, slashed by a broken beer bottle she spied sticking out of the earth like a mini-skyscraper. If she hadn't been gawking...

"Are you hurt?" The deep voice reverberated in her ears, and she lifted her eyes to Adam Chase's concerned face.

"Oh, uh." She nodded. "Yes. I'm cut."

"Damn kids," he said, glancing at the broken bottle. He took her hand and placed it on the bridge of her foot. "Put pressure here and hang on a sec. I'll be right back."

"Th-thanks."

She applied pressure, squeezing her foot tight. It began to feel a little better, and the stinging dissipated. She glimpsed Adam as he jogged away. Her rescuer was just as appealing from the backside. Tanned legs, perfect butt and a strong back. She sighed. It was hardly the way she'd hoped to meet the very private Adam Chase, but it would have to do.

He returned a few seconds later holding a navy-blue-and-white beach towel. He knelt by her side. "Okay, I'm going to wrap it. That should stop the bleeding."

A huge wave crashed onto the shore, and water washed over her thighs. Adam noticed, his gaze darting through amazingly long lashes and roving over her legs. A warm rush of heat entered her belly. She wore white cotton shorts and a turquoise tank top. She'd wanted to appear like any other beachgoer taking a leisurely morning stroll along the water's edge, when in fact she'd deliberated over what to wear this morning for thirty minutes.

Now Adam Chase was touching her cautiously. His head down and a few strands of hair falling on his forehead, he performed the task as if it were an everyday occurrence. She had to admire him. "You seem to know what you're doing."

"Three years lifeguarding will do that to you." He glanced up and smiled, flashing a beautiful set of white teeth.

That smile buoyed her spirit a little.

"I'm Adam," he said.

"Mia."

"Nice to meet you, Mia."

"Uh, same here."

He finished his work, and her foot was tied tightly but with an excess of material hanging down. She'd never be able to walk away with any dignity. The makeshift tourniquet was ugly and cumbersome, but it seemed to do the trick. The bleeding was contained.

"Do you live close by?" he asked.

"Not really. I thought I'd go for a stroll along the beach this morning."

"Do you have any beach gear?"

She nodded. "It's about a mile up the beach." She pointed north. "That way."

Adam sat up on his knees and peered down at her, rubbing the back of his neck. "You really should have that cleaned and bandaged right away. It's a sizable gash."

She shivered. "Okay."

The water crept up to their legs again.

Adam frowned and glanced at her encumbered foot.

Pushing off from the sand, she tried to rise. "Oh!" Putting her weight on her foot burned like crazy. She bit her lip to keep from crying out any more and lowered herself back down onto the sand.

Adams's eyes softened. "Listen, I know we've just met, but I live right over there." He gestured to the biggest modern mansion on the beach. "I promise you, I'm not a serial killer or anything, but I have antiseptic and bandages in my house, and I can have you patched up pretty quickly."

Mia glanced around. No one else was on the beach. Wasn't this what she'd wanted? A chance to get to know Adam Chase? She knew darn well he wasn't a serial killer. All she knew was that he liked his privacy, he didn't go out much and—most important of all—he was Rose's father.

She could write volumes about what she didn't know about Adam Chase. And that's exactly why she'd come here—to find out what kind of man he truly was.

Rose's future was riding on it.

"I guess that would be okay."

Come to think of it, no one knew where she was today. Rose was with her great-grandmother. If Adam did have evil on his mind, it would be a long time before anyone came looking…

The mountain of a man scooped her up, and she gasped. *Pay attention, Mia.* Her pulse sped as he nestled her into his chest. His arms secure about her body, he began to carry her away from the water's edge. On instinct, she roped her arms around his neck. Water drops remained on his shoulders, cooling his skin where her hands entwined.

"Comfy?" A wry smile pulled at his lips.

Speechless, she nodded and gazed into his eyes. There were steely flecks layered over gray irises, soulful shadows and as mysterious as a deep water well. Oddly, she didn't feel *un*comfy in his arms, even though they were complete strangers.

"Good. Couldn't think of a faster way to get you to the house."

"Thank you?" she squeaked.

He didn't respond, keeping his eyes straight ahead. She relaxed a little until her foot throbbed. Little jabs of pain wound all around the bottom of her foot. She stifled a shriek when a few bright red drops of blood seeped from the towel onto the sand.

"Does it hurt?" he asked.

"Yes, this is…*awful*." She barely got the word out. Adam Chase or not, she wanted to crawl into a hole. What a way to meet a man. Any minute now, she'd probably bleed all over his gorgeous house.

"Awful?" He seemed to take exception with that. She wasn't complaining about his sudden caveman move, how he'd plucked her into his arms so easily. No, that part had been, well, amazing. But she felt like a helpless wounded animal. She couldn't even stand on her own two feet.

"Embarrassing," she muttered.

"No need to be embarrassed."

His stride was long and smooth as he moved over the sand toward his mansion. Up close, the detail of his craft showed in the trim of wide expansive windows, the texture of the stucco, the unique decorative double glass doors and the liberating feel of an outdoor living space facing the ocean—a billionaire's version of a veranda. Fireplaces, sitting areas with circular couches, overhead beams and stone floors all made up the outskirts of his house. The veranda was twice the size of her little Santa Monica apartment, and that was only a fraction of what she could see. Inside must be magnificent.

"Here we are," he said, steps away from the dream house.

"Uh, do you think we could stay out here?" She pointed to the enormous outside patio.

He blinked, those dark gray eyes twinkling. "Sure. If you feel safer outside."

"Oh no, it's not that."

His perfectly formed eyebrows arched upward. "No?"

"I don't want to ruin your carpeting or anything." Lord knew, she made a decent living at First Clips, but if she destroyed something in the mansion, it could take years to pay off a replacement.

"My carpet?" His smile could melt Mount Shasta. "There's not a shred of carpet in the house. I promise to keep you away from any rugs lying about."

"Oh, uh. Fine then."

He moved through the front doors easily and entered a massive foyer, where inlaid marble and intricate stone patterns led to a winding staircase. She gulped at the tasteful opulence. She clamped her mouth shut and held back a sigh from her lips. Was it the unexpected nuances she found in his stunning home, or was it the man himself who caused such a flurry in the pit of her stomach? His size commanded attention, the breadth of his shoulders, the bronze tone of his skin and, yes, the fact that he was shirtless and wet, his moisture clinging to her own clothes, his hands gripping the backs of her thighs.

A thrill ran through her, overriding her embarrassment.

He began to climb the stairs.

"Where are we going?" Up to his lair?

"The first aid supplies are in my bathroom. Mary is out shopping, or I'd have her go get them for us."

"Mary? Your girlfriend?"

His gaze slipped over to her. "My housekeeper."

"Oh." *Of course.*

"Have you lived here long?" She needed lessons in small talk.

"Long enough."

"The house is beautiful. Did you decorate it yourself?"

"I had some help."

Evasive but not rude. "I'm sorry about this. You probably have better things to do than play nursemaid to me."

"Like I said, I have mad lifeguarding skills."

Yes. Yes, he did.

Adam set the woman down on the bathroom counter. Long black lashes lifted and almond-shaped eyes, green as a spring meadow, followed his every movement. From what he could tell, she didn't have an ounce of makeup on her face. She didn't need it. Her beauty seemed natural, her face delicately sculpted, glowing in warm tones. Her mouth was shaped like a heart in the most subtle way, and her skin was soft as butter. His palms still tingled from holding the underside of her thighs as he'd lifted her off the hot sand. "Here we go. Just let me get a shirt and my glasses."

He grabbed the first shirt he found in his bedroom drawer and then came up with a pair of wire-rimmed glasses. Next he selected the medical supplies he'd need out of a closet in his bathroom. He found what he needed easily: gauze, peroxide, antibacterial cream. When it came to keeping things organized, he was meticulous. It was the way he rolled, and he'd taken more than a fair share of heat about it from everyone who knew him. That aside, he'd bet he'd shock his college pals if they saw the worn, tattered and faded to ghost-blue UCLA Bruin T-shirt he'd just thrown on. Adam almost cracked a smile. It was so unlike him; yet once a Bruin, always a Bruin. He wouldn't part with his shirt. He set his glasses onto the bridge of his nose. "Okay. Here goes. Ready?"

She nodded. "Go ahead."

Gently, he unwound the towel from her foot. "I want to take a better look at that gash."

"You're really nice for doing this," she said softly.

"Hmm."

"What kind of work do you do?" she asked.

He didn't take his eyes off her foot. It was small and delicate, and he was careful with her, surveying the damage and elevating the heel. "Uh, I'm self-employed."

"It's just that, well, this house is magnificent."

"Thank you."

"Is it just you and Mary living here?"

"Sometimes. Mia, do you think you could swivel the rest of your body up on the counter, near the sink, so I can see the foot a little better?"

"I think so." Holding the heel of her foot, he helped guide her legs onto the counter. She had to scoot back and pivot a bit until she filled half the length of the long cocoa marble commode. She couldn't be more than five foot five. Her foot hovered over the sink.

A tank top and white shorts showed off her sun-kissed body. Her legs were long and lean like a dancer's. Seeing her sprawled out before him, the entire Mia package was first-class gorgeous. He caught himself staring at her reflection. *Focus, Adam. Be a Good Samaritan.*

"So you went to UCLA?" she asked.

"Yeah. Undergrad." He stroked his chin and hesitated, staring at her foot. It had been years since his lifeguarding days. He'd never had qualms about giving first aid before. He'd done it a hundred times, including giving CPR to a man in his sixties. That hadn't been fun, but the man had survived and, years later, gratefully commissioned Adam to design a resort home on the French Riviera. It had been one of his first big architectural projects. But this was different somehow, with Mia, the beauty who had landed at his feet on the beach.

"Adam?"

He looked at her. A fleeting thought entered his head. For a woman in distress, she sure asked a lot of questions. It wouldn't be the first time someone tried an unorthodox way to interview him. But surely not Mia. Her foot was slashed pretty badly. Some women liked to talk when they were nervous. Did he make her nervous?

"Is it okay if I wash your foot?"

Her lovely olive complexion colored, and a flash of hesitation entered her eyes. "Do you have a foot fetish or anything?"

He grinned. Maybe he did make her nervous. "Nope. No fetishes at all."

She made a little noise when she inhaled. "Good to know. Okay."

He filled the sink with warm water. "Let me know if it hurts."

She nodded, squeezed her eyes shut and clenched her legs.

"Try to relax, Mia."

Her expression softened, and she opened her eyes. He rotated her slim ankle over the sink with one hand and splashed warm water onto her foot. Using a dollop of antibacterial liquid soap, he cleansed the area thoroughly with a soft washcloth. Heat rose up his neck. It was about as intimate as he'd been with a woman in months, and Mia, with her cotton-candy-pink toenails, endless legs and beautiful face was 100 percent woman. "The good news is, the bleeding has stopped."

"Wonderful. Now I can stop worrying about destroying your furniture."

"Is that what you're worried about?" He furrowed his brow.

"After the foot fetish thing, yes."

He shook his head and fought the smile trying to break his concentration. Not too many people made him smile, and Mia had already done that several times. "You can stop worrying. I don't think you'll need stitches either. Luckily, the gash isn't as deep as it looked. It's long, though, and it might be painful for you to walk on for a day or two. You can have a doctor take a look, just to make sure."

She said nothing.

He dabbed the cut with peroxide, and bubbles clustered up. Next he lathered her wound with antibiotic cream.

"How're you doing?" He lifted his head, and her face was there, so close, obviously watching his ministrations. Their eyes met, and he swallowed hard. He could swim a mile in her pretty green eyes.

She took a second to answer. "I'm, uh, doing well."

It was quiet in the house, just the two of them, Adam's hand clamping her ankle gently. "That's…good. I'll be done in a second." He cleared his throat and picked up the bandages. "I'm going to wrap this kind of tight."

He caught Mia glancing at his left hand, focusing on his ring finger, as in no white tan lines, and then her lips curled up. "I'm ready."

Suddenly, he'd never been happier that he was romantically unattached than right at that moment.

After Adam had patched her up, Mia's stomach had shamefully grumbled as he'd helped her down from the bathroom counter. She'd probably turned ten shades of red when the unladylike sound echoed against the walls. Luckily, he'd only smiled and had graciously invited her to breakfast. She had to keep her foot elevated for a little while, he'd said, and Mia had been more than willing to continue to spend time with him.

To get the scoop on him. It would take some doing; he was tight-lipped. Making conversation was not in his wheelhouse. But so many other things were. Like the way he'd immediately come to her aid on the beach, how thoughtful he'd been afterward, carrying her into his house, and how deadly handsome he looked behind those wire-rimmed glasses. *Oh, Mama!*

She sat in a comfortable chaise chair in the open-air terrace off a kitchen a chef would dream about. Part of the terrace was shaded by an overhead balcony. Adam was seated to her right at the table. Her foot was propped on another chair. Both faced the Pacific.

The morning gloom was beginning to lift, the sun breaking through and the sound of waves hitting the shore penetrating her ears. White curtains billowed behind her as she sipped coffee from a gold-rimmed china cup. Adam knew how to live. It was all so decadent, except that Adam, for all his good looks and obvious wealth, seemed down-to-earth even if he didn't talk about himself much. And she had to admit, her Viking warrior looked more like a beach bum in khaki shorts and a beaten-down Bruins T-shirt. But she still hadn't found out much about him.

"So you work as a hairdresser?" he said.

"Actually, I own the shop but I don't cut hair. I have two employees who do." She gauged his reaction and didn't elaborate that First Clips, her shop, catered to children. The hairdressers wore costumes and the little girls sat on princess thrones, while the boys sat in rocket ships to have their hair cut. Afterward, the newly groomed kids were rewarded with tiaras or rocket goggles. Mia was proud of their business. Anna had developed the idea and had been the main hairstylist while Mia ran the financial end of things. She had to be careful about what she revealed about First Clips. If Anna had confided in him about their business, he might connect the dots and realize Mia wasn't exactly an innocent bystander out for a beach stroll this morning.

Mary, his sixtysomething housekeeper, approached the table and served platters of poached eggs, maple bacon, fresh biscuits and an assortment of pastries.

"Thank you," she said. "The coffee is delicious." Adam had brought it out from the kitchen earlier.

"Mary, this is Mia," he said. "She had an accident on the beach this morning."

"Oh, dear." Mary's kind pale blue eyes darted to her bandaged foot. "Are you all right?"

"I think I will be, thanks to Adam. I stepped on a broken bottle."

Mary shook her head. "Those stupid kids…always hanging around after dark." Her hand went to her mouth immediately. "Sorry. It's just that they're in high school and shouldn't be drinking beer and doing who knows what else on the beach. Adam has talked about having them arrested."

"Maybe I should," he muttered, and she got the idea he wasn't fully committed to the idea. "Or maybe I'll teach them a lesson."

"How?" Mary asked.

"I've got a few things bouncing around in my head."

"Well, I wish you would," she said, and Mia got the impression Mary had some clout in Adam's household. "It's very nice to meet you, Mia."

"Nice meeting you, too."

"Thanks, Mary. The food looks delicious," he said. Mary retreated to the kitchen, and Adam pointed to the dishes of food. "Dig in. I know you're hungry." His lips twitched. When he smiled, something pinged inside her.

She fixed herself a plate of eggs and buttered a biscuit, leaving the bacon and pastries aside, while Adam filled his plate with a little of everything. "So you said you're self-employed. What kind of work do you do?"

He slathered butter onto his biscuit. "I design things," he said, then filled his mouth and chewed.

"What kind of things?" she pressed. The man really didn't like talking about himself.

He shrugged. "Homes, resorts, villas."

She bit into her eggs and leaned back, contemplating. "I bet you do a lot of traveling."

"Not really."

"So you're a homebody?"

He shrugged again. "It's not a bad thing, is it?"

"No, I'm sort of a homebody myself, actually." Now that she was raising Rose, she didn't have time for anything other than work and baby. It was fine by her. Her heart ached every time she thought about giving Rose up. She didn't know if she could do it. Meeting Adam was the first step, and she almost didn't want to take any more. Why couldn't he have been a loser? Why couldn't he have been a jerk? And why on earth was she so hopelessly attracted to him?

Had he been married? Did he have a harem of girlfriends? Or any nasty habits, like drugs or gambling or a sex addiction? Mia's mind whirled with possibilities, but nothing seemed to suit him. But wasn't that what people said about their neighbors when it was discovered they were violent terrorists or killers? "He seemed like such a nice man, quiet, kept to himself."

Okay, so her imagination was running wild. She still didn't know enough about Adam. She'd have to find a way to spend more time with him.

Rose was worth the trouble.

Rose was worth…everything.

"You're not going to be able to walk back," Adam said.

She glanced at her foot still elevated on the chair. Breakfast was over, and her heart started thumping against her chest the way it did just before panic set in. She needed more time. She hadn't found out anything personal about Adam yet, other than he was filthy rich and truly had mad first aid skills. Her foot was feeling much better, wrapped tightly, but she hadn't tried to get up yet. Adam had carried her to her seat on the shaded veranda.

She knew her flip-flops would flop. She couldn't walk in them in the sand, not with the bandage on her foot.

"I don't have a choice."

Adam cocked his head to the side, and his lips twisted. "I have a car, you know."

She began shaking her head. "I can't impose on your day any more. I'll get back on my own."

She pulled her legs down and scooted her chair back as she rose. "You've already done en—" Searing jabs pricked at the ball of her foot. She clenched her teeth and keeled to the right, taking pressure off the wound. She grabbed for the table, and Adam was beside her instantly, his big hands bracing her shoulders.

"Whoa. See, I didn't think you could walk."

"I, uh." Her shoulders fell. "Maybe you're right."

And for the third time today, she was lifted up in Adam's strong arms. He'd excused himself while Mary was cooking breakfast and taken a quick shower and now his scent wafted to her nose—a strong, clean, entirely too sexy smell that floated all around her.

"This is getting to be a habit," she said softly.

He made a quick adjustment, tucking her gently in again, and gave her a glance. "It's necessary."

"And you always do what's necessary?"

"I try to."

He began walking, then stopped and bent his body so she could grab her turquoise flip-flops off the kitchen counter. "Got them?"

"I got them."

"Hang on."

She was. Clinging to him and enjoying the ride.

Two

Adam carried Mia down a long corridor heading to the garage. After traveling about twenty steps, the hallway opened to a giant circular room and a streamlined convertible Rolls-Royce popped into her line of vision. The car, a work of art in itself, was parked showroom-style in the center of the round room. She'd never seen such luxury before and was suddenly stunningly aware of the vast differences between Adam Chase and Mia D'Angelo.

She took her eyes off the car and scanned the room. A gallery of framed artwork hung on the surrounding walls and her gaze stopped on a brilliant mosaic mural that encompassed about one-third of the gallery. Her mouth hung open in awe. She pressed her lips together tightly and hoped her gawking wasn't noticed.

"Adam, you have your own bat cave?"

His lips twitched. He surveyed the room thoughtfully. "No one's ever described it quite like that before," he said.

"How many people have seen this?"

"Not many."

"Ah, so it *is* your bat cave. You keep it a secret."

"I had this idea when I was designing the house and it wouldn't leave me alone. I had to see it through."

Score one for his perseverance.

"I don't know much about great works of art, but this gallery is amazing. Are you an art junkie?" she asked.

"More like I appreciate beauty. In all forms." His eyes

touched over her face, admiring, measuring and thoughtful. Heat prickled at the back of her neck. If he was paying her a compliment, she wouldn't acknowledge it verbally. She couldn't help it if having a gorgeous man hold her in her arms and whisper sweet words in her ear made her bead up with sweat. But she wasn't here to flirt, fawn or fantasize. She needed to finesse answers out of him. Period.

He stepped onto the platform that housed the car and opened the passenger door of the Rolls-Royce. "What are you doing?"

"Taking you home."

"In this? How? I mean, the car's a part of your gallery. And in case you haven't noticed, there's no garage door anywhere." She double-checked her surroundings. No, she wasn't mistaken. But just in case the bat cave had secret walls, she asked, "Is there?"

"No, no garage door, but an elevator."

Again her gaze circled the room. "Where?"

"We're standing on it. Now let me get you into the car."

Buttery leather seats cushioned her bottom as he lowered her into the Rolls, his beautiful Nordic face inches from her. The scent of him surrounded her in a halo of arousing aroma. Her breath hitched, she hoped silently. Mia, stop drooling.

"Can you manage the seat belt?" he asked.

Her foot was all bandaged up, not her hands, but still a fleeting thought touched her mind of Adam gently tucking her into the seat belt. "Of course."

He backed away and came around to the other end of the car and climbed in. "Ready?"

"For?"

"Don't be alarmed. We're going to start moving down."

He pressed a few buttons, and noises that sounded like a plane's landing gear opening up, filled the room. Mia had a faint notion that they were going to take off somehow. But then the platform began a slow and easy descent as the main floor of Adam's house began to disappear. Grandma Tess would call it an "E" ticket ride.

She looked up and the ceiling was closing again, kind of like the Superdome. Adam's gallery had a replacement floor. If he designed this, he was certainly an architectural and mechanical genius.

Score one more for Adam Chase.

Smooth as glass, they landed in a garage on the street level. More noises erupted, she imagined to secure the car elevator onto the ground floor. Inside the spacious garage, three other cars were parked. "Were these cars out of gas?" she asked.

A chuckle rumbled from his throat. "I thought this would be fastest and easier for you. And to be honest, it's been a while since I've taken the Rolls out."

She liked honesty, but surely he wasn't trying to impress her? He'd already done that the second he'd strode out of the ocean and come to her aid.

A Jag, an all-terrain Jeep and a little sports car were outdone by the Rolls, yet she wouldn't turn any one of them down if offered. "So, are you a car fanatic?"

He revved the engine and pressed the remote control. The garage door opened, and sunshine poured in. "So many questions, Mia. Just sit back, stretch out your leg and enjoy the ride."

What choice did she have? Adam clearly didn't like talking about himself. Anna's dying words rang in her head and seized her heart. Clutching her sister's hand, her plea had been weak but so determined. "Adam Chase, the baby's real father. Architect. One night…that's all I know. Find him."

Anna had been more adventurous than Mia, but now she understood why she'd known little about the man who'd fathered her child. Anna had probably done most of the talking. It had been during the lowest part of her sister's life, when she thought she'd lost Edward forever. Maybe neither one of them had done much talking.

She glanced at Adam's profile as he put the car in gear, his wrist resting on the steering wheel. Chiseled cheekbones, thoughtful gray eyes, strong jaw. His hair, kissed by the sun, was cropped short and straight. No rings on his fingers. Again, she wondered if he had a girlfriend or three. Everything about him, his house, his cars, his good looks, screamed babe magnet, yet oddly, her gut was telling her something different, something she couldn't put her finger on. And that's why she had to find a way to delay her departure. She didn't have enough to go on. She certainly couldn't turn her sweet-cheeked baby Rose over to him. Not yet.

He might not even want her.

Perish the thought. Who wouldn't want that beautiful baby?

"Are you sure you don't want me to drive you home?" he asked. "You can have someone pick up your car later if you can't drive comfortably."

"Oh no. Please. Just drive me to my car. It's not that far, and I'm sure I can drive."

Adam took his eyes off the road and turned to her. "Okay, if you're sure." He didn't seem convinced.

"My foot's feeling better already. I'm sure."

He nodded and sighed, turning his attention back to the road.

"How far?"

"I'm parked at lifeguard station number three."

"Got it."

It was less than a mile, and she kept her focus on the glossy waters of Moonlight Beach as he drove the rest of the way in silence. Too soon, they entered the parking lot. "There's my car." She pointed to her white Toyota Camry. He pulled up next to it. The Rolls looked out of place in a parking lot full of soccer-mom vans and family sedans. A mustard-yellow school bus was unloading a gaggle of giggling children.

"Hang on," he said. "I'll get your gear. Just show me where it is on the beach."

Whoops. She'd lied about that. She didn't have so much as a beach towel on the sand. Blinking, she stalled for time. "Oh, I guess I forgot. I must have put everything in my trunk before I took my walk."

Adam didn't seem fazed, and she sighed, relieved. He climbed out of the car, jaunted around the front end of the Rolls and stopped on the passenger side. She opened the car door, and he was there, ready to help her out.

His hands were on her again, lifting her, and a warm jolt catapulted down to her belly. She'd never felt anything quite like it before, this fuzzy don't-stop-touching-me kind of sensation that rattled her brain and melted her insides.

He set her down, and she put weight on her foot. "I'm okay," she said, gazing into eyes softened by concern.

"You're sure?"

"If you can just help me to my car, I'll be fine."

He wrapped his arm around her waist, and there it was again—warm, gooey sensations swimming through her body. She half hopped, half walked as he carefully guided her to the driver's side of the car.

"Your keys?" he asked.

She dug her hand into the front pocket of her shorts and came up with her car key. "Right here."

He stared at her. "Well, then. You're set."

"Yes."

Neither one of them moved. Not a muscle. Not a twitch.

Around them noises of an awakening beach pitched into the air, children's laughter, babies crying, the roar of the waves hitting the shore, seagulls squawking, and still, it was as if they were alone. The beating of her heart pounded in her skull. Adam wasn't going to say anything more, although some part of her believed he wanted to.

She rose up on tiptoes, lifted her eyes fully to his and

planted a kiss on his cheek. "Thank you, Adam. You've been very sweet."

His mouth wrenched up. "Welcome."

"I'd love to repay you for your kindness by cooking you one of my grandmother's favorite Tuscan dishes, but—"

"But?" His brows arched. He seemed interested, thank goodness.

"My stove is on the blink." Not exactly a lie. Two burners were out and the oven *was* temperamental.

He shook his head. "There's no need to repay me for anything."

Her hopes plummeted, yet she kept a smile on her face.

"But I love Italian food, so how about cooking that meal at my place when you're up to it?"

At his place? In that gorgeous state-of-the-art kitchen? Thank goodness for small miracles. "I'd love to. Saturday night around seven?" That would give her three days to heal.

"Sounds good."

It was a date. Well, not a date.

She was on a mission and she couldn't forget that.

Even if her mouth still tingled from the taste of his skin on her lips.

Adam removed his glasses and set them down on the drafting table. He leaned back in his seat and sighed. His tired eyes needed a rest. He closed them and pinched the bridge of his nose as seconds ticked by. How long had he been at it? He turned his wrist and glanced at his watch. Seven hours straight. The villa off the southern coast of Spain he was designing was coming along nicely. But his eyes were crossing, and not even the breezes blowing into his office window were enough to keep him focused. He needed a break.

And it was all because of a beautiful woman named Mia. He'd thought of her often these past two days. It wasn't often a woman captured his imagination anymore. But somehow this beautiful woman intrigued him. Spending those few hours with her had made him realize how isolated he'd become lately.

He craved privacy. But he hadn't minded her interrupting his morning, or her nosy questions. Actually, coming to her aid was the highlight of his entire week. He was looking forward to their evening together tomorrow night.

"Adam, you have a phone call," Mary said, bringing him his cell phone. Few people had his private number, and he deliberately let Mary answer most of the calls when he was working. "It's your mother."

He always took his mother's calls. "Thanks," he said, and Mary handed him the phone. "Hi, Mom."

"Adam, how's my firstborn doing today?"

Adam's teeth clenched. The way she referred to him was a constant reminder that there had once been three of them and that Lily was gone.

"I'm doing okay. Just finished the day's work."

"The villa?"

"Yeah. I'm happy with the progress."

"Sometimes I can't get over that you design the most fascinating places."

"I have a whole team, Mom. It's not just me."

"It's your company, Adam. You've done remarkable things with your life."

He pinched the bridge of his nose again. His mother never came right out and told him she was proud of him. Maybe she was, but he'd never heard the words and he probably never would. He couldn't blame her. He'd failed in doing the one thing that would've made her proud of him, the one thing that would've cemented her happy life. Instead, he'd caused his family immense grief.

"Have you spoken with your brother yet?"

He knew this was coming. He braced himself.

"Not yet, but I plan to speak with Brandon this week."

"It's just that I'm hoping you two reconcile your differences. My age is creeping up on me, you know. And it's something I've been praying for, Adam…for you and Brandon to act like brothers again."

"I know, Mom." The only justice was that he knew his mother was giving Brandon the very same plea. She wanted what was left of her family to be whole again. "I've put in a few calls to him. I'm just waiting to hear back."

"I understand he's in San Francisco, but he'll be home tonight." Home was Newport Beach for his brother. He was a pilot and now ran a charter airline company based out of Orange County. He and Brandon never saw eye to eye on anything. They were as different as night and day. Maybe that's why Jacqueline, his ex-girlfriend, had gotten involved with his brother. She craved excitement. She loved adventure. Adam would never be convinced that she hadn't left him for Brandon. Brandon was easygoing and free-spirited, while Adam remained guarded, even though he'd loved Jacqueline with all of his heart.

"Don't worry, Mom, I'll work it out with Brandon. He wouldn't want to miss your birthday party. We both know how important it is to you."

"I want my boys to be close again."

Adam couldn't see that happening. But he'd make sure Brandon would come to celebrate their mother's seventieth birthday and the two of them would be civil to one another. "I understand."

It was the best he could do. He couldn't make promises to his mother about his relationship with Brandon. There was too much pain and injury involved.

"Well, I'd better say goodbye. I've got a big day tomorrow. A field trip to the Getty Museum. It's been a few years since I've been there."

"Okay, Mom. Is Ginny going?"

"Of course. She's my Sunny Hills partner. We do everything together."

"And you haven't gotten on each other's nerves yet?"

A warmhearted chuckle reached his ears. It was a good sound. One he didn't hear enough from his mother. "Oh, we have our moments. Ginny can be overbearing at times. But she's my best friend and next-door neighbor, and we do so love the same things."

"Okay, Mom. Well, have fun tomorrow."

"Thanks, dear."

"I'll be in touch."

Adam hung up the phone, picturing his mom at Sunny Hills Resort. It was a community for active seniors, inland and just ten miles away from Moonlight Beach. Thankfully his mother hadn't balked about leaving Oklahoma and the life she'd always known after his father died. Adam had bought her a home in the gated community, and she seemed to have settled in quite nicely, her middle America manners and charm garnering her many friendships. The activities there kept her busy. He tried to see her at least once or twice a month.

Mary walked into his office. "It's dinnertime. Are you hungry, Adam?"

"I could eat. Sure."

"Would you like me to set you up on the veranda? Or inside the kitchen?"

"Kitchen's fine."

Mary nodded.

Mary asked him every night, and he always had the same answer for her, but he never wanted her to stop asking. Maybe one night he'd change his mind. Maybe one night he'd want to sit outside and see the sun set, hear distant laughter coming from the shoreline and let faint music reach his ears. Maybe one night he wouldn't want to eat in solitude, then watch a ball game and read himself to sleep.

"Oh, and Mary?"

She was almost out of the doorway when she turned. "Yes?"

"Take the day off tomorrow. Enjoy a long weekend."

Sundays and Mondays were her days off. Adam could fare for two days without housekeeping help, unless something important came up. He made sure it didn't. He had an office in the city where he met with his clients and had meetings with his staff. He often worked on his designs from home. His office was fully equipped with everything he needed.

"Thank you, Adam. Does this have anything to do with that lovely girl you met the other day?"

Mary had been with him since before he'd moved into his house. Some said she had no filter, but Adam liked her. She spoke her mind, and he trusted her, maybe more than some trusted their own relatives. She was younger than his mother but old enough to know the score. "If I told you yes, would you leave it at that?"

A hopeful gleam shined in her blue eyes. "A date?"

Of course she wouldn't leave it alone. "Not really. She's coming over to cook for me. As a thank-you for helping her."

Mary grinned, her face lighting up. "A date. I'll make sure the kitchen is well stocked."

"It's always well stocked, thanks to you, Mary. Don't worry about it. I imagine she's bringing over what she needs. So enjoy your Saturday off."

"And you enjoy your date," she said. "I'll go now and set the table for dinner."

She walked out of the room and Adam smiled. Mia was coming over to make him a meal. For all he knew, she felt obligated to reciprocate a favor. Not that what he'd done had been a favor; anyone with half a heart—that would be him—would've helped her out. Who wouldn't stop for a woman bleeding and injured on the beach?

A beautiful woman, with a knockout body and skin tones that made you want to touch and keep on touching.

He had to admit, the thought of her coming over tomorrow got his juices flowing.

And that hadn't happened in a very long time.

"Gram, this is so hard," Mia said, shifting her body to and fro, rocking baby Rose. The baby's weight drained her strength and stung her arms, but she didn't want to stop rocking her. She didn't want to give up one second of her time with Rose. Her sweet face was docile now, so very peaceful. She was a joy, a living, breathing replica of her mama. How could she lose Anna a second time? "I can't imagine not seeing her every day. I can't imagine giving her up."

"She's ours, too, you know." Grandma Tess sat in her favorite cornflower-blue sofa chair. As she smiled her encouragement the wrinkles around her eyes deepened. "We won't really be giving her up," she said softly. "I'm sure… this Adam, he'll do the right thing. He'll allow you contact with the baby."

"Allow." A frown dragged at her lips. She'd raised Rose from birth. They'd bonded. Now someone would have the power to *allow* her to see Rose?

"He may not be the father, after all. Have you thought about that?"

"I have," she said, her hips swinging gently. "But my gut's telling me he's the one. Rose has his eyes. And his hair coloring. She's not dark like us."

"Well, then, maybe you should get going. Lay the baby down in the playpen. She'll probably sleep most of the night. We'll be fine—don't you worry."

"I know. She loves you, Gram." Tears formed in her eyes. Her heart was so heavy right now. She didn't want to leave. She didn't want to see Adam Chase tonight. She wanted to stay right here with Rose and Gram. She caught the moisture dripping from her eyes with a finger and sighed. "I won't be late. And if you need me for anything, call my cell. I'll keep it handy."

She laid the baby down in the playpen that served as the crib in Gram's house. Wearing a bubblegum-pink sleep sack, Rose looked so cozy, so content. Mia curled a finger around the baby's hair and, careful not to wake her, whispered, "Good night, Sweet Cheeks."

She left the baby's side to lean down to kiss Gram's cheek. Her skin was always warm and supple and soft like a feather down pillow. "Don't bother getting up. I'll lock you in."

"Okay, sweetheart. Don't forget the groceries."

"I won't," she said.

As she passed the hallway mirror, she gave herself a glance. She wore a coral sundress with an angled shoulder and a modest hemline. Her injured foot had healed enough for her to wear strappy teal-blue flat sandals that matched her teardrop necklace and earrings. Her hair was down and slight waves touched the center of her back.

"You look beautiful, Mia."

"Thanks, Gram." She lifted the bag of foodstuffs she'd need to make the meal, glanced at Rose one more time and then exited her grandmother's house, making sure to lock the door.

The drive to Adam Chase's estate was far too short. She reached his home in less than twenty minutes. Her nerves prickled as she entered the long driveway and pressed the gate button. After a few seconds, Adam's strong voice came over the speaker. "Mia?"

"Yes, hello… I'm here."

Nothing further was said as the wrought-iron gates slid away, concealing themselves behind a row of tall ivy scrubs. She drove on, her hands tight on the steering wheel, her heart pumping. She had half a mind to turn the car around and forget she'd ever met Adam Chase. If only she had the gumption to do that. He would never know he had produced a child. But how fair would that be to him or to Rose? Would she wonder why she didn't know her father and try to find him once she grew up? Would she pepper her aunt Mia with questions and live her life wondering about her true parents?

In her heart, Mia knew she was doing the right thing. But why did it have to hurt so much?

She parked her car near the front of the house on the circular drive. Adam waited for her on the steps of the elaborate front door, his hands in the pockets of dark slacks. Her breath hitched. A charcoal silk shirt hugged arms rippling with muscle and his silver-gray eyes met hers through the car window. Before she knew it, he was approaching and opening the car door for her. His scent wafted up, clean and subtly citrus.

"Hello, Mia." His deep voice penetrated her ears.

She took a breath to calm her nerves. "Hi."

"How are you?" he asked.

"I'm all healed up thanks to you."

"Good to hear. I've been looking forward to the meal you promised." He stretched his hand out to her and she took it. Enveloped in his warmth, she stepped out of the car.

"I hope I didn't overstate my talents."

His gaze flowed over her dress first and then sought the depth of her eyes. "I don't think you did." A second floated by. "You look very nice."

"Thank you."

He spied the grocery bag on the passenger seat and without pause lifted it out. "Ready?"

She gulped. "Yes."

He walked alongside her, slowing his gait to match hers. As they climbed wide marble steps, he reached for the door and pushed it open for her. Manners he had. Another plus for Adam Chase. "After you," he said, and once again she stepped inside his mansion.

"I still can't get over this home, Adam. The bat cave is

one thing, but the rest of this house is equally mind-blowing. I bet it was a dream of yours from early on, just like your gallery garage."

"Maybe it was."

He was definitely the king of ambiguity. Adam, guarded and private, never gave much away about himself. Already he was fighting her inquiries.

"I've got wine ready on the veranda, if you'd like a drink before you start cooking."

"We."

"Pardon me?"

"You're going to help me, Adam." Maybe she could get him to open up while chopping vegetables and mincing meat.

He rubbed the back of his neck. "I thought I'd just watch."

"That's no fun." She smiled. "You'll enjoy the meal more knowing you've participated."

"Okay," he said, nodding his head. "I'll try. But I'm warning you, I've never been too good in the kitchen."

"If you can design a house like this, you can sauté veggies. I'm sure of it."

He chuckled and his entire face brightened. Good to see. She followed him into the kitchen, where he set her bag down on an island counter nearly bigger than the entire kitchen in her apartment. Oh, it would be a thrill cooking in here.

"So what's the dish called?"

"Tagliatelle Bolognese."

"Impressive."

"It's delicious. Unless you're a vegetarian. Then you might have issues."

"You know I'm not."

She did know that much. They'd shared a meal together. "Well, since the sauce needs simmering for an hour or two, maybe we'll have our wine after we get the sauce going."

"Sounds like a plan. What should I do?"

She scanned his pristine clothing. "For one, take your shirt off."

A smile twitched at his lips. "Okay."

He reached for the top button on his shirt. After unfastening it, he unbuttoned the next and the next. Mia's throat went dry as his shirt gaped open, exposing a finely bronzed column of skin. She hadn't forgotten what he looked like without a shirt. Just three days ago he'd strode out of the sea, soaking wet, taking confident strides to come to her aid.

"Why am I doing this?" he asked finally. He was down to the fourth button.

Her gaze dipped again and she stared at his chest. "Because, uh, the sauce splatters sometimes. I wouldn't want you to ruin your nice shirt."

"And why aren't you doing the same? Taking off that beautiful dress?"

Her breath hitched. He was flirting, in a dangerous way. "Because," she said, digging into her bag and grabbing her protection. "I brought an apron."

She snapped her wrist and the apron unfolded. It was an over-the-head, tie-at-the-waist apron with tiny flowers that didn't clash with her coral dress. She put it on and tied the straps behind her back. "There. Why don't you change into a T-shirt or something?"

He nodded. "I'll be right back."

By the time Adam returned, she had all the ingredients in place. He wore a dark T-shirt now, with white lettering that spelled out Catalina Island. "Better?"

The muscles in his arms nearly popped out of the shirt. "Uh-huh."

"What now?" he asked.

"Would you mind cutting up the onions, celery and garlic?"

"Sure."

He grabbed a knife from a drawer and began with the

onions. While he was chopping away, she slivered pieces of pork and pancetta. "I'll need a frying pan," she said. Her gaze flew to the dozens of drawers and cabinets lining the walls. She'd gotten lucky; the chopping blocks and knives were on the countertop.

"Here, let me." Adam reached for a wide cabinet in front of her and grazed the tops of her thighs with his forearm as he opened the lower door. She froze for a second as a hot flurry swept through her lower parts. It was an accidental touch, but oh how her body had reacted. His fingertips simply touched the drawer loaded with shiny pots and pans and it slid open automatically. "There you go."

She stood, astonished. "I've never seen anything like that. You have a bat cave kitchen, too."

"It's automated, that's all. No pulling or yanking required."

"I think I'm in heaven." How wistful she sounded, her voice breathy.

Adam stood close, gazing at her in that way he had, as if trying to figure her out. His eyes were pure silver gray and a smidgen of blue surrounded the rims. They reminded her of a calm sea after a storm. "I think I am, too."

She blinked. His words fell from his lips sincerely, not so much heady flirtation but as if he'd been surprised, pleasantly. Her focus was sidetracked by compelling eyes, ego-lifting words and a hard swimmer's body. *Stop it, Mia. Concentrate. Think about Rose. And why you are here.*

She turned from him and both resumed their work. After a minute, she tossed the veggies into the fry pan, adding olive oil to the mix. The pan sizzled. "So, did you help your mother cook when you were a boy?" she asked.

Grandma Tess always said you could judge a man by the way he treated his mother.

"Nah, my mom would toss us boys out of the kitchen. Only Lily was— Never mind."

She turned away from the clarifying onions and steaming veggies to glance at his profile. A tic worked at his jaw, his face pinched. "Lily?"

"My sister. She's gone now. But to answer your question, no, I didn't help with meals much."

He'd had a sister, and now she was gone? Oh, she could relate to that. Her poor sweet Anna was also gone. He didn't want to talk about his sister. No great surprise. She'd already learned that Adam didn't like to talk about himself. "Do you have brothers?"

"One."

He didn't say more. It was like the proverbial pulling teeth to get answers from him.

She added the pork to the mix and stirred. "Did you grow up around here?" she asked matter-of-factly.

"No, did you?"

"I grew up not far from here. In the OC." She didn't like thinking about those times and how her family had been run out of town, thanks to her father. She, her mama and sister had had to leave their friends, their home and the only life they'd ever known because of James Burkel. Mia had cried for days. It wasn't fair, she kept screaming at her mother. But it hadn't been her mother's fault. Her mother had been a victim, too, and the scandal of her father's creation had besmirched the family name. The worst of it was that an innocent young girl had lost her life. "Here, stir this for me," she said to Adam, "if you wouldn't mind. We're caramelizing the meat and veggies now and don't want them to burn. I'll get the sauce."

"Sure." He grabbed the wooden spoon from her hands and stood like stone, his face tightly wound as he concentrated on stirring. She was sorry she'd made him uncomfortable with her questions. But they had to be asked.

"Okay, in goes the sauce. Stand back a little."

He turned her way. "What's that?"

She gripped a tube of tomato paste in her hand and squeezed. Red paste swirled out. "Tuscan toothpaste."

He laughed, surprised. "What?"

"That's what we call it. It's concentrated sauce. Very flavorful. Take a taste."

She sunk her spoon into the sauce and then brought it to his mouth. His lips parted, his head bent and his eyes stayed on hers as she gave him a taste. "Might be a little hot."

He swallowed, nodding his head. "It's so good."

"I know. Yummy."

His eyes twinkled. There was a moment of mischief, of teasing, and his smile quickened her heart. "Yummy," he repeated.

The staunch set of his jaw relaxed and she stared at his carefree expression. She liked the unguarded Adam best.

After tossing in the herbs and the rest of the ingredients, she set the pan to simmer and they left the kitchen for the open-air veranda. "I don't usually come out here," Adam said, pulling out a chair for her. "But I thought you might like it."

The sun was dipping, casting a shimmering glow on the water. Hues of grape and sherbet tangled through the sky. It was glorious. There was nothing better than a beachside view of the horizon at this time of day. "Why not, Adam? If I lived here, I'd spend every night watching the sunset."

"It's…" His face pinched tight again, and she couldn't figure out if it was pain or regret that kept him from saying more. Maybe it was both? "Never mind."

Lonely. Was that what he was going to say? Was this intelligent, wealthy, physically perfect specimen of man actually lonely?

"Would you like a glass of wine?"

"Yes," she answered.

"Cabernet goes well with Italian."

"It does."

He poured her a glass, and she waited for him before taking her first sip.

"Mmm. This is delicious."

The veranda spread out over the sand in a decking made entirely of white stone. A circular area designated the fire pit and off to the side, a large in-ground spa swirled with invigorating waters. She'd been here before, sat close to this very spot, but she'd been too immersed in her mission to really take note of the glorious surroundings. Sheer draperies billowed behind them.

"I'm glad you like it."

What was not to like? If only she could forget who Adam Chase really was.

They sipped wine and enjoyed the calm of the evening settling in. A few scattered beachgoers would appear, walking the sands in the distance, but other than that, they were completely alone.

"Why did you leave Orange County? For college?" he asked.

"No, it was before that." The wine was fruity and smooth and loosened her tongue, but she couldn't tell Adam the reason her mother had picked up and left their family home. She'd been careful not to share the closest things about herself to Adam, in case Anna had divulged some of their history to him. While Anna had kept the last name Burkel, Mia had legally changed her name to her mother's maiden name, D'Angelo, as an adult. Mia was dark haired with green eyes, while her sister had been lighter in complexion and bottle blonde. She wondered if Adam would even remember much about Anna. It had been a one-night fling, and a big mistake, according to Anna. "After my mother and father got divorced, we came to live with my grandmother."

It was close to the truth.

"I see. Where did you go to school?"

"I graduated from Santa Monica High and put myself through community college. I bet you have multiple degrees."

"A few," he admitted and then sipped his drink. His gaze turned to the sea.

"You're very talented. I'm curious. Why did you decide to become an architect?"

He shrugged, deep in thought. Oh no, not another evasive answer coming on. Was he trying to figure out a way out of her question? "I guess I wanted to build something tangible, something that wouldn't blow over in the wind."

"Like the three little pigs. You're the smart pig, building the house made of bricks."

His lips twitched again and he lifted his glass to his mouth. "You do have a way of putting things. I've never been compared to a pig before." He sipped his drink.

"A *smart* pig, don't forget that. You build structures that are sturdy as well as beautiful."

He nodded. "Foundation comes first. Then I layer in the beauty."

She smiled. "I like that."

He reached for her hand. "And I like you, Mia." The hand covering hers was strong and gentle.

His eyes were warm, darkening to slate gray and as liquid as the sensations sprinting through her body right now. This wasn't supposed to happen. This intense, hard-to-ignore feeling she got in the pit of her belly. She couldn't be attracted to him. It was impossible and would ruin everything.

She slipped her hand from his and rose from her seat. "I think I'd better check on the meal."

His chair scraped back as he stood. Always the gentleman. "Of course."

She scurried off, mentally kicking herself. An image of Adam's disappointed face followed her into the kitchen.

Three

"Damn it." Adam squeezed his eyes shut. He'd almost blown it with Mia. She was skittish, and he couldn't blame her. She didn't know him. It had been his MO not to let people in, and he'd done a good job of avoiding her questions tonight. He'd lost the fine art of conversation years ago, if he'd ever had it. If only he wasn't so darn smitten with her. *Smitten?* Now that was a corny word. Hell, he was attracted to her, big-time. She was a breath of fresh air in his stale life.

He entered the kitchen holding two wineglasses he'd refilled and found her by the oven, wearing her little blue apron again. His throat tightened at the domestic scene. How long had it been since a woman cooked him a meal? Well, aside from Mary. A long, he couldn't remember how long, time. "Me again." He set down her wineglass. "What can I do?"

"How are you at making a salad?"

"I can manage that."

She stirred the sauce as he opened the refrigerator and grabbed a big wooden bowl covered with plastic wrap. He set it in front of her.

"How's this?"

"Looks beautiful." She smirked. "You work fast."

"Thank Mary. She anticipates everything." He opened a drawer and revealed a loaf of fresh crusty Italian bread. "Yep, even bread."

Mia smiled. "Thank you, Mary. The sauce is almost ready. I brought homemade tagliatelle. But I can't take credit for making it. There's no way I could duplicate my gram's recipe. She's the expert. She made it."

Several sheets of thin pasta were laid out on a chopping block. Mia rolled a sheet all the way up until it was one rather long log and then she cut inch wide strips and then narrower strips all the way down the line. "Tagliatelle doesn't have to be perfect. That's the beauty in the recipe. Once you've made the pasta, cutting it is a breeze." She unrolled two at different lengths and widths and showed it to him. "See?"

She added a sprinkling of salt to a boiling pot. "Here you go. Want to put these in as I cut?"

"I think you can double as a chef, Mia D'Angelo." They worked together, her cutting, him adding the pasta to the bubbling water.

"That's nice of you to say. But judge me in two minutes, when it's done."

"If it tastes anything like it smells…" The scent of garlic and herbs and the meaty sauce spiked his appetite. The homey aroma brought good memories of sitting down to a meal with his mom and dad, brother and sister. "It'll be delicious."

"I hope so."

He helped Mia serve up the dish, and they sat down outside again. It was dark now; the moonlight over the ocean illuminated the sky. Mary had placed domed votive candles on the table, and he lit them. He couldn't remember having a more relaxed evening. Mia didn't seem to want anything from him. She was the real deal, a woman he wouldn't have even met, if she hadn't injured herself practically on his doorstep. She was curious, but she wasn't overbearing. He liked that she made him laugh.

Steam billowed from the pasta on his plate and he hunkered down and forked it into his mouth before his stomach started grumbling. The Bolognese sauce was the best he'd ever tasted, and the pasta was so tender, it slid down his throat. The dish was sweet and savory at the same time, just the right amount of…everything. "Wow," he said. "It's pretty damn good."

She grinned. "Good? Your plate is almost empty."

"All right. It's fantastic. I'm going in for second helpings. If that's okay with you?"

"If you didn't, I'd be insulted." She ladled another portion of pasta onto his plate and grated parmesan cheese in a snowy mound over it. "There—that should keep you happy for a while."

"I'll have to double my swim time tomorrow."

"How long are you out there usually?"

"I go about three miles."

"Every day?"

He nodded. "Every day that I'm home."

She swirled pasta around her fork. "Do you travel much?"

"Only when I have to. I'm doing a big job right now on the coast of Spain. It might require some traveling soon."

"I'd love to travel more. I rarely get out of California. Well, there was this one trip to Cabo San Lucas when I graduated high school. And my father's family was from West Virginia. I spent a few weeks there one summer. But oh, your life sounds so exciting."

It wasn't. He didn't enjoy traveling. He liked the work, though, and it was necessary to travel at times. Adam pictured Mia on the southern coast of Spain with him, keeping him company, lounging in a villa and waiting for him to return home from work. He saw it all so clearly in his mind that he missed her last comment. He blinked when he realized he'd been rude. "I'm sorry—what did you say?"

"Oh, just that I've always wanted to see Italy. It's a dream of mine, to see where my mother's family was from. That's all."

He nodded. Many people would love to trace their roots, but if Adam never entered the state of Oklahoma again, he wouldn't miss it. Not in the least. After Lily died, their family had never been the same. Some nights he woke up in a sweat, dreaming about the natural disaster that had claimed his sister's life. "I can understand that. Italy is a beautiful country."

"Have you been there?"

"Once, yes."

She took a long sip of wine. His gaze was riveted to her delicate throat and the way she took soft swallows. He didn't want the evening to end. If he had his choice, she'd be staying the night, but that would have to wait. Mia couldn't be rushed, and he wasn't one to push a woman into something she wasn't ready for. "After dessert, would you like to take a walk on the beach? I promise I'll bring a flashlight, and we'll be careful."

Mia turned her wrist and glanced at the sparkly silver bracelet watch on her arm. "I would love to, but it's getting late. Maybe just dessert this time. But I'll take a rain check on that walk."

Late? It was a little after ten. "You got it. Another time then."

They brought the dishes inside and Adam pulled out a strawberry pie from the refrigerator. "Mary brought this over this morning. That woman is a saint. I gave her the day off, yet she still came over with this pie."

Fresh whipped cream and split strawberries circled the top of the pie.

Mia took a look. "Wow, it's beautiful. Mary reminds me of my gram. Eating is a priority. And she makes enough food for an army. You'll never go hungry if my gram is around."

"I think I like her already." Adam grabbed a cake knife from the block.

"You would. She's the best."

Adam made the first cut, slicing up a large wedge of pie. "Whoa," Mia said, moving close to him. "I hope that piece is for you."

Her hand slid over his as she helped guide the knife down to cut another thinner wedge. Instant jolts hit him in the gut. Mia touching him, the softness of her flesh on his. She'd gotten under his skin so fast, so easily. Her scent, something light, flowery and erotic, swam in his head, and he couldn't let her go.

"Mia," he said. Turning to her, the back side of his hand brushed a few strands of hair off her face. Her eyes lifted, jade pools glowing up at him. They both dropped the knife, and he entwined their fingers, tugging her closer until her breasts crushed against his chest. "Mia," he said again, brushing his mouth to her hair, her forehead and then down to her mouth. His lips trembled there, waiting for invitation.

"Kiss me, Adam," she whispered.

His mouth claimed hers then, tenderly, a testing and tasting of lips. Oh God, she was soft and supple and so damn tempting. He was holding back, not to frighten her, holding back to give her time to get used to him. Every nerve in his body tingled.

She touched his face, her fingertips tracing the line of his jaw. A sound emerged from his throat, raw and guttural, and as her willing lips opened, he drove his tongue into her mouth. Her breath was coming fast—he could feel it, the rapid rise and fall of her breasts against his chest. His groin tightened, and he fought for control. He had to end the kiss. Had to step away. She turned his nerves into a crazed batch of male hormones. He swept his tongue into her soft hollows one more time, then mastered half a step back, breaking off the connection.

It was too much, too soon and crazy. She brought out his primal instincts. The jackhammering in his chest heated his blood. He held her in his arms, his forehead pressed to hers; then he brushed a kiss there. "Go out with me tomorrow night, Mia," he whispered. There was raw urgency in his request. Did he sound desperate?

Her expression shifted from glazed-over passion to concentration. Her silence worried the hell out of him. "Okay," she finally whispered back, her voice breathy and as tortured as his. "I'd better go now, Adam."

He didn't want her to leave. He couldn't get enough of her, but he wasn't going to press his luck. She wasn't a one-night-stand type of woman, and he was glad about that. "I'll see you out." He took her hand, the strawberry pie forgotten, and walked her to the front door. Rubbing the back of his neck, he gazed into her eyes. "Thanks for the meal."

"My pleasure."

"It was delicious." So was she. "I'll need your address."

"Six four, six four Atlantic. It's easy. Apartment ten, first floor."

He repeated her address, cementing it into his brain, and then opened the door for her. "I'll walk you to your car."

It was only a few steps, but he took her hand again, fitting it to his and she turned her leaf-green eyes his way. He melted a little inside. It would be a long twenty hours. "I'll pick you up at seven?"

"That's perfect."

Breath released from his lungs. "See you then."

He bent his head and placed a chaste kiss on her lips. Her sweet taste and softness seared him like a sizzling-hot branding iron.

He shut her car door. As she started the engine he gave her a smile, lifting his hand in a wave. Mia wiggled her fingers back and drove down his driveway, turning onto Pacific Coast Highway.

He stood rooted to the spot, breathless.
Mia D'Angelo had literally stumbled into his life.
What kind of fantastic dumb luck was that?

Four

"It's gonna cost you, Mia." She glanced in the ladies' room mirror of the nightclub, frowning at the reflection staring back at her. She was going to tell Adam the truth, sometime tonight during their date. She couldn't put it off any longer. Deep down in her heart, she knew Adam Chase was a decent man. She could feel it in her bones. She'd had a few boyfriends who'd been bad mistakes. Boyfriends who had cheated on her or given her a sob story every time they ran out of cash. How many times had she dipped into her own pocket to lend them a hand only to be taken advantage of again?

She wasn't that naive woman any longer. She'd learned from her mistakes, especially after she'd been burned by a master, her dear old dad, who was a terrible father and an even worse husband. He'd cheated on her mom and done much worse. A drunk and a womanizer, he'd brought shame and heartbreak to the family. He'd taken a life, running down an innocent young girl while under the influence. Gin was his poison of choice, and he'd reeked of it when he'd been hauled off to jail.

But Adam Chase, swimmer, rescuer, talented architect, wasn't a mistake. It was a feeling she got every time she was with him. Even though trying to delve into his past to learn more about him proved fruitless—the guy didn't like talking about himself—Mia owed it to Rose and to Adam to reveal her secret.

It had been on the tip of her tongue to reveal the truth a couple of times tonight. Once, just as she was about to say something, the waiter had come by with their meal and she'd lost her nerve. And later, as she was about to speak up again, the band had kicked up, drowning out her thoughts. Adam had asked her to dance then, and she couldn't refuse those expectant eyes gleaming at her. She'd taken his hand and danced close to him, losing herself in the music. Losing herself in him.

Now she had no excuse. She was going to march right out here, sit down next to him and ask for his patience and understanding. This was it. The time for stalling was over. This was going to be the hardest thing she'd ever had to do in her life. Tears stung her eyes and threatened to ruin her mascara. She dabbed at them with a tissue, took a breath and bucked up.

Her high heels clicked against the wood floors like a death march as she made her way back. The room was dark, the blues music in tune with her edgy mood. Keeping her eyes averted, unable to look Adam in the eye, she reached their table. Her mouth dropped open and she quickly clamped it shut. Sitting next to her date was none other than Dylan McKay.

Movie star. Sexiest man of the year. Box office gold. So much for her well-rehearsed confession. Her mind fuzzed over. She was looking at Hollywood royalty.

Both men instantly rose to their feet. "Mia D'Angelo," Adam said. "I'd like you to meet my neighbor Dylan."

"Hi, Mia." He extended his hand.

"Hello." She placed her hand in his and smiled casually as if she met megastars every day of the week. "Nice to meet you."

"Same here. I have to say I'm impressed. Not too many people can get Adam out of the house. Lord knows, I've tried a hundred times."

Adam shot him a glare. "Give it a rest, McKay."

Dylan flashed a brilliant ultrawhite smile, mischief playing in his eyes. "Adam and I have been neighbors for a few years now. He keeps to himself, but he's a good guy." Dylan winked, and Adam seemed to suffer through it. It was hard not to smile, Dylan was a charmer. Gosh, she'd seen every one of his films. Dylan pulled out the seat for her before Adam could get to it. She caught him frowning.

"Thank you," she said. She lowered herself down, and he scooted the chair in.

"Don't you have to be going?" Adam remarked, giving Dylan McKay some sort of male signal with his eyes. Mia stifled a chuckle.

"Yes, actually. I have a hot date with an older woman. She loves jazz."

Adam's brows shot up. And then he seemed to catch on. "Your mom's visiting?"

Dylan nodded. "She loves jazz. She brought my little sis with her this time. I'd bring them over, but I don't want to bust in on your date."

"The way you did?" Adam said drily, taking his seat.

Dylan didn't take offense. "Hey, I didn't want to be rude and not say hello." Dylan bent over to Mia, and she peered directly into his clear blue eyes. "Are you Italian?"

She nodded. "My family's from Tuscany."

"It's a beautiful country. I want to do another film there, just to absorb the culture and the food. Have you ever been?"

"No, it's a dream of mine to go one day. My gram tells some great stories of the old country."

"You'll get there. Nice meeting you, Mia. Adam. Have a nice evening, you two."

"Thanks." Adam rose to shake his hand. They seemed to have an easy friendship.

As he took his seat, Adam said, "Well, now that Dylan gave me his seal of approval as a nice guy, will you dance with me again?"

He was already rising, taking her hand and piercing her with those sharp metallic eyes. A soft, sultry, bluesy tune whispered over the conversational hum of the night-club. He tugged her to the middle of the dance floor and brought her in close, folding her hand in his and placing it on his chest. "Thank you for not going all fan-crush crazy for Dylan. His ego's big enough."

"He came across very down-to-earth."

"He's easy with people. That's probably why he's loved by the masses."

Adam was the exact opposite of Dylan, quiet and closed off. For all she knew, the only thing they had in common was that they both lived on Moonlight Beach, and were probably billionaires or close to it. "You like him."

Adam gave a short nod. "He's a good friend." He tightened his grip on her and whispered, "Are you enjoying yourself tonight?"

"Very much."

Adam brushed a soft kiss to her hair, and she melted into him. "So am I," he whispered into her ear.

As they danced silently, his heartbeat echoed into her chest. Feeling the music, moving to the rhythms, the saxophone delivering gloriously soulful notes, she was floating on air. When the music stopped, Adam didn't move. He pushed a strand of hair from her face, gazing at her as if she was made of something precious and fine. Then he touched his mouth to hers, a tender claiming of her lips that stole her breath. His hands roamed over her partially backless dress possessively; her skin tingled where his fingers touched her skin.

His breath hitched, a small guttural sound emanating from his throat, as he continued to kiss her. Luckily, they were still ensconced on the crowded dance floor with couples waiting for the next song to begin. When the music started up again, he tugged her off the floor and they returned to their table, but he didn't sit down. Instead he took her face in his palms, gave her another wonderful kiss and gazed deeply into her eyes. "Mia, I have to get you home."

Why? Would he turn into a pumpkin at the stroke of midnight? But then he inched closer. Restraint pulled his face tight, his eyes pleading, and she instantly understood why he needed to get out of the nightclub.

She nodded, a beam of hot tingling heat spreading through her body. "I'm ready."

The courtyard near her apartment was dimly lit. Rays of moonlight reflected off a pond and flowed over the hibiscus bushes by her front door. "Thank you for a lovely evening," she said, turning to Adam. He let go of the hand he held and mumbled something she didn't quite hear. Her brain had scrambled during the limo ride home between bouts of sensual caresses and kisses that sent her soaring into the stratosphere.

She'd lost her nerve, once again. And she vowed, tomorrow, after all this heat and energy died down, she'd meet with him on neutral turf and tell him the truth.

"I'm sorry—what did you say?" she asked.

He braced his arms against the front door and trapped her into his body's embrace. His scent, a hint of lime and musk emanating from his pores, did wild things to her. Her thoughts, her body, were keyed into him. Below her belly, she ached and tingled, the pressure building. Her breasts pressed the boundaries of decency and the pebbly tips jutted out, stretching the material of her dress.

"Invite me in, Mia."

And then his lips were on hers again, taking her in another mind-numbing kiss. Her soul was seared, branded by a man she hardly knew. Yet it felt right. So very right. How could she be so attracted to the same man her sister had slept with? Conceived a baby with? This wasn't going to happen. It couldn't.

Her little plan was backfiring.

Because as much as the battle raged inside her head with all those thoughts, she couldn't stop kissing Adam. She couldn't stop wanting him. She hadn't yet said yes or no, and his kisses kept coming, delving and probing her mouth, his lips teasing and tempting hers. She tingled and ached for him, and when he placed the flat of his palm across her chest, rubbing at the sensitive tip through her clothes, a flood of warmth pooled down below, and a strangled sound rose from her throat. "Adam."

She was breathless, out of oxygen and falling fast.

He was an amazing kisser.

He was probably an amazing lover.

How long had it been since she'd been flipped inside out like this?

Maybe never.

She slipped a hand into her beaded purse, grabbed for her key and pressed it into his hand. "You're invited in," she said, her voice a raspy whisper.

"Thank God." Adam blew out a relieved breath.

She moved slightly away from the wall, her body ragged and limp already, just from his kisses.

A thought scurried into her mind of the baby's gear. *Oh no!* Was it all tucked away? Mentally picturing each room, she summed up that the coast was clear. For now, and that was all that mattered.

She didn't want to think further than this moment. She couldn't refuse Adam anything. In seconds, she was inside her apartment, deep in his embrace.

If she expected him to rip at her clothes, he didn't. He took her hand in his and brushed a soft caress to her mouth. More deliberately now, he spoke over her lips. "This is crazy. I don't want to rush you, Mia."

Adam, always rational. She was beginning to understand that about him. Even in the heat of passion, he thought of her feelings. His eyes were hot embers, his body on fire, yet he slowed down enough to make sure he wasn't taking advantage of her or the situation. "I don't feel rushed, Adam." Her voice softened as she confessed the truth.

He drew breath into his lungs as if he'd prayed for that answer and nodded.

She pushed his dinner jacket off his shoulders and he wiggled out of it. He wore no tie, but he unfastened the top buttons on his shirt. She took his hand and led him to the sofa. He sat first and tugged her down onto his lap. "You're beautiful." The heat in his eyes bored straight into her, and then his lips were on her again, his tongue mating with hers.

She gripped his shoulders, touched his hot sizzling skin from beneath his shirt. His strength rippled through her body and heightened her thrill. A low guttural growl rose up from his throat and touched something deep and tender in her heart. Nothing else existed in the world. It was all Adam. Adam. Adam.

He lowered her down slightly, holding her by one strong arm as the heat of his palm covered her breast. It swelled even more, aching for his touch. It was easy for him to slip down the one shoulder strap of her dress. The material and her strapless bra edged down; cool air hit her exposed chest. She arched for him, and he bent his head, taking her into his mouth.

She moaned as he suckled gently, his tongue moistening her extended nipples. Mia wiggled, and he held her arms firm, stroking her over and over, torturing her with swipes that left her breathless. The apex of her legs began to throb, a deep building of pressure that would soon need release.

His mouth left her breast then to reclaim her lips. The hem of her dress was pushed up and the rough planes of his hand cupped her leg, skimming the underside of her thigh, back and forth.

Her mind swam with delicious thoughts as pressure climbed. His fingertips came close to her sweet spot, and she ached for his touch.

"You want this, right?" he rasped, his fingers teasing closer.

"Yes," she breathed, her pulse racing. "I want it."

It wouldn't take much to send her over the edge. She was almost there already. She'd never been so in tune with a man before. She'd never had this kind of immediate response. And she wasn't ashamed that she was practically begging him to take her.

His fingers slipped beneath her bikini panties, and his touch brought a sudden sharp breath from her lips. "Easy, sweetheart. I won't hurt you."

She nodded, unable to utter a word.

As he moved over her, moisture coated his fingers, and, ever so slightly, her body began to rock and sway as he stroked her. Sensations swirled, and she gave herself up to the wondrous feeling. Adam's mouth on hers, his tongue inside her and his fingers working magic—she was too far gone to hold back. She let go and moved with him now. He pressed her harder, faster and she climbed as high as she could go.

"Mia." His voice tight, he seemed just as consumed as she was.

Her body gave way, releasing the strain, the heavy weight loosening up and shattering. Her eyes closed, she merely allowed herself to feel. And it felt mind-blowingly wonderful.

She opened her eyes to Adam's stare. The hunger on his face told her he was ready for more.

He brought down the hem of her dress and replaced the strap over her shoulder. She was being lifted again, tucked into his arms. Kissing her throat, he whispered, "Where's your bedroom, sweetheart?"

She pointed toward the darkened hallway. "The last door on the left."

He began to move slowly, cradling her. "Are you okay?"

She gave a slow nod. "I'm perfect." There was no shame.

She couldn't wait to be with him again, to have him inside her. She was just getting started. How many years had she gone without? Now, having Adam as a partner, her bones jumped to life.

"I agree. You are."

The compliment seeped into her soul.

He walked past Rose's bedroom. The door was shut, hiding her nursery, but a jolt of guilt-ridden pain singed her. She didn't want to think about that right now. Things were getting complicated.

They neared her bedroom door.

And then she was nearly falling out of his arms.

He tripped, and she went down with him. The stumble brought him to his knees. He never let go of her, though— good lifeguarding skills—and he laughed in her ear. "I've still got you. Sorry for the stumble. I must've stepped on something."

He set her down gently and searched the floor, picking up the mystery item that caused the fall.

Her eyes squeezed shut.

"What the hell is this?"

He groped at the stuffed snowman with the giant carrot nose. Olaf, the character from *Frozen*. She remembered Rose dropping it as she was getting ready to go to her grandmother's house. She'd meant to grab it but had totally forgotten.

"It's a toy I forgot to pick up."

"Do you moonlight as a babysitter or something? Or do you have a thing for weird-looking snowmen?"

She sighed. Then stood up and flipped the light switch on.

Adam squinted and gazed at her through narrowed eyes. "Mia? I was just kidding. Why are you frowning?"

Her heart sank, and tears burned behind her eyes. The night would bring on so many changes. Rose's innocent face flashed. For a split second, she thought about bailing. About lying to Adam and sending him packing. In her dreams, Rose was hers, Gram would live forever and they'd be a family.

"Mia?" Adam rose from the floor. She couldn't put this off any longer. It was time. She had the perfect opportunity to tell Adam about Rose. To lie now would only prolong the inevitable and make things harder than they already were.

"Adam, that's Olaf. It's, uh…it's your daughter's favorite toy."

It took all of her effort to get Adam to sit down at the kitchen table so she could explain. As she filled the coffeemaker, she sensed his gaze boring into her like a pinpointed laser beam and her neck prickled. He kept looking at her as if she were from outer space.

"This is some kind of joke, isn't it, Mia?"

"No joke. You have a daughter."

He shook his head. "I'm still waiting for your explanation. You can't just blurt out I've got a daughter and then decide we need to discuss this over coffee, as if we were talking about the weather. Christ, Mia. I've had people try to infiltrate my territory and invade my privacy. I admit you're good. You found a way to get my attention. Even it if did cost you pain and a little bleeding. Hell, you had me fooled. Whatever you want, just spill it out, so we can get this over with."

Her head whipped around, her eyes burning hot. "I'm not trying to fool you or invade your precious privacy, Adam. And you wouldn't say that if you knew Rose. That baby is the sweetest thing on this earth." She simmered down. She so didn't want to have a confrontation. "We need to discuss this calmly, rationally."

"How do you know I have a daughter? Who is she to you?"

"She's…my niece."

"Your niece?" His voice rose, piercing her ears. He hadn't expected that, but the truth deserved to be told now.

"Yes, my niece. About a year ago, you spent some time with my sister. Her name was Anna Burkel."

Adam frowned and darted his eyes away, as if trying to recall.

"She was dark blonde and pretty and, well, you spent one night with her."

Adam turned back to her and blinked. "She's your sister?"

Trembling, she poured coffee into mugs and brought them to the table in her small kitchen. Steam rose up and she stared at it a second. All of her mistakes came bounding back at her, and her hand shook as she set the mug down in front of him. "Yes, she was my sister."

"Was?"

"She died after giving birth to Rose. It was a complicated delivery."

Adam didn't offer condolences. He was in shock, staring at her face, but seeing straight through her. "Keep going, Mia. I'm not connecting the dots."

Her heart pounded. This wasn't going well. And it was probably going to get a lot worse. "I'll try to explain. When you met Anna, she was at a low point in her life. She was in love with Edward, her fiancé of two years. They had planned to get married that summer, but then Edward broke it off with her. I doubt she told you any of this, on… on that night."

He shook his head. "No, she didn't. I only remember that she looked lonely. I was at an art museum in the early hours, just when it opened," he said, gazing out the window to the dark sky. "I only make rare visits. But she was there, too, wandering around, and we were enthralled with the same piece. She said something that intrigued me about the artist. She seemed to know a lot about art. We had that in common. We struck up a conversation and ended up spending the day together. Are you saying she got pregnant that night?"

"Apparently."

"Apparently," he repeated. "Well, what is it Mia? Yes or no?" He rose from his seat and began pacing. "Are you trying to hustle me?"

"No! Damn it, Adam. I'm not doing that. And, yes, she got pregnant that night."

"So why didn't she try to find me and tell me about the baby?"

"Because she didn't tell anyone she was carrying your baby. She kept the secret from everyone, including her fiancé. She got back together with Edward just one month later and, and…" Oh, man, this was harder to admit than she'd thought. Saying the words out loud made her sister's deed seem conniving and sinister. What she'd done was wrong, and Mia had been shocked to learn the truth on Anna's deathbed. But how could she blame her sister now? She'd paid the worst price, dying before she got to know her sweet child.

"And she pretended that the kid was his?" Adam's lips twisted into a snarl. She didn't think his handsome face could ever appear ugly, but right now it did.

She nodded.

He stopped pacing and closed his eyes as if absorbing it all. "I'm not convinced the child is mine. How can you be so sure?"

"Because my sister was dying when she confided the truth to me, Adam."

"And?"

She bristled. "If that's not enough, Rose has your eyes."

"What does that mean?"

"How many children do you know have silver-gray eyes?"

"I don't know many children, Mia."

Now he was being obtuse. Yes, it was a lot to lay on him and she hadn't planned on his finding out this way… accidentally. It would've been much better if she could have confessed the truth to him during a long soulful talk, the way she'd hoped.

"How old is the baby?" he asked.

"Rose is four months."

His hands went to his hips. He might've been a gun-slinger, eyeing his opponent. He stood ramrod stiff and ready to do battle. "Four months? The child is four months old?" He paced again, moving briskly, and she imagined his head was ready to spout steam any second. "So what was all this about?" He gestured to her apartment, the couch where she'd come undone in his arms and all the rest, by making a circle with his hand. "Were you trying to soften the blow? Because, Mia, you're good. I'd say you're a pro."

The "pro" comment had her walking up to him, her nerves absolutely raw. "Don't insult me, Adam. Bullying doesn't work on me."

She'd been called many names in high school after her father had sullied the Burkel name. It had hurt her be-yond belief. She'd felt dirty and shamed. Mean-spirited folks aimed their disgust and revulsion at her entire fam-ily, instead of the one person who'd actually been guilty of hideous crimes. James Burkel deserved their distrust, but not the rest of her family. They'd been innocent vic-tims, as well.

From that day on, Mia had vowed not to allow anyone to bully her again.

"You sure had me fooled." And then Adam's eyes wid-ened and he pointed a finger at her. "Did you plant that broken bottle on the beach, just to meet me?"

"Don't flatter yourself, Adam. I was trying to meet you, yes, that's true, but I wouldn't bloody myself. That was an accident."

"But it did the trick, didn't it?"

Oh man. She couldn't deny it. "Yes, it served my pur-pose."

"And that was to what? Screw me, as many ways as you could. And I'm not talking about sex, but honey, after to-night, if the shoe fits."

Fury blistered up and her hand lifted toward his face. He stared her down, and she dropped her hand, not because she was afraid of Adam, but because she didn't approve of physical violence of any kind. There had been one too many slaps to her mother's face by dear old dad for her to ever want to repeat that behavior.

He sensed her displeasure and backtracked a little. "I apologize for that. But just tell me why you waited for four months and why, when we first met, you didn't immediately tell me about Rose?"

"For one, my sister died before I could get much information out of her. She told me your name and that you were an architect. Do you know how many Adam Chases there are in the United States? Logic had me narrowing it down to a handful of men, but then I found a recent picture of you…which, by the way, wasn't easy to find. You're not exactly press happy, are you?" She didn't expect him to answer. It was common knowledge that he was a recluse, or whatever kind of label fit a man who didn't like people or being out in public. "When I saw a picture of you, and homed in on your eyes, well, then I knew it had to be you."

"What else?"

"Nothing else. Isn't that enough? I was right. You were with my sister."

"What about this Edward guy? Does he still believe the baby is his?"

An exhausted sigh blew through her lips. This had been a trying day, and her emotions were tied up into knots. "No, Anna left it up to me to tell him. He didn't believe me at first and I understood that. He didn't *want* to believe it. He had already bonded with Rose. When the DNA test came back, he was devastated. He'd lost Anna, and then to find out Rose wasn't his… I've been raising Rose ever since."

"Where is the baby now?"

"With my gram." Taking her eyes off Adam, she glanced at the wall clock. "I have to get her soon. She'll be fast asleep."

"I want to see her, Mia. Tomorrow morning. First thing." It was the first time Adam Chase barked an order at her.

"I'll have to make arrangements. I'm expected at work, but I'll be there."

"See that you are. Who watches the baby when you're working?"

"I do. She's too much for my gram all day. I take her to the shop, and she's pretty good. She takes naps. And some days I work part-time or work from home. She's my little mascot."

"You never explained why it took you so long to reveal this little secret. Why didn't you just come out and tell me about her?"

His eyes locked in on her, and it was clear he wouldn't let her off the hook. She could tell him she was charmed and mesmerized by him. But that would only compound the problem. Her palms began to sweat. "You're not going to like it."

"I've liked nothing about his evening, so why stop now?"

Ouch, another sharp blow. She felt something for Adam Chase, and it hadn't been one-sided. But that was beside the point. "Rose is precious to me. She's all I have left of my sister and she's an amazing, beautiful, smart baby. I'd die for her, Adam. I couldn't just turn her over to a stranger. I had to get to know you as a person."

"Those nosy questions you kept asking me."

She nodded. "But you gave nothing away about yourself. I mean, other than you're a brilliant architect and you're pretty handy with a first aid kit."

A low guttural laugh crept out of his mouth. The sound

made her skin crawl. "You've got to be kidding? You were judging me? If Rose is my baby, where do you come off not telling me immediately?"

She had to make him see her logic. Certainly, he wouldn't condemn her for her actions. He had to see she had the baby's welfare at heart. "It's only because I was trying to protect Rose. Think about it, Adam. All I knew about you is that you had a one-night stand with my sister. That doesn't make you father material. I had to make sure you weren't—"

"What? An ax murderer? A criminal?" Blood rose to his tanned cheeks.

She nodded slowly. "Well…maybe," she squeaked. "I had to know you weren't a jerk or a loser or something."

His eyes widened.

Stop talking now, Mia.

"So you made yourself my judge and jury? Did I pass your test? I must have…since you practically let me—" His eyes roamed over her disheveled dress. "Never mind." He pushed his fingers through his hair. "I can't believe this."

"I was going to tell you tonight. I had it all planned, but then we kept getting interrupted."

"If I hadn't stepped on that toy, I might never have learned the truth."

"That you have a daughter?"

"Whether this child is actually mine remains to be seen. I meant I would've never found out what a liar you are."

He grabbed his jacket from the sofa and strode toward the front door. Handling the knob, he stopped and stared at the door, refusing to look at her another second. "Bring her over in the morning. If you don't show, I'll come for her myself."

"We'll be there, Adam."

He walked out, and the sound of the door slamming made her embattled body jump.

So far her "daddy test" plan was an epic fail.

Five

Adam gazed out his bedroom window to view overcast morning skies. His eyes burned like the devil. He shut them and flopped back against his mattress. "Ow."

Hammers pounded away in his skull, but he'd have to ignore the rumble. He had more pressing things to think about than his hungover state. He'd had too much mind-numbing vodka last night. In just a few hours, he'd come face-to-face with Mia again. The conniver. The liar. The woman who'd deceived him for days. He'd let down his guard, just like he had with Jacqueline, and look how that had ended. He'd given her his heart and trust and shortly after, she'd broken it off with him, falling madly in love with his brother instead. Nice.

He pinched the bridge of his nose and filled his lungs with air.

And now Mia claimed he'd fathered her sister's child. He didn't trust Mia D'Angelo as far as he could toss her. But the baby was another matter. If she was his, he'd make things right. Last night, before he'd taken to drink, he'd put the wheels in motion to find out his legal rights in all this. And to find out who Mia really was.

He remembered more and more about the night he'd shared with Anna. It had been on the anniversary of his sister's death, some twenty years ago. He'd gone out, because staying in always made him think too hard about Lily and then the guilt would come. So he'd escaped to the museum and had met an equally lonely woman and they'd had a nice time. Nothing too earth-shattering, and, afterward, they'd both agreed it was best not to see each other again. No phone numbers were exchanged. They'd barely known each other's names. It had been an impetuous fling.

A knock at the door sounded loudly. "It's Mary. I brought you something to make you feel better."

"Come in." He sat up. His head was splitting like an ax to logs. The tomato drink flagged with a celery stem popped into his line of vision. "I thought you might need this."

How did she always know what he needed?

"I saw an empty Grey Goose bottle on the counter and figured this might be a welcome sight this morning."

"Thanks. It's exactly what I need."

She handed him the glass. "Bad night? Or an extremely good one?"

He took a sip. "Might be a little bit of both. Take a seat." He gestured to the chair by the window. "I have something to tell you. We're going to have two visitors today…"

Two hours later, Adam walked out of his bedroom showered and dressed in a pair of jeans and an aqua-blue polo shirt. He was too keyed up to eat breakfast and his head-shredding hangover didn't allow his usual morning swim. Instead, he grabbed a mug of coffee and wandered outside. He walked to the outer edge of his stone patio and gazed at the steady waves pounding the shore. He sipped coffee, staring out.

The last time he'd thought about fatherhood, he was getting ready to ask Jacqueline to marry him. He'd fallen hard for her and thought they were in tune with one another. So much so, he'd wanted to spend the rest of his life with her. But life never turned out as expected. He'd been shell-shocked when Jacqueline broke it off with him. Shortly after, he'd accidentally found out she'd fallen in love with Brandon.

There'd be no marriage. No family with Jacqueline for him.

As it turned out, Brandon hadn't lasted long with Jacqueline. She'd left him three years later, after a tumultuous relationship, and finally married a college professor. She was living a quiet life on the East Coast now. His mother had given him the scoop, though he kept telling her it wasn't any of his business anymore.

Now his every thought revolved around being a father. A chill ran down his spine thinking of all the ways his life would change after meeting Rose. But first and foremost, he had to find out if she was his daughter.

Mary's voice from behind startled him. "Adam, they're here."

He pivoted around to see Mia holding the baby in her arms. Behind them, long sheer drapes flapped gently in the breeze, fanning around them as if framing the Madonna and her child. He held his breath; his limbs locked in place. They both wore pink, Mia in a long flowery summer skirt and a pale blouse. The baby, wrapped in a lightweight blanket with only her face peeking out, had sandy-blond hair. That was all he could see of her as he stood a good distance away. Mia gazed at the child she held, her eyes filled with love and adoration, and the sight of her again packed a wallop to his gut. She didn't look like the conniving liar he'd pegged her for last night. But he wouldn't be fooled again. Too much was at stake.

This could be a scam. Mia could be a gold digger. Maybe she'd conjured up all of this after learning about the fling he'd had with her sister. The baby might be an innocent pawn in the sick game she was playing. *Remember that, Adam.*

His gaze went to Mary, standing near them, her hand on her heart, her light eyes tender on the baby. "I'll take it from here, Mary. Thanks."

"Yes, thank you, Mary." The women exchanged a glance. "She's precious."

"Yes, she is," Mia responded.

"I'll leave you two to talk it out."

Adam waited for Mary to leave. Then he set the coffee mug down and strode the long steps toward them. Mia cradled the baby possessively, holding her haughty chin up, suddenly defiant. What did she think he'd do, wrestle the baby out of her arms and banish her from his house forever?

He faced Mia and swiveled his head to see the baby's face. Soft gray eyes, circled with a hint of sky blue, looked up at him. Adam's heart lurched. Oh, God, she did have his eyes.

"This is Rose."

He nodded, his throat tight.

"She was born on May first."

Mia unfolded the blanket, showing him her chubby little body outfitted in a frilly cotton-candy-colored dress. Ruffles seemed to swallow her up. Her little shoes and socks matched her dress. "She weighed seven pounds, seven ounces. She's almost doubled her birth weight now."

"She's a beauty," he found himself saying. His child or not, he couldn't deny the truth. "Let's get her inside the house."

"Good idea. She's probably going to need a diaper change soon. She feels a little wet."

Adam gestured for her to go first. She stepped inside the kitchen. He pressed a button on the wall and the sliding doors glided shut. "Where do you want to change her?"

"Mary said she put her diaper bag in the living room."

"In here," he said and moved ahead of her.

She followed him down the hallway and into a room he barely used, filled with sofas, tables and artwork. A bank of French doors opened out in a semicircle to a view of the shoreline.

"Mary says I don't use this room enough," he muttered,

lifting the diaper bag overflowing with blankets, bottles, rattles and diapers. "All this stuff is hers?"

"That's only part of it."

Mia's lips twitched, not quite making it to a smile. Her eyes were swollen and her usual healthy-looking skin tone had turned to paler shades.

"Where do you want to change her?" asked Adam.

"On the floor always works. She's starting to roll and move a lot. It's safer for her than putting her on the sofa where she might topple. Hand me a diaper and a wipe out of there, please?"

Adam dug into the bag, pulling the items out, while she kneeled onto the floor, laid the baby's blanket down and then placed Rose on top of it. "That's right my little Sweet Cheeks—we're going to clean you right up."

The baby gave her a toothless grin and Adam had to smile. She was a charmer. Mia pressed a kiss to the top of her forehead. "Bloomers off first," she said, pushing them down beautifully chunky legs. "Now your diaper."

The baby kicked and cooed, turning her inquisitive little body to and fro. Something caught his eye on the back of her leg as the ruffles of her dress pulled up. A set of light brown markings, triangular in shape, stained her skin on her upper back thigh. Mia laid a hand on her stomach to hold her still while she cleaned the area with a diaper wipe. Adam kneeled down beside her to get a better look at that mark. He pointed to her thigh. "What's that on the back of her leg?"

Mia rolled the baby over ever so gently to show him. "This? It's nothing. The pediatrician said it's a birthmark. She said it'll fade in time and would be hardly noticeable."

Adam drew a deep breath. "I see."

The birthmark caught him by surprise. Up until now he hadn't been convinced about Rose's bloodlines. Gray-blue eyes were rare but not proof enough. But a family birthmark? Now that wasn't something he could ignore.

He'd been born with the exact marking in the same location, upper back thigh. Adam's father had had it, but as far as he knew, Lily and Brandon had escaped that particular branding. "I have the same birthmark, Mia."

Her eyes flickered.

"I still want a DNA test." His attorney had told him it was a must. For legal reasons, he needed medical proof. "But now I know for sure. Rose is my child."

The moment had finally come. Adam understood he was Rose's father. The birthmark she hadn't given a thought to had convinced Adam. Mia wanted this, but where did they go from here? How should they proceed? Adam hadn't said much of anything as to his plans. He'd asked countless questions about Rose, though. What was she like? Did she sleep through the night right away? Had she ever been ill? What foods did she like to eat?

Calmly and patiently she answered his questions as they sat on the sofa that faced the Pacific Ocean. Adam gawked as Mia fed the baby a bottle of formula.

He reached out to touch her hair, wrapping a finger around a blond curl. "She's been good, hasn't she?"

"She's usually very good. Not too many things upset her. She only makes a peep when she's tired. I rock her to sleep and that calms her."

"Do you sing to her?"

"I try. Thank goodness she's not a critic."

Adam laughed, a rich wholesome sound that would've had her smiling, if the situation was something to smile about.

"When she's done with her bottle, I'd like to hold her."

Mia drew breath into her lungs. The thought of handing her over to Adam, if only for a little while, turned her stomach. Soon she'd lose Rose to him forever. She had a right to see her from time to time, but it wouldn't be the same as raising her, day in and day out. Nothing would be the same.

Oh, how her heart ached. "Sure."

The baby slurped the last drops of formula, and Mia sat her on her lap and burped her, explaining to Adam how to do it in an upright position. The baby belched a good one, and she smiled. "That's my little trouper."

She hugged Rose to her chest, kissed her forehead and turned to Adam. "Are you ready?"

"Yes, but keep in mind, I haven't held a baby since my sister was born. And then I was only a kid."

"Just put your arms out, and let me give her to you."

He did just that, and she placed Rose into his arms. "She holds her head up now all by herself, but just make sure she doesn't wobble."

Mia positioned Adam's hand under the baby's neck and extended his fingers. Adam darted a glance at her. Their eyes connected for a second, and then he was focused back on the baby.

Rose squirmed in his arms, her face flushed tomato red. And then her mouth opened, and she let out an ear-piercing wail.

Adam snapped his head to her for help. "What do I do?"

"Try rocking her."

He did. It didn't help.

"What am I doing wrong?" he asked.

She didn't know. Usually Rose wasn't fussy. "Nothing. She doesn't know you."

Her wails grew louder and louder, and Mia's belly ached hearing her so unhappy.

"Maybe that's enough for right now," she said, reaching for the baby.

Adam was more than willing to give her back. "Hell, I don't know what I did to upset her."

"Please don't swear around the baby. And you did nothing wrong."

Mia put her onto her shoulder and rocked her. She stopped crying.

Adam shook his head. "Okay. What now?"

"Well, I'm due at First Clips in a little while. Rose and I should get going."

Adam's gaze touched upon the baby, a soft gleam shining in his eyes. He opened his mouth to say something, and then he clamped it shut. Was he going to refuse to let Rose leave? That could never happen. He wasn't properly equipped to have a baby here. And clearly he didn't know what to do with her. "I want to see her tomorrow. I want her to know me."

"I'll stop by again. Same time?"

He nodded and then helped her pack up the baby's stuff. He looked on fascinated as she strapped Rose into the car seat. "You'll have to teach me how to do that."

"It's not that hard." A man who designed state-of-the-art houses shouldn't find it a challenge to buckle a baby up. "Tomorrow, you'll fasten her in."

"All right."

She slung the shoulder bag over her shoulder and Adam lifted the bucket, walking her outside to her car. On the way out, little Rose peered up, watching him holding the handles of her car seat, and squawked out several complaints. Once at the car, they made an exchange. He took the diaper bag off her arms and she lifted the bucket onto its base and snapped it in, giving it a tug to make sure it was in tight. "There you go, little one."

"The baby rides backwards?" Adam asked.

"Until she's much older, yes."

He shrugged. "I guess there's a lot to learn."

"Tell me about it. I was petrified when I first took Rose home from Edward's house. It was a hard day for everyone."

Adam glanced at Rose again. Maybe he didn't have much sympathy for what she'd gone through, losing her sister, telling Edward the truth and then raising Rose these past months, but she'd done what she thought was right.

"I'll call you tonight," Adam said.

"Why?"

"She's my daughter, Mia. I've already missed enough time with her." There was no mistaking his condemning tone. He held her guilty as charged. "I want to know everything about her."

Yes, she was right. No sympathy.

She drove off his property as he stood in the driveway, hands in his pockets, watching her drive away and looking like he'd lost his best friend.

"Morning, Mia. Bad news. The rocket ship's on the fritz again." Sherry greeted her at the back entrance of First Clips and opened the screen door for her. Situated in the heart of the Third Street Promenade, the shop catered to an elite clientele of children from ages one to twelve years. "How about I watch the baby while you do your magic on that crazy machine."

Mia sighed. "I wish you and Rena would learn how to fix the darn thing. It's just a matter of replacing shorted fuses."

"I can calm a kid and cut hair on the wildest child, Mia, but you know I'm not good with mechanics. Luckily, our next client isn't due for another fifteen minutes. And she'll be sitting on the princess throne."

Baby Rose loved to watch the lights flicker on and off on the First Starship seat but she also loved the shiny tiaras and lighted wands the girls played with while seated on the Princess Throne.

Mia handed Sherry the handle to the baby's car seat. "Here you go. Auntie Sherry will watch you while I make all the pretty lights work again."

"Hello there, Rosey Posey. How's my little angel today?"

Rose cooed at her aunt Sherry. Today Sherry wore a

carnation-pink chambermaid costume with white ruffle sleeves. Her thick blond hair was up in a fancy do and she looked fit to coif the hair of the finest royalty. Sherry was a stylist extraordinaire.

Mia set about fixing the dashboard on the rocket ship. It took her all of five minutes to replace the fuses, and when the mission was accomplished she found Sherry rocking Rose to sleep in her office, which doubled as the baby's nursery. "Shh...she's out," Sherry whispered. "Sweet little thing." Sherry lowered her into the playpen as Mia looked on.

Sherry and Mia strolled into a small lounge that consisted of a cushy leather sofa and a counter with a coffee machine on top and a small refrigerator underneath.

"She's such a doll," Sherry said.

Mia smiled, grabbing two mugs and setting them out. "For everyone but her father." Steam rose up as she poured the coffee. She handed Sherry a cup, took her own and they both sat down. They held their mugs in their laps.

"Still? It's been how many days?"

"Today makes four. She's not warming to him, and I think he's really frustrated. He thinks if she sees him for more than an hour or two, she'll get used to him. And he has to get used to her, too. He's very unsure when he's holding her."

"It doesn't seem like a wealthy guy like that would be unsure of anything."

Mia sipped her coffee. "Babies are in a category all their own. They throw most men off-kilter. Doesn't matter how powerful or rich they are, there's something about babies that frighten them. They think of them as fragile little creatures."

"My brother has a six-month rule," Sherry said. "He won't hold a baby until they're sturdy little beings."

"What about little Beau? Did he back off from holding his own son?"

"He made an exception for Beau, but he still waited a good couple of weeks before he held him."

"Wow."

"I know. Me? I couldn't wait to get my hands on Beau. And you know how I feel about Rose. I love her like she's my own niece."

"I know, Sherry. She loves you, too. You're her auntie Sherry."

"I love that. So what about Adam?"

"What do you mean?"

"Well, you said he doesn't venture out much, he's sort of a recluse and he's got his head stuck in a computer all day. So, is he a geek?"

A sound rumbled up from her chest. "Not at all."

An image of Adam striding out of the ocean, toned and tanned, shoulders broad, arms powerful, beads of water sliding down his body as he made his way to her, wouldn't leave her head alone.

Rena stepped into the room wearing a metallic silver jumpsuit with triangular collar flaps. She was the First Starship captain. "Oh I came just in time." She poured herself a cup of coffee. "Tell us more about Adam."

"You know all there is to tell," Mia said. "As soon as he found out who I really was, he turned off completely. Shut me down. He's only interested in Rose. And right now she's not cooperating with him. It's sort of sad, seeing the disappointment in his eyes every time we leave."

"Turned off, completely? Does that mean he was turned *on* at one point?" Sherry asked.

Mia rubbed at the corner of her eyes, stretching the skin to her temples. She hadn't told her friends about her dates with Adam or the kisses they'd shared. Or the way he'd made her come undone on her living room sofa that night. It seemed like eons and not days ago since that happened. She couldn't tell Gram the details of what had transpired with Adam that night. Goodness no. "Well, maybe. As I told you before, we spent some time together. I was trying to get to know what kind of person he was and, yes, judging him to see if he was worthy of Rose."

"You had every right," Sherry said.

"You couldn't just drop her off and hope for the best," Rena said.

"Thanks for the support. It means the world to me, but, unfortunately, Adam doesn't see it that way. And well, I thought we might have had something pretty special."

Two sets of eyes pierced her, waiting for juicy news.

She went on. "Let's just say on a scale of one to ten, our date was an eleven. I know enough to believe it wasn't one-sided. He is very charming when he lets down his guard."

"You didn't tell us you went on a date!" Rena said.

"Was it flowers and chocolates?" Sherry asked.

"More like an amazing dinner and lots of dancing," she explained.

"Holding tight. Whispers in the ear?" Rena asked.

Mia nodded.

"And good-night kisses?"

"Oh yes, delicious good-night kisses."

"Mia, did you do it with him?" Sherry asked, darting a bright-eyed glance at Rena.

"Of course not." But almost, she wanted to add. Something made her hold that part back. She wasn't ready to tell them she'd come close to giving Adam her heart and her body that night. She'd lost her head and been fully consumed with passion. Had it been desperation that drove her or something else?

Their shoulders slumped; the fire in their eyes snuffed out. Her love life disappointed her friends. Oh well, what could she say? It disappointed her, too.

"He's filthy rich," Rena said.

"And rock-star handsome," Sherry added. "We wouldn't blame you."

"Or judge you," Rena said. "You've had it rough lately."

"You guys are the best. But he's Rose's father. And I have to watch my step from now on. Her future is on the line. That's all that matters to me right now."

"You're late." Adam grumbled, opening her car door for her.

His *pleasant* greeting grated on her already shot nerves. "Only by fifteen minutes. It's Friday night. There was a ton of traffic on the PCH." She climbed out of the driver's seat, taking the diaper bag with her.

Adam scratched his head. "If you'd let me have a car pick you up, we wouldn't run into this problem."

"Adam, we've been over this. Does your car drive *over* traffic? Because if you had one that did, I'm sure it would replace the Rolls in your gallery."

Adam's mouth clamped shut. A tic worked at his jaw. He didn't like her attitude? Well, she wasn't crazy about his. This was her third stop today. She'd worked long hours, then rushed out of the salon just so she could get here on time. She'd hit bad traffic, which was no joy. And when she'd pulled up to his house, he was waiting for her outside like an irate parent, his displeasure written on the tight planes of his face. Where was that beautiful man she'd met on the beach?

"Come inside," he said.

He reached for the handle of the baby seat but thought better of it. Rose was awake, her gaze glued to his. One false move could start her on a crying jag. Once again, disappointment touched his eyes as he took the diaper bag off her shoulder and grabbed her purse. She followed him inside to the living area. It was after six, a beautiful time of day at the beach. The sun was fading and a glow of low burning light flowed in through the bank of opened French doors. A slight breeze blew into the room, ruffling the leaves on the indoor plants.

"If it's cold for the baby, I can shut the doors."

"No, this is fine. She's been inside all day. She could use a little air." And so could she. Her nerves were frazzled and the temperature was just right to cool off her rising impatience with Adam.

Once they were situated, Mia unfastened Rose from her restraints and picked her up. "There we go, Sweet Cheeks." Mia kissed both of the baby's cheeks, and Rose opened her mouth to form a wide toothless smile. Then she propped the baby on her lap and cradled her in the crook of her elbow.

Adam looked on. Longing was etched on his perfect features, and a twinge of guilt and sorrow touched her heart. He wanted to bond with Rose so badly, and she was having none of it.

"I'd like to hold her," Adam said.

"Okay. Come sit down next to me first."

He did. The scent of him—sand and surf and musk—packed a wallop. He was a towering presence beside her. If only she wasn't so darn attracted to him. "Let's give her a few minutes."

"Okay."

"Talk to me. Let her get used to the sound of your voice again." They'd done this before, and it hadn't worked. Maybe tonight it would make a difference.

"What would you like to know?"

"Everything. But you can start by telling me how your day went."

Adam hesitated. His face was pinched tight. She pictured the debate going on in his head before he finally agreed to open up. "Well, I took my usual swim this morning, after you left."

"Don't you swim just after dawn?"

"I'm a stickler about that, yes. But I woke up later than usual today and I didn't want to miss seeing Rose."

"How far did you swim this morning?"

He glanced at the baby. Rose's eyes were intent on him. It was uncanny how she measured him.

"Four miles."

"Four? I thought you usually did about three?"

"I, uh, had a little more energy to work off this morning."

"Why?"

He glanced at Rose.

"Oh." Rose had been unusually clingy and wouldn't let Adam get anywhere near her.

He didn't say more. "So then, what did you do after your swim?"

He lifted his head and stroked his chin thoughtfully. "My mother called."

"How nice. Do you speak with her often?"

"About once a week. It was a short conversation."

How she missed her own mother and the conversations they used to have. With Anna and her mother gone, she had only Gram. Her grandmother was wonderful, and Rose's arrival had given Mia's life more purpose.

"After that it was business as usual. I did some drafting, took a few calls. Went into the office for a few hours and got home in time to meet you."

"You didn't hesitate to scold me about being late."

Adam shot her a glance, bounded up from the sofa and walked over to the French doors, running his hands through his hair. Turning to her, his eyes were two tormented storm clouds. "Look, I'm sorry about that. I was worried about her. Do you have any idea how much I want to be a part of her life? I've already missed her first four months. I don't want to miss any more time with her."

She nodded. "Okay. I can understand that."

"Well, that makes me feel a whole lot better that you understand I want to know my daughter. I want to love and protect her."

"Adam."

"Let me hold her, Mia."

"Let's play a game with her first. She loves peekaboo. It might make her warm up to you."

"All right, fine." He softened his tone. "How do we do that?"

"I'll show you." She laid the baby down on a blanket on the floor. "Want to play peekaboo, Sweet Cheeks?" Rose's eyes followed her movement as if anticipating something more fun than a diaper change. "Come down here with me, Adam."

Adam scooted next to her, his thigh brushing hers as he positioned himself. Her body zinged immediately, which annoyed her. He didn't think much of her these days, and she should get the hint already. "Reach over to the bag and hand me a receiving blanket," she ordered.

Adam rummaged through her bag and came up with one. "This good?"

"Yes, thank you," she said and softened her tone. "Now watch."

Mia brought the blanket very close to Rose's face and left it there for three seconds so that she couldn't see them, and then quickly removed it. "Peekaboo!"

Rose broke out in cackles. It was the sweetest sound.

"See, she loves this game. Now you do it, Adam." She handed him the blanket.

"Okay, I'll give it a try. Here we go."

Adam repeated the same moves. "Peekaboo!"

Rose stared at him, her mouth curving up slightly, but no real smile emerged. Her legs were kick, kick, kicking. It was something she did when she was excited.

"Try it again. At least she's not crying."

"Okay."

He went through the peekaboo ritual again. The baby studied him. Her inquisitive eyes roamed over his face as if she couldn't quite figure him out. Mia felt like she had the same problem.

"I'm going to pick her up now," Adam said. He bent

and gently lifted her, cradling the back of her head and her buttocks. "That's it, little Rose," he said, carefully rising with her in his arms.

As if Rose finally realized what was happening, she turned abruptly in his arms, her body stretching out, stiffening up. Adam caught her before she wiggled free of his hold. She reached for Mia, her arms extended and pleading. Then she let out a scream.

Mia jumped up. "Rose!"

Adam held her back, firming up his grip. "Let me hold her, Mia. I'll walk her around and talk to her. She can't cry forever."

Mia bit her lip. Her stomach ached. It was torture hearing Rose cry and seeing her desperately reaching for her. "It might be longer than you think."

"Be positive, Mia. Isn't that what you tell me?"

"But she's crying for me."

"Maybe she wouldn't if she didn't see you. I'll take her in to see Mary."

He headed toward the kitchen, gently bouncing the baby in his arms. "Sing to her," she called to him. "She loves music."

Adam nodded and walked out of the room. She closed her eyes. But that only concentrated the baby's screeching cries over Adam's rendition of "Old McDonald Had a Farm." Her heart lurched, and she bit down on her lower lip to keep from calling to her.

She couldn't stand it.

She walked over to the French doors and stepped outside.

Mia sat across from a stony-faced Adam at the dinner table. Mary had left for the day, and Rose slept on her blankets on the floor of the living room. Mia pushed chicken Florentine around on her plate. Mary had outdone herself today with the meal, but Adam's quelling silence soured her stomach of any appetite she might've had.

He sipped wine, a fine Shiraz that went well with the meal. But Adam hadn't touched his food, either. He stared off, his gaze on the shoreline and the high tide rising. A gentle breeze blew by, coming in through the expanse of the open kitchen area, and she shuddered.

Adam glanced at her. She shook her head—she wasn't cold.

Not from the winds anyway.

"She wouldn't go to Mary, either," Adam said, mystified. "And Mary is good with children."

"I know. I heard Mary trying to calm her."

"She cried for twenty minutes in my arms. I tried everything."

He had. He'd sung out of tune to her. He'd bounced her. He'd taken her outside to see the beach. Then he'd sat down on a glider and swayed back and forth, trying to keep her from squirming out of his arms. Mia had hidden herself from the baby's sight and stolen quick glances. She couldn't help worrying over Rose. She'd taken care of her every need for four solid months. It had been a very hard twenty minutes, seeing the baby's anguish and knowing she needed her aunt Mia.

"She's too attached to you, Mia."

She jumped at his comment. "What does that mean?"

"It means that I want my daughter to know me. And that's not happening right now."

"Give it time, Adam."

"You keep saying that. How much time? The longer she's with you and you alone, the more attached she'll become. Isn't that obvious?"

"No, it's not obvious. She'll warm up to you. These are new surroundings, and she's only known you for a few days. She's fine with Rena and Sherry at the salon. She goes to them—so I know it's not just me she wants."

"Is it supposed to make me feel better knowing my daughter will go to perfect strangers, but she won't let her own father hold her, not even for a minute, without exercising her very healthy lungs?"

"Rena and Sherry are not perfect strangers. They are her family."

Adam's face reddened. "I'm her family, Mia."

Oh man. This evening wasn't going well. Her stomach lurched. Dread crept along her spine and knotted her nerves.

He bounded up and pushed his hands through his hair. He always did that when he was agitated. Several sandy-blond strands stood straight up, but Adam could get away with that look. It was appealing on him, a little muss to disrupt his perfectly groomed appearance.

"There's only one solution, Mia."

Her throat constricted. She buttoned her lips.

"Rose has to live here with me."

Oh God. Oh God. Oh God.

Her worst fears were coming true. She knew this day would eventually come, but hearing him say it ripped her apart. "No."

"No? Mia, she belongs with me. I've already missed so much time with her. Four months to be exact. I may not be a perfect father to her right now, but I've got to keep trying. I know if she's here, she'll come to accept me quicker. You can visit her any time you'd like. It's a promise."

Her eyes burned; the tears threatening to flow were white-hot flames. Her body shook, her lips quivering. "No, Adam. I can't leave her."

Adam watched her carefully. This was so hard. She tried to be brave, to put up a good front, but she was ready to fall apart. Any second now, she'd shatter into a mass of tears.

"I'll hire you on as a babysitter," he said, softer.

"A babysitter?" What was he saying? She sobered a little. Grabbing the table for support, she rose on wobbly legs. She couldn't sit still another second. "You want to pay me to take care of my beautiful niece? My own flesh and blood?"

"Hell Mia, do you have a better idea?"

"I already have a job, thank you very much. I own First Clips. I'm needed there."

His lips tightened to a thin line. His eyes became two stormy gray clouds. A battle seemed to rage inside his head. Seconds ticked by. Finally, he sighed as if he'd lost something treasured. "Fine, then. Just move in with me."

"M-move in with you? You couldn't possibly want that."

A wry laugh rumbled from his chest. "I don't see that I have a choice. If I want Rose here…"

"Then you're stuck with me, is that what you were going to say?"

"Don't put words in my mouth, Mia." He gave his head a shake. "You don't have any idea how important this is to me, or I wouldn't even consider inviting you into my home."

"But we'd be living together."

She caught his shudder. No, he didn't want this any more than she did.

"It's a big house," he countered, "and a solution to our problem. You both move in. You can come and go as you please, and I'll be able to see Rose whenever I want. She'll be here every day and night. And she'll come to accept me."

"I don't know," Mia said, stalling. The idea was sprung on her so quickly, she needed time to think it through.

"Mia, it's the only way to ease Rose into this transition more comfortably. It's best for her."

She didn't know if that was true. Adam wasn't thrilled with having her live with him. How could he be? It wasn't for romantic reasons. For all she knew, he hated her or at best resented her for the lies she'd told.

"I don't know if I can do it, Adam."

"And I don't see that we have any other choice. You want to be with Rose as much as I do."

"I know she's your daughter and you want to get to know her, but I don't understand why you are so insistent about this since you're clearly not comfortable around babies."

He stared at her, or rather, stared straight through her as if thinking hard about her question.

Finally, he sighed. "I have my reasons."

She shrugged, palms out gesturing to him for an answer.

"It's personal."

Of course. How could she believe he'd give her an up-front honest reason. That would mean he'd have to divulge something about himself.

She didn't see that she had any choice in the matter. "When and for how long?"

"Move in by the end of the week." He blinked, and then added, "We'll have to take it one day at a time from there."

She gulped.

"Just say yes, Mia."

It probably *was* the best solution for Rose. And Mia couldn't give her up cold turkey. She'd be getting what she ultimately wanted, a chance to keep Rose with her most of the time. Nothing would change other than her location. They'd just hang their hats at this gorgeous beach house instead of at her small apartment.

Her mouth opened and she heard a squeak come out. "Yes?"

Adam nodded, satisfied.

But just as he turned away, a shadow of fear entered his eyes.

The recluse's life was about to change dramatically.

And so was hers.

Six

The guest room on the second story of Adam's home was amazing. It wasn't cozy like her own bedroom, but she could certainly make do with the king-size bed, bulky light wood furniture and much more square footage than she'd need for her yoga workouts. There was a one-drawer desk by the window, a view of the ocean she couldn't complain about, a lovely white brick fireplace and a sixty-inch flat-screen television hanging on the wall. All her clothes would fit into two dresser drawers and one-tenth of the walk-in closet. Adam had let her choose her room and she'd chosen the one that suited her tastes the most. Namely, it was right next door to Rose's nursery.

"Oh listen, Rose. Hear the big trucks? They are coming with your brand-new furniture." Propped on pillows on the bed, Rose kicked her legs and watched her put her clothes away in the closet. The baby was learning how to roll, though she hadn't quite gotten the hang of it yet. Even so, Mia kept an eye on her every second. It was a long way down to the floor for a four-month-old.

Last night, Adam had enlisted her help in picking out nursery items the baby would need from a catalog, including a crib and dresser. Less than twenty-four hours later, they had arrived. Through the magic of…Chase money.

She sighed, although she was glad Adam insisted on buying Rose all new furniture. The baby deserved as much and it meant that Mia could keep Rose's nursery intact at her apartment for those times, if ever, she would take Rose there.

With a fold and a tuck, the last of her sweaters were stacked neatly into the dresser drawer. As she closed the drawer slowly with the flat of her hands, a shiver coursed through her body. Her future was uncertain. She'd been driven out of one home already. How long before Adam added to her pain? How long before she felt like that same unwanted, sullied guest that had overstayed her welcome and been asked to leave? And how could she leave Rose?

Grandma Tess hadn't taken the news lightly of Mia moving into Adam Chase's mansion. Mia had put a happy face on it, trying not to worry Gram with her own doubts. Gram didn't want her getting hurt. There'd been enough heartache in their family recently. Mia couldn't disagree. But she did point out the obvious. Adam was Rose's legal father—the DNA test results had come back positive—and he could provide Rose with a great future.

Sherry and Rena had a different opinion. They saw her move as an opportunity for Mia to spruce up her nonexistent love life. Mia had been dating the vice president of a financial firm six months ago, and her two pals had been sorely disappointed to learn that she'd broken it off with him weeks later. He'd been a player, fooling with women's hearts. Mia recognized the signs and the lies immediately. And she wanted none of those games. She'd seen what her mother had gone through, putting up with her father. Mia didn't want to make the same mistake. Rena and Sherry saw moving in with the mysterious, deadly handsome Adam Chase as a romantic adventure. Mia only saw it as a necessity. He'd given her no other option.

A sudden quiet knocking broke into her thoughts. She turned to the door she'd left partially open, and Adam popped his head inside. "How's it going?"

"We're doing fine. I'm just about unpacked."

Adam glanced at the baby on the bed. "May I come in?"

She nodded.

He took a few steps inside and gave the room a once-over, his gaze stopping on the items she'd put on the dresser—a framed photo of her mother and Gram in the early days and another of her holding the baby along with her gal pals at First Clips—then walked over to the bed, making eye contact with Rose.

She'd thought better of putting out Anna's picture right now, but she would eventually give it to Rose. The child had a right to know all about her mother.

"The movers are downstairs, ready to come up," he said, turning to her. "Would you mind showing them where you'd like everything to go?" He shrugged. "I haven't got a clue."

The irony hit her hard. The master designer needed help arranging baby furniture. "I can do that."

"Great."

Mia bent and gathered Rose into her arms. "Come on, Sweet Cheeks. We're gonna see your new digs."

Adam's lips twitched and a beam of love glistened in his eyes. He reached his hand out as if to stroke the baby's head, then retracted it quickly.

Mia pretended not to notice.

Thirty minutes later the movers were gone and the nursery was almost all set up. She sat on a glider, entertaining Rose with a game of patty-cake while Adam sat cross-legged on the floor staring at screws and nuts and wooden slats of the crib he'd laid out. "So you're telling me you put Rose's crib together all by yourself?" He spared her a glance over his shoulder.

"I sure did."

He scoured over the small-print instructions for all of ten seconds, his brows gathering. "I see."

"What?" she asked. "If a mere woman can do it, you should be able to knock it out without a problem?"

"I didn't say that," he said, his tone light.

She chuckled. "It was implied. I'm curious—why didn't you have the movers set it up?"

He swiveled around to face them, those gray eyes soft now on the baby. "It's the least I can do for Rose. A father usually sets up his baby's crib, doesn't he?"

A lump formed in her throat. Her heart grew suddenly heavy. The man who had everything wanted to do something meaningful for his child. "Y-yes. I suppose he does."

He nodded and turned back to his task.

"I'll put her sheets and towels into the wash," she said, rising. "They'll be ready for her tonight."

"Mary's got that covered."

"But does she have the right—"

"She raised three children," Adam said. "She knows all about laundering baby clothes."

"Oh, right. Okay."

"If you don't mind, I'd like you to stay in here until I get this thing put together."

"Don't mind at all. I can lend a hand if you get confused."

Adam turned to her. She grinned ear to ear and the frown on his face disappeared. Gosh, the man almost cracked a smile. "Smart aleck."

The house was finally quiet of noises that would fill his life from now on. Rose playing with her toys, Rose taking a bath, Rose crying for her bottle. Adam breathed a sigh of relief. This was his daughter's first official night in her home. He'd built the crib she was sleeping in now, his heart bursting as he looked at her small chest rising and falling with steady breaths.

Assembling the crib hadn't been too much of a challenge after all. His only struggle had been afterward, when he'd discovered eight leftover screws and bolts. He'd checked over the crib twice, pulling and tugging at it, testing the sturdy factor and only after Mia told him that the same thing had happened to her had he relaxed about it. The leftovers, she said, are either spares or a result of incompetence on the manufacturer's part. Either way, she'd given him her seal of approval on the crib.

And somehow, that had mattered to him.

Adam touched a small curl on Rose's head. If only he could bend over and kiss her sweet cheeks, wish her a good-night the way a father should. But he couldn't chance waking her and, worse yet, having her scream mercilessly at him.

She'd warm up to him. She had to. How long could he go without holding his own child?

He'd been given a second chance with Rose. He'd do better than he had with Lily. His sister had counted on him and when he'd let her down, it had cost her her life. That pain was always with him and drove him to the outskirts of life. He vowed solemnly not to ever let Rose down. Raising her, he'd try to make up for his failures with Lily and then maybe, he'd find a way to forgive himself.

Having Mia move into the house seemed like the only solution to keep Rose happy and content while living under his roof. For Rose's sake, he'd do anything to make up for lost time. Neither he nor Mia wanted it this way, but for all his business smarts and college degrees, he couldn't figure a way around it.

The architect couldn't draft a better design than the plan he'd come up with, so now he had two new females living under his roof.

Adam left his sleeping daughter and walked downstairs to the kitchen. Mary was long gone. She'd been smitten by Rose and had stayed longer than usual to make sure all was right with the nursery. Rose hadn't warmed to her either yet. Seemed she was all about Mia right now.

He dropped two ice cubes into a tumbler and poured himself a shot of vodka. Stepping outside, the cool salty air aroused his senses and he inhaled deeply. It was cleansing and peaceful out here.

To his left, movement caught his eye. He found Mia standing at the outer rim of the veranda where a low white stone wall bordered the sand. She watched the waves bound upon the shore. And Adam watched her. Breezes lifted the hem of her loose-fitting blouse, her long dark hair whipping at her back, her feet bare. She looked beautiful in the moonlight, and Adam debated going to her. He couldn't trust her. The lies she'd told him, the deceit she'd employed that had gotten them all to this point, painted an indelible mark on his soul. He'd be a fool to let her get under his skin again.

And Adam Chase was no fool.

Yet, he was drawn to her… Something was pulling at him, urging him to walk toward her and not stop. He had to see her. To talk to her. It was unlike anything he'd ever felt before. He took the steps necessary to reach her.

His footfalls on the stone alerted her to his presence. She turned to him. "Adam."

"Can't sleep?"

She shook her head. "I'm kind of keyed up. All these changes." Her shoulder lifted. "You know what I mean?"

"I think I do."

He shook his glass and the ice clinked. "Would you like a drink?"

Her eyes dipped to his glass. "No thanks. It's late. I should go check on Rose."

"I just did. I was in there before I came outside. She's sleeping."

Mia held a remote video receiver in her hand. She glanced at it and nodded. "I can see that."

"A pretty cool invention," he said.

"The best. I don't know how I'd ever get more than five feet away from her room without it. Even so, I get up during the night to check on her. It's a habit. Like I said, I really should go in."

"Am I disturbing you, Mia?"

Her gaze drifted to his mouth, then those amazing eyes connected to his. "It's your house, Adam," she said softly. "I might ask you the same thing. For all I know, you might have a nightly ritual of having a drink outside by yourself."

"Just me and my thoughts, huh?" If she only knew the pains he went through not to think. Not to let the demons inside. He sipped vodka and sighed. "You don't have to walk around on eggshells while you're here. For now, this is your home. Do whatever you please." Under a beam of moonlight her smooth olive complexion appeared a few shades lighter. He remembered touching her face, the softness under his fingertips when he'd kissed her. "We're going to be seeing each other a lot. I mean, my main focus is Rose. I want her to get used to me."

She turned away from him. "I get it. You're stuck with me. If you want to see Rose, I come along with the deal. Is that what you're trying to say?"

"It's just fact, Mia. And I can think of a lot of worse things than being stuck with a gorgeous woman living under my roof."

Mia snapped her head around, her eyes sharp and searching, her lips trembling.

Just days after meeting her, she'd gotten to him. She'd warped his defenses and he'd let her in a little. She'd made him think long range…he hadn't been that happy in a long time. But the path she'd led him down was broken and dangerous. He was too careful a man to venture in that direction again.

Boisterous voices carried on the breeze and reached his ears. Adam peered down the shoreline and made out half a dozen teens tripping over themselves, slinging loud drunken words, many of them profane.

He grabbed Mia's hand. "Shh. Come with me," he said leading her into the shadows behind a five-seat sofa. "Duck down."

He slouched, tugging her with him. They landed on their butts on the cold stone.

"What are you doing?"

"Shh," he repeated. "Lower your voice. It's the kids who've been vandalizing the beach," he whispered. "I still owe them for leaving that broken bottle in the sand and hurting you."

"How can you be sure they're the same kids?"

"Doesn't matter. News travels fast. They'll put the word out not to come here anymore."

"So, what's the plan?"

"Come with me and I'll show you."

Moving through the shadows, they entered the house. Adam left Mia at the foot of the stairs. "I'll check on the baby on my way back," he said.

Three minutes later, dressed in shorts and running shoes, he nodded at Mia as he reached the bottom step. "Not a peep out of her. She's still sleeping. Come—follow me outside."

They stayed out of the light as they returned to the spot near the sofa. "Okay, here's what I want you to do. Give me five minutes and be sure to watch. You'll get a kick out of it."

Adam explained the plan. Then he slunk through the darkness to the house next door that he'd once leased to his friend, country superstar Zane Williams. Zane was gone now, living back in Texas with his fiancée, and the house was empty. Well out of view, he trekked down to the shoreline and began jogging along the bank, heading toward the kids. He came upon them appearing as a midnight runner working up a sweat and breathing hard. Just as he reached them, he dug his heels in the sand and hunched over, hands on knees, and pretended to be out of breath. "Hey…guys." A dozen eyes watched him. "Anybody…have…some water?"

"Water?" one of the kids said. "Does it look like we have water?"

The kid tipped his bottle and slurped down beer. Then the big shot slung the bottle and it whizzed right by Adam's head. A crash competed with the roar of the waves as the bottle shattered against a metal ice bucket. Shards of glass scattered onto the sand. Adam ground his teeth. Maybe he should call the police.

Then one curly-haired boy stepped up and a plastic bottle of water was pushed into his hand. "Here you go, man. Drink up. You look like you could really use this."

The kid had compassion in his eyes. Okay. No cops. They were just stupid kids. They couldn't be more than sixteen years old. "Hey, thanks a lot. You know," he said, rising to his height and uncapping the bottle. "Just a heads-up, but you should be more careful. I mean, coming here and boozing it up right under the nose of a retired police captain."

"What?" the big shot said. "No way."

"Yeah, he moved into that house a few weeks ago." He pointed to the empty house. "I see his wife outside most nights watching the waves as I run by."

The boy craned his head in that direction. "That's far away. I can't see anything. Which means they can't see us."

"Okay, suit yourself. But I hear the captain's a hard-ass about underage drinking. Just a warning to you. Thanks for the water." Adam began jogging away. A siren bellowed, the sound screaming and urgent, disrupting the quiet of the night. Adam turned and looked into the big shot's eyes, wide now and panicked, his innocent years showing on his frightened face. The boys jumped to attention, all six of them darting fearful glances at each other.

One of them shouted, "Run!"

And they flew out of there, leaving their booze behind, kicking up sand and bumping into each other as they dashed down the beach. They'd run a good mile before they'd stop. The run and fright alone should sober them up.

Adam jogged over to Mia, who came out of hiding, holding the siren in her hand. She turned it off. "Did you see them run?" he asked.

"I sure did. Wow. This thing sounds like the real deal. Where did you get it?"

"It's a long story, but it's from my lifeguarding days. Sounds authentic because basically it is." Adam glanced down the beach, his mouth beginning to twitch. He hadn't had that much fun in a while. "I doubt they'll ever come back. Some might've learned a lesson. I can only hope."

He turned to find Mia smiling at him, her eyes warm and gentle. His heart began to thump, and blood pumped hard and fast through his veins.

One smile. One gentle look.

It shouldn't be that easy for Mia to affect him.

"You did this because they hurt me?"

"Yeah," he admitted. "They shouldn't be drinking at their age. Disturbing the peace and—"

Her lips touched his cheek in a kiss that was chaste and thankful. Her hair smelled of sweet berries.

"Mia," he said, folding her into his embrace.

"Adam, what are you doing?"

He whispered, "If you're going to thank me, do it right."

Mia came up for air a minute later. Her lips were gently bruised from Adam's kisses. The taste of him still lingered on her mouth. As he held her in his arms under the moonlight, she trembled.

It was crazy. This couldn't happen. They had a tentative relationship at best, and throwing romance into the mix would complicate everything. Adam clearly wasn't her biggest fan, and yet how could she forget how wonderful those first few days had been between them, when he didn't know who she was or what she'd done?

She hadn't forgotten about how his touch once made her giddy. How, before the truth was revealed, she had been lost in the moment and had almost given herself to him. Good thing that hadn't happened,

"Now, that was a proper thank-you." His hot breath hovered over her lips and she thought he would kiss her again. And once again, she might not stop him.

The baby's cries interrupted him. "Rose," she said, reaching for the baby monitor on the sofa and glancing at it. "She's awake, Adam. Fussing around."

Adam took the monitor from her hand and also looked.

"I've got to go to her," she said, walking quickly toward the doors.

"I'm coming."

Adam caught up to her and entwined their fingers. They headed upstairs together and when they reached the threshold to the nursery, Mia stopped and turned to him. "Maybe you should stay out here," she said.

Adam's head shook. "No, I'm coming in. She has to see me here. It's better that I'm with you."

"Okay." Rose's cries stopped the minute she saw Mia. She picked her up and cupped her head, kissing her rosy soft cheeks. "I know, my baby girl. This is all so new for you. But I'm here now. And so is your daddy."

Mia turned Rose toward Adam. She took one look at him and immediately swung her head in the opposite direction.

"Hi, Rose," he said anyway. "Sorry you can't sleep. Daddy can't, either."

Something lurched in Mia's heart as Adam spoke so tenderly and patiently to Rose. And hearing him call himself "Daddy" brought tears to her eyes. Her stomach ached. It seemed to do that a lot lately. Losing Rose would destroy her, she was sure, but how could she possibly not encourage the baby to know and love her father?

Mia turned so that Rose faced Adam. "Will you let Daddy hold you while I get you a bottle?"

Adam put out his arms to his daughter. Rose tightened her grip around Mia's neck, squirming up her body. Mia tried to pry her off, but Rose was determined not to go to her daddy. Mia didn't fight her. She stepped away from Adam and strode to the other side of the room. "It's okay, baby girl. It's okay. Adam, maybe you could warm up her bottle? I'll rock her."

Adam nodded and walked out of the room.

While he was gone, Mia changed the baby's diaper and then plunked down on the glider and began rocking the baby. By the time Adam returned, Rose was calmer and relaxed. Quietly, he handed Mia the bottle and sat cross-legged on the floor, facing them. Rose sucked on the bottle, keeping a vigilant eye on Adam. He said nothing, merely watched as Rose's eyes eventually closed. There were a few halfhearted attempts to suck the last inch of the formula down before Rose fell back to sleep.

"She's out," Mia whispered.

Adam nodded, the yearning in his expression touching something deep inside.

"Do you want to put her into the crib?" she asked.

"She'll wake if I do that." His voice was quietly bereft. Adam believed Rose had a sixth sense about him.

"No, I can almost guarantee you she won't wake up. She's out."

A childlike eagerness lit in his eyes and he stood. "Yes, then. Hand her to me."

Mia rose from the glider and transferred the baby carefully into Adam's arms. The baby didn't move a muscle. Mia sighed, grateful Rose didn't make a liar out of her.

Holding the infant in his arms, Adam's expression changed. The hard planes of his face softened. His gunmetal-gray eyes melted into longing, pride and love. It was beautiful to see.

But heartbreaking, too.

Mia stood back, away from Adam, overseeing him putting Rose down to sleep.

Not a whimper from Rose as her body touched down on the baby mattress.

Standing over the crib, Adam watched the baby sleep. Mia turned away, leaving the two of them alone. The bonding was happening right before her eyes. She was facilitating it to some degree. It was the right thing to do, but that didn't stop fearful jabs from poking her inside reminding her, her days with Rose at Moonlight Beach were numbered.

Saturday afternoon, Mia was just walking into the house with Rose after working a half a day at First Clips when she spotted Adam at the edge of the patio in very much the same place they'd kissed the other night. "Come on, Rose," she cooed. "Your daddy didn't see you this morning." Adam had made it clear he expected to see Rose at every opportunity. Mia couldn't balk at that. Or that Rose needed the fresh air. Most of her days were spent inside the salon.

She plopped a sunbonnet on Rose's head to shield her eyes from the sun. The hat matched a purple-and-white Swiss polka-dotted dress and bloomers that Adam had given her. She pictured him venturing out to shop for baby clothes and, well, she just couldn't grasp that notion. Yet Mary had insisted Adam had done the shopping with no help from her. She had to admit Rose looked especially adorable today.

With Rose in her arms, kicking her bootie-socked feet happily, Mia ventured outside. That beautiful kiss he'd planted on her hadn't been discussed or repeated. She'd thought that after she'd helped Adam chase off those teens, they'd broken new ground. Not the case apparently. Adam had retreated, probably kicking himself for letting down his guard and showing some emotion.

"Adam, we're home."

He turned around, but it wasn't Adam at all. The man had similar sharp features, a chiseled profile, strong jaw and shoulders just as broad. Stepping closer, she noted he wasn't nearly as tall and his eyes were a deep and mesmerizing blue. There was kindness on his face and a grin that touched something delicate in her heart as he gazed at the baby. "Sorry to disappoint. I'm Brandon. Adam's younger brother."

He put out his hand. "And you are?"

"Mia." She blinked. Adam hadn't told his brother about her and the baby?

They shook hands. "And who's this pretty little thing?"

She couldn't help responding kindly to him. He had a beautiful baritone voice that elevated as he asked about the baby. "This is Rose."

"Rose? Named after a flower," he said, his voice lowering, a veil dimming over his eyes. "Well nice to meet you two stunning ladies," he said. His eyes shined again. "I'm waiting for Adam. Mary said he's due back soon."

"He must be at the office. I think he had a meeting."

Brandon eyed her curiously, the smile never leaving his face. She didn't know what to say to him. Should she spill the beans? Adam was such a private person he might never forgive her if she did. It might be grounds for him tossing her out of the place.

"Is there something I should know? Am I an uncle?"

Mia shuddered.

Brandon's affable expression changed. "Sorry. She's got my brother's eyes."

There was no way around it. Brandon had guessed the truth. "Yes, Rose is Adam's child. I'm her aunt Mia."

"Aunt?"

She nodded. "It's a long story—better to be told by Adam, I think."

Brandon stared at her and then focused on his niece. "I'm an uncle."

Footsteps on stone had her turning to find Mary heading their way. *Thank goodness for the interruption.*

"Lunch is waiting, if you're hungry. I've got coffee, tea and lemonade ready in the kitchen."

Mia was famished. She'd eaten very little that morning. Rose had been in a mood and she'd missed breakfast. She should refuse, but how rude would it be to make Adam's brother eat alone? "Thanks, Mary."

"Shall I warm up a bottle for the little one?" Mary asked.

"I gave her a bottle a little while ago, but I appreciate the offer."

They entered the kitchen and ate lunch together, while the baby played quietly in the playpen. Brandon respected her wishes and didn't ask too many questions about the situation with Rose, other than how much she weighed at birth, how old she was and how Adam was taking to fatherhood. She skirted around the last question and turned the conversation to him. She found out he was a charter pilot working out of an Orange County airport and loved flying. He spent the remainder of their lunch speaking about his escapades in foreign countries, dealing with Homeland Security, and he told a few outrageous stories about the celebrities he'd flown around the world.

Rose began to cry and Mia rose immediately. As she lifted her out of the playpen, the baby whimpered still and Mia knew she had no time to lose. Rose could bellow with the best of them. "Sorry, she's hungry now. I've got to warm a bottle."

Brandon stood and walked over to her, holding out his arms. "No problem. Can I help?"

Mia tried not to let her eyeballs go wide. He didn't know

what he was asking. "Oh…uh. She's squeamish around strangers. I don't think she'll go to you."

"Can we try?" He had persuasive eyes, clear and so startling crystal blue a person could definitely lose their way in them.

"Sure." One second and he'd be handing her back.

"This is your uncle Brandon, Sweet Cheeks. He wants to hold you while I make your bottle."

Mia made the transition carefully, and Rose, the little sprite, didn't make a peep as Brandon settled her into his arms. He began moving, walking, pacing and rocking her as Mia looked on. Astonished, she'd almost forgotten about warming her bottle. "She's a sweet one," he said.

Mia gulped before giving him a smile. The baby was putty in his arms. Was that a good thing? Maybe Rose was finally coming around.

She made quick work of heating the formula in a bottle warmer. Once done, she placed the bottle above her arm and let a few drops drip onto her wrist. Brandon watched. "A test in case it's too hot."

"Gotcha." The baby was fascinated by him. She kept looking into his eyes, responding to his voice.

"I usually feed her in the living room. Mary likes that we're using that room."

Brandon followed her and sat down fairly close on the sofa. "Mind if I feed her?"

"Uh…no, I don't mind." The baby might even let him.

Mia handed him the bottle and the baby latched on to the nipple right away. She slurped and made sucking noises. "She's quite a guzzler." He chuckled and seemed comfortable holding an infant.

"She is growing like a weed."

Brandon took his eyes off the baby to give Mia a look. "I knew a Mia once, an older Italian woman who herded sheep. I can tell you stories…"

"Please do," she said. She enjoyed his company. He

was a charming, funny man who wasn't afraid to talk about himself, and she didn't mind the distraction from his brother, who would rather have a root canal than smile.

They were quietly laughing, Brandon just finishing a story about his crazy stay in Siena, the baby peacefully asleep in his arms, when Adam walked into the room. He stopped midway and gave Mia a cold glance before sending a grim look to his brother. His eyes were filled with indignation.

"Brandon." He kept his voice low, menacing. "What are you doing here? I didn't expect you until Monday."

"There was a change in plans."

Adam's mouth twisted in an unbecoming snarl. "There always is."

"Sorry, bro. I didn't think it would be a problem."

"It is a problem."

Adam frowned at Mia. There'd be no more smiles today for anyone.

"The baby is a stunner, Adam. Congratulations."

Adam blinked, his gaze shifting from her to the baby. "It's none of your concern, Brandon."

"Hey, you're a father, Adam. And that makes me this one's uncle. That's something to celebrate. Isn't she the reason you summoned me here?"

Adam's teeth clenched. He kept his focus on Rose now, in his brother's arms. Mia could only imagine what thoughts plagued his head. The baby wouldn't go to him, yet she took to Brandon, Adam's obviously estranged brother, like peanut butter to jelly.

"Does Mom know she's a grandmother?" Brandon asked.

Adam shook his head. "Not yet."

Mia rose from her seat. "Maybe I'd better let you two talk this out. Brandon, I'll take the baby—"

"Leave her be, Mia." Adam's voice was rough, his gaze

chillier than a deep freeze. "I don't want to break up your little party."

"It's not a party, for heaven's sake, Ad—"

He faced her, betrayal shining in his eyes. "Did you tell him everything?"

"She told me nothing," Brandon interjected in her defense, which only seemed to irritate Adam further.

"I'm asking Mia," he said, enunciating each word.

Defusing the situation was tricky. "No, I only told him that Rose was yours and that I'm her aunt. I thought it best for you to explain the details," she said.

He pinned her down. "That's all?"

She nodded and glanced at Brandon. "He was kind enough not to pressure me with questions."

"My brother's a regular Mr. Nice Guy."

Brandon rose now, careful with the baby in his arms. "Adam, don't take your sour mood out on Mia. Okay, so I showed up a few days early. My bad. Obviously, you've got issues going on here that you need to work out. I'll leave and come back another time."

Adam gave his head a shake. If he hoped to clear away his foul mood, it didn't work. "No. I need to talk to you. Tonight. We'll talk after dinner."

Brandon approached Adam with the baby, ready to hand her to him. Mia immediately stood and intervened. "I'll take her."

Wouldn't that just put a perfect ending on this afternoon for Rose to leave Brandon's arms only to start sobbing uncontrollably when Adam took hold of her. The scene played out in her head with HD clarity. She couldn't allow that to happen.

Brandon swiveled around, and opened his arms enough for Mia to gently take Rose from him. Little sleepyhead kept on sleeping, thankfully.

"Like I said, don't let me break up your little party. I have work to do."

Adam stalked out of the room leaving Brandon and Mia standing there, dumbfounded.

Seven

Adam pushed his hands through his hair half a dozen times as he paced the floor in his home office. He'd deliberately set his office in the front of the house, so he wouldn't be distracted by the roar of the ocean, beachgoers' voices carrying inside the room or a brilliant sun setting over the California shoreline. His windows open, sea breezes blew inside and ruffled the papers lying on his drafting table. He walked over and put a pewter paperweight over them. He wasn't going to get any work done today.

Brandon was here. It had been two years last Christmas since he'd seen him. His mother had insisted her boys share the holiday with her. They'd gone to her home at Sunny Hills and spent nine hours of rigid politeness being around each other. His mother's attempt at reconciliation hadn't worked and it had been awkward as hell. Adam wasn't ready to forgive Brandon for stealing Jacqueline away. Brandon, in one way or another, had been the source of pain for him all of his life. Yet, Brandon was the son whom his mother loved most. Deep down, Adam thought his mother had never forgiven him for what happened to Lily, though she'd never admitted that to him. Adam gnashed his teeth. Hell, he'd never forgiven himself. And he'd never divulged to his mother Brandon's part in Lily's death. Only Adam knew the absolute truth about what had happened that day.

Earlier today, when he'd seen Brandon holding Rose,

acid had spilled into his gut. He'd held back a barrage of curses. Brandon, the charmer, had already won Rose over, while Adam stood on the sidelines waiting and hoping his little baby would come to accept him.

Later that night over dinner, all was quiet. Mia didn't say a word that wasn't directed to the baby. Brandon was treading carefully, too. Several times, he'd caught Brandon shooting Mia conspiratorial sideway glances. Somehow Adam had become the villain.

Fine by him.

He was too wound up to give a damn.

Mia rose from the table after her meal and lifted the baby from her playpen. Rose clung to her neck so sweetly Adam ached inside. "I think we'll turn in early tonight," she said. "Good night, Brandon. Adam."

The sun had just set and it was especially early for her to hit the sack. Even little Rose didn't go to bed until nine. Mia wasn't fooling him. He'd behaved badly earlier this afternoon and she was annoyed with him. He probably deserved her scorn. And it was better that he speak with Brandon in private anyway. He was ready with a condensed version of the story to tell his brother about Rose. He didn't need Mia interjecting facts.

"Good night, Mia," Brandon said, rising to his feet. "Nice meeting you. And give that little one a good-night kiss from Uncle Brandon."

Mia smiled warmly at him. "I'll be sure to."

She was halfway out the door, when Adam spoke up. "I'll be up in a little while. Keep her awake until I get there."

Mia whirled on him instantly, shooting him twin green daggers with her eyes.

Great.

"Rose will sleep when she's tired, Adam, which I think was about five minutes ago. We're not waiting up."

He rolled his eyes. "Fine. Good night, then."

As soon as she left the room, Brandon grinned like a schoolboy. "You sure know how to charm them."

He bounded up, striding out of the kitchen to the bar outside on the patio. Fresh briny air smacked him in the face, and it was far gentler than Mia's reprimand. Technically, he could demand that she obey his wishes. He was Rose's father. He had all rights when it came to his daughter, but he'd never pull that card on Mia. Not unless she gave him good reason to.

He grabbed two highball glasses from underneath the white-and-black granite-topped bar and poured them both a drink. Brandon preferred bourbon, but Adam wasn't feeling especially generous tonight. He poured vodka into both glasses and handed him one as he walked up. "I'm going to make this quick. Want to take a seat?"

"Okay." The iron legs of the chaise scraped across the stone decking as Brandon pulled the chair out and sat down. He lifted his glass. "Thanks," he said and took a sip. His facial muscles tightened as he swallowed the strong liquor and leaned back.

Adam didn't want to start out on a bad note with his brother. He was ready to put the past behind him for his mother's sake, but having Brandon show up unannounced today and finding him holding his baby, his perfect little child who couldn't stand the sight of her own father, had snapped his patience.

He didn't like seeing Mia's eyes go warm and gooey over Brandon, either.

He dismissed that notion. Mia wasn't his concern. His mother and his child were his priorities now.

"So, tell me about the kid, Adam. She's yours—that much I know. And her mother is gone?"

He nodded. "Mia's sister died shortly after the birth."

"That's rough. Were you two close?"

"No, it wasn't like that. We barely knew each other."

"But you're certain the baby is yours?" Brandon asked.

"She is. DNA tests confirmed it. She's got the Chase birthmark, if DNA wasn't enough proof." A wry laugh erupted from his chest.

"No kidding. And what about Mia?"

"She spent months raising her and now she's moved in here, helping to make Rose's transition easier."

"Man, you sound like you're talking about some business merger or something. It's clear Mia loves that child. What about you?"

"Of course I love Rose. She's my daughter." It was love at first sight. On his part, anyway.

"You didn't pick her up when I tried to hand her to you. I haven't seen you hold her. And what's with you ordering Mia around like she's your indentured servant?"

Adam drew oxygen into his lungs. The chilly air helped keep his hot temper at bay. "None of that is important right now." He wasn't going to reveal how Mia had duped him when they first met. How she'd been doing her own form of investigation to make sure he was father material. Or that his daughter screamed blue murder when he tried to hold her. Wouldn't Mr. Charming have a good laugh over that one? "Look, I had an affair with Mia's sister. It wasn't serious and it ended mutually. I only learned weeks ago from Mia that Rose was conceived when we were together.

"So now I've got the baby here and we're trying to figure it out. Rose will always live with me."

"So you and Mia aren't…"

Adam shook his head a little too vehemently. "No. She's gone as soon as we feel Rose has acclimated to…the surroundings."

"Gone? Isn't that cold, Adam? She loves that child. It's clear Rose has formed a strong attachment to her. Who wouldn't? Mia's sweet and gorgeous and—"

"Brandon, lay off, okay? I said we're trying to figure it all out. And what makes you an expert on Mia D'Angelo anyway? You've known her for less than six hours."

"We talked. I have good instincts about people. She's a keeper."

Adam clenched his jaw. Was his brother really trying to give him romantic advice? "Do you want to know why I asked you to come here?"

"Has something to do with Mom. Her birthday's coming up." Brandon sipped his drink.

"That's right. It's her seventieth, and she wants only one thing from us."

"I can only guess."

"You got it. She wants us to patch up our differences. She wants to see her family whole again." It would never be, without Dad and Lily, but that was beside the point.

Brandon shoved the tumbler aside and leaned in from his nonchalant position on the chair. His elbows came to rest on the patio table. "I've tried, Adam. But you weren't ready to hear me."

Adam stared toward the ocean. The swells were high now, breaking on the shore in white foam that cleansed the sand. If only he could cleanse away the bitter pain that seeped into his soul that easily. Maybe that's what he was hoping for with those daily dawn swims, to wash away all the bad things in his life.

Brandon had always been at the very core of his pain. He'd been selfish and self-serving as a young boy, but Adam had never told his mother the true story. Because ultimately, he'd been the older one. He'd been responsible for Lily. "I'm listening now, Brandon."

"You're doing this for Mom."

He shrugged. "Does it matter why?"

Brandon drew a deep breath. "I guess not. I never meant to hurt you, Adam. As much as you may not want to hear this, I swear to you—Jacqueline and I never went behind your back."

Adam looked into his tumbler, sighed and then polished off the rest of it. He let the burn of alcohol settle in his gut before turning to face his brother. "No. You did it right in front of me."

"Not true. I admit, I fell for her from almost the moment I met her. Right here in this house. But she was your girlfriend, Adam. And I saw how much you cared for her. I never acted on my feelings. I never flirted. I never—"

"You were just your usual charming self."

"I am who I am."

Adam scoffed. "You're saying you couldn't help yourself?"

"No, that's not what I'm saying. You have to believe me. I fell hard for her, but never once thought about trying to come between you. I pretty much kept out of your hair. If you remember, I hardly showed up around here while you were dating. And when you two broke up, I struggled with that, but I didn't call her. I wanted to. I was in love with her, Adam. I'm sorry, but that's the truth. And I tried not to think about her. I figured out of sight, out of mind. Then one day, out of the blue, she called me. She had a friend who wanted to charter a flight for a special anniversary party. It began just by talking on the phone. A few dinners later, we were both in love. That's exactly how it happened, Adam. She didn't break up with you because of me."

Adam's mouth tightened. He gazed out to sea again, nodding his head. What was done was done. He'd have to live with Brandon's explanation for now. It had been six years. Jacqueline was out of the picture and his sister Lily wasn't ever coming back. If mending fences with Brandon would make his mother happy, he'd do it. "Okay. I understand."

Brandon slumped back against the chaise, his eyes incredulous. "You do? Just like that? For years, you've kept your distance. Now, you believe me?"

He'd recently discovered that he no longer cared about the situation with Brandon and Jacqueline. As far as he was concerned, it was ancient history. "I believe you didn't know how much it would affect me."

"We didn't sneak behind your back."

"Got it."

Though in Adam's rule book, he'd never go after his brother's girl, broken up or not. "Now, can we talk about Mom's birthday?"

"Sure…" Brandon smiled with a gleam in his eyes, reminding him of the young boy who'd always gotten away with stealing the last cupcake in the batch.

Adam tiptoed up the stairs after he and Brandon hashed out the details of their mother's birthday party. An hour had passed since Mia had taken the baby up to bed and he was certain the baby had already fallen asleep. Just watching Rose sleep was a relaxing balm, a way to calm his nerves and smooth out the kinks going on in his brain. She did that for him. He loved her with all of his heart, and it unnerved him how much she already meant to him.

He walked into the nursery lit by a Cinderella night-light and peered inside the crib, only to find it empty.

Slowly, he turned and crept out of the room. The door to Mia's room was ajar. He peeked inside and found the two of them asleep on the bed. Mia wore the same dress she'd had on during dinner, the hem of soft periwinkle cotton hiked up to her thighs. Her tanned legs were exposed and bent at the knees, protecting the baby with her body. She lay on her side facing him, two perfect breasts partially spilling out of her neckline and long raven strands of hair tickling her flesh as she took easy breaths. As sexy as she was in sleep, Adam only saw beauty now as she lay beside his child swathed with pink-and-brown teddy bears on her nightdress. Her breaths were strong and steady.

Tears stung his eyes, and the allure of their peaceful sleep brought him into the room. He stood over both of them for several seconds and recognized the yearning eating at him. He hadn't spent any time with Rose today. He'd missed his nightly ritual of holding her as she slept and laying her into the crib. It was such a small thing. One he never wanted to miss.

Nimbly, Adam kicked off his shoes and lay down on the bed. The mattress groaned and he winced, freezing in place. When no one stirred, he took great precautions stretching out his body, inching his way, trying not to wake either of them. Then he positioned his body exactly like Mia, a matching opposite bookend to complete the fortress around Rose's little sleeping self.

She was so small, so precious. Moving only the muscles necessary, he wound a curl of her blond hair around his finger. It was soft and as fine as silk. His eyes closed. He wanted to plant a loving kiss on her sweet cheeks. He wanted to speak to her, without her going ballistic on him, and tell her eye to eye how much he loved her.

When he opened his eyes, Mia was staring at him, those jade shards of ice from before melting to a bright warm glow. "Hi," she whispered over the baby. He could barely hear her.

"Hi."

"We tried to wait up."

So that's why they are on her bed tonight. After all her blistering, she thought enough to try to wait for him.

"Thanks. It took longer than I thought."

"You were grumpy tonight." She moved hair off her face, pushing the strands from her eyes. God, she was beautiful.

"My brother brings that out in me. He's gone. For now."

"Do you want to put her down in her crib?"

"Will that wake her?"

Mia glanced at the slumbering baby. "I doubt it. She's pretty tired."

He nodded. "Okay, then."

"You go on and do it. I'll stay here."

He stared at her for the beat of a second. "You're sure?" She wasn't going to oversee him putting the baby to sleep? He'd never done it without her watchful eye before.

"Yes."

Mia was a mystery to him. She'd lied to him, pretending to be an innocent bystander on the beach when they'd first met, and had kept up the deceit for days. Normally, Mia was extremely possessive about Rose. He didn't know what to make of her sudden generous attitude toward him. He certainly didn't trust her. Days earlier, he'd put the wheels in motion to find out what he could about her. More than she was willing to tell him. And he'd be interested in learning who Mia D'Angelo really was. Did she have any skeletons in her closet? He felt justified in his investigation because she had great influence over his daughter. A father had to protect his child, even from possible unknown threats.

Never taking his eyes off Rose, he slipped gently from the bed and bent to scoop her up. Fitting her little body across his arms, he braced her head with his right hand. She smelled of fresh diapers and baby shampoo, innocence and sweetness. He cradled her closer, absorbing all that goodness. She stirred from his movements, her hands fisting and her body arching in a stretch. He rocked her back and forth the way Mia had taught him, and she settled back into a peaceful sleep. Then he headed to the nursery and stood over the crib, hating to give her up. These were the only minutes in the day he could be this close to her. He could hold her all night and not tire of it, but he couldn't chance waking her. He laid her down, and she immediately turned her face toward the wall. She slept the same way he did. He smiled and after a few minutes inched away, his eyes on her as he backed out of the room.

Mission accomplished. He'd put his baby down all by himself. He felt over the moon.

Mia was waiting for him in the hallway. "Is she down?"

"Yeah, she stirred for a second but didn't wake up."

She smiled. "She does that."

Adam gazed into the warm glow of Mia's eyes again, the love shining through clearly despite the dim lighting. She looked mussed, a little tumbled and sexier than any woman he'd ever known.

"I'm glad you were able to put her down tonight."

"You waited up for me. Why?"

She shrugged. "You ordered it."

He took a step closer to her. Dangerous but he couldn't help himself. "If it came out that way, I apologize."

"I'm teasing, Adam. Do I look like a woman who'd cave to bullying tactics?"

"Definitely not." She looked like a woman who needed to be kissed and then some. "Why then?"

Her delicate shoulder lifted. "You were so tense around your brother, I figured you'd need Rose to soothe you."

"Oh, so *she* soothes *me*? Not the other way around. Is that what you're saying?"

"Uh-huh. Are you denying it?"

After a moment of thought, he replied, "No, I can't deny that."

"I didn't think so. Adam, what's up with you and your brother?"

He sighed and gave her a long look. He didn't want to have this conversation with her. He didn't want to have *any* conversation with her. "I don't want to talk about Brandon right now," he whispered, taking a step closer. "There are better things to do."

She gulped, and her gaze dipped to his mouth and lingered.

"Thank you for waiting up for me."

"It wasn't anything—"

"It was plenty," he whispered. His lips hovered over hers. Her breath smelled sweet and minty and when she sighed over his mouth, he could almost taste her.

"Adam," she whispered. A warning?

He thought she'd deny him a kiss, but instead she reached for his shirt collar and then slowly glided her fingers to the back of his neck. She locked her hands in place behind his head. The woman was unpredictable, and it only made her more appealing. Roping her around the waist, he pulled her closer.

She gazed at him, her eyes filled with the same warm glimmer she reserved for Rose. Resisting her now was impossible. He'd seen her laughing with Brandon, and that was all it had taken. If he had anything to say about it, Brandon wouldn't get within a mile of her.

He pressed his mouth to hers, and she fell into his kiss with a whimper of longing. A shudder ran through him. She affected him. And he couldn't help himself.

Her lips parted, and he didn't hesitate to plunge deeper and sink into the sweetness of her mouth.

He hadn't forgotten about that night in her apartment. He'd been lost in her and the heady way she'd responded to him. He'd touched the most intimate parts of her body, and she'd loved every second of it. During these past few nights, he'd lain awake in his bed thinking about her sleeping down the hall. Thinking about where that night would've led, if she hadn't dropped that bombshell on him.

There would be no bombshells tonight and he was ready to finish what he'd started.

Eight

"Adam, we can't." The words fell from her lips limply. They *were*, and she was helpless how to stop it.

His palm flattened against the center of her chest as he forced her back up against the wall. She was trapped by his body, cocooned in his heat. It was so unexpected, so thrilling a move her heartbeat began to pound up in her skull. His aggression excited her and his kisses wiped out any idea of a real protest. "Mia, tell me you don't want this and I'll back off."

He pulled away from her lips to trail hot moist kisses on her throat, gently nipping at her skin with his teeth. A path of fiery heat sprinted down her belly. She was dying with want, her traitorous body giving in to his passion, while a banner across her mind shouted no.

He whispered in her ear, "I'll take your silence as a yes."

A shiver ran through her, yet her mouth refused to open.

Adam kissed her then until she was breathless. His fingers fumbled with the spaghetti straps of her dress, sliding them down. Then with a few hastened tugs, the garment fell to a puddle on the floor around her feet.

She stood before him in her black bra and French-cut panties. He scanned over her body with a sharp intake of breath. "Mia," he said almost painfully. "What am I going to do with you?"

She had a pretty good idea and it didn't scare her. Well, just a little bit, considering who Adam was. He'd been her sister's lover once. She'd resigned herself to that already and didn't relate the mystery man she'd searched for with this living, breathing, sexy man who'd just picked her up into his arms.

He kissed her again and she held on to him as he carried her to his room.

She was lowered down on the bed, and he stood in front of her, flipping the buttons of his shirt. His chest appeared before her eyes, toned, rippled and solid. She sat there shaking, in awe of his upper body. If the lower half matched his brawn…

His eyes bored into her. "Come here, Mia."

The tone of his voice insisted on full obedience. Not that she would've disobeyed his command. She knew what she wanted and rose from the bed.

And then her world tipped upside down. Adam claimed her lips again and again and then he found other places to tease and torture with his mouth. His touch was magical, his hands knowing how to please, his fingers strumming her like a finely tuned instrument. Those firm demanding lips took her to heaven and back. He wreaked havoc on her body, one hand holding her in place while the other elicited moans of agonized pleasure.

"That's it, Mia. Fall apart in my arms."

His urgent command did the trick. The magician made her come apart at the seams, and she crumbled into a thousand wonderful satisfying pieces. She had the feeling Adam was just getting started.

He held her against him, cradling her so close she heard his rapid-fire heartbeat. Her hair was gently pushed off her face, tucked behind her ear and he placed easy quick kisses there to soothe her. She was loose like a rag doll and beautifully sated.

"Do what you want with me," he whispered.

Another thrill traveled south to regions of her body just satisfied. To have him at her mercy made liquid of her bones. Trembling, wicked thoughts entered her head. She was needy and throbbing again, and as she reached out to touch his slick moist skin, her hands shook. He was perfect, trim and muscled and as firm as granite. He shuddered under her hands, and she gazed into his eyes. They were soft, wistful, almost pleading. She had power over him. It was a heady notion and the biggest turn-on.

She lifted up to kiss him as she continued to probe his body. When her splayed hand reached beyond his belt buckle to tease the tip of his manhood, his breath came out as a sharp potent gasp. He was firm and large below the waist, another big-time turn-on.

"Touch me, sweetheart."

It was as much a dare as a request.

Mia wasn't one to back down from a dare. She covered the length of him with one hand and stroked over his trousers again and again. *Oh my.*

A deep barrel of a groan rose from his throat. And then she was being lifted again, Adam's soft curses ringing in her ears about enough foreplay or something. She hid a grin and was lowered rather unceremoniously onto a massive bed. "You said do what I want with you."

"And you're going to pay for that one."

"I'm waiting," she shot back. Where did she get her nerve?

He unbuckled his belt and removed his pants in a rush and joined her on the bed. *Oh my, again.* He had impressive architecture.

He rolled away from her and fiddled with a drawer in the end table. While he was doing that, she calmed herself by looking over the amazing bedroom. The corner room was angled and two entire walls were windows that looked out to sea. The rooms were tastefully decorated and—

He dumped five condom packets on the bed.

Her brows lifted. She had no idea Adam had such lofty plans for her. "Still waiting."

He groaned and grabbed her waist, lifting her above him. She settled, facing him in a straddle position over his thighs. "I want to see your face when I make love to you." Reaching up, he unhooked her bra and signaled for her to remove her panties.

No more fooling around. This was serious. *He* was serious, and the intensity in his eyes scared her a little. Her arms were braced by his hands and he began to massage them, up and down, caressing her limbs as if she were a precious jewel. It was pure heaven, and her anticipation grew. With a simultaneous tug of her arms, she fell forward, and he captured her mouth and kissed her soundly on the lips. The tips of her breasts touched his chest. The coarseness of his skin abraded her nipples, making them pebble up. He flicked his thumb over each one, and a shot of liquid heat poured down her body. She was beginning to ache in pleasant, searching ways. Adam kept it up, kissing her, touching her, making her come alive again.

She couldn't ignore his need, pressing firm against her belly. She touched him there and more soft curses rang from his lips. Hot silk in her hand, she pleasured him as he'd pleasured her, his moans and grunts encouraging her to go on.

Adam's eyes were wild now, smoky and dangerous. He hissed through his teeth, a warning for her to stop. Then his palms were on her waist, guiding her up onto him. They were both ready. She sank down into his heat and two instant moans of relief fell from their lips.

"So good," Adam muttered.

It was. She was filled with him, and it was only more beautiful when he began moving, his hands still on her waist, leading her, helping her find a rhythm that suited them both. He moved with her, slowly building up to a speed neither could maintain for too long. His hands went to her hips, and he rose up partway, encouraging her to wrap her legs around him. And it was like that for a while, each coming together, moving, looking into each other's eyes as he drove farther and farther.

He kissed her breasts, her throat, her chin, and when he reached her lips, he fell back against the pillows, taking her with him.

He arched his hips and pumped, keeping his eyes trained on her. Her hair spilled over the sides of his face and once again, he pushed the strands back, maintaining eye contact.

"Are you there?" he asked.

She nodded.

And then he unleashed the power of his body, sinking farther into her. She whimpered, her cries oddly quiet. It was so damn good, she was stunned almost silent.

Adam climbed with her, his body taxed but relentless. She let go a powerful release, and this time her mouth opened to a scream of pleasure.

Adam, too, made manly noises that seemed to promote his inner caveman. He huffed and grunted, and then she fell on top of him in a heap of boneless rapture.

By far, Adam Chase had given her the best night of loving in her life.

Mia rose from Adam's bed and tiptoed past the nightstand, where two remaining condom packets were left untouched. She was sore in places she hadn't been sore in years, but that wasn't the worst of it. She'd managed to have sex with Rose's father three times during the night. After the first time, the baby had woken and Mia went to her. Adam hadn't been far behind; he'd apparently become a light sleeper, since Rose had arrived here. Adam had warmed her bottle while Mia diapered her. Together, in the night-lighted room, they'd taken care of the baby. Once Rose had fallen back to sleep, Mia handed her off to Adam to put her down.

She'd been halfway to her own room when Adam took her hand and led her back to his big master bed. She hadn't

gone kicking and screaming, and that was part of the problem. It had been so good between them she hadn't wanted
the night to end. Adam hadn't let up on her and she'd met
him touch for touch, kiss for kiss. After bout three, Adam
held her tenderly in his arms, whispered soft words of her
beauty, but he hadn't asked her to stay the night with him.

And once he'd fallen asleep, she'd returned to her own
bed.

Now footsteps approached her room, and she listened
carefully. Her door creaked open and Adam poked his
head inside. They made eye contact and the door opened
wider. Adam stood in the threshold, gazing at her in the
predawn light. Disapproval marred his handsome features.
"I'm going for a swim," he said. "Mary's not due for three
more hours."

"Okay," she said. "I'll listen for Rose." If that's what
he was getting at. She always listened for Rose, and this
morning was no different.

He nodded, his gaze sharp on the covers she held up to
her throat. After what they'd done to each other last night,
it was a silly thing to do. But she felt vulnerable now and
didn't know what he was thinking. Or feeling. Adam wasn't
one to show emotion. Even now, after the passionate night
they'd shared, his face was blank, his eyes unreadable, except for that note of disapproval she couldn't miss.

"Fine," he said. "You feeling all right?"

She'd had a hot night of sex with the handsomest man on
the beach and all she could do was nod and answer, "Yes."

He blinked, stood there a few seconds and then closed
the door.

Mia knocked her head against the pillows. What was
that all about? Damn him. Why was he so closed off?

Was he not a morning person? How would she know—
he never talked about himself. He didn't let anyone in. And
what made her think he would ever let *her* in? Just because

they'd satisfied their base needs last night didn't mean he would actually confide in her about anything.

She refused to think of last night as a mistake, but a little voice inside her head told her that very thing, over and over.

Where they went from here was anyone's guess.

Grabbing the baby monitor, she rose from bed and walked to the bathroom. She used a dimmer switch to adjust the lighting just so, and set the controls on the whirlpool tub. The jets turned on with a blast and bubbles rioted around the oval bathtub. She lit a few scented candles and soon vanilla and raspberry flavored the air, the flickering flames reflecting off the water. She was never one to pamper herself, but today luxury was called for. With luck, the baby would sleep another hour or two.

It would give her time to come to grips about her strong feelings for Adam Chase.

The genius recluse.

Adam stood at the edge of the veranda, his foot atop the stone border, gazing at Mia and the baby playing a game at the water's edge. The baby was smiling and every so often a breeze would carry Mia's animated voice to his ears as she played toe-tag with the incoming waves. He sipped coffee from a steaming mug. How had his life gotten so complicated?

He'd woken up early this morning to find Mia gone from his bed. He'd wanted her there last night. And this morning, he'd wanted to wake to the sweet scent of her luxurious body, to see her hair splayed across the pillow. He'd wanted to trail kisses across her soft shoulders and whisper good morning to her.

He'd worried that he'd been too rough with her, too forceful, too demanding of her body. When he found her gone from his bed, he'd worried that he'd hurt her. Thoughts of last night flashed before his eyes. There wasn't a doubt in his mind that he'd given her pleasure, but how much was too much? And had it been a stupid, mindless mistake, to take his daughter's aunt to bed? Carnal desire aside, he didn't want to ruin things between them. Mia would be in Rose's life forever.

"Here Adam—take this to Mia." Something was shoved into his free hand. He hadn't heard Mary come up behind him, and he looked down at the wicker basket he now held.

"What is it?"

"Mia's breakfast. Yogurt and granola, toast and juice. She has the day off, but she didn't eat anything this morning. There's some other things in there, too, if you'd like."

He gazed at Mia again. She'd taken a seat on a blanket under one of his multicolored umbrellas, the baby propped in her arms. "No, I'm good right now."

Mary relieved him of his coffee mug. "Go on now. Take her the basket. I know you want to."

Mary's eyes twinkled. He nodded. "Fine, if you want to shirk your duties."

"That's me—always finding my way out of doing work around here."

Mary was the best housekeeper he'd ever had. She'd been with him since before he'd come to Moonlight Beach. He wouldn't want anyone else taking care of his home.

"Fine. Shirker."

"I'll be eating bonbons on the sofa in you need me," Mary said as she walked away.

"Smart aleck," he muttered and stepped onto the beach barefoot.

It was a short walk to where Mia had planted herself. He supposed she'd want to have *the talk*. Adam hated those "what happens now" questions that he couldn't answer. Since Jacqueline, the women he'd been with had been few and far between, but almost all of them wanted to know where they'd stood with him after a night of sex.

Once he reached the blanket, he crouched down, setting the basket next to Mia. "Here you go. Compliments of Mary. Breakfast."

Mia turned to him, her sunglasses shielding her eyes. She removed them and glanced at the basket. "That's very nice of her," she said and finally looked at him. Her eyes were a gorgeous shade of rich green, reminding him of morning grass on the pastures in Oklahoma. He was struck silent for a second. "I'll thank her when I go in," she said.

The baby stared at him, her lower lip jutting out and trembling. Her pout broke his heart all over again. What would it take for Rose to accept him?

"Mind if I join you?" he asked.

She hesitated for longer than he would've liked. "No, be my guest."

He scooted onto the blanket on the other side of the baby. He hated that he had to keep his distance from her to keep her happy. Maybe he should keep his distance from Mia, too.

Too late for that.

"You weren't hungry this morning?" He looked into the basket and found a dish of vanilla yogurt topped with granola and raisins, pastries, a bottle of orange juice and fruit.

"Not really. I had coffee."

"Yeah, me, too."

He watched the waves bound in and out. Her silence unnerved him. Had he done something wrong? Other than the obvious, making love to a woman he had no right making love to.

Her hair was pulled into a ponytail that extended to the middle of her back. She wore black shorts and a pretty white scoop-neck tank with a glittery pink tiara painted over her chest. Mia looked delicious in anything she wore.

"You didn't stay the night with me," he said finally. It had been on his mind all morning. "Why?"

He braced himself for her answer. While he knew darn well they shouldn't be entering into an affair, hearing her put a halt to it wouldn't be welcome news. He couldn't imagine not touching her again. She was under his roof and so darn beautiful; it would be the greatest test to his willpower to keep away from her.

"You didn't ask me to."

His mouth nearly dropped open. "I figured you'd know that I'd want to wake up with you."

"Adam," she said, sighing. "Are we really going to have this talk?"

This talk? *The talk?* "Well, hell yeah, we should talk. Don't you think so?"

"I don't see the point."

He clenched his teeth. "You don't see the point?"

"It's weird, Adam. That's all. You and me, after what happened between you and my sister. Are you making comparisons? Did I measure up?"

He blinked, obviously surprised. "Mia, what's going on between you and me has nothing to do with that. Well, indirectly it does, since if Rose wasn't born, I wouldn't have gotten to know you. What's done is done, Mia. I can't change the past. Is that why you're upset?"

"No, Adam. That's not it."

"Then what is it?"

Their voices were raised, and Rose's lips began to quiver. Her face flushed red, a precursor to crying that he'd come to recognize. Mia scrambled to her feet, taking the baby with her. "It's nothing," she said, her voice lower and steady for the baby's sake. "Nothing whatsoever. I'm going inside. The sun's getting too hot for the baby."

A few scattered rays of sunlight beamed through the clouds, hardly enough heat to warrant taking the baby inside. He rose to his feet. "Wait a minute, Mia. Don't leave. We need to figure this out."

"Is that an order?"

He sighed. He hated that she played the martyr. If she was confused, well, so was he. But what they shared last night, all night, was pretty damn amazing. "It's a request. What's gotten into you today?"

"You, Adam. You've gotten into me. How does it feel not having your questions answered? Not knowing where you stand? Not good? Well, welcome to my world."

Crap. He stood there mystified, watching her walk away.

What on earth did she want from him?

And when he figured it out, would he be able to give it to her?

"I can't believe my son didn't tell me about this little one, the minute he learned he was a father," Alena Chase said to Mia.

Mia sat next to Adam's mother on the sofa, with Rose seated comfortably on her lap. Alena's birthday celebration was set for six o'clock that night, and Adam had picked up his mother early to give her the news. He was off somewhere now, speaking to Mary and the catering staff.

Alena had a pleasant voice that hinted at her southern beginnings. Her eyes were a brilliant blue-gray very similar to Adam's, and she wore her thick white hair curled just under her chin in a youthful style. Her face was smooth for a woman her age and only crinkled when she smiled. There were plenty of smiles. She absolutely glowed around Rose. Mia could relate. She'd thought she might feel threatened by yet another Chase laying claim to Rose, but she didn't feel that way about Alena.

"I think it's taken Adam a while to come to grips with it himself," Mia said. She didn't come to his defense for any reason other than to keep Alena's feelings from being hurt. Leave it to Adam to let two weeks go by before he told his mother the truth. "I think he wanted to surprise you for your birthday."

Alena took Rose's small hand in hers and gave it a little shake and then stroked the baby's soft skin over and over.

"Such a sweet surprise. I can't even fault Adam—I'm too happy about becoming an instant grandmother today. It's the best gift in the world. Now I have my entire family here for my birthday."

Brandon sat down and scooted close to Mia, his arm resting behind her on the back of the sofa cushions. "That's just what you wanted, right, Mom?"

She nodded, her gaze never leaving Rose. "Yes. Just what I wanted."

Alena hadn't judged her. She hadn't asked a lot of questions, either. She wondered how much of the true story she'd gotten from Adam when he'd picked her up this morning. Adam, the great communicator.

Mia had made a special point to keep her distance from him all week. She couldn't out and out ignore him, because he expected to see the baby, but she'd found excuses to work later than usual at First Clips every day. There were a dozen good reasons why she needed to avoid him, but the main one popped into her head day and night and wouldn't leave her alone.

She was falling for him.

And that was a disaster in the making.

Adam walked into the room and all eyes turned to him. He took in their cozy scene on the sofa, his gaze lifting to Brandon's arm nearly around her shoulders. His nostrils flared a bit, and a tic worked his jaw. Surely, he didn't think that she and Brandon…

He took a seat opposite them, his back to the ocean, and spoke to his mother. "All is set for the party tonight."

"That's fine, son. I can't wait to introduce this little one to my friends."

Adam nodded. "She'll steal everyone's heart."

"She looks so much like Lily did at this age," his mother said, her eyes misting up.

Adam stared straight ahead, not saying a word. His throat moved in a giant swallow. On a Richter scale of curiosity, Mia registered the highest magnitude. Adam's life was one big mystery to her.

"Sorry Adam, I know you don't like to talk about Lily, but it's just that I feel she's—"

"Mom, she looks more like Adam, I think." Brandon intervened, giving each of them a glance.

"Actually, the baby has her mother's nose and mouth," Mia said softly, gazing at the baby in her arms. Her heart lurched. "She looks a lot like Anna."

Alena blinked, and then lowered her head. "Oh, dear. I'm sorry if I'm being callous." She seemed genuinely contrite. "I'm sure Rose has many of your sister's features. That poor girl, losing her life that way. You must miss her terribly."

"I do. Every day. We were close."

"I'm so smitten with the baby, I can hardly think straight. Can you forgive me?"

Mia nodded. "Yes. Of course. I understand."

Mary walked into the room to announce that lunch was being served on the veranda outside. It was her cue to escape the tension surrounding Adam's family. There seemed to be many unspoken words between them. "Rose needs a diaper change and a nap before the party. I'll take her upstairs now."

"I'll bring up your lunch if you'd like," Mary said.

"Oh, that's not necessary. I'm not very hungry. I'll come down later and eat something."

Mary tilted her head, a note of disapproval in her expression.

"I promise," Mia said. "I'll eat something in a little while."

Mary let it go with a nod. It was sweet the way Mary mothered her.

She made her escape to their rooms upstairs. It would be a big day for Rose, and she really did need a nap. She took one look at the baby making clicking noises and searching with her mouth for the bottle Mia had forgotten to bring up. "Oh, baby. What a dummy your auntie is."

"Is this what you're looking for?" Mia jumped and turned to Adam. He gestured, holding Rose's bottle. "It's ready to go. And, no, you're not a dummy. Maybe you're a little too anxious to get away from my family, though."

Mia's shoulders slumped. "Was I that obvious?" Adam looked a little worn around the edges. His face sported stubble, his eyes appeared sleep weary and not every hair on his head was in place. He looked approachable, normal, but still hot enough to heat her blood.

"Only to me."

"It's not your family, Adam. It's me. I feel…out of place. I know nothing about them, and I have no idea what you've told them about me."

"They know only what they need to know about you. All good things."

"You didn't tell them the entire truth?"

He cracked a rare smile. "Mia, really? You think I'd want them to know how I really came to meet you? What purpose would it serve?"

He was right and it eased her mind that he'd protected her from his family's mistrust and scrutiny.

"So they know nothing about how I—"

"No. They know you had trouble finding out who I was and that once you found me, you immediately told me I had a daughter. That's all they need to know."

"Okay, but I did what I did only because—"

"I know your reasons, Mia. No need to rehash them."

Adam set the bottle down beside the diaper changer and glanced at Rose. Mia had her diaper off and was cleansing her bottom. Adam reached for a diaper and opened it, his eyes, as tired as they appeared before, now beamed with love for his daughter. It transformed his whole face, and Mia would never tire of seeing that adoring expression on Adam. She lifted the baby's legs up a few inches, and Adam slid the diaper underneath her soft-cheeked bottom.

"We're becoming a well-oiled team," Adam said. "I'd like to think so anyway."

Mia finished diapering her and sat down on the glider. The baby latched on to the bottle instantly, guzzling the nipple and taking long pulls of formula.

Adam sat down on the floor beside the glider, watching her feed the baby. It was becoming a ritual, Adam waiting for the time when the baby slept, so he could hold her for precious moments and put her down into her crib.

Only minutes later, the bottle was sucked dry and the baby's eyes had drifted closed. When Mia nodded to Adam, he helped her up and the hand he'd placed on her shoulder sparked a riot of emotion. He hadn't touched her for days and she'd hoped to be immune, but that night of shared passion was never far from her mind. She'd done a good job of keeping her distance from him since, yet her body responded to him like no other man she'd ever met before. Drawing in her lips, she nibbled on them and sighed.

"Here you go." Carefully, she handed Rose off to him and walked out of the room. It was his special time with his daughter and Mia could grant him that. At any other part of the day, Rose didn't want to have anything to do with her father.

Mia was standing at the window in her room watching the tide roll in, when she heard a knock on her door. She turned to find Adam there. "Do you have a minute?"

"Is Rose down?" she asked.

"Sleeping like an angel."

"Shouldn't you be having lunch with your family?"

"I'll go down in a few minutes. My mother never tires of being with Brandon."

There it was again, spoken with no sarcasm, yet Adam's choice of words was very revealing.

"Come in."

He approached her and for a few seconds was quiet, standing by her side watching the surf curl into waves that beat upon the shore.

"What is it, Adam?"

He sighed and his gaze flowed over her. "It's you, Mia. You're doing your best to avoid me."

"I won't deny that."

His brows lifted as if he didn't expect her to be so blunt. "Why?"

Did he really want to have this conversation now, on the day of his mother's party? "Let's just say I don't find you…" She stopped. Was she really going to say she didn't find him appealing, attractive—she wasn't into him? Yeah, right. And the sun didn't rise in the east every day. "You and I aren't compatible." She shrugged. That would have to do.

"Liar."

"What?"

"We're very compatible. In case you're forgetting that pretty fantastic night together. I'm having a hard time forgetting it. And I heard no complaints from you that night."

She blushed. "I mean outside of the bedroom."

"How so?"

"Adam, you're a recluse. Not only do you hide inside your house—you don't engage with people. You're closed off. You give nothing of yourself away, and I already have trust issues with men. So, you see, it's impossible. Besides, there's Rose to think about."

"Leave Rose out of this. What do you mean, you have trust issues?"

"Something's clearly eating at you, and you won't tell me what it is."

"I don't know what you're talking about," he said, eyes wide as a schoolboy's.

"Okay, fine, Adam. If that's how you want to play this. There's really nothing much more to talk about. Now, if you don't mind, I have some work to do before the party tonight."

"Mia, don't dismiss me."

She lifted her face to his, shaking her head and wishing for things to be different. "Then tell me the truth, Adam." The plea in her voice was softly spoken. "Talk to me."

"I'll tell you one truth." He cupped her face in his hands and, before she knew what was happening, placed a solid, smoldering kiss on her lips. A guttural moan rose from her throat as he drew her closer, his body pressed to hers, hips colliding, chests crushing.

He ended the kiss abruptly and spoke over her bruised lips. "Compatible."

He was almost to her door, when he turned to her and tossed out, "For your own sake, stay away from my brother, Mia. He's trouble."

Nine

Trouble was charming. *Trouble* offered her a drink and bantered with her during the party, while Adam stayed back overseeing the celebration with his foot braced against the wall on the veranda. *Trouble* wasn't trouble at all. He seemed like a man eager to get to know his niece. Brandon would leave Mia and Rose's side and venture to the opposite end of the patio to entertain one of his mother's guests and then come back to say something clever to Rose. Mia had no interest in Brandon, other than he was Rose's uncle and so far, proved to be a pretty nice guy, yet Adam hadn't balked at the chance to warn her about him. Why?

"I can't believe she's my granddaughter," Alena said, rocking the baby gently, with the expertise only a mother would know. Rose seemed to enjoy it. So far, not a peep out of her as Alena held her. Adam had given Rose the outfit she wore today. It was a lavender satin little thing, with frills and lace, made by a designer. Her shoes and socks and bonnet all matched. Several of Alena's friends surrounded her, their gazes focused lovingly on grandmother and baby. Alena was in birthday heaven.

"She's lucky to have you," Mia said. She couldn't begrudge the baby the love of her grandmother. Rose deserved to be loved by everyone in her family.

Alena's eyes welled with tears. "Thank you. It's nice of you to say. I hope to be seeing a lot of her. She's the blessing I've been praying for."

"I think Rose would enjoy spending time with you, Alena."

Rose, as if on cue, began to fuss.

"There, there," Alena said, changing her position and rocking her a little more forcefully. Rose was having none of it. Her mouth opened to tiny cries that grew increasing louder. "Whoops, I think she needs her auntie Mia."

Alena transferred the baby into Mia's arms, just as a hush came over the twenty-five other partygoers. Mia turned to see what the big deal was all about. In walked Dylan McKay, only the most celebrated movie star of this decade, with a young woman on his arm. He smiled amiably at everyone and strode directly over to Alena. He took her hands in his. "Alena, happy birthday," he said, giving her a big smooch on the cheek.

Women had swooned over far less attention from Dylan McKay.

"Dylan, I'm very glad you came."

"I wouldn't miss it." Alena's face was in full bloom.

"This is Brooke, my little sis."

"Hi," Brooke said. She was very attractive and up until that moment, Mia suspected she knew what had been on everyone's mind when Dylan had walked in with her. Dylan McKay was fodder for the tabloids and the entire world supposedly knew who he was dating, made-up scandals or not. "Nice to meet you."

"The very same here, my dear. Thank you both for coming."

"I hear there's someone else for me to meet." Dylan turned her way. "Hi again, Mia," he said. "We've met once before." His daunting blue eyes bored into her, and she almost swooned herself.

"Yes, we have. Hello, Dylan. It's nice to meet you, Brooke."

Alena sent an adoring look at Rose. "And this gorgeous little babe is my granddaughter, Rose."

Mia wasn't new to celebrities. First Clips catered to a

high-end clientele, but she'd never spent time with anyone in the same caliber as Dylan McKay. Adam never mentioned to her he'd invited them, but of course, why would he break the mold? After that kiss today, her relationship with him was even more complex than ever.

Adam finally left his wall space and approached the group. "Dylan, Brooke," he said amiably. "Welcome."

Dylan nodded, his focus solely on Rose. "She's beautiful, Adam. Congratulations."

He extended his hand, and the two men shook. "Thanks. Can I get you and Brooke a drink?"

"Sure, I'll go with you. Brooke, are you okay here?" Dylan asked.

"Of course. You know I love babies. Do you mind if I hang out with you?" she asked Mia.

"Not at all," Mia said. "I'd like that."

"Great," Dylan said. "I'll be back in a little while."

Dylan walked off with Adam and Brooke turned her attention to Rose. "May I hold her?"

Mia smiled warmly. "You can try."

"So you're a daddy now?" Dylan said, taking a sip of Grey Goose. They stood a few feet from the bar, out of the way of the bartender, who was making cocktails for the guests.

Dylan's appearance impressed his mother's friends, but that was not why he'd been invited. Dylan truly cared for Alena Chase. She reminded him of his own mother, who was living a quiet life in Ohio as a retired school principal. And in his own way, Dylan McKay was old-fashioned about family. He was a good son and brother from what Adam could tell.

"It appears that way. It came as a shock, but I'm getting used to the idea."

Dylan glanced into the crowd surrounding Mia and the baby. "The baby also came with a pretty hot-looking nanny.

Or haven't you noticed?" He grinned that winning mega-watt grin that earned him millions.

"I've noticed. But don't let your imagination run wild. Mia isn't her nanny. She's Rose's aunt and she's off-limits." To every man here under the age of sixty, he wanted to add, which meant Dylan and Brandon.

"Possessive," Dylan said.

Adam shrugged. It did no good explaining the situation to Dylan. The guy formed his own impressions and usually they were dead-on. "Not really. Just looking out for my daughter's welfare."

"Hmm. Yeah, I can see that. She's living with you, isn't she?"

"Rose? Yes, she's my daughter."

"I meant Aunt Mia."

Of course that's what he meant. "It's a temporary arrangement. Now change the subject, Dylan."

"Okay, but first let me say I'm very happy for you. It may not be a perfect situation, but that baby will bring you a world of joy."

Dylan wanted to find a woman he could settle down and raise a family with. He'd dated a bunch of women already and hadn't found *the one*. The man loved kids and wanted a few of his own. Sometimes, fame came with a huge price, and he was never sure who he could trust, who was the real deal.

Adam could relate. He didn't trust easily anymore. He thought he knew what love was, but apparently he'd been wrong. Having his heart carved up and laid out on a silver platter could do that to a man.

"Your mom looks happy, Adam."

"She's getting exactly what she wants. Brandon and I have patched up our differences. The baby is the icing on the cake for my mother. A baby bonus."

"Yeah, well, babies have a way of softening people. So, you've forgiven Brandon?"

One night over a bottle of fifty-year-old Chivas Regal whiskey, Adam had divulged his heartache about Jacqueline and his brother to Dylan. He was the only person who remotely knew the story. Apparently, Dylan had been dumped once, too, before he'd become famous, and the scars had left an indelible mark on him.

"For the most part, yeah."

He glanced over to the fire pit. Brandon was standing beside Mia, and their laughter drifted to his ears. What did the two of them always seem to find so funny? Adam fisted his free hand as he sipped his drink.

Dylan followed the direction of his gaze "You sure? Because you're looking a lot like the jealous husband right out of my last movie about now."

Adam glared at Dylan.

"Hey, don't kill the messenger. Listen, if you're interested in her, you should do something about it. She's the whole package."

"How on earth do you know that?"

"Hell, Adam. I read people. And if she wasn't, you wouldn't trust your baby with her or look like you want to strangle your brother right about now."

Adam drew a sharp breath. "Shut up."

"You know I'm right."

"What happened to changing the subject?"

"Okay, fine. Are you going to Zane's wedding next week?"

Country superstar Zane Williams had been his other next-door neighbor on Moonlight Beach until he'd fallen in love with Jessica Holcomb, his late wife's sister, and moved back to Texas. "I am. How about you?"

"I'm bummed that I can't. I'm set to film up north next week."

"Are you taking Brooke with you?"

Dylan's gaze reverted to his foster sister, who was playing with little Rose. "No, Brooke's too busy with her new business. She's moving into her own apartment this week," he said. "Things are going well for her."

The chef interrupted his next thought. "Dinner is ready, Mr. Chase. Would you like to announce it, or shall I?"

"You do it, Pierre, and thank you."

Adam and Dylan walked over to the fire pit where Rose was staring at the stone gems casting off light and heat. She seemed fascinated by the crystallized display, and Adam got a kick out of seeing life through her untarnished eyes.

"Mom, we're ready for dinner. Chef made all of your favorites."

His mother looked up. "Mia and Rose will sit with us at our table?"

"Yes."

"And Brandon, too?" she asked.

"Of course, Mom. Today is all about family."

Mia's head lifted. Her eyes softened as they met his, and Adam winked at her.

She tilted her head to one side.

Then she smiled, a beautiful, heart-pulling smile that settled around his heart.

"The party was really nice," Mia said to Sherry on Monday morning as they prepared to open the doors at First Clips. The first appointments were due at nine. Sherry arranged her hairbrushes, combs and scissors, while Mia looked over the appointment book. Rose was perfectly happy swatting at the toys hanging over the handle of her infant seat. "Adam's mother is smitten with Rose. She said it was the best birthday of her life."

"I would imagine. Learning that she had an adorable granddaughter could only put a smile on her face. But, Mia, was it hard seeing her with the baby?"

Mia thought about it a second. "Not really. I thought it would be. Gram is the only grandmother Rose has known, so I worried that it might seem strange and, I don't know, kind of disloyal. But it wasn't that way at all. Alena is a warm person and she's careful not to be heavy-handed when it comes to Rose. She stayed over the weekend, and we got to know each other a little. For her birthday, I had a picture of Rose taken shortly after her birth blown up and framed. Alena cried when I gave it to her and told me how much she appreciated it. She left this morning and you should've seen her when she kissed Rose goodbye. It was really touching. "

"So, now it's just you and the hunky architect living in that big old mansion again?"

"Technically yes. But it isn't like that, Sherry."

"Okay, if you say so. Did I tell you how jealous I am that you partied with Dylan McKay? Mia, you're mingling with Hollywood royalty."

"About ten times this morning."

"Oh man, Mia. If I didn't love you so much, I'd hate you."

"Thanks… I think."

Rena walked in wearing a cerulean satin princess gown à la Cinderella. Her hair was piled up on her head; a tiara dotted with gemstones caught the overhead lighting. "Morning ladies. How's everyone today?"

"Dylan McKay was at the party over the weekend," Sherry announced.

"No way he was," Rena said. Contrary to her words, her face lit up. "He wasn't there, was he?"

"If I promise to tell you, you have to promise not to hate me."

Rena gave Sherry a glance. She was feigning a frown and nodding her head. Rena's eyes widened. "I promise," she said. "Now tell me all about it."

She recounted the brief conversations she'd had with Dylan to her friends, and as they worked through the morning, they managed to keep all their appointments on schedule. Five boys and seven girls were clipped and groomed and had walked out with smiles on their faces. By eleven-thirty, Mia's stomach growled. She hadn't eaten much that morning. As she headed to the back lounge, taking the diaper bag with her, she spotted Rena and Sherry ogling a man through the shop window.

"He's heading this way," Rena said. "Would you look at him? He's a ten, if I ever saw one."

"Ten and a half," Sherry added. "Bone structure counts extra, you know."

"I take it you're not talking about shoe sizes," Mia said, preoccupied with getting Rose's bottle out of the diaper bag.

"No, but oh man, Mia. This guy is hot. I bet he'd put your Adam to shame."

"He's not *my* Adam." She was curious enough to move over to the window beside her friends. She followed their line of vision and oh! Thump. The overfilled diaper bag slipped from her hand. She gulped. "That *is* Adam."

The girls shrieked. "That's Adam," Sherry said. "Oh, Mia. Now I really do hate you."

"Me, too," Rena said.

"Oh, be quiet, you two." What was he doing here? Adam was too busy perusing the storefront sign to notice the three of them all lined up, gawking at him.

The next thing she knew, he was reaching for the door-knob. The overhead chime rang out a rendition of the *Star Wars* theme and he walked in. The girls bumped shoulders, waiting in attendance. They probably looked like the Three Stooges on a bad day.

"Hello," he said, eyeing the girls first. Mia had to admit, their starship captain and princess getups were a bit distracting.

"Hi," the two chorused in unison.

Mia stepped up. "Adam, what are you doing here?"

He shrugged. After he lifted his shoulders, the beige

zillion-dollar suit he wore slipped right back into place. "I came to see your shop."

Rena made an obvious throat-clearing sound, and Mia got the hint.

"Oh, right. Adam, let me introduce you my friends. They staff the shop along with me. This is Rena and Sherry. Adam Chase."

He took both of their hands and gave a gentle one-pump handshake. "Nice to meet you ladies. I've heard good things from Mia about you."

"Same here," Sherry said. "I mean, Mia talks about you all the time."

Mia nibbled her lip.

Adam glanced at her, and she looked away.

"Where's Rose?"

"She's in the lounge, napping," Rena volunteered. "We take turns with that precious bundle. Sherry and I are her honorary aunties."

Adam nodded. "I know she's in good hands." He turned to Mia. "If you have a minute, I'd like to speak with you."

"Now? Here?" She was curious. Why couldn't it wait until she got home?

"Yes, if you have the time."

"Oh, um. Sure. Follow me and I'll give you the nickel tour. We can talk in the back room, and you can see Rose."

"Sounds like a plan."

It really did only take two minutes to show Adam the entire shop. They wound up in the lounge area where Rose was sleeping. "She's still asleep," she whispered. "Sometimes she sleeps in the infant seat and sometimes I put her down in the playpen. I keep this place spotless and she's in good hands with Rena and Sherry, so you don't—"

Two of his fingertips brushed over her mouth, stopping her from saying more. The pads were rough over her lips, but a sweet tingle washed through her anyway. "Mia, you don't have to explain. I'm not here to inspect the place."

"Then why are you here?"

"I came by to see where my daughter spends a lot of her time. And I came to ask you to lunch."

"Lunch? You want to have lunch with me?"

"You look surprised. Don't you take a lunch break?"

"Yes, but…why?"

He released a big sigh. "I'm trying, Mia."

"Trying to do what?"

"Not be so closed off."

They sat across from each other in a hole-in-the-wall restaurant in Santa Monica, three blocks away from her shop. Seaboard Café boasted the best seafood in town. The baby enjoyed the short walk in the stroller and was now sitting in her infant seat next to Mia, taking in the surroundings with inquisitive eyes. Mia's heart seemed to be in a perpetual state of melt mode lately. She'd gone gooey soft inside when Adam confessed he was trying not to be so closed off. For her? If only she could be sure. But oh wow, that seemed to come out of the blue. And it made her giddy.

Adam stood for a moment and removed his jacket. "You mind?"

She shook her head. He could undress in front of her anytime he wanted.

He unfastened his tie and folded it into his jacket pocket and then unbuttoned the first two buttons on a crisp cocoa-brown shirt. He'd come into the shop looking sharp and handsome, but he was no less gorgeous now. The girls would never let up on her now that they'd laid eyes on him.

He sat down, shot his daughter an adoring look and said, "I like your shop. It was hard to picture in my mind. Now, I can visualize children sitting in those chairs getting their hair cut."

"We still have our challenges. Sometimes we get a child who is frightened or stubborn. All the bells and whistles in the world won't get them to sit in the chair. Sherry has actually cut a child's hair, sitting in the rocket ship, while the child stood up. The kid absolutely refused to do it any other way. We have learned to be flexible."

"It's a great idea, though. A very unique approach for a hair salon. Was it your idea?"

"No, I'm not that imaginative. It was Anna's. She was the mastermind of First Clips."

Adam nodded. And then hesitated. His lips pursed, tightening up. He seemed to have something to say, but he kept silent.

"What is it?" she asked.

"Your sister. I'm sorry she died, Mia."

Mia's heart pounded hard, the way it did whenever Anna's death was brought up. "Thank you."

"What you said about me comparing you to her, that isn't true. It never crossed my mind."

Mia's eyes narrowed on him. "Not even a little?"

"No. Not even a little."

"I wasn't too happy with you when I said those things."

"I know."

The waitress came by to take their order. Mia ordered a bay shrimp salad to Adam's grilled salmon. A loaf of pumpernickel bread and cheesy biscuits were placed on the table along with garlic-infused butter. Mia's mouth watered. When Adam offered her the bread, she grabbed a cheesy biscuit.

"Hungry?"

"Starving."

"Dig in. So when does the baby eat?"

"She'll be fussing the minute my food arrives, I'm sure. She has an inner time clock that keeps Aunt Mia in shape. My hips are grateful."

"So am I." A wicked smile graced his face.

"Is that so?" She chuckled and didn't know what to make of Adam today. "Tell me that when it happens to you."

"I'm waiting for the day when Rose lets me feed her."

"The pediatrician said he might give me the okay to start feeding her solid foods. She might be eating with a spoon soon."

"So soon? I'll never get to feed her with a bottle."

"Yes, you will, Adam. She'll come around. And she'll be drinking from a bottle for a long time."

"I'd like to go to her next pediatrician's appointment with you. When is it?"

"Next week. I was going to ask you to join us, if you weren't too busy."

"I'm never going to be too busy for Rose," he said emphatically.

After their meals arrived, Mia got two bites of her salad in before the baby squawked and squirmed uncomfortably in her seat. "See, I told you. She has a sixth sense." She smiled at Rose. "You don't want your auntie Mia getting chubby, do you?"

"I'm recognizing her different cries now. That's definitely a hunger cry." He dug into the diaper bag and grabbed the bottle. He gave it a few shakes and handed it to her. "I wish she'd let me help you more."

Mia lifted the baby out of the infant seat. "You're welcome to try anytime you want, Adam." She gestured with the bottle.

"Not now. I wouldn't want to get kicked out of this place. The food is good. I'd like to come back."

"Chicken," Mia said, grinning. Rose was getting good at holding the smaller four-ounce bottles on her own. Mia fed the baby with one hand and picked up her fork and took bites of her salad with the other.

"You make it all work, Mia." Adam's note of admiration wasn't lost on her. "You multitask like a pro."

"Thanks. Are you buttering me up for something?"

He cut into his meal and chewed thoughtfully. "Why, because I'm paying you a compliment?"

"Well, yes. There is that."

"You caught me. But I'd give you the compliment even if I didn't have something to ask you."

"So, I was right?"

"Yes." He braced his arms on the table's edge and leaned forward, capturing her attention. "I want to take you and the baby away for the weekend."

"What?" She couldn't possibly have heard him correctly.

"I'm going to a wedding, and I want to take you with me."

She absorbed that for a moment. "You want me or the baby?"

"Both of you, of course."

Meaning, he wanted Rose with him, and the only way that could happen was if she went, too. They were a package deal.

"My friend is getting married, and you're both invited. It's in a small town in Texas. We'll leave Friday morning and be home by Sunday afternoon. It's short notice, but I'm hoping you'll say yes."

"I don't know, Adam." She began shaking her head. "Taking Mia on a plane can get complicated. I'd have to check it out with her doctor. Wouldn't it be easier for you to go without us?"

"I'm chartering one of my brother's planes. So we'd have a ton of room and all the conveniences we'd need. The trip is less than four hours, Mia. And well, I don't want to stall the small amount of progress I've made with Rose. The truth is, I don't want to miss a minute of time with her."

It was a tough situation. Mia was pretty much at his mercy. If he wanted to take his daughter somewhere, Mia would always be the tagalong. "Texas?"

"It'll be fun. A change of scenery. The wedding is being held in a barn on his property."

"Whose property?"

"Zane Williams."

Mia shrieked. "*The* Zane Williams. The country superstar?"

He nodded, blinking at her outburst.

"For heaven's sake, Adam. Don't you know any normal people?"

He chuckled. "Zane is as down-to-earth as they come. He's a great guy, and he wants to meet my daughter. Mia, I really want you there with me. It's not just about the baby."

Could she believe that? Should she trust him enough to believe he genuinely wanted her with him? "Give me some time to think about it."

"Okay. I can do that."

The meal was over, and Mia fastened Rose into her infant carrier again. Adam paid the check and picked up the carrier, inserting it into the stroller base. With a click, the baby was latched in. He was getting good with the baby's gadgets.

Adam assumed the position, taking hold of the stroller handle. "Ready, my pretty little Rose? Daddy's going to take you for a walk." She lagged behind as he strolled the baby out of the restaurant and onto the sidewalk, heading back to the shop.

There would be nothing left of her heart if Adam continued being so sweet and loving. He wanted to be a father in every sense of the word. How could she stand in his way?

She already knew what her answer to the weekend trip had to be.

She couldn't seem to deny Adam Chase anything anymore.

Ten

The plane trip was as comfortable as Adam said it would be. Rose slept most of the time in her car seat, and Mia and Adam played games with her during the rest of the trip. Mia had half hoped the pediatrician wouldn't give Rose permission to fly, but that hadn't been the case at all. Rose had gotten the all clear. And now Adam sat facing Mia in a stretch limo loaded down with baby equipment, heading toward Beckon, Texas.

"Tell me about Zane and his fiancée," Mia asked Adam, keeping her voice low. The baby's eyes were drifting closed again. Mia wished she could join her in a nap. "You told me that he'd leased the house next door to you and that you'd become friends during that time. But that's all I know, really."

Adam poured her a glass of lemonade from the bar and extended his arm to hand it her. "Thanks."

"You haven't read about it? It's big entertainment news. I guess the story got leaked out about Zane falling for his late wife's sister. They fell in love when Jessica came to Moonlight Beach to heal her wounds from being dumped at the altar."

"I don't have much time to read that stuff, Adam."

Adam poured himself a glass of lemonade, too, and took a sip. "Jessica is a nice woman. You're going to like her. She's a schoolteacher. I got to know her a bit when she lived here."

"And so will this wedding be a three-ring circus?"

"It shouldn't be. They were keeping their wedding plans a secret. Zane had rumors spread that they were hoping to get married next summer on the beach where they met. So, hopefully, this small farm wedding won't attract attention."

"I hope not, for their sake. They deserve to have a private ceremony."

His eyes flickered as he flashed a smile. That killer rare smile did things to her insides. Then he slid across from his seat to sit beside her and brought his hand up to her face. The gentle touch had her lifting her chin, and their eyes met as his arm wrapped around her shoulder. "I'm glad you're with me, Mia."

"Me, too," she said, taking a swallow of air.

His head bent toward her, and her mouth was captured in a long delicious kiss that was sweet, soothing and different from the way he'd kissed her before. "It's a long ride," he said. "Why don't you close your eyes and get some rest?"

It was just what she needed. The plane trip and all the preparations beforehand had worn her out. "Sounds perfect."

He cradled her in his arms and coaxed her head onto his chest. He smelled of musk and man, so strong and so good. The sound of his heart beating, the rapid thump, thump, thumping, calmed and comforted her as she drifted off.

A kiss to her forehead snapped her eyes wide-open. "Wake up, sweetheart."

Mia pushed up and away from Adam's grasp to get her bearings. The limo was parked in front of a hotel. All those miles of flatlands were behind them. "Did I sleep the whole way?"

"You and Rose were sleepyheads."

She gazed at Rose in the car seat. Her eyes were just now opening. "Wow, I didn't mean to sleep so long." She fiddled with her mussed hair. She must look a wreck.

"You needed the rest. You do a lot, holding down a job and taking care of Rose."

"I love it."

"I know, but that doesn't mean it doesn't wear you down at times."

She couldn't disagree. She'd been getting up with Rose twice a night the last few days. The baby was cutting teeth and wasn't sleeping through the night.

The chauffeur opened the door, and Adam unsnapped the baby out of the infant seat. He handed her off to Mia before she fussed and then extended his hand to help them out of the car. After Adam gave the driver instructions regarding the baby equipment, he guided her to the front desk and checked them into the only two-room suite on the premises.

Beckon wasn't a destination stop, but Zane Williams had put their little town on the map. He was their pride and joy. That much she knew about the country star.

As they entered the elevator, Adam whispered in her ear. "I can't promise you a five-star hotel. But I was assured it's a decent place."

"All I need are clean sheets and a nice bathtub and I'm happy."

"Is that all it takes to make you happy?"

"Uh-huh." She glanced at him. There was a lightness to Adam lately that kept her on her toes. "And what makes you happy?"

"Whatever makes you happy, Mia."

If he wanted her to jump his bones, he was halfway there. She liked this new Adam. He was charming and sweet. It sort of unsettled her, though. His abrupt turnaround seemed too good to be true.

"Right answer," she said as she stepped out of the elevator to face their suite.

Adam opened the door and they stepped inside. "Wow, this is nice," she said immediately. It was spacious with a flat-screen television on the wall and two lovely sofas facing a fireplace. A double door opened to one large bedroom and a master bath.

A large bouquet of pink lilies filled a glass-blown lavender vase that sat on the fireplace hearth. Adam walked over to it and read the card. "It's from Zane and Jessica, welcoming us to Beckon."

"Nice of them," she said. Rose was getting heavy in her arms. "Adam, can you lay a blanket down, please?"

He jumped to help her, retrieving the blanket from the diaper bag. Kneeling down, he placed it in the center of the room, and Mia met him there as she laid the baby down on her stomach. "Tummy time," she said. Then she gazed at Adam. "There's only one bedroom," she blurted. It was one of the first things she'd noticed about the suite.

"You and the baby take the bedroom. I'll sleep in here," he said. "I'm sure the sofas fold out into beds."

Their eyes locked, and warmth heated her cheeks. It was one thing living under Adam's roof in a huge mansion of sixteen rooms. A person could go all day without bumping into anyone else, but here? *Awkward.*

"You're pretty when you blush," Adam said.

Her shoulders slumped. No sense skirting the issue. "It's not as if we haven't slept together, Adam. But we have to be careful for Rose's sake that we don't make a mistake."

"I agree. We're on the same page, Mia."

"We are? Okay, good." As long as she made herself clear. Adam had no clue how hard it would be to go to bed tonight knowing he was only steps away. She wasn't as immune to him as she pretended, especially lately. He'd been a dream these past few days. "So what's on the agenda today?" she asked.

"Well, first we take a little rest and get settled. And later tonight there's a welcome barbecue at the farm. Zane's in the process of building Jessica a house, so it'll be on his property, but prepare to rough it a bit."

"You didn't design the house by any chance?"

"It's their wedding present. Zane had specifics and I helped him along."

"It's probably going to be fantastic, a dream home."

"I hope so."

"If you designed it, it will be."

Adam's expression softened and warmth filled his eyes. "Thank you."

She stared at him. "You're welcome."

Their luggage arrived at the door, breaking the moment, and they spent the next twenty minutes unpacking and setting up the baby's equipment.

By six o'clock they were standing on Zane Williams's property, a vast amount of land accented by cottonwoods and lush meadows. Off in the distance, she saw the house under construction and could only imagine how beautiful it would be when it was done. Adam told her there were balconies and terraces to the rear of the home facing a lake.

The party invitation had said ultracasual. Mia wore a soft cotton paisley dress and tall tan leather boots. Adam told her she looked very much like a country girl. Adam did the cowboy thing justice, too. He wore jeans, a belt buckle, boots and a black Western shirt with white snaps. He could easily play the sexy villain in a Western movie in that getup.

"Ready?" he asked.

She nodded and Adam placed a hand to her back as they headed on foot toward the festivities held under tall thick oaks shading the area. Mia pushed the stroller, and when the terrain got a little too rough, Adam took over. As they approached a set of picnic benches with candles burning and vases filled with willowy wildflowers dotting the length of the dressed tables, intense hickory scents flavored the air and worked at her appetite. Beyond the benches, smoke billowed from three giant smoker barbecue grills.

"Howdy," said a voice she recognized. She owned at

least three of Zane Williams's albums. And sure enough, he was approaching them, holding the hand of a pretty blonde woman. "Adam, I'm glad you could make it. Congratulations on being a daddy."

The men shook hands and the woman placed a kiss on Adam's cheek. "Yes and congrats from me, too, neighbor. So glad you all made it for our wedding."

"I am, too, Jess. You're looking beautiful and very happy," Adam said.

She winked. "Never could pull the wool over your eyes, Adam. And who are these gorgeous ladies?"

Adam made the introductions. Mia couldn't believe Zane Williams actually gave her a warm hug and thanked her for coming. "Nice meeting you and congratulations. Little Rose, is she?"

"Yes, she was named after my mother," she told the couple.

"Pretty name," Zane said, crouching down to get a better look at Rose. "She's got your eyes, Adam. Such a pretty little thing."

"And you're the baby's aunt?" Jessica asked softly, eyeing the baby.

"Yes, I'm Aunt Mia." There was no need to go into further detail. She didn't know how much Adam had told them, but she was certain it wasn't all that much.

"Well, I hope you have a nice time this evening," Zane said. "We've invited our closest friends and family. Before we eat, we'll go around and introduce you to everyone."

"Sounds good," Adam said.

Mia raised her brows. There must be fifty people in attendance. Small for wedding standards, but would Adam make the rounds to meet everyone or stay in the shadows like he always did?

"Would you like to sit down?" Adam asked after Jessica and Zane left. "Looks like we can take our pick of seats."

"Actually, I'd like to walk around a bit. If you don't mind trudging around with the stroller."

"Not at all." They headed away from the festivities, staying to flat grounds, Rose cooing and gurgling as they bumped along a grassy path. "I didn't know Rose was named after your mother."

"She was. Rose was her middle name."

"Makes me wonder what else I don't know about you. And don't say, welcome to my world."

Mia's breath caught. At some point, she'd wanted to tell Adam about her life and share her innermost secrets. But did she know him well enough? So far the men in her life had only disappointed her. If Adam hurt her, she'd be devastated. She'd wait for the time when Adam met her halfway. Right now, he already knew much more about her than she knew about him. "How about, welcome to my universe?"

"Very funny, Mia." But Adam was smiling, and he didn't press her.

They walked along in silence and returned in time to meet Zane and Jessica's family and friends. All the while, Adam stayed by her side and was cordial to everyone, shaking hands, making small talk.

They sat down to the best barbecue Mia had ever eaten. She tasted a little of everything. The spareribs were to die for. The corn on the cob smoked in their husks and flavored with honey butter, insane. The chicken, shrimp and brisket were all tender and tasty. Mia had never eaten so much in her life.

Zane and Jess sat down with them after the meal. Mia was enamored by the love they shared. Zane's eyes gleamed when he looked at his fiancée and spoke about the house they'd live in and the children they hoped to have one day. Mia's heart did a little tumble. How lovely to see two people so blessed by love. Her mother had never had that. And Mia's track record with the opposite sex wasn't all that good, either. She'd met too many men like her father. Flakes, liars or losers. She'd weeded out quite a few, and what was left in the dating pool hadn't been all that inspiring.

From under the table, Adam's hand sought hers and he entwined their fingers. It seemed like such a natural move and yet it meant something monumental. She glanced at his strong profile as he bantered with Zane and clung on to her hand, his thumb absently stroking over her skin.

Sweet, amazing sensations whipped through her. Somehow, after their arguments, their intense lovemaking and their time spent with Rose, after pranking those teens on the beach, kissing under the moonlight and holding hands under the table, Mia had fallen fully and deeply in love with Adam Chase.

She loved him. There wasn't anything she could do about it.

She'd put up a good battle. She'd tried to talk herself out of it. She'd tried to keep her distance, falling short of her goal a time or two, but it was no use. Adam wasn't a flake, a liar or a loser. He was pretty wonderful. And she was about to give him the one thing she hadn't given another man. Her full trust.

"Well, it's time for me to punish y'all with a song or two," Zane was saying. The sun had set and glass lights slung from tree to tree lit the night. "We've got a fire going. Come on around to the fire pit and bring the baby, too. I'll sing her a lullaby."

"I'll round up our guests," Jess said "Mia, I'll come sit with you in a while."

"I'd like that."

Adam helped her up and gave her a kiss on the cheek. "What was that for?"

"Just because," he said and squeezed her hand before he let her go.

Could he be feeling the same sentiment and mood as

her? Was being outdoors under the stars with all the talk of love and marriage getting to him?

With darkness came cooler breezes, and Mia shivered a bit. "Rose is going to need a sweater," she said.

"I'm right on it." Adam reached into the basket under the stroller and gave her a choice of a blue knit sweater or a black-and-pink sequined Hello Kitty jacket.

"Such a good daddy."

"Unless you think it's too cold for the baby," he added. "If you want to head back to the hotel, I'm fine with it."

"And miss a private performance by Zane Williams? Not on your life." She nabbed the jacket out of his hands.

Adam laughed.

It was such a beautiful sound.

Adam laid the sleeping baby into the play yard, her own personal bed brought from home. Mia loved the way he handled Rose now, confident but also so tenderly it made her heart sing. Standing together in the hotel bedroom, they watched her take peaceful breaths. Adam reached for Mia's hand again, and their fingers naturally entwined. She could stay this way forever, in the quiet of the night, with the man she loved and their little bundle of sweetness.

"The party knocked her out," Adam said.

"It's been a long day."

"Are you tired? Should I leave you, so you can get some sleep?"

"No, stay." The night had been perfect and she didn't want it to end.

"Let's have a drink." He lingered one more second over Rose and then led her into the living room. "Have a seat," he said, leaving her by the sofa. "I'll get us something from the bar."

Instead Mia walked over to him and laid her hand on his arm. "Adam, I don't need a drink."

He turned to her, his brows lifting. "You don't?"

She shook her head. "I don't," she said softly, staring into his eyes.

His lids lowered, and his arms wrapped around her waist. "What do you want, sweetheart?" he rasped.

Mia rose up on tiptoes and pressed her lips to his. She'd taken him momentarily by surprise, but Adam was fast on his feet, and she loved that about him. He drew her up, cradling her body to his, deepening the kiss and letting her know with deep-throated groans that he wanted her as much as she wanted him.

Their kisses led to the shedding of their clothes and the two of them falling onto the sofa cushions. Adam's hands roved her body, his touches eliciting white-hot sensations that brought her to the brink of ecstasy. She cried out quietly, muting her sighs with closed lips. Adam was an expert at drawing her out. And when he coaxed her to do the same to him, she didn't disappoint. Her caresses led to bolder moves as she explored his body and made love to him in every way she knew how.

She gave him her whole self, holding nothing back. Making love on a sofa brought out Adam's inventive side. He positioned her in ways that heated her blood and made her ache for more. Mia was happy, so happy she didn't want to think about where this would lead. She shut her mind off to anything but good thoughts and as she climbed higher and higher, Adam wringing out every last ounce of her energy, each powerful thrust brought her closer to completion. And then it happened. His name tumbled from her lips over and over and her body splintered.

Adam wasn't far behind, and as he held her, his face inches from hers, his eyes locked on hers, he bucked his body one last time and shed a release that brought them both earth-shattering pleasure.

He collapsed on top of her, and she bore his weight. Her hands played in his sweat-moistened hair as his mouth found hers. His kiss was gentler now, easy and loving. "Are you okay, sweetheart?" he murmured.

"Mmm." She was humming inside, feeling wonderful, filled with love.

Adam rolled off her, taking her with him so she wouldn't fall off the sofa. It was a tight fit, but there wasn't anywhere she'd rather be. "Mia, we're good together." He kissed her forehead.

It was hardly a declaration of love, but if it was the best he had to offer, she'd take it. "We are."

A cool blast of air made her shiver. It was hard to believe since Adam's body was a hot furnace. But the air conditioner was running and the room was growing chilly.

"You're cold?"

"A little."

"Let me get the sofa bed ready, Mia. I want you with me tonight. Will you stay?"

"I'll stay."

"Good." She was lifted off him and kissed soundly on the lips. "You go check on Rose. I'll only be a minute."

She grabbed Adam's shirt, fitting her arms through the sleeves and scooted out of the room. The baby was still peaceful and sleeping on her back, her cheeks as rosy as ever, such a pretty sight. She was plenty warm in her sleep sack.

When she returned to the room, the bed was made up and Adam was waiting. He patted the spot beside him and she climbed in next to him. The back of the sofa as their headboard, they used pillows to prop up. Adam put his arm around her shoulders and she snuggled in, bringing a sheet over them. "Better?" he asked.

"Much. The baby is still asleep."

He kissed her forehead. "I haven't been this happy in a long time."

She let those words sink in. "Since when, Adam?"

He was silent for a while. Had he been thinking out

loud? Did he regret revealing that much to her and had she overstepped again, trying to get information out of him? He let go a deep sigh, and her breath caught. Then he spoke. "I was almost engaged once. I thought we were perfect together. Her name was Jacqueline."

"What happened with her?" she asked in a whisper.

"She broke it off. Pretty much broke my heart. I thought we were crazy in love, but it turned out I'd been wrong about our relationship. I'd never been poleaxed like that before. You know, it was like a sucker punch to my gut."

"I'm so sorry, Adam."

"That's not all. About a month later, I called her. It was late at night and I couldn't sleep. I'd been rehashing everything and it all seemed so wrong. I thought surely she was having doubts about the breakup. It was all a big mistake. I can still remember the shock I felt when I heard my brother's voice on the other end of the phone. For a few seconds, it didn't quite click. I thought I'd dialed the wrong number. And when it hit me, my head nearly exploded. I'm surprised I didn't grind my teeth to the bone. Of course, Brandon made all sorts of excuses, but he didn't deny the fact that he and Jacqueline were together."

"Oh, Adam. Really? Brandon and Jacqueline? That was the ultimate betrayal."

"I thought so. Believe me—I wasn't happy with either one of them. I didn't speak to Brandon until they broke up three years later. He cheated on her, and she finally wised up and dumped him."

"Wow. So that's what you have against him. I get it now. You must've loved her a lot."

"It was years ago, Mia. I'm over her, and Brandon is who he is. My mother has been after me for years to mend fences. Somehow it's my fault all of this happened. She believes Brandon didn't go after Jacqueline until after she broke up with me. I can't blame Mom. She wants us to be close like we once were."

"What happened is clearly not your fault," Mia said. "But you have forgiven your brother, haven't you?"

"There's a difference between forgiving and forgetting. I'm not holding a grudge. But I can't forget who Brandon is."

"Is that why you warned me about him?"

She set her hand on his chest and stroked him tenderly, sliding over his skin, hoping to soothe him, calm him, make the pain go away. He reached for her hand and lifted it to his lips, placing a kiss on her palm. They were finally connecting, finally making headway.

"If he goes anywhere near you, there's no telling what I'd do to him."

Warmth spiraled through her body, a slow flow of heat that surrounded her entirely. "You don't have to worry— there's only one Chase I'm interested in." She kissed his shoulder, and he gazed into her eyes. There was no mistaking the gratitude and relief she found in them.

"I'm glad." He sighed heavily as if relieved of his burden. "I feel like I've been given a second chance with my life. I don't want to blow it again."

"Adam, what do you mean, second chance? Are you talking about your sister? Is it about Lily?"

His eyes closed then, as if the pain was too much. He shook his head. "Yes, but I can't talk about Lily now, Mia. I can't talk about my sister."

"Okay." There was enough force in his voice to make her a believer. "You don't have to tell me."

"Thank you, sweetheart."

Adam was trying. It was all she could ask of him.

The old barn was decorated with wildflowers, lilies and white roses. Sprays of color splashed over haystacks, and snowy sheer curtains were draped from rafter to rafter overhead. Hundreds of flameless candles cast romantic lighting over the entire interior of the barn and lanterns on pickets defined each row of white satin chairs tied with big bows.

"It's beautiful," Mia said. She sat beside him in the last row. A precaution, she'd said, in case the baby fussed, she could duck out and make a quick escape.

"*You're* beautiful," he whispered. "The place is okay."

The jade in her eyes brightened, and he winked playfully. Mia wore a stunning pastel-pink dress that met her waist in delicate folds, accented her sexy hips and flowed to her knees. Her hair was down and curled, and her olive skin absolutely glowed. Rose looked cute as a button. She wore pink, too, her dress a mass of fancy ruffles. A big matching bow wrapped around her forehead. She was smiling now, her eyes gleaming as she took in the candles and colorful flowers surrounding her.

Adam knew a sense of peace. This moment in time couldn't be more perfect. He reached for Mia's hand— he'd been doing that lately, sometimes without realizing it—and held it on his knee.

Violins began to play, and people milling about promptly took their seats.

Zane appeared, walking in from the side entrance, wearing tuxedo tails and his signature cowboy hat, looking happier than he'd ever seen him. Zane took his place next to the minister at the back of the barn. A ray of sunshine poured over him from the loft window—he had his own personal spotlight—as he searched the aisle for signs of his bride.

And then the orchestra kicked up, playing a classic version of "Here Comes the Bride."

A hush fell over the barn.

Jessica stepped up and all eyes turned toward her. Chairs creaked and shuffling sounds echoed against the walls as everyone rose to their feet.

"I love her dress," Mia whispered.

Ivory and satin, with lace everywhere, Jessica made a lovely bride.

She'd been jilted at the altar once before, but if Adam knew Zane, he was more than going to make up for that.

Jessica made her trip down the aisle, smiling, her face beaming, the bouquet of star lilies and gardenias trembling in her hands.

She reached Zane, and everyone settled back into their seats.

The minister gave a lovely speech about second chances, and something hit home for Adam as he reached for Mia's hand again. He'd liked waking up with her this morning. Almost as much as he'd enjoyed taking her to bed last night. And afterward, he'd managed to give her a glimpse into his life. He'd told her things about Brandon and Jacqueline he'd never shared before with another human being. He'd shared his heartache with her, the betrayal that ruined him for love.

He'd been over Jacqueline for a long time. But he'd never get over Lily. Mia hadn't pressed him last night about her, and he'd been relieved. He kept those memories buried.

Rose began to kick in her infant seat. She had a shelf life of about twenty minutes, before things got out of hand. Her complaints started quietly and Mia took out a long-necked giraffe teething toy. She handed it to Rose, and that seemed to settle her.

Zane and Jessica exchanged vows, making mention of the woman they'd both loved and lost, Janie Holcomb Williams, and promised to do her memory honor by living a good and happy life. Adam had never met Zane's first wife, but he knew the heartache her death had caused to both Jessica and Zane. It was a touching moment, and even Mia shed a tear or two.

Now the minister was asking if anyone knew a reason why the couple shouldn't be joined in holy matrimony, and Rose's mouth opened as if on cue. A belch blasted from her lips, so loud it was hard to believe the uncouth sound had come from such a tiny person.

The entire assembly laughed. Zane and Jessica glanced over their shoulders and chuckled, too.

Mia gasped and looked at Adam in wide-eyed shock, but then a slow grin spread across her face and they both burst out laughing, like everyone else.

The minister made a joke about that not counting, garnering a few more chuckles and he proceeded with the ceremony.

After the wedding, the barn was transformed into a reception hall. The orchestra was replaced by Zane's country band, and a dance floor was laid down. Appetizers were passed around and a bar was set up. It all flowed smoothly.

Mia had the baby out of the infant carrier now and was swaying to the music. Rose was cackling, making those little sounds of happiness that ripped into his heart. He wound his arms around both of them, Rose sandwiched in between, and swayed with them, rocking back and forth to the music. It seemed as long as Mia was present, his finicky little daughter would tolerate him.

"Now that's a sight to behold."

Adam turned to the smiling groom. "Hey, buddy. Congratulations." He shook his hand and gave him a light slap on the back. "Great ceremony."

"Thanks. Thanks. We did it. Jess is a beautiful bride, isn't she?"

"She is." Mia stepped up to give him a hug. "Congratulations. I feel honored to have been invited."

"Hey, well, you and this little one are part of Adam's family now." Zane smiled and playfully wiggled Rose's toes. "She even participated in the ceremony."

Mia's gaze shot up. "Oh, gosh. I'm sorry about the disruption. You never know what these little ones are going to do. Leave it to Rose to make her presence known," she said.

"She's a glutton for attention. She doesn't get that from me," Adam said.

"Oh, so you're saying it comes from my side of the family," Mia teased.

"Hey, we didn't mind. Honestly," Zane said.

"Not at all," Jessica said as she joined Zane, slipping her hand in his. "It was just what the ceremony needed, a little levity."

Jessica's appearance brought another round of hugs and congratulations. And shortly after, the announcement was made that dinner was ready.

Halfway through the meal, Adam's phone vibrated. He pulled it out of his pocket and frowned when he saw the name lit up on the screen. He wanted to ignore the call and finish his meal with Mia, but something told him he needed to answer his brother's call. He kissed Mia's cheek, breathing in her intoxicating scent and rose. "Excuse me. I've got to take this call. Are you going to be all right?"

"We'll be fine. Rose needs a diaper change. I was just about to take her."

"Okay, I'll meet you back here and we'll finish our meal."

He walked out of the barn and strode toward the construction site, away from the music and conversations and picked up on the fifth ring. "Brandon, it's Adam. I'm at a wedding in Texas. What's up?"

"Adam. You need to come home right away. Mom's had a heart attack."

Eleven

Adam held his mother's pasty hand, gazing into her soft blue eyes. A pallor had taken over her skin as she lay in the hospital bed. She was hooked up to IV tubes and oxygen, yet she managed to smile. "Hi, Mom."

"Adam, you came." Her voice was weak.

"Of course I came." He squeezed her hand. He'd flown half the night to get back to Los Angeles, hoping he wouldn't be too late. He'd had a limo waiting at the airport and had come first thing. Mia and the baby were driven to Grandma Tess's home so she could spend time with Rose.

"I'm so glad you both are here," Mom said, glancing at Brandon, too.

Brandon stepped up. "Of course we're here."

"I'm sorry to worry you. I don't know what happened. One minute I was fine, shopping with Ginny, and the next thing I know, my legs went out from under me. I felt terribly weak, and a few kind people at the mall brought me over to a bench and sat me down. Someone called nine-one-one."

"I'm glad they did. You need to be here," Brandon said. He'd been in constant contact with Adam, letting him know the status of the tests they were doing. "Mom, you've had a bad attack of angina. It's not life-threatening, but you do have to take it easier now. Eat better, watch your diet. You'll probably be put on medication, too."

"They're keeping me here for a few days."

"Just for observation," Brandon said. "They've got a few more tests to run, and they want to monitor you. I think it's a good idea."

"I do, too," Adam said, greatly relieved the emergency wasn't more serious. He wasn't ready to say goodbye to his mother.

Tears filled her eyes. "I was shopping for Rose. Oh dear… I want to see her grow up, Adam. I want to be around for all of it."

"You will, Mom." She didn't get to see her own daughter grow up. She didn't have the chance to raise Lily. "You'll see Rose as much as you want. I'll make sure of it, Mom. I'll be sure to keep my baby safe." His voice cracked. Fatigue, worry and regret had him spilling out words he'd always wanted to say. Words that he'd harbored for years. "I won't let you down the way I did with Lily."

"Oh no…you didn't… Please don't feel that way. I don't blame you. I never did, son. And that was before Brandon told me the truth earlier today." Her face tightened, the wrinkles around her eyes creasing.

Adam whipped his head around. "Brandon, what did you tell her?"

"The truth, Adam," his brother said. His jaw tight, the hard rims of his eyes softened. "I told Mom about how you covered for me during that storm. How you wanted to leave the storm cellar and check for Lily and how I lied to you. I told you Lily was with Mom, when I knew it wasn't true. I was too scared to let you go looking for her up at the house. I didn't want you to leave me alone. You were my big brother and I needed you to protect me." Brandon put his head down.

Adam let that sink in. Seconds ticked by, his mind scrambling for answers. "Why now?" he asked Brandon.

"Because he thought I was dying, Adam."

He stared at his mother. Then blinked. She'd shocked him, but her expression now was solid and more alive than when he'd first walked into her room. "It's been bothering him for years—isn't that what you said, Brandon? And today you thought I might die before you could confess the truth to me."

"Mom, you're not dying." His brother's voice was deep and compassionate.

"From your lips to God's ears." Her pained sigh resounded in the quiet room. Her head against her bed pillows, she closed her eyes. "The truth is, I've been blaming myself all these years. I shouldn't have left Lily alone with you boys." Her voice was soft, reverent and full of regret. She peered at both of them. "She was only six. You were twelve, Adam, and Brandon was eight. I knew we lived in tornado country. It was to be a quick trip to the grocery store, but I should've taken Lily with me. She wasn't your responsibility—she was mine. I'm more to blame than anyone. I'm only grateful, when that tornado ripped through our land, you boys didn't die along with her. Adam, you took your brother to safety and kept him there. Or maybe all three of you would've died."

Brandon had tears in his eyes. "I told Adam I saw Lily go in the car with you, so he wouldn't leave me alone. I lied, and Lily died."

"You were so young, Brandon," Mom said. "I understand how scared you must've been. But have you ever once considered that you might have saved both of your lives that day?"

"No, Mom, I never did. And I've hated myself ever since." Brandon spoke quietly, his voice nearly breaking.

Adam winced and breathed deep, keeping his emotions at bay. He couldn't break down now. He couldn't show the world, or his family, his vulnerability, yet the scars within him were on fire. He was burning and didn't know how to stop it.

He'd never known Brandon felt guilty about Lily's death. They'd never spoken of it. Adam had always blamed himself for not seeing through Brandon's lies, for not knowing his little brother had been too frightened to let him go after Lily. He was older, the responsible one when his mother wasn't around. He should've checked on his sister regardless of what Brandon told him. But often he questioned whether he would've actually taken those steps up from the storm cellar even if Brandon hadn't stopped him. He'd been afraid, too; the noises outside had been horrifying. Adam had always wished he would've done something different. Been stronger. Acted braver.

His head pounded. All these years, he'd resented Brandon and had been more than willing to hate his brother when he'd discovered his involvement with Jacqueline, but now... He wasn't sure about anything.

"I'm sorry, Adam," Brandon said, his face flushed. He was trying valiantly to hold back tears.

It was a genuine, heartfelt apology. He never thought he'd hear those words from Brandon, and in the course of a few weeks, he'd heard them twice.

"I've let you carry this burden all these years. The truth is, I think I intentionally sabotaged my relationship with Jacqueline because I knew I didn't deserve her and because I'd hurt you. I've been a coward. About everything."

Adam swallowed.

"I know you've despised me. I can't blame you, Adam. But I'm apologizing for all I've done that has hurt you."

"I don't despise you, Brandon."

"You boys were always fighting," his mother said. "But I knew back then, just as I know now, you love each other. So shake hands once and for all. Heaven knows there's enough guilt in this room to feed the devil. The past has hurt all of us. It's time to move on."

They looked at each other now, and the hope and apology in Brandon's eyes had Adam extending his hand. Brandon clasped it. "You're a good man, Adam. Always have been."

He nodded, too choked up to speak.

The nurse walked in. "Excuse me, but you have another visitor," she said to his mom. "But I'm afraid we can allow only two visitors at a time. One of you will have to leave."

Mia stood at the door, holding a vase of spring flowers. "Is it okay?"

Adam gazed at Mia. She was a bright and wonderful light shining through all of his past darkness.

"I'll leave, so you three can spend time together." Brandon offered. He walked to the door and gave Mia a kiss on the cheek. "Thanks for coming," he said and walked out of sight.

"I don't want to interrupt," she said to Adam, still not moving.

And it hit him, just like that. He *wanted* her there. He needed her support. Especially after the conversation he'd just had with Brandon. She'd come, and that meant a lot to him. "Please, come in."

"Yes," his mother said quietly. "It's good to see you, dear."

"I was worried about you, Alena," Mia said, walking into the room. Adam took the flowers and placed them on a small table under the television where his mother could see them easily.

"The flowers are lovely," his mother said. "Thank you."

"I was hoping you'd enjoy them," Mia said.

"Mia, I'm sorry to interrupt your plans with my son this weekend. I feel awful about that."

"Don't think of it. Your health is important to us. You've just got to concentrate on getting better." Mia reached for her hand. "How are you feeling now?"

"Better. It was frightening, I will admit. I had an angina attack that knocked me for a loop. I have to stay a day or two for monitoring, but then I'll be going home."

"That's great news," Mia said, her eyes so beautifully hopeful.

"Where is Rose today?"

"My grandma Tess is watching her for a few hours."

"That's nice. I hope you'll let me babysit one day, too."

"I'm sure you will."

"Come sit and tell me all about the trip. How did Rose do at the wedding?"

Mia lowered down on the edge of the bed. "Well, uh…" Her eyes met his, and they shared a conspiratorial moment. Little Rose was the maker of many stories, and this one would surely bring a smile to his mother's face. She could use a little levity. The last few minutes had been laden with grief, guilt and regret.

Adam breathed a sigh of relief, taking a step back, allowing Mia to comfort his mother.

"She did fine, except for this one moment during the ceremony…"

The next day, Mia walked through the door lugging Mia in her infant seat in one arm and a file folder she'd brought from First Clips tucked under the other arm. Since the wedding and Alena's health scare she wanted to work from home more these days, to be closer to Adam. Rose had a way of cheering him up, even if she still wasn't too keen on him. Adam adored being with her. And one day soon, his daughter would come to accept him. Every day together brought them closer and closer. Mia sensed that Rose was warming to him.

She was heading upstairs to her room, when she spotted a young woman sitting on the living room sofa speaking with Mary. She set down her files on the entry table and unfastened the straps of the carrier, lifting Rose into her arms. "Let's see what's going on," she said, kissing the baby's forehead. The baby gurgled, and Mia's heart warmed. Casually, her curiosity getting the better of her, she strolled into the living room.

"Hi, Mary. We're home," she said.

The woman popped up from her seat immediately and

turned to her. The spunky blonde was all smiles as her gaze locked on to the baby. "This must be the little darlin', Rose."

One glance at Mary's sheepish expression sent dread to her belly. "Hello, Mia."

Mia waited, staring at the woman who couldn't be more than twenty-two.

"Mia D'Angelo, this is Lucille Bridges," Mary said. "She's from Nanny Incorporated."

"I have an appointment with Adam Chase this afternoon," the woman added.

Nanny Incorporated? Adam had called a nanny agency? The blood in her veins boiled. The girl wouldn't take her eyes off Rose. Mia hugged her tighter and stepped back.

"I was just explaining to Miss Bridges that Adam isn't home. He must've forgotten about his appointment with all the commotion this past week. I've called him, but he hasn't answered his phone."

"He's at the hospital visiting his mother." She eyed the girl cautiously. "I'm sure he won't be home for quite a while."

"That's okay. I understand. I've left my references with Mary. I've been with the agency for three years and I have impeccable referrals," she said.

Wow, three whole years.

"Do you think I can say hello to the baby while I'm here?"

Mia's nerves jumped. She shot a glance at Mary.

"Uh, I think Aunt Mia was just about to put Rose down for a nap. It's past her naptime, isn't it, Mia?"

"Right," she gritted out. How could Adam do this to her? "Rose is quite a handful when she's tired."

"I know how babies can be. I helped raise four siblings."

Mia couldn't take it another second. Adam's betrayal and deceit didn't sit well in her gut. "I'm sure Mary can show you out. I've got to take the baby upstairs now."

"Oh, uh, sure. Bye-bye, Rose. Nice meeting you, Mia."

She headed for the stairs without responding.

She couldn't. Her throat had closed up.

She was in shock.

Trembling, she stood in the kitchen doorway, watching Adam forage through the refrigerator. It was after seven, and he'd just come home.

"I asked Mary to go home early," she said.

Adam backed up and peeked at her. "Good idea. I see she left us dinner." He pulled out covered dishes and set them on the counter. Lifting a lid, he said, "Looks like we're having rosemary chicken and—" he lifted the next lid "—glazed carrots."

"I won't be having dinner…w-with you." Her darn throat constricted again. Her anger had never subsided; neither did the hurt. She'd cried and cried all afternoon. Like a fool.

Adam stopped what he was doing to really look at her. "Why, sweetheart?" He approached her. "You're pale as a ghost. Are you feeling sick?"

He wrapped his arms around her, and for one instant, she relished it, squeezed her eyes closed and sought the pleasure of him, before she set both hands on his chest and shoved with all her might. Surprise more than force made him stumble back, his eyes wide and confused. "Yes, I'm sick, Adam. Of you. And all your secrets, lies and deceit. When were you going to tell me you were hiring a nanny for Rose? Were you going to hire someone, then toss me out onto the street? Was that your plan all along?"

Adam's tanned face flushed with color instantly. "Mia, for goodness' sake, calm the hell down."

"No, Adam. I will not calm down," she shouted. "How do you think I felt coming home to find a blonde bimbo nanny sitting on the couch, waiting for you?"

"Mia," he said, exasperated. "I meant to speak to you

about it. But then Mom had her attack and it slipped my mind."

"It slipped your mind!" Mia was one step away from losing it entirely. "It should've never *been* on your mind. Do you think I can't care for Rose? Am I lacking in some way? Or has the recluse in you decided that I'm getting too close, invading your precious privacy?" She gestured an air check with her index finger. "Checked me right off, didn't you?"

"No, of course not!"

She folded her arms. "I don't believe you."

"Shh, Mia, keep your voice down. Where's Rose?" he asked.

"Sleeping upstairs." She grabbed the monitor attached to her belt and showed him. "Regardless of what you might think of me, I'd never put Rose in danger. See, I'm watching her. She's my baby, too, Adam. You had no right. No right, going behind my back like that."

"Mia." His voice was an impatient rasp. "I know you'd never put Rose in danger. And if you'll let me explain what I was thinking."

"Apparently, you weren't thinking. Adam, that girl was a kid. I don't care that she claimed to have impeccable references—she doesn't know Rose, not the way I do."

Adam walked to the bar at the end of the huge granite counter and slapped a shot glass down. He filled it with vodka and downed it in one gulp. He didn't hesitate to pour a second shot.

"Alcohol never solved any problems, Adam."

He gulped the second shot and poured a third. "Don't lecture me, Mia. I won't get behind the wheel of my car and slaughter some poor innocent girl."

Mia froze. The swirling tirade in her head ready to lash out of her mouth vanished. She hadn't heard right, had she? "What?"

He slugged back the third shot and hunkered down, bracing his elbows on the counter. "Nothing."

"It was something, Adam." She walked over to him and spoke to his profile. "How do you know about that?"

"Know what?" He refused to look at her. It wasn't a coincidental statement. Adam Chase didn't leave things up to chance.

"About my father."

Silence.

"Adam, if you care one iota about me, you'll tell me how you know that right this minute."

Silence again.

Adam didn't care. Maybe he never had. She was through with Adam Chase. He would never let her in, never trust her. She turned her back on him and walked away. She was almost out of the kitchen when his voice broke the silence.

"I had you investigated."

A gasp exploded from her mouth. She whirled around. "You did what?"

He turned to face her. His expression was coarse, his eyes raw, not filled with the apology she'd expected. "I didn't know a thing about you, Mia. And when you came to me with that story about your sister and Rose, I didn't know if I could believe a word out of your mouth. After all the lies you'd told me when we first met, I had to find out more about you. I had to know who was coming to live in my house and help raise my daughter."

"You didn't trust me to tell you the truth."

"No, I didn't."

"I would have one day, Adam. I was waiting for you to open up to me. But I can see that will never happen." She sighed, the conversation sapping her strength. "So, you know everything?"

He nodded.

Shame washed over her. She was the young Burkel girl again, whose father had mowed down a young teenager, a girl who'd had a full life yet to live. He'd been drunk, coming home from a scandalous affair with a married woman. The town scorned the Burkels. She couldn't go anywhere without being harassed or whispered about. It was equally painful going to school. Young Scarlett Brady, the victim, had been a classmate and the daughter of a revered police captain. Everyone knew and loved Scarlett. When her mother decided to move them to Grandma Tess's home, their neighbors put up balloons in celebration on the day they'd moved out. The memory brought fresh shivers.

"You didn't even tell me your real name, Mia. What was I to think?"

He'd had her investigated like a common criminal. She cringed at the thought. How so like Adam, though. Sweeping heartache invaded her from top to bottom. "That maybe I didn't lead a charmed life. That maybe my family suffered and we'd paid a big price for my father's deeds. That maybe I make mistakes, unlike you."

"I make mistakes, Mia."

"Yes, you're right. *This* was a big mistake. But that doesn't make what you've done any easier to take."

Adam wadded up the note Mia had left for him on the kitchen table that morning. She needed time to think, away from him. She had taken Rose with her, but she'd call often and let him know how Rose was doing. She'd be at her grandma Tess's home for the next few days. He was welcome to come visit her anytime. And please, don't call the police—she hadn't kidnapped his daughter.

What the hell. He'd never accuse her of kidnapping. That last part really gutted him through and through. Mia would never allow any harm to come to his daughter. He trusted Mia with Rose and knew he wasn't equipped to take care of the baby on his own. Not yet. Not like Mia could. He missed the both of them, like crazy.

Adam tossed the note, missing the trash can in his

office, and rubbed his temples. He had a headache that wouldn't let up. How had he thought he'd get any work done today? It was a foolish notion. Mia had called him twice already today with an update about Rose. She'd eaten a good breakfast. She'd pooped her diaper. She'd taken her for a walk around the neighborhood with her grandmother this morning.

"When are you coming home?" Adam had asked.

"I don't know, Adam," she'd replied coolly. The aloof tone of her voice worried him.

He knew when she did come home, nothing would be the same.

"Adam, Brandon's here," Mary announced at his doorway. "He's waiting for you downstairs."

"It's about damn time," he said, bounding up from his desk. "Thanks, Mary."

He strode down the stairs to find Brandon in the living room with a drink in his hand, a whiskey. He'd also had a tumbler of vodka ready for him. "So, Mia's gone?" Brandon held out the glass to him.

He should refuse the drink. Last night, he'd nearly polished off half a bottle and his head still throbbed. "Just one." He took it from his brother and nodded. "Yeah, she's gone."

"Let's sit outside, Adam. It's a cool afternoon. It'll help clear your head."

"Is that what I need?"

"Oh, I think so, brother." He led the way outside, where breezes took away the heat of the day. The sun, lowering on the horizon, cast a brilliant gleam on the water. "I have to say, I was surprised to get your call."

Adam shrugged. He was surprised he'd called his brother, too. Just went to show how crazy confused he was right now. "We might as well start behaving like brothers."

"You had no one else to call," Brandon stated and then sat down on a lounge chair.

Adam chuckled, taking a seat, as well. "Okay, guilty." He really didn't confide in anyone about personal matters. Trusting his brother didn't come easy, but Mia and Rose were important to him and oddly, he believed Brandon could help him sort this out. "You know women, Brandon. And you know me."

"I'm glad to help, bro. Go on. Tell me what happened with Mia."

"All of it?"

"Everything. I'm no relationship expert, but I've made enough mistakes now that I've gotten pretty good at rectifying them. And, yes, I do know women."

Adam spelled it out for Brandon. Telling him exactly how he'd met Mia on the beach. Explaining Rose's negative reaction to him and how Mia coming to live with him had been necessary, at least in the beginning. He recounted the past few weeks, up to a point.

"Have you slept with her?" Brandon asked.

"Why does that matter?" Adam shot back.

"Just the fact that you're asking, means you need more help than I originally thought."

"Okay, yes. Damn it. We've been together, more than once. That's all you need to know. And I think she had feelings for me."

"Had?"

"I blew it with her."

"Yeah, well, going behind her back to search for a nanny might do that."

"I explained the reason I did that."

"To me, but you never told Mia your reasons."

"I never had the chance. I wanted her to calm down so I could explain it rationally to her, but then I made that slip about her family and I was forced to tell her I'd had her investigated."

"The final nail in the coffin."

Adam nodded and admitted quietly, "I did it for Rose."

"I believe you, but you're going to have a hard time convincing Mia about your intentions, because you won't open yourself up. She's been telling you all along that's what she wants. Why are you holding back? It's obvious you're crazy about her."

"It is?"

"Aren't you?"

Adam gave it some thought. "With Rose came Mia. I think of them as one. I guess I never realized it before. They were a package deal almost from the beginning."

"You adore Rose. *And Mia.* They are a gift. All tied up into a bow for you. So what are you afraid of, Adam?"

Adam rubbed his temples again. The pain in his head pounded with the truth. He'd been plagued by guilt and uncertainty for years, safeguarding his heart so securely, that he'd kept himself away from serious relationships and love. He'd hidden behind his work and his need for privacy. "Mia was right. I've been closed off a long time. I don't know how to let anyone in."

"You let me in, Adam. Of course it took Mom's health episode to accomplish that, but I think you're ready to let Mia in. If she wasn't important to you, you wouldn't have called me. And don't give me that business that you were worried about how to get Rose home without hurting Mia in the process. If you want Rose back, all you have to do is go get her. You have legal rights to her, Adam. But you want more than that. And I'm telling you, don't wait until it's too late. The clock is ticking. Go after what you want right now. Tell Mia how you feel. And hurry the hell up."

"I hate it that you're right," Adam said, finishing his drink.

"And I hate it that you've got a gorgeous woman and child waiting for you." Brandon smiled. "I've had to live knowing you'd saved my life and there was no damn way for me to reciprocate. At least now I feel I may have helped save yours."

Adam smiled back. "That makes us even."

"Get your child and woman back first. Then we'll be even."

The front porch swing moaned as Mia rocked Rose in her arms. The quiet sound lulled the baby to sleep. This house had been her home once, when Grandma Tess had taken all of them in, and now she was back, feeling that same sense of loss, the hurt blistering her up inside. Her grandmother was a rock, a solid, rational, wise woman and Mia needed to be here with her now. She needed the comfort Grandma Tess provided. She always knew the right thing to say. Mia was wounded. She'd begun to trust again. She'd believed in Adam Chase. She'd let go her fears and put her faith in the power of her intense feelings for Adam. He'd sure had her fooled.

Initially she and Adam had spoken about her nanny duties and taking it day by day with no real end in sight. Now that the time had come, Mia couldn't face leaving Rose in the hands of another…a stranger. No matter what had happened between her and Adam, Mia was prepared to forgive and forget in order to live under Adam's roof and care for her niece, if he allowed it.

If that meant swallowing her pride, she would do it. She'd return to Moonlight Beach and keep out of Adam's life the best she could. If she didn't do that, what kind of life would Rose have? She'd have every material thing she might want—Adam's wealth could provide that—but what about love? What if Adam couldn't open himself up to loving his own daughter? What if he held back with her, the same way he'd held back with Mia?

She peered at the slumbering angel in her arms. "Sweet Cheeks, your auntie Mia will not abandon you," she whispered. "Don't worry."

Mia was almost lulled to sleep, too. Gentle breezes reaching this far inland soothed her tired bones until the humming roar of an engine coming down the street reached her ears. She opened her eyes and leaned forward in the swing, watching a Rolls-Royce park in front of the house. The gorgeous car stuck out on this middle-class street, like a diamond among mere stones.

Adam climbed out of the car, and their eyes met. She wasn't surprised to see him. She knew he wouldn't let Rose out of his sight for long, but they'd agreed that he'd call before coming over. Of course, Adam hadn't abided by that rule.

As he wound around the car and approached, a bouquet of lavender roses in his hand caught her attention. Did he think flowers would solve anything? He reached the porch and set one foot on the first step. "Hello, Mia."

She gasped inside, her heart racing like crazy.

"Adam."

He glanced at Rose, love beaming in his eyes. "How long has she been sleeping?"

"Only a few minutes."

"Is your grandma Tess home?"

"Yes."

"I would like to meet her."

"Now?"

"Yes, right now. It's about time I met her. Don't get up. Let the baby sleep. I'll knock and see if she comes to the door."

He walked past her and gave three light raps to the door.

Adam was full of surprises today. Of course Grandma Tess came to the door, and she graciously greeted Adam, bleeder of her heart, and let him inside.

"What on earth?" Mia muttered.

Rose stirred restlessly, stretching out her arms, and Mia pushed off with her bare feet to start the swing swaying again while she strained to listen to the quiet conversation going on in the house.

She sighed. She couldn't hear a thing.

A short time later, Adam walked out the door, minus the flowers. "Mind if I sit with you?"

She shrugged and he sat down. "I like your grandmother, Mia. She's a nice lady."

They spoke softly to keep from waking the baby.

"You were supposed to call to let me know you were coming."

"I didn't want to chance you telling me no."

Adam pushed a hand through his hair. He breathed deeply and turned to face her. "I've missed you, Mia."

"You miss Rose."

"I miss both of you." His eyes narrowed as if he was choosing his words carefully. "You know what I saw when I pulled up to the house just now? I saw my family. You and Rose and me, we're a family. And it doesn't scare me anymore to think it, to say it or to feel it."

"Don't, Adam. You don't have to pretend. I've already decided for Rose's sake I'll come back to Moonlight Beach."

Adam's eyes gleamed and he smiled. "Oh, so you've decided that you can tolerate me. You're making the ultimate sacrifice for the baby by being in my presence."

Had he gone crazy since she'd left him? "Why are you smiling?"

"Because you are so full of it, Mia." What *did* Grandma Tess say to him?

"I beg your pardon?"

"You are. And if you just listen to me for one minute, I'll explain about the nanny."

"Don't forget about the investigation. I'd love to hear your excuse for that one."

"Fine. I'll tell you everything. I hope that'll make up for hurting you. Because, sweetheart, the very last thing in the world I want to do is hurt you again."

He was getting to her. His body nestled next to hers, the tone of his voice and the sincere way he spoke only added to her slow melt. "Start from the beginning, Adam. Leave nothing out."

As Adam spoke about Lily, his little sister who'd looked up to him, who'd followed him around like a lost puppy, who'd trusted him like no other, Mia bit her lip to keep tears from spilling down her cheeks. His voice broke a few times, recounting that horrible day when the tornado ripped through his town and took Lily with it. He spoke of grief and guilt and heartache. About his relationship with his mother and his brother, about how he'd shouldered the blame and let that come between him and his family. He spoke about Brandon, too, and how they'd finally patched up their differences and about how he'd asked Brandon for advice today, needing his brother now more than he ever had before.

Mia was seeing a side of Adam that he'd never revealed. She could relate to the pain they'd endured as a family, the loss, the heartache. "I'm glad you told me."

"I want there to be no secrets between us, Mia." He put his arm on the back of the porch swing and even though he wasn't touching her, his presence surrounded her and she felt safe and protected.

"About the nanny," he said. "It was just a thought to make your life easier. I've seen how hard you work. You come home looking tired and drained at times. I know how much Rose means to you, and you do it without complaint. But you hold down a full-time position, take care of Rose and your grandmother and have to put up with me. It's a lot of responsibility. The nanny idea came to me, only as a means to provide you with some backup. Believe me, I was going to run it by you, but then we started getting closer and I didn't want to ruin what we had going. Being with you two in Texas was wonderful. I've never been happier, and I did tell you that."

"You did," Mia admitted.

"And then Mom got sick and we had to rush home. The

whole thing slipped my mind. Mia," he said, his arm wrapping around her shoulder. "No one could replace you." The depth of his voice had her believing him.

A tear trickled down her cheek. "Thanks."

He went on, "Do you remember how we met?"

"Of course, I cut my foot and bled all over you."

Adam chuckled. "Not quite. But you came to Moonlight Beach to find out what you could about me, right? Why did you do that?"

"I've already told you. I couldn't just turn Rose over to a stranger. I needed to find out what kind of person you were."

"Exactly. I regret having you investigated now, but weeks ago when all I knew about you were the lies you'd told me, I needed to know the same thing. You were going to live under my roof and help me raise my daughter. What I did wasn't too different than what you did. We just had different ways of going about it. We were both trying to protect this little girl." He pointed to Rose, love shining in his eyes. "Because she's precious to both of us."

"Adam, the difference is I would've answered all of your questions truthfully. You, on the other hand, went out of your way to evade mine."

"True. That was the old Adam. I don't like to talk about myself."

"You really mean you don't like letting people know you."

"You know me now, Mia. You know everything about me. And I'm happy about it. Loving you has changed me."

Hot tingles rose up from her belly. "What did you just say?"

Adam grinned. "I love you, Mia. At first I thought my feelings were just for Rose, but Brandon, of all people, helped me see what was right in front of me. I'm in love with you, Mia. You and Rose own my heart."

"We do?"

"Yes, you do."

Adam leaned over and brushed his lips over hers. She'd never known a sweeter kiss. "Oh, Adam." Tears spilled down her cheeks freely now. She could hardly believe this was happening. She moved closer to him on the porch swing, and his next kiss wasn't sweet at all, but soul-searching and magical.

"I love you, Adam Chase. I tried really hard not to."

"I'll take that as a compliment, sweetheart, and thank God you love me. Must've been my mad first aid skills."

A chuckle burst from her lips. "That was it. That's why I love you so much I can hardly stand it." The baby fussed, a little sound of displeasure. "Adam, I think the baby wants her daddy."

"I'll take her," Adam said, and she transferred Rose into his arms. Adam cuddled her close and turned to face Mia. "Before she wakes up and howls, I have a question for you." A hopeful glint entered his eyes.

"What is it?"

"I've asked for your grandmother's blessing and she's given it to me."

Mia took a big swallow at the reverent tone in his voice.

"I've never asked this of another woman. Will you come home to Moonlight Beach and be my wife? You, me and our little Rose, we're already a family, but I want to make it official because I love both of you with all my heart. I'm asking you to marry me, Mia."

Mia touched his arm and gazed into his beautiful eyes. She no longer had to hold back her love for him; she let it flow naturally, and it was liberating and wonderful. "Yes, Adam. I'll marry you."

"We'll have a good life, Mia. I promise. I want to take you to Italy. We'll honeymoon there, the three of us."

"It's always been a dream of mine."

"I know, sweetheart. I want to make your dreams come true."

Their gazes locked, and warmth seeped into her heart. She loved this man like crazy. He would be a wonderful father and an attentive, loving husband. She had no doubt.

"Uh-oh," Adam said. "Looks like little sleepyhead is waking up. Do you want her back?"

"No, you hold her, sweetheart."

"Okay, but she's not going to like this."

Rose's eyes opened, she fidgeted and took a glance around. Her lips parted and they waited for her complaint.

"Coo, coo." Precious sounds reached their ears.

She gurgled a few times, and then her chubby hand reached up to touch Adam's face.

His brows lifted, creasing his forehead. "Would you look at that."

"I'm looking," she said, awed. Her little Rose had perfect timing.

The baby peered at her daddy's handsome face. Her mouth opened and spread wide, revealing a gummy toothless beautiful smile.

Adam's eyes welled up. "I think I've won her over, Mia."

"Adam Chase, only you can win two female hearts in one day."

"Our sweet little matchmaker helped make that happen."

"She's brilliant, just like her daddy."

Adam kissed her then, and Mia's heart swelled. Their baby Rose did have a way about her. She was going to wrap them both around her finger.

And there was no place either of them would rather be.

* * * * *

"Look at me," she ordered. "You know me, Luc."

Blowing out a breath, Luc hung his head. "I... It's on the tip of my tongue. Damn, why can't I remember?" Worry filled his dark eyes.

This was not good, not good at all. She was going to have to get her boss back to the house and call the palace doctor. Obviously Luc's memory wasn't cooperating if he couldn't remember that they worked together. But she didn't want him panicking; she could do that enough for both of them.

"My name is Kate." She watched his eyes, hoping to see some recognition, but there was nothing. "I'm your—"

"Fiancée." A wide smile spread across his face. "Now I remember."

Before she could correct him, Luc leaned in to capture her lips with a passion she'd never known before.

A ROYAL
AMNESIA SCANDAL

BY
JULES BENNETT

Published in Great Britain 2015
by Mills & Boon, an imprint of Harlequin (UK) Limited,
Eton House, 18-24 Paradise Road, Richmond, Surrey, TW9 1SR

© 2015 Jules Bennett

ISBN: 978-0-263-25270-5

51-0715

Harlequin (UK) Limited's policy is to use papers that are natural, renewable and recyclable products and made from wood grown in sustainable forests. The logging and manufacturing processes conform to the legal environmental regulations of the country of origin.

Printed and bound in Spain
by CPI, Barcelona

Award-winning author **Jules Bennett** is no stranger to romance—she met her husband when she was only fourteen. After dating through high school, the two married. He encouraged her to chase her dream of becoming an author. Jules has now published nearly thirty novels. She and her husband are living their own happily-ever-after while raising two girls. Jules loves to hear from readers through her website, www.julesbennett.com, her Facebook fan page or on Twitter.

I have to dedicate this book to the fabulous
Andrea Laurence and Sarah M. Anderson
who always come through for me when I need a plot
fixed five minutes ago. Wouldn't go through
this crazy journey without you guys!

One

Escaping to the mountains would have been much better for his sanity than coming to his newly purchased private seaside villa off the coast of Portugal.

Kate Barton fully clothed was enough to have any man panting, but Kate running around in a bikini with some flimsy, strapless wrap that knotted right at her cleavage was damn near crippling. The woman had curves, she wasn't stick-thin like a model and damn if she didn't know how to work those dips and valleys on that killer body. Not that she ever purposely showcased herself, at least not in the professional setting, but she couldn't hide what she'd been blessed with, either. Even in a business suit, she rocked any designer's label.

Luc Silva cursed beneath his breath as he pulled his Jet Ski back to the dock and secured it. His intent in coming here was to escape from the media, escape from the woman who'd betrayed him. So why was he paying a penance with yet another woman?

To ensure privacy for both of them, he'd given Kate the guesthouse. Unfortunately, it and the main house shared the same private beach, damn it. He'd thought purchasing this fixer-upper on a private island, barely up to civilization's standards, was a brilliant idea at the time. With no internet access and little cell service, it was a perfect hideaway for a member of Ilha Beleza's royal family. He didn't want to be near people who knew of or cared about his status. Luc had only one requirement when searching for a hideout: a place to escape. Yet here he was with his sexy, mouthy, curvy assistant.

Not only that, the renovations to the property were only half-done, because he'd needed to get away from reality much sooner than he'd thought he would.

A lying fiancée would do that to a man.

"Your face is burning."

Luc fisted his hands at his sides as he approached Kate. Was she draped all over that lounge chair on purpose or did she just naturally excel at tormenting men? She'd untied that wrap and now it lay open, as if framing her luscious body covered only by triangles of bright red material and strings.

"I'm not burned," he retorted, not slowing down as he marched up the white sand.

"Did you apply sunscreen?" she asked, holding an arm over her forehead to shield her eyes from the sun.

The movement shifted her breasts, and the last thing he needed was to be staring at his assistant's chest, no matter how impressive it was. When she'd started working for him about a year ago, he'd wanted her... He still wanted her, if he was being honest with himself.

She was the absolute best assistant he'd ever had. Her parents still worked for his parents, so hiring Kate had been an easy decision.

A decision he questioned every single time his hormones shot into overdrive when she neared.

He never mingled with staff. He and his parents always kept their personal and professional relationships separate, so as not to create bad press or scandal. It was a rule they felt very strongly about after a scandal generations ago. Rumor had it the family was quite the center of gossip for a while after an assistant let out family secrets best left behind closed doors.

So once Luc had become engaged to Alana, he'd put his attraction to Kate out of his mind.

For the past three months, he'd been ready to say "I do" for two very valid reasons: his ex had claimed to be expecting his child, and he needed to marry to secure his crown to reign over Ilha Beleza.

Now Alana was gone and he was trying like hell to hang on to the title, even though he had just a few months to find a wife. And the second he was in charge, he'd be changing that archaic law. Just because a man was nearing thirty-five didn't mean he had to be tied down, and Luc wanted nothing to do with holy matrimony... especially now that he'd been played.

"You're frowning," Kate called as he passed right by her. "Being angry isn't helping your red face."

There were times he admired the fact she didn't treat him as if he was royalty, but just a regular man. This wasn't one of those times.

Before climbing the steps to the outdoor living area, Luc turned. "Did you cancel the interview with that journalist from the States?"

Kate settled back into her relaxed position, dropping her arm to her side and closing her eyes as the sun continued to kiss all that exposed skin.

"I took care of canceling all media interviews you

had scheduled regarding the upcoming wedding, or anything to do with Alana," she told him. "I rescheduled your one-on-one interviews for later in the year, after you gain the title. By then I'm positive you'll have everything sorted out and will be at the top of your game."

Luc swallowed. Not only was Kate his right-hand woman, she was his biggest supporter and advocate. She made him look good to the media, occasionally embellishing the truth to further boost his family's name.

"I simply told each of the media outlets that this was a difficult time for you, playing up the faux miscarriage, and your family's request for privacy."

Kate lifted a knee, causing a little roll of skin to ease over her bikini bottoms. Luc's eyes instantly went to that region of her body and he found himself wanting to drop to his knees and explore her with more than his eyes.

"If you're done staring at me, you need to either go inside or put on sunscreen," she added, without opening her eyes.

"If you'd cover up, I wouldn't stare."

Her soft laugh, drifting on an ocean breeze, hit him square in the gut. "If I covered up, I wouldn't get a tan. Be glad I'm at least wearing this. I do hate those tan lines."

Gritting his teeth, Luc tried but failed at keeping that mental image from his mind. Kate sunbathing in the nude would surely have any man down on his knees begging. Forcing back a groan, Luc headed up the steps and into the main house. She was purposely baiting him, and he was letting her, because he was at a weak spot in his life right now. He also couldn't hide the fact that his assistant turned him inside out in ways she shouldn't.

He'd been engaged, for pity's sake, yet before and after the engagement, he'd wanted to bed Kate.

Sleeping with an employee was beyond tacky, and he wasn't going to be so predictable as to fall into that cliché. Besides, the house rule of no fraternizing with employees was something he stood behind wholeheartedly.

He and Kate were of like minds, and they needed to remain in a professional relationship. Period. Kate stood up for him, stood by him, no matter what, and he refused to risk that by jumping into bed with her.

She had been just as shocked as he was when Alana's deception had been revealed. For once, Kate hadn't made a snarky comment, hadn't tried to be cute or funny. She'd instantly intervened, taking all calls, offering up reasons why the engagement had been called off.

In fact, it was Kate's brilliant plan that had saved his pride. She'd informed the media that Alana had miscarried, and the couple had opted to part ways as friends. At first he'd wanted to just come out with the truth, but he'd been so hurt by the personal nature of the lie, he'd gone along with the farce to save face.

So, for all the times Kate got under his skin with their verbal sparring and her torturous body, he couldn't manage this situation without her.

There were times, even before the fiancée debacle, that he'd just wished he had a place to run to and escape all the chaos of being royalty. Purchasing this home— even though it needed some updating—was like a gift to himself. The view had sold him immediately. With the infinity pool overlooking the Mediterranean Sea and the lush gardens, the previous owners obviously had to have been outdoor enthusiasts. At least Luc had a dock for his Jet Ski and his boat.

Too bad he'd had to come here before all the remodeling was complete. Kate had informed the workers they would have the next two weeks off because the house would be in use. The contractors had managed to get a few of the rooms fully renovated, and thankfully, Luc's master suite was one of them.

He stripped off his wet trunks and stepped into his glass-enclosed shower, which gave the illusion of being outside, but in fact was surrounded by lush tropical plants. The shower was an addition to the master suite and one of his favorite features in the house. He loved having the feeling of being outdoors while being ensured of the privacy he craved. That had been his top priority when he'd bought the house.

An image of sharing this spacious shower with Kate slammed into his mind, and Luc had to focus on something else. Such as the fact she was ten years younger than him, and when he'd been learning to drive, she'd been going to kindergarten and losing her first tooth. There. That should make him feel ridiculous about having such carnal thoughts toward his assistant...shouldn't it?

Water sluiced over his body as he braced his hands against the glass wall and leaned forward. Dropping his head, he contemplated all the reasons why bedding his assistant was wrong. Not only would things be awkward between them, but any bad press could threaten his ascension to the throne. Not to mention the no-fraternization rule, which had been implemented for a reason. He didn't want to be the cause for a black mark on his family's name. One major issue was all he could handle right now. Unfortunately, the one and only reason for wanting to claim her kept trumping all the mounting negatives. He had to find a way to keep her at arm's length, because if he kept seeing her parading around in that skimpy gear, he'd never make it through these next two weeks alone with her.

Scrolling through the upcoming schedule, Kate jotted down the important things she needed to follow up on once she was back at the Land of the Internet, aka the palace. Even though Luc was taking a break from life, she had no such luxury, with or without cyberspace. He might be reeling from the embarrassment of the breakup, and dodging the media's speculations, but she still had to stay one step ahead of the game in order to keep him pristine in the eyes of the people once the dust cloud of humiliation settled. Damage control had moved to the top of her priorities in her role as assistant.

Being the assistant to a member of the royal family hadn't been her childhood aspiration. Granted, he wasn't just any member of the royal family, but the next king of Ilha Beleza, but still.

At one time Kate had had notions of being a dress designer. She'd watched her mother, the royal seamstress, often enough, and admired how she could be so creative and still enjoy her work. But Kate's aspirations hit the wall of reality when she'd discovered she excelled at organizing, being in the thick of business and playing the peacemaker. The job appealed to the do-gooder in her, too, as she felt she could make a real difference in the lives of others.

Once she'd received her degree, Kate knew she wanted to work with the royal family she'd known her entire life. She loved them, loved what they stood for, and she wanted to continue to be in that inner circle.

Kate had first met Luc when she was six and he was sixteen. After that, she'd seen him at random times when she'd go to work with her parents. As Kate grew

older and well into her teens, Luc had become more and
more appealing to her on every level a woman starts to
recognize. Of course, with the age gap, he'd paid her
no mind, and she would watch as he'd parade women
in and out of the palace.

She'd never thought he would settle down, but as
his coronation fast approached, with his thirty-fifth
birthday closing in, the timing of Alana's "pregnancy"
couldn't have been better.

Too bad the spoiled debutante had had her hopes of
being a queen shattered, tarnishing the tiara she would
never wear. Alana had tricked Luc into believing she
was expecting their child, which was absurd, because
there's only so long that lie could go on. Alana hadn't
planned on Luc being a hands-on type of father, so
when he'd accompanied her to a doctor's appointment,
he'd been stunned to realize there was no baby.

At least now Kate wouldn't have to field calls for
"Lukey" when he was in meetings and unable to talk.
Kate was glad Miss D Cup was out of the picture...not
that there was room in the picture for Kate herself, but
having that woman around had seriously kept her in a
bad mood for the past several months.

As she glanced over Luc's schedule after this two-
week hiatus, all she saw was meetings with dignitaries,
meetings with his staff, the wedding ceremony and the
ball to celebrate the nuptials of his best friend, Mikos
Alexander, and a few outings that were just "spontane-
ous" enough for the media to snap pictures but not get
close enough to question Luc. A quick wave as he entered a building, a flash of that dimpled grin to the cam-
era, and the paparazzi would be foaming at the mouth
to post the shots with whatever captions they chose.

For the past year Kate had tried to get him to take

on charity projects, not for the media hype, but because he had the power to make things happen. Good things, things that would make a difference in people's lives. What good was power and money if they weren't used to help those less fortunate?

But Luc's focus had always been on the crown, on the bigger prize, on his country and what it would take to rule. He wasn't a jerk, but his focus was not on the little guys, which occasionally made Kate's job of making him look like a knight in shining armor a little harder.

Still, working for a royal family had its perks, and she would have to be dead to ignore how sexy her boss was. Luc would make any woman smile with a fantasy-style sigh. But no matter how attractive the man was, Kate prided herself on remaining professional.

She may have daydreamed about kissing him once. Okay, fine. Once a day, but still. Acting on her attraction would be a colossal mistake. Everyone knew the royal family's rules about not fraternizing with staff. The consequences could mean not only her job, but also her parents'. A risk Kate couldn't take, no matter what she ached for.

With a sigh, Kate rose to her feet and set her day planner aside. Luc had warned her that she'd be "roughing it" at this guesthouse, but she sort of liked the basic charm of the place. The rooms were pretty much bare, the scarred hardwood floors desperately in need of refinishing and the kitchen was at least thirty years out of date, if not more. But she was in her own space and had water, electric power and a beach. She wasn't working nearly as much as she had been at the palace in the midst of wedding-planning chaos. All of those media interviews had been canceled or rescheduled, and she was on a secluded island with her hunky boss. So roughing it wasn't so "rough" in her opinion.

Kate headed out her back door, breathing in the fresh scent of the salty ocean breeze. Following the stone path lined with overgrown bushes and lush plants, which led to the main house, she was glad she'd come along even if the circumstances made Luc only edgier, grouchier and, well, difficult. He had every right to be furious and hurt, though he'd never admit to the pain. Luc always put up a strong front, hiding behind that tough-guy persona.

Kate knew better, but she still chose to refrain from discussing the incident too much. Keeping things more professional than personal was the only way she could continue to work for him and not get swept away by lustful feelings.

When Kate had first started working for Luc, they'd had a heated discussion that led to a near kiss before he'd pulled back. He'd informed her right then that under no circumstances did he bed, date or get involved with employees.

Still, long nights spent working together, trips abroad and even the close quarters of his office had led to heated glances and accidental brushes against each other. The attraction most definitely wasn't one-sided.

Then he'd started dating Miss D Cup, and the obvious physical attraction between boss and employee had faded…at least on Luc's side. Typical playboy behavior. Kate had chided herself for even thinking they would eventually give in to that underlying passion.

Yet here they were again, both single and utterly alone. So now more than ever she needed to exercise this ability to remain professional. In reality, she'd love nothing more than to rip those designer clothes off him and see if he had any hidden tan lines or tattoos, because that one on his back that scrolled across his taut muscles and up onto his left shoulder was enough to have her lady parts standing at attention each time he took his shirt off.

As tempted as she was to give in to her desires, too much was at stake: her job, her parents' jobs, the reputation she'd carry of seducing her boss. That wouldn't look good on a résumé.

Kate had left her phone behind and contemplated changing. But since she was comfortable and would be only a minute with Luc—five at the most—she wanted to see if he'd take her up on this venture she'd been requesting his help with for the past year. Now that his life was turned inside out, perhaps he'd be a little more giving of his time.

With her sandals slapping against the stone pathway, Kate rehearsed in her head everything she wanted to say as she made her way to the house, passing by the picturesque infinity pool.

The rear entrance faced the Mediterranean. Of course, there wasn't a bad view from any window or balcony that she'd seen, and her guest cottage was definitely on her list of places she never wanted to leave. Regardless of the updates that needed to be done, this house was gorgeous and would be even more so once Luc's plans were fully executed.

When she reached the glass double doors, she tapped her knuckles against the frame. The ocean breeze lifted her hair, sending it dancing around her shoulders, tickling her skin. The wind had kicked up in the past several minutes and dark clouds were rolling in.

Storms…she loved them. Kate smiled up at the ominous sky and welcomed the change. There was something so sexy and powerful about the recklessness of a thunderstorm.

When she knocked again and Luc still didn't answer, she held her hand to the glass and peered inside. No Luc in sight. The knob turned easily and she stepped inside the spacious living area. It led straight into the kitchen, which was only slightly more modern than hers. Basically, the main house looked the same as the cottage, only supersized, with the entire back wall made up of windows and French doors.

"Luc?" she called, hoping he'd hear her and she wouldn't startle him.

What if he'd decided to rest? Or what if he was in the shower?

A smile spread across her face. Oh, yeah. What if he *was* in the shower? Water sliding over all those glorious tanned muscles…

Down, girl.

She wasn't here to seduce her boss. She was here to plant a seed about a charity project close to her heart. If Luc thought he'd formulated the plan, then he'd be all for it, and she desperately wanted him to donate his time and efforts to an orphanage in the United States she'd been corresponding with on his behalf. For reasons he didn't need to know about, the place held a special spot in her heart. She didn't want him to go there out of pity. She wanted him to do so on his own, because he felt it was the right thing to do.

But Kate couldn't get the twins who lived there, Carly and Thomas, out of her mind, and she was driving herself crazy with worry. For now, though, things were out of her control, so she had to focus on getting Luc on board with funding and volunteering. What would that little bit hurt him, anyway? In all reality, the visit and the monetary gift wouldn't leave a dent in his time or finances, but both would mean the world to those children.

"Luc?" She headed toward the wide, curved staircase with its scrolled, wrought-iron railing. She rested her hand on the banister, only to have it wobble beneath her palm. Definitely another item for the list of renovations.

She didn't even know what room he'd opted to use as the master suite, as there was one downstairs and one upstairs. "Are you up there?" she called, more loudly this time.

Within seconds, Luc stood at the top of the stairs, wearing only a tan and a towel. Kate had seen him in swimming trunks, knew full well just how impressive his body was. Yet standing here looking up at him, knowing there was only a piece of terry cloth and a few stairs between them, sent her hormones into overdrive. And she had to keep reminding herself she was only his assistant.

Still, that wouldn't stop her from appreciating the fact her boss was one fine man. Her "office view" was hands down the best she could ever ask for.

"I'm sorry," she said, forcing her gaze to stay on his face. If she looked away she'd appear weak, as if she couldn't handle seeing a half-naked man. If her eyes lowered to the flawless chest on display, he'd know all her fantasies for sure. "I'll just wait until you're dressed."

Before she made a fool of herself by staring, babbling or drooling, Kate turned and scurried back to the living area, where she sank onto the old sofa that had been draped with a pale yellow cover until the renovations were completed and new furniture arrived. Dropping her head against the saggy cushion, she let out a groan.

Lucas Silva was one *atraente* prince. Sexy prince. After living in Ilha Beleza for a full year now, she was growing more accustomed to thinking in Portuguese as opposed to English. Even thinking of Luc in another language only proved how pathetic she was.

Get a grip.

She should've waited in the living room, or just come back later after her walk. Then she wouldn't have been tortured by seeing him wearing nothing but that towel and the water droplets that clung to those taut muscles. Had he been standing closer, the temptation to lick away all the moisture from his recent shower might have been too much to handle.

She'd held on to her self-control for a year and didn't intend to let it snap now. A man like Luc would enjoy that too much, and Kate refused to be like all the other women who fawned over the playboy prince.

Smoothing her floral, halter-style sundress, she crossed her legs, hoping for a casual look instead of the assistant-hot-for-her-boss one. The second she heard his feet crossing the floor, she sat up straighter and silently scolded herself for allowing her thoughts and hormones to control her.

"Sorry I interrupted your shower," she told him the second he stepped down into the sunken living area. "I was heading out for a walk, but I wanted to run something by you first."

He'd thrown on black board shorts and a red T-shirt. Still, the image of him wearing next to nothing was burned into her mind, and that's all she could focus on. Luc fully or even partially clothed was sexy, but Luc practically in his birthday suit was a much more dangerous thought.

"I'm not working, if that's what you want to discuss." He strode across the room and opened the patio doors, pushing them wide to allow the ocean breeze to stream in. Kate came to her feet, ready to be firm, but careful not to anger him, because this project was too important to her.

"It's just something you need to think about," she retorted as she went to stand near the open doors. "I know we've discussed charity work in the past—"

He turned, held up a hand to cut her off. "I'm not scheduling anything like that until I have the crown. I don't want to even think beyond right now. I've got a big enough mess on my hands."

Crossing her arms, Kate met his gaze…until that gaze dropped to her chest. Well, well, well. Looked as if maybe he wasn't immune to the physical attraction between them, after all.

"I was working on your schedule for the next several months and you have a gap that I could squeeze something into, but you have to be in agreement."

The muscles in his jaw clenched as Kate waited for a response. Whenever he stared at her with such intensity, she never knew what was going through his mind. If his thoughts had anything to do with the way he'd been staring at her moments ago, she was totally on board. Sign her up.

Before she realized what he was doing, Luc reached out and slid a fingertip across her bare shoulder. It took every bit of her willpower not to shiver beneath such a simple, yet intimate touch.

"Wh-what are you doing?" she asked, cursing the stammer.

When his finger trailed across her collarbone, then back to her shoulder, Kate continued to stare, unsure what he was doing. If he was trying to seduce her, he needn't try any harder. With the way he kept looking at her, she was about to throw out the window all the reasons they shouldn't be together. One jerk of the knot of fabric at her neck and that halter dress would slide to the floor.

She waited, more than ready for Luc to make her fantasy come true.

Two

Luc fisted his hands at his sides. What the hell had he been thinking, reaching out and touching Kate like that? He was nothing but a *tolo*, a fool, even to allow himself the brief pleasure.

With all Kate's creamy skin exposed, silently inviting his touch, his last thread of willpower had snapped. And as much as he hated to admit it, even to himself, he was too emotionally drained to think straight. Part of him just wanted someone as a sexual outlet, an escape, but he wouldn't use his assistant...no matter how tempted he was.

Luc hadn't tried hard enough to keep himself in check, which was the main problem. He was still reeling from the fact that Kate had stood at the base of the steps looking as if she might leap to the second floor and devour him if he even hinted he was ready. And *misericórdia*, mercy, he was ready for some no-strings affection. Still, not with his employee. How did this number-one rule keep slipping from his mind?

"You're burned," he replied, surprised when his tone came out stronger than he'd intended. "Looks like you should've taken your own advice about that sunscreen."

With a defiant tilt of her chin, a familiar gesture he'd come to find amusing, she propped her hands on her hips, which did amazing things to the pull of the fabric across her chest. The woman was slowly killing him.

The no-dating-staff rule also covered no sleeping with staff. Damn it, he was a mess after Alana. More so than he feared if he was thinking even for a second of risking his family's reputation, and his own reputation as a worthy king, by sleeping with Kate. Nothing good would come from his moment of weakness, and then he'd be out an amazing assistant, because he couldn't allow her to work for him further. And she'd have a wealth of fodder for the press if she chose to turn against him.

That was precisely the reason he needed to keep his damn hands off his assistant.

"Maybe tomorrow we can rub it on each other, then," she suggested with a mocking grin. "Anyway, back to the charity."

Charity, the lesser of two evils when compared to rubbing sunscreen over her luscious curves… But he wasn't getting into this discussion again. He sponsored several organizations financially, but his time wasn't something he'd considered giving. The main reason being he didn't like it when people in power used that type of opportunity as just another publicity stunt. Luc didn't want to be that type of king…that is, if he actually got the crown.

"We need to figure out a plan to secure my title first," he told Kate. "Everything else can wait."

Pursing her lips, she nodded. Apparently, she was backing down, which was a first. She never shied away from an argument.

"You're plotting something," he said, narrowing his gaze. "You may as well tell me now."

"I'm not plotting anything," she replied, that sweet grin still in place, confirming his suspicion. "I've been thinking about your title, but I haven't come up with a solid solution, other than a quick wedding, of course."

She turned and started through the patio doors, but Luc reached out, grabbing her arm to halt her exit. Her eyes darted down to his hand, then back up to his face, but he didn't release her.

"Why is this particular charity so important to you?" he asked. "You mention it so often. If you give me the name, I'll send as much money as you want me to."

Her eyes softened, filled with a sadness he hadn't seen there before. "Money isn't what I wanted."

Slipping from his grasp, she headed down the stairs toward the beach. Money wasn't what she wanted? Had he ever heard a woman say that before? Surely any organization could benefit from a sizable donation.

Kate was always surprising him with what came out of her mouth. She seemed to enjoy a good verbal sparring as much as he did. But something about the cause she kept bringing up was bothering him. Obviously, this was something near and dear to her, and she didn't feel like opening up about it. She'd worked for him for a year, but he'd known her longer than that, though they didn't exactly hang in the same circles. Didn't she trust him enough to disclose her wishes?

Luc shook his head as he watched her walk along the

shoreline. The woman was mesmerizing from so many different angles, and it was a damn shame she was his assistant, because having her in his bed would certainly help take the edge off this title-throne nightmare.

Glancing up at the sky, he noticed the clouds growing darker. A storm was on the horizon and he knew how much Kate loved Mother Nature's wrath. She'd always been fascinated by the sheer power, she'd told him once. And that summed Kate up in a nutshell. She was fierce, moved with efficiency and had everyone taking notice.

Part of him wanted to worry, but he knew she'd be back soon, most likely to watch the storm from her own balcony. Luc still took a seat on his patio to wait for her, because they weren't done discussing this charity business. She was hiding something and he wanted to know what it was. Why was this mysterious organization such a secret? And why did discussing it make her so sad and closed off?

He sank down onto the cushioned bench beside the infinity pool. Everything about this outdoor living space was perfect and exactly what he would've chosen for himself. From the stone kitchen for entertaining to the wide, cushioned benches and chaise lounges by the pool, Luc loved all the richness this space offered.

Glancing down the beach where Kate had set out, he found he couldn't see her any longer and wondered when she'd start heading back. Ominous clouds blanketed the sky, rumbles of thunder filling the previous silence.

When the first fat drop of rain hit his cheek, Luc continued to stare in the direction she'd gone. Since when did he give anyone such power over his mind? He didn't like this. Not one bit.

He was next in line for the throne, for pity's sake.

How could his hormones be led around so easily by one petite, curvy woman, and how the hell could he still want her after months and months of ignoring the fact?

This pull was strong, no doubt, but Luc just had to be stronger. There was no room for lust here. He wouldn't risk his family's stellar reputation, or his ascension to the throne, just because he was hot for his assistant.

The wild, furious storm had been magnificent, one of the best she'd seen in a long time. Kate had meant to get back to the house before the weather got too bad, but she'd ended up finding a cove to wait it out in and couldn't resist staying outside. She'd been shielded from the elements, but she'd gotten drenched before she could get hunkered down.

With her dress plastered to her skin, she headed back toward the guesthouse. Even being soaking wet and a bit chilly from the breeze caressing her damp skin didn't dim her mood. She had to walk up the steps to Luc's patio in order to reach the path to her place. Noticing a light on the dock and lights on either side of the patio doors, she realized she'd been gone longer than she'd intended. It was clearly very dark and not because of the storm.

"Where the hell were you?"

Startled, Kate jumped back at the sound of Luc's angry, harsh tone. He stood in the doorway to his living area, wearing the same clothes as he had before, but now his hair stood on end, as if he'd run his fingers through it multiple times.

"Excuse me?" She stepped closer to him, taking in his flared nostrils, clenched jaw and the firm line of his mouth. "I told you I was going for a walk. I wasn't sure I had to check in, Dad."

Luc's lips thinned even more. "That storm was nasty. I assumed you'd have enough sense to come back. What the hell were you thinking?"

The fact he'd waited for her warmed something in her, but the way he looked as if he was ready to throttle her had her defensive side trumping all other feelings. This had nothing to do with lust or sexual chemistry.

"I purposely left the palace, the guards and everyone to get away from my troubles," he went on, his voice laced with irritation. "You're here to help me figure this whole mess out. But if you can't be responsible, you can either go back to the palace or I'll call in one of my guards to stay here and make sure you're safe."

Kate laughed. "You're being ridiculous. I'm a big girl, you know. I was perfectly fine and I sure as hell don't need a keeper. Next thing you know you'll be calling my parents."

With her father being head of security and her mother the clothing designer and seamstress for the family, Kate had been surrounded by royalty her entire life… just without a title of her own. Oh, wait, she was an assistant. Equally as glamorous as queen, princess or duchess.

Actually, she liked being behind the scenes. She had an important role that allowed her to travel, make great money and do some good without being in the limelight. And she would continue to try to persuade Luc to visit the orphanage so close to her heart. They'd taken care of her there, had loved her and sheltered her until she was adopted. Now she was in a position to return some of their generosity.

"Your father would agree with me." Luc stepped forward, closing the gap between them as he gripped her arm. "Don't go anywhere without your phone again. Anything could've happened to you."

"You can admit you were worried without going all Neanderthal on me, Your Highness." She jerked from his grasp, but he only stepped closer when she moved back. "What is your problem? I was out, I'm back. Don't be so grouchy because you can't admit you were scared."

"Scared?" he repeated, leaning in so close she could feel his warm breath on her face, see the gold flecks in those dark eyes. "I wasn't scared. I was angry that you were being negligent."

Kate really wasn't in the mood to be yelled at by her boss. She didn't deserve to be on the receiving end of his wrath when the issue he had was clearly with himself.

Her soggy dress needed to go, and she would give anything to soak in a hot bubble bath in that sunken garden tub in her master bathroom. She only hoped it worked. She hadn't tested it yet, and the sink in her kitchen was a bit leaky...

"I'm heading home." Kate waved a hand in the air to dismiss him and this absurd conversation. "We can talk tomorrow when you've cooled off."

The instant she turned away, she found herself being jerked back around. "I'm getting real sick of you manhandling—"

His lips were on hers, his hands gripping the sides of her face, holding her firmly in place as he coaxed her lips apart. There was nothing she could do but revel in the fact that Prince Lucas Silva was one potent man and quite possibly the best kisser she'd ever experienced.

And he was most definitely an experience. Those strong hands framed her face as his tongue danced with hers. Kate brought her hands up, wrapping them around his wrists. She had no clue if she should stop this before it got out of hand or hang on for the ride, since he'd fueled her every fantasy for so long.

Arching against him, she felt his firm body do so many glorious things to hers. The chill she'd had from the rain was no longer an issue.

But just as quickly as he'd claimed her mouth, he released her and stepped back, forcing her hands to drop. Muttering a Portuguese curse, Luc rubbed the back of his neck and kept his gaze on the ground. Kate honestly had no clue what to do. Say something? Walk away without a word?

What was the logical next step after being yelled at by her boss, then kissed as if he needed her like air in his lungs for his survival? And then pushed away with a filthy term her mother would blush at…

Clearing her throat, Kate wrapped her arms around her waist. "I'm not quite sure why you did that, but let's chalk it up to the heat of the moment. We'll both laugh about it tomorrow."

And dream about it tonight.

"You just push me too far." His intense gaze swept over her, but he kept his distance. "For a year I've argued with you, but you've always had my back. I know there've been times you've intervened and stood up for me without my even knowing. As far as employees go, you're the best."

Confused, Kate ran her hands up and down her arms as the ocean breeze chilled her damp skin. "Okay. Where are you going with this?"

"Nowhere," he all but yelled, flinging his arms out. "What just happened can't happen again because you're an employee and I don't sleep with staff. Ever."

Kate couldn't help the laugh that erupted from her. "You kissed me. Nobody mentioned sex."

His gaze heated her in ways that a hot bubble bath never could have. "I don't have to mention it. When I look at you I think it, and after tasting you, I feel it."

If he thought those words would deter her, he didn't know her at all. Kate reached forward, but Luc stepped back.

"Don't," he growled. "Just go on back to your cottage and we'll forget this happened."

Smoothing wet tendrils off her forehead, Kate shook her head. "Oh, no. You can't drop that bomb, give me a proverbial pat on the head and send me off to bed. You went from arguing to kissing me to throwing sex into the conversation in the span of two minutes. You'll understand if I can't keep up with your hormonal swings tonight."

The muscle tic in his jaw, the clenched fists at his sides, were all indicators he was irritated, frustrated and angry. He had no one to blame but himself, and she wasn't going to be caught up in his inner turmoil.

"This is ridiculous," she said with a sigh. "We're both obviously not in a position to talk without saying something we don't mean."

"I always mean what I say," he retorted. "Otherwise I wouldn't say it."

Rolling her eyes, Kate again waved a hand through the air. "Fine. You meant what you said about wanting to have sex with me."

"Don't twist my words," he growled.

Kate met his leveled gaze, knowing full well she was poking the bear. "Did you or did you not say you thought of having sex with me? That you actually feel it."

He moved around her, heading for the steps leading to the beach. "This conversation is over. Go home, Kate."

She stared at his retreating back for all of five seconds before she took off after him. Just because he was royalty and she was his assistant didn't mean he could dismiss her anytime he wanted. Rude was rude no matter one's social status.

She didn't say a word as she followed him. Luc's long strides ate up the ground as he headed toward the dock. Surely the man wasn't going out on his Jet Ski now. Granted, the water was calm since the storm had passed, but it was dark and he was angry.

Just as she was about to call his name, he went down. The heavy thud had her moving faster, her thighs burning from running across the sand. She prayed the sound of him falling was much worse than any injury.

"Luc," she called as she approached. "Are you all right?"

He didn't move, didn't respond, but lay perfectly still on the wet dock. Dread consumed her. The second she stepped onto the dock, her feet slid a bit, too, and she tripped over a loose board that had warped slightly higher than the others.

The dock obviously hadn't been repaired like the rest of the outdoor spaces on this property.

Kate crouched next to him, instantly noticing the swollen knot at his temple. He'd hit his head on a post, from what she could tell.

"Luc." She brushed his hair off his forehead, afraid to move him, and hoping he'd only passed out. "Can you hear me?"

She stroked his cheek as she ran her gaze down his body to see if there were any other injuries. How could he be up one second and out cold the next? Fear threatened to overtake her the instant she realized she didn't have her phone.

Maybe she was irresponsible, but she'd have to worry about that later. Right now she had no clue how serious Luc's injury was, but the fact he still hadn't moved had terror pumping through her.

Shifting so her knees weren't digging into the wood, Kate sat on her hip and kept patting Luc's face. "Come on, Luc. Wake up. Argue with me some more."

Torn between rushing back to the house for her phone to call for help and waiting to see if he woke on his own, Kate started patting down his shorts, hoping he carried his cell in his pocket.

One pocket was empty, and before she could reach to the other side, Luc groaned and tried to shift his body.

"Wait," she told him, pressing a hand to his shoulder as he started to rise. "Don't move. Are you hurt anywhere?"

He blinked as he stared up at her. Thankfully, the bright light from the lamppost was helping her assess his injuries, since the sun had set.

Luc's brows drew together in confusion. "Why were you feeling me up?"

Relief swept through her. "I wasn't feeling you up," she retorted, wrapping her arm around his shoulders and slowly helping him to sit up. "I was checking your pockets for a cell phone. You fell and hit your head on the post. I was worried because you were out for a few minutes."

Luc reached up, wincing as his fingers encountered the bump on his head, which was already turning blue. "Damn, that hurts."

"Let's get you back up to the house." Kate helped

him to his feet, then slid her arm around his waist to steady him. "You okay? Feeling dizzy or anything?"

He stared down at her, blinked a few times and frowned. "This is crazy," he muttered.

"What?"

With his thumb and index finger, he wiped his eyes and held the bridge of his nose. He probably had the mother of all headaches right now. All the more reason to get this big guy moving toward the house, because if he went back down, she couldn't carry him.

"I know you," he murmured. "I just… Damn it, your name isn't coming to me."

Kate froze. "You don't know my name?" This was not good. That ball of fear in her stomach grew.

Shaking his head, he wrapped an arm around her shoulders and started leading them off the dock. "I must've hit my head harder than I thought. Why isn't it coming to me?"

Kate pressed a hand to his abdomen, halting his progress. She shifted just enough to look him in the eyes. Since she wasn't a medic and never had any kind of training other than a basic CPR course, she had no idea what signs to look for with a head trauma.

"Look at me," she ordered. "You know me, Luc. You know my name."

Blowing out a breath, he hung his head. "I… It's on the tip of my tongue. Damn, why can't I remember?"

He glanced back up at her, worry filling his dark eyes. This was not good, not good at all. She was going to have to get him back to the house and call the palace doctor. Obviously, Luc's memory wasn't cooperating. But she didn't want him panicking; she could do enough of that for both of them.

"My name is Kate." She watched his eyes, hoping

to see some recognition, but there was nothing. "I'm your—"

"Fiancée." A wide smile spread across his face. "Now I remember you."

Luc leaned in to capture her lips once more, with a passion she'd never known.

Three

Fiancée? What the hell?

Mustering all her willpower, Kate pushed Luc and his intoxicating mouth away as his words slammed into her.

"Let's get you inside," she told him, trying not to focus on how hard he must've hit his head, because he was clearly not in his right mind. "I'm not comfortable with that knot you have, and you may have a concussion. I need to call your doctor. Hopefully, with the storm gone, we'll have cell service."

Luc stared at her another minute, then nodded. Slipping his arm around her shoulders again, he let her lead him up to the house. Something was definitely wrong with him. The Luc from only twenty minutes ago would be arguing that he didn't need a doctor, and he certainly wouldn't be leaning on her for support.

She couldn't even think about the fact that he believed they were engaged. Because if he thought they were sleeping together, this situation would get extremely awkward really fast.

Though she'd be lying if she didn't admit to herself just how much she liked him thinking they were a couple. How long would his mind play this trick on him? How would he treat her now that he believed they were together?

Once she had him inside and settled on the sofa, she stood up and caught her breath. Luc was one massive, thick, muscular man. She'd known he was cut, but she'd had no clue how solid and heavy he would be.

His body had leaned against hers, twisting her dress on their walk. As Kate readjusted herself, trying to refill her lungs with air and not panic, she found him staring up at her, that darkened gaze holding her in place. Shivers rippled through her at the intensity of the moment—and the man.

"What?" she asked.

"Why are you all wet?"

Plucking at the damp material that clung to her thighs, Kate shook her head. "I got caught outside in the storm earlier."

Those eyes continued to rake over her body. "You're sexy like this," he murmured as his heated stare traveled back up. "With your dress clinging to your curves and your hair messy and wavy."

Kate swallowed, because any reply she had to those intimate words would lead to a lie, and she couldn't let him keep thinking they were anything more than employee-employer, servant-royal.

"Where's your cell?" If she didn't stay on task, she'd get caught up in all those sultry looks he was giving her...and she desperately wanted to get caught up in the promise behind those sexy stares. But he wasn't himself right now. "I need to call the doctor. I hope we have service."

Luc glanced around, raking a hand through his hair. "I have no idea. I don't even remember why I was outside."

He slapped his hand on the cushion beside him and let out a string of curses. "Why can't I remember anything?"

The worry lacing his voice concerned her even more than the fact he thought they were engaged. Luc Silva never let his guard down. Even when faced with losing the crown, the man was the epitome of control and power. Sexy and strong and she wanted him. Plain and simple…or maybe not so simple considering she could never have him.

"It's okay," she assured him as she leaned down to pat his shoulder. "I'll find it. Once the doctor comes, we'll know more. Maybe this will only last a few minutes. Try not to panic."

That last bit of advice was for herself as much as him, because she was seriously in panic mode right now. She didn't know much about memory loss, but the fact that something had set his mind so off balance concerned her. She couldn't even imagine how he felt.

Kate walked around the spacious but sparsely decorated living room, into the dated kitchen and then back to the living room. Crossing to the patio doors they'd just entered, she finally spotted his cell lying on the old, worn accent table most likely left by the last tenants.

Thankfully, she knew the passcode to get into the phone. "I'm just going to step out here," she told him, trying to assure him he wouldn't be alone. "I'll be right back."

She didn't want Luc to hear any worry in her tone when she described the incident to the doctor. And for now, she wasn't going to mention the whole "fiancée" bit. She would ride this out as long as possible. Yes, that was selfish, but, well…everyone had their moments of weakness and Luc Silva was definitely her weakness.

Kate was relieved to get the doctor on the phone and even more relieved when he promised to be there within the next hour. For the next sixty minutes, Luc would most likely believe they were engaged and she would play right along until she was told otherwise.

Luc's private beach villa just off the coast of Portugal wasn't far from his own country. He was pretty much hiding in plain sight. This way he could be home quickly in an emergency—or someone could come to him.

Kate was grateful the doctor could use the private boat to get to the island. There was no airstrip and the only way in or out was via boat. Only yesterday she and Luc had been dropped off by her father, so Luc could keep his hideout a secret.

When she walked back inside, Luc had his head tipped back against the sofa cushions. Eyes closed, he held a hand to his head, massaging his temples with his fingers.

"The doctor is on his way."

Without opening his eyes, he simply gave a brief nod.

"I know you're hurting, but I don't want to give you anything before the doctor can examine you."

What if his injuries were more serious than she thought? Amnesia, temporary or not, wasn't the worst thing that could happen. People died from simple falls all the time. Even when they felt fine, they could have some underlying issue that went unnoticed.

The possibilities flooded her mind as she continued to stand across the room and stare at Luc. Should he be resting or should she keep him awake? She prayed she didn't do the wrong thing. She would never forgive herself if something happened to him because they'd been fighting and he'd stormed off. If she didn't always feel the need to challenge him, this wouldn't have happened.

The kiss wouldn't have happened, either, because that was obviously spawned from sexual frustration and anger. Luc's full-on mouth attack had been forceful, not gentle or restrained. She'd loved every delicious second of it. But now she needed to focus, not think about how good it had felt to finally have him touch her the way she'd always wanted.

As she watched him, his lids kept fluttering, and finally remained closed for a minute.

"Luc," she said softly. "Try not to fall asleep, okay?"

"I'm not," he mumbled. "The lights are too bright, so I'm just keeping my eyes closed."

Crossing to the switches, she killed the lights in the living room, leaving just the one from the kitchen on so she could still see him.

"Does that help?" she asked, taking a seat beside him on the couch, relishing in the warmth from his body.

He opened one eye, then the other, before he shifted slightly to look at her. "Yeah. Thanks."

When he reached over to take her hand, Kate tensed. This wasn't real. The comfort he was seeking from her was only because he was uncertain—and he thought they were engaged.

Oh, if they were truly engaged, Kate could hold his hand and not feel guilty. She could wrap her arms around him and give him support and love and...

But no. She wasn't his fianceé so thinking along those lines would get her nowhere.

For now, she could pretend, she could keep her fingers laced with his and feel things for him in ways she never had before. This was no longer professional… they'd crossed that threshold when he'd captured her mouth beneath his.

"I'll be fine." Luc offered a wide smile, one rarely directed at her. "Just stay right here with me."

Swallowing the truth, Kate nodded. "I'm not going anywhere."

She tried not to relish the fact that Luc's thumb kept stroking the back of her hand. She tried to fight the thrill that he was looking at her as more than just an employee.

None of this was reality. He was trapped in his own mind for now. She didn't know if she should focus on the kiss earlier or the nasty knot on his head. Both issues made her a nervous wreck.

The hour seemed to crawl by, but when Dr. Couchot finally knocked on the back door, Kate breathed a sigh of relief. Beneath her hand, Luc tensed.

"It's okay." She rose to her feet, patting his leg. "We'll figure this out and you'll be just fine."

Dr. Couchot immediately came inside, set his bag down and took a seat on the couch next to Luc.

"Tell me what happened," he said, looking at Kate. Worry was etched on the doctor's face. This man had cared for Luc since the prince had been in diapers, and held all the royals' medical secrets.

Kate recounted the events, omitting the fiancée bit, and watched as the doctor examined his patient while she spoke. He looked at Luc's pupils with his minuscule light, then lightly worked his fingertip around the blue knot. With a frown, he sat back and sighed.

"Have you remembered anything since I was called?" he asked.

Luc shook his head. "I know Kate, but she had to tell me her name. I know I'm a member of the royal family because of my name, and I believe I'm the prince. I know this house is mine and I know I wanted to fix it up, but apparently I didn't get too far, so I had to have just bought it."

All this was right. A little burst of hope spread through Kate. Maybe his injuries weren't as bad as she'd first feared.

"From what I can tell, you've got temporary amnesia," the doctor stated. "I'm not seeing signs of a concussion and your pupils are responsive." Dr. Couchot looked up at Kate. "I would like him to have a scan to be on the safe side, but knowing Luc, he'll be stubborn and refuse."

"I'm sitting right here," Luc stated, his eyes darting between Kate and the doctor. "I don't want to get a scan. I'd have to go home and face too many questions. Unless I'm at risk for something more serious, I'm staying here."

Kate shared a look with the doctor. "What about if I promise to monitor him? You said there was no concussion, so that's a good sign."

"Fine," Dr. Couchot conceded. "I won't argue. But Kate will have her eyes on you 24/7 for the next few days and I'll be in contact with her. At the first sign of anything unusual, she will get you back to the palace, where we can treat you. No exceptions."

Luc nodded. "Agreed."

After receiving her instructions and a list of things

to look for in terms of Luc's behavior, Kate showed the doctor out.

Once they reached the edge of the patio, Dr. Couchot turned to face her. "Make sure you don't force any memories on him. It's important he remembers on his own, or his mind could become even more confused and his condition could actually worsen. It's a blessing he remembers as much as he does, so I believe he's only lost a few months of his memories."

A few months. Which would explain why he didn't recall the real fiancée or the fake pregnancy.

"I'll make sure not to feed him any information," Kate promised. Smoothing her hair back, she held it to the side in a makeshift ponytail. "Can he see photos or listen to his favorite music? Maybe just subtle things that will spark his thoughts?"

"I think that would be fine. Just don't push all of that on him at once. Give this some time. He may wake tomorrow and be perfectly fine, or he may be like this for another month. Every mind is unique, so we just don't know."

Kate nodded, thanking the doctor for coming so quickly. She watched as he made his way back down to the boat, where a palace guard was waiting. Thankfully, it wasn't her father, but his right-hand man.

Kate gave a wave to the men and took in a deep breath. When the doctor mentioned unusual behavior, did that include believing you were engaged to the wrong woman?

Weary and worried, she stepped back through the doors. All her stuff was at the guesthouse, but she would need to stay here.

Luc's eyes were instantly on hers when she returned to the living room. That warmth spread through her once again as she recognized that look of need. She couldn't let him keep this up. There would be no way she could resist him. And based on his reaction after that kiss, he wouldn't be happy that he'd indulged his desire for her, no matter how good together they might be.

The warning from the doctor played over in her mind. She couldn't force memories, so for now she'd have to let him think what he wanted, until his mind started to cooperate.

"Sit with me," he whispered, holding his hand out in invitation.

Kate cringed, wanting nothing more than to take his hand and settle in beside him. "I need to go get some of my things."

Lowering his hand, he frowned. "Where are your things?"

Coming up with a quick excuse, she tried to be vague, yet as honest as possible. "I have some things next door at the guesthouse. Let me get them and I'll be all yours."

Okay, she didn't necessarily need to add that last bit, but it just slipped out. She'd have to think through every single word until Luc fully regained his memory. For now, she'd have to play along...and still try to maintain some distance, or she could find herself in a world of hurt when he snapped out of his current state. Getting wrapped up in this make-believe world, even for a short time, wasn't the wisest decision. Still, he would need her during this time and they were on this island together. How could she resist him? How could she resist more touching, more kissing?

"Why do you have anything next door?" he asked.

"I was working there earlier." Still not a lie. "Give me five minutes. I'll be right back."

She escaped out the back door, unable to look at the confusion on his face any longer. If she got too far into the truth as to why she had things at the cottage, she'd have to come clean and produce the information his mind wasn't ready for.

As quickly as she could, she threw a change of clothes into her bag, adding a few essential toiletries. Everything else she'd have to smuggle over a little at a time, provided she stayed at the main house for longer than a few days.

Her biggest concern now was the fact she hadn't packed pajamas, assuming she'd be living alone. She stared at her pile of silky chemises in various colors. There was no getting around this. She didn't even have an old T-shirt to throw on for a sleep shirt.

With no other choice, she grabbed the pink one and shoved it in her bag before heading back to the main house. There was no way she could let Luc see her in this chemise, but how could she dodge a man who thought they were engaged? Most likely he assumed they slept together, too.

Kate froze on the path back to the main house. There was no way she could sleep with Luc. None. If they shared the same bed, she'd be tempted to give in to his advances.

As the moonlight lit her way back, Kate was resigned to the fact that things were about to skyrocket to a whole new level of awkward.

Four

Kate glanced over her shoulder, making sure she was alone as she slipped back out onto the patio to call her mother. There were times in a woman's life she just needed some motherly advice, and for Kate, that time was now.

"Darling!" Her mother answered on the second ring. "I was just thinking of you."

"Hey, Mama." Kate leaned against the rail on the edge of the patio, facing the doorway to make sure Luc didn't come up behind her and overhear things he shouldn't. "Are you busy?"

"Never for you. You sound funny. Everything all right?"

Not even close. Kate sighed, shoving her hair behind her ear. "I'm in a bit of a bind and I need your advice."

"What's wrong, Katelyn?"

Her mother's worried tone slid through the line. Kate swallowed back her emotions, because tears wouldn't fix this problem and they would only get her a snotty nose and red eyes. Not a good look when one was shacking up with one's sexy boss.

"Luc fell earlier."

"Oh, honey. Is he okay?"

"Well…he has a good-sized goose egg on his head. And he has temporary amnesia."

"Amnesia?" her mother repeated, her voice rising an octave. "Katelyn, are you guys coming back to the palace? Do his parents know?"

"I actually called them before I called you. Dr. Couchot was just here and he's assured us that Luc is okay, no concussion or anything. He isn't sure when Luc will regain his memory, but he's confident it's a short-term condition."

"I can't even imagine how scary this must be," her mother commented. "What can I do to help?"

"Right now Luc and I are staying here as planned," Kate stated, her eyes darting to the patio doors on the far side of the house. Luc stood there for a moment, looking out at the ocean, before he turned and disappeared. "The doctor said keeping him relaxed and calm is best for now. Luc had wanted to get away, so staying here is still our best option."

"I agree. So what else has you upset? If the doctor has assured you this is temporary, and you're staying there as planned, what's wrong?"

Pulling in a deep breath, Kate blurted out, "He thinks we're engaged."

Silence settled over the line. Kate pulled her cell away from her ear to make sure the connection hadn't been cut.

"Mom?"

"I'm here. I just need to process this," her mother stated. "Why does he think you're engaged?"

"He's only lost the past few months. He knew I was familiar, but at first he couldn't place me. When I told him my name, he assumed we were engaged. I was worried and didn't say anything, because I wanted the doctor to look him over. Dr. Couchot said not to feed Luc any information, because giving him pieces of his recent past could mess up his memory even further."

Kate rambled on. She knew she was talking fast, but she needed to get all this out, needed to get advice with Luc out of earshot.

"The doctor and Luc's parents have no clue that Luc believes we're engaged," Kate went on. "That's what I need your opinion on. What do I do, Mom? I don't want to go against the doctor's orders, but at the same time, I can't have him thinking we're a couple, but he doesn't even recall I work for him. You know how this family feels about dating or having such personal relationships with their staff."

"Oh, Katelyn." Her mother sighed. "I would wait and see how tonight goes. If this is temporary, maybe Luc will wake up tomorrow and everything will be fine. You can't go against the doctor's wishes, but I wouldn't let this lie go on too long. Luc may cross boundaries that you two shouldn't cross if he thinks you're his fiancée."

Cross boundaries? Too late. The kiss they'd shared moments before his fall flashed through her mind.

"Thanks, Mom. Please don't say anything. You're the only one who knows Luc thinks we're getting married. I don't want to humiliate him any further or have anyone else worry. I just needed your advice."

"I'm not sure I helped, but I'm definitely here for you. Please, keep me posted. I worry about you."

Kate smiled, pushing herself off the railing and heading back toward the doors. "I know. I'll call you tomorrow if the cell service is good. It's pretty sketchy here."

"Love you, sweetheart."

"I love you, Mama."

Kate disconnected the call as she grasped the doorknob. Closing her eyes, she pulled in a deep breath and blew it out slowly. She needed strength, wisdom and more self-control than ever.

And she needed to remember that Luc was healing. That he was confused. Whatever emotions she'd held on to after that kiss had no place here. Being this close to grasp onto her fantasy, yet not being allowed to take all she wanted was a level of agony she hadn't even known existed.

Luc stood in the spacious bedroom. Apparently, his master suite and luxurious attached bath, with a most impressive shower that gave the illusion of being outdoors, had been at the top of his list for renovations. Fine with him, because this room was fit for romance, and his Kate had looked all sorts of sexy the way she'd worried over him, assuring him he would be okay.

When she'd said it, her sweet, yet confident words had sliced through the fear he'd accumulated. He'd seen the worry in her eyes, but she'd put up a strong front for him. Was it any wonder she was the one for him? Dread over the unknown kept creeping up, threatening to consume him, but Luc wasn't giving up. Being unable to recall bits of his life was beyond weird and frustrating. He actually didn't have the words to describe the emotions flooding him. All he knew was that his beautiful fiancée was here, and she was staying by his side, offering support and comfort.

His eyes drifted from his reflection in the glass patio doors back to the king-size bed dominating the middle of the room. Sheers draping down from the ceiling enclosed the bed, giving an impression of romance and seduction. There was a reason this bed was the focal point of the room, and he had to assume it all centered around Kate. He could already picture her laid out on those satin navy sheets, her black hair fanned out as they made love.

Damn it. Why couldn't he remember making love to her? Why couldn't he recall how she felt against him? How she tasted when he kissed her? Maybe their intimacy would help awaken some of those memories.

Luc cringed inwardly. No, he wasn't using sex or Kate in that way. He wanted to remember their love on his own, but he definitely wanted her by his side tonight while he slept. He wanted to hold her next to him, to curl around her and lose himself to dreams. Maybe tomorrow he'd wake and all this would be a nightmare. His memory would be back and he and Kate could move forward.

There had to be something lying around, some clue that would spark his memory. Granted, he hadn't really brought anything personal to the place, judging by the hideously dated furniture in the majority of the rooms, but surely there was something. Even if he looked through the clothes he'd brought, or maybe there was something in his wallet that would kick his mind back into the proper gear. Perhaps he'd packed something personal, like a picture, or maybe he should go through the contacts on his cell. Seeing a list of names might be just the trigger he needed.

Luc searched through his drawers, finding nothing of interest. It wasn't as if his underwear drawer would reveal any hidden clues other than the fact that he liked black boxer briefs.

Slamming one drawer shut, he searched another. By the time he was done looking through the chest and hunting through his bathroom, he was alternating between being terrified and being furious. Nothing new popped up except a healthy dose of rage.

There had to be something in his cell phone. He started out the bedroom door, only to collide chest to chest with Kate. Her eyes widened as she gripped his biceps in an attempt to steady herself.

"Sorry," she said, stepping back. "I just got back with my things. I called your parents and gave them the rundown. They're worried, but I assured them you would be fine and you'd call them yourself tomorrow. I also called my mother. I didn't mean to be gone so long. Are you heading to bed?"

Was she shaking? Her eyes darted over his shoulder toward the bed, then back to meet his gaze. The fact she had been rambling and now kept chewing on her lip was proof she was nervous. About the amnesia?

"Are you all right?" he asked, reaching out to smooth her hair away from her forehead. He tipped her chin up, focusing on those luscious, unpainted lips. "You seem scared, more than you were just a few minutes ago."

Kate reached up to take his hand in hers. "I guess all the events finally caught up with me. I'm tired and worried. Nothing more."

"That's more than you need to handle," he told her, stroking his thumb over her bottom lip. "Let's go to bed."

That instant, holding Kate completely trumped finding his phone and seeking answers. There was a need inside him, an ache he had for this woman that was so primal he couldn't even wrap his mind around it. His phone would be there when he woke up, and right now all he wanted was to lose himself in Kate. She looked dead on her feet, and she still hadn't changed from her wet dress, which had now mostly dried. There was no way she was comfortable.

"Why don't you grab a shower and meet me in bed?" he asked.

Her eyes widened. "Um…I'm not sure we should…"

Luc waited for her to elaborate, but she closed her eyes and let out a soft sigh. When her head drooped a little, Luc dropped his hand from her chin and squeezed her shoulder.

"Are you afraid to be with me because of the memory loss?"

Her lids lifted, her dark eyes searching his. "I'm not afraid of you, Luc. I think it would be best if we didn't… you know…"

"Make love?"

A pink tinge crept across her tan cheeks. "Yes. You're injured. You need to rest and relax. Per the doctor's orders."

Luc snaked his arms around her waist as he pulled her flush against his body. "I plan on relaxing, but I want you lying beside me. It's obvious we came here to get away, and I don't want to ruin this trip for you."

Delicate hands slid up his chest, fingers curling up over his shoulders. Just her simple touch was enough to have his body quivering, aching. Everything about her was so familiar, yet so new at the same time.

"You're not ruining anything for me." She offered a tired, yet beautiful smile. "Let's just concentrate on getting you better, and everything else will fall into place."

"So no sex, but you'll lie down with me?"

Her eyes held his as she nodded. "I'll lie with you."

He hadn't recalled her name at first, but he'd instantly felt a pull toward her. No wonder they were engaged. Obviously, they shared a special, deeply rooted bond. Their chemistry pushed through the damage to his mind, and that alone would help him pull through this.

"I'll just go shower in the guest bath, real quick," she told him, easing away from his embrace. "Give me ten minutes."

Confused at her need to retreat, Luc crossed his arms over his chest. "Why not just use the shower in here? The other bathroom hasn't been renovated and this one is much more luxurious."

She looked as if she wanted to argue, but finally nodded. "You're right. A quick shower in here would be better. I just didn't know if I would disturb you trying to rest."

"You won't bother me. You can take advantage of the sunken garden tub, you know." He took her hands, leading her farther into their bedroom. "No need to rush through a shower. Just go soak in a tubful of warm water and relax."

"I'll be quick in the shower. Why don't you lie down?"

He leaned forward, gently touching his lips to hers. "Don't take too long or I'll come in after you."

She shivered beneath his touch, and it was all Luc could do to keep from hauling her off to the bed and taking what he wanted, throwing every reason he shouldn't straight out the window.

Retreating into the bathroom, she closed the door. Luc frowned. Was she always so private? Why did some things seem so familiar, while other, mundane things had disappeared from his mind?

As he stripped down to his boxer briefs, he heard the

shower running. An image of a wet, soapy Kate flooded his mind. He couldn't wait to get beyond this memory lapse, beyond the annoyance of the headache, and make full use of that spacious shower with her.

He would make this up to her, somehow. His Kate was exhausted, and still worried about him. She was sacrificing, when this was supposed to be a romantic trip away.

As of right now he only remembered they were engaged. He recalled some buzz about wedding invitations and upcoming showers. He'd let his assistant handle all of that…but he couldn't recall who his assistant was at the moment.

Raking a hand down his face, Luc sighed. Now wasn't the time to think of staff, not when he was about to crawl into bed with his fiancée. Right now he wanted to focus on Kate, on their trip and somehow making this up to her.

Kate showered quickly, constantly watching the door she'd closed. She should've known he'd want her in his room, that he wouldn't even question the fact.

But sleeping with him under false pretenses was an absolute no.

No matter how Luc made her body tingle and the nerves in her belly dance…she couldn't let her thoughts go there.

She was still Luc's assistant, which meant looking out for his best interest. And it was in the interest of both of them to keep their clothes on. Easier said than done.

Kate dried off, wrapped her hair up in a towel and slid into her chemise. She truly had no other option unless she asked Luc for a T-shirt, but she didn't know if he was one of those guys who would be even more turned on by seeing a woman in his clothes, so she opted for her own gown.

Rubbing the towel through her wet hair, she got all the moisture out and took her time brushing it. Perhaps if she stayed away a few extra minutes, Luc would get tired and fall asleep before she went back out there.

Their argument before his fall had taken on a life of its own, and she still couldn't get that kiss from her mind. Of course, if her lips weren't still tingling, maybe she could focus on something else. Such as the fact that the man was suffering from memory loss and was scared and angry over this sudden lack of control with his own mind.

Still, between the toe-curling kiss and the fact she was about to slide between the sheets with her boss, Kate didn't know how to act at this point. What was the proper protocol?

After applying some lotion on her legs and shoulders, Kate hung up her towel and faced the inevitable: she was going to have to go out into the bedroom and get in that bed. The sooner she moved beyond the awkward, uncomfortable stage, the sooner she could breathe easily. All she needed to do was go in there, lie beside Luc and wait for him to fall asleep. Then she could get up and go to the sofa or something. No way could she lie nestled next to him all night. The temptation to pick up where their kiss had left off would be too strong.

But the doctor had been adamant about not saying too much, to allow the memories to return on their own. Kate didn't want to do anything that would cause Luc more damage.

Somehow she had to abide by his no-fraternization

rule and still manage to play the doting fiancée. Was that combination even possible?

Taking a deep breath, she opened the bathroom door. The darkened room was a welcome sight. At least this way she wouldn't have to look him in the eye and lie. Now the only light spilled from the bathroom, slashing directly across the bed in the center of the room as if putting all the focus on Luc and his bare chest. The covers were up to his waist; his arms were crossed and resting on his forehead.

"Turn off the light and get in bed."

The memory loss didn't affect his commanding ways. The man demanded, he never asked, and he expected people to obey. Still, the low, powerful tone he used was enough to have her toes curling on the hardwood. This was her fantasy come to life, though when she'd envisioned Luc ordering her into bed, she never imagined quite this scenario.

What a way for fate to really stick it to her and mock her every dream with this false one.

"Is your head still hurting?" she asked, remaining in the bathroom doorway.

"It's a dull pain, but better than it was."

Kate tapped the switch, sending the room into darkness, save for the soft moonlight sweeping through the balcony doors. The pale tile floor combined with the moon was enough to light her path to the bed.

Pulling the covers back, she eased down as gently as possible and lay on her back. On the edge. As stiff as a board. And the ache for him only grew as his masculine scent surrounded her and his body heat warmed the minuscule space between them.

The bed dipped as Luc rolled toward her. "Are you okay?"

His body fitted perfectly against hers. Just the brush of the coarse hair on his legs against her smooth ones had her senses on alert…as if they needed to be heightened.

Was she okay? Not really. On one hand she was terrified. On the other she was completely intrigued…and spiraling headfirst into arousal. And arousal was taking the lead over so many emotions. With his breath tickling her skin, she was fully consumed by the one man she'd wanted for so long. It would be so easy, yet so wrong, to roll over and take what she wanted.

"I'm fine," she assured him.

With the darkness surrounding them, the intimacy level seemed to soar. She should've insisted on a small light or something. But then she would see his face. Honestly, she had no clue what was more torturous.

"You're tense."

Understatement of the year.

Luc's hand trailed up her arm, moving to rest on her stomach. If he thought she was tense before, he should just keep touching her. She was about to turn to stone.

She needed to regain control of her body, her hormones. Unfortunately, her mind and her girlie parts were not corresponding very well right now, because she was getting hot, restless, as if she needed to shift toward him for more of that delicate touching he was offering.

No. This was wrong. Her even thinking of wanting more was wrong. Just because he'd kissed her earlier didn't mean a thing. He'd done so to shut her up, to prove a point and to take charge as he always did.

Yet given the way he'd masterfully taken over and kissed her with such force and passion, there was no way he'd been unmoved. And she would've called him on it, but now she was dealing with a new set of issues surrounding her desires.

"If you're worried about me, I'm fine," he assured her. "I just want to lie here and hold you. Scoot over against me. I feel like you're about ready to fall out of the bed."

Just as she started to shift, her knee brushed against him. His unmistakable arousal had her stopping short.

"Ignore it," he said with a laugh. "I'm trying like hell."

Squeezing her eyes shut, Kate sighed. "I can't do this."

Five

Luc grabbed Kate around the waist just as she started to get up. Pulling her flush against him, her back against his chest, he held on tight. Her silky gown slid over his bare chest, adding fuel to the already out-of-control fire.

"Don't," he whispered in her ear, clutching the silk material around her stomach, keeping her body taut against his own. "Just relax."

"You need to be sleeping."

Her body was still so stiff, so rigid beneath him. Something had seriously freaked her out and she wasn't telling him what it was. Damn it, was it something he already knew but couldn't recall? Or was this not about her at all, but something to do with his fall?

A sliver of fear slid through him.

"Did the doctor say something you're not telling me?" he asked.

"What? No."

She shifted, relaxing just a touch as she laid her hand over his on her stomach. The first contact she'd initiated since climbing into bed.

"He didn't say much when I walked him out," she went on. "Just that he felt it necessary for you to remember on your own."

"The only thing I want to do right now is to get you to relax."

Luc slid his hand out from beneath hers, to the lacy edge of her silk gown. Her body stiffened briefly, then arched as if she was fighting her own arousal. When she sucked in a breath, Luc knew he had her.

"Luc, you need to rest."

Her shaky voice betrayed her, indicating she was just as achy and excited as he was. He pushed one of her legs back, easing his fingers beneath the silk until he found the delicate elastic edge on her panties.

"What I need to do is pleasure my woman," he whispered in her ear, pleased when she trembled.

Kate's back arched again and her head fell against his shoulder. "Luc, you don't have to—"

He nipped at the tender flesh of her earlobe as he eased his hand inside her panties to stroke her. "I want to."

Her soft moans, her cry when he found just the right spot, left his mouth dry. It didn't take long for her body to give in and shudder beneath his touch. She gasped, trembled all the while Luc trailed kisses along her shoulder, her neck when she'd turn just so and the soft spot below her ear.

Yet nothing triggered any memories.

All the same, he didn't regret giving her pleasure. Everything about this private moment only made him want her, yearn for her more.

"Are you always this responsive?" he whispered.

Slowly, she rolled toward him, rested a palm on his chest. With the pale glow from the moon, he didn't miss the shimmer in Kate's eyes.

"Baby, don't cry."

She blinked, causing more tears to slide down her flushed cheeks. "You didn't remember, though, did you?"

He smoothed her damp hair away from her face. "No."

When her hand started down his abdomen, toward the top of his boxer briefs, he gripped her wrist.

Kate had been through a rough time, and even though he was the one suffering the medical concern, he wasn't about to let her think he'd given her pleasure only to get his own. This moment was all about her, reassuring her that he—no, that they—would be okay.

"We both need to rest right now," he told her, dropping a kiss to her forehead. "You're exhausted, I'm recovering. We'll make love tomorrow and I'll make this up to you, Kate. Our trip won't be ruined. I promise."

So stupid. Foolish, careless and flat-out irresponsible.

First she'd let him touch her, then she'd cried. The tears came instantly after she'd crashed back into reality after the most amazing climax she'd ever had.

The moment had been so consuming, so mindblowing. That's when she knew Luc hadn't remembered anything, or he would've been angry to be in that position with her.

So when the tears fell, she'd had no way to stop them.

What should've been a beautiful moment was tarnished by the situation. She hadn't expected Luc to be so powerful in bed. She truly had no idea how she'd hold him off from becoming intimate now that they'd shared such passion.

Kate had eased from the bed early this morning. Her vow to leave and sleep on the couch as soon as he fell asleep had gone out the window. After his mission to relax her had been a success, she'd been dead to the world.

How had this bizarre scenario spiraled so far out of control? She'd just spent the night in her boss's arms, a boss who was a prince, a boss who thought she was his fiancée. He was a man who prided himself on control and keeping his professional and personal lives separate. The rule was very clear at the palace.

Everything that had happened in the past eighteen hours was a colossal mess.

Kate had hurried back to her cottage early this morning while Luc slept. She'd managed to smuggle a couple sundresses and her swimsuit over. That should get her through the next few days, though she prayed she wouldn't be here that long.

Her cell phone vibrated in the pocket of her short dress. Pulling it out, she was thankful the service seemed to be holding up. The doctor's name lit up her screen.

"Good morning, Dr. Couchot," she said, as if she hadn't had the most life-altering night she'd ever experienced.

"Kate, how is Luc this morning?"

Glancing over her shoulder toward the open patio doors, she saw him still sprawled out on the bed, asleep. She kept checking on him, but he'd grumble and roll back over. She had to assume he was fine, since he was resting so well.

"He's sleeping in today," she told the doctor, turning back to watch the gentle waves ebb and flow against the shoreline. "He was exhausted last night."

"I imagine so. Still nothing new to report? No change in the memory or new symptoms?"

Kate leaned against the wrought-iron railing and wondered if the toe-curling intimacy was worth reporting. Probably best to leave that out of the conversation.

"No. He's the same."

The same sexy, determined, controlling man he always was, just with a sweeter side he was willing to share. And he was oh so giving between the sheets...

Dr. Couchot reiterated how Kate was to just let Luc think on his own, let the memories return as slowly or as fast as his mind needed them to. As if she needed reminding. Nearly all she could focus on was keeping this colossal secret.

Once she hung up, she turned, leaning her back against the rail. Watching him sleep was probably wrong, too, but why stop now? She hadn't done anything right since she'd gotten here. In the span of three days she'd fought with him, kissed him, come undone in his bed and played the part of the doting fiancée. How could she make things any worse?

Kate just prayed he'd get his memory back so they could move on. The lies were eating at her and she didn't know how she could keep up this charade.

Luc was a fighter in every way. He wouldn't let this memory loss keep him down. He'd claw his way back up from the abyss and then...

Yeah, that was the ultimate question. And then... what? Would he hate her? Would he fire her? Would he look at her with disdain?

A sick pit formed in the depths of her stomach. Would her parents lose their jobs? Surely her mom and dad would be disappointed in her for breaking the royal protocol.

This couldn't go on. Luc had to remember. So far she hadn't given Luc any extra information regarding his past, and she didn't intend to because she didn't want to make his issue worse. But there was only so long she could go on not telling him things. The man wanted to sleep with her.

How did she keep dodging that fact when she wanted it, too?

The way he'd looked at her, with affection, was so new and so tempting. And all built on lies.

Luc called out in his sleep. Kate straightened as she slowly moved closer. When he cried out again, she still couldn't make out what he was saying. She set her phone on the nightstand and eased down on the edge of the bed. His bronze chest stared back at her and Kate had a hard time not touching him, not running her fingertips over the tip of the tattoo that slid perfectly over one shoulder.

The sheet had dipped low, low enough to show one hip and just the edge of his black boxer briefs. She'd felt those briefs against her skin last night. More impressively, she'd felt what was beneath them.

"Tell me," he muttered, shifting once again. His eyes were squeezed tight, as if he was trying to fight whatever image had him twisting in the sheets.

Kate froze. Was he remembering something? Would his memory come back and play through his mind like a movie?

When his face scrunched even more and his chin started quivering, she knew he was fighting some demon, and she couldn't just sit here and watch him suffer. She might not be able to fully disclose the truth, but she didn't have to witness the man's complete downfall, either.

"Luc." She placed her hand on his shoulder and shook him gently. "Luc."

Jerking awake, he stared up at her, blinking a few times as if to get his bearings. Kate pulled her hand back, needing to keep her touching at a minimum.

Raking a hand down his face, his day-old stubble rustling beneath his palm, he let out a sigh. "That was insane. I was dreaming about a baby," he murmured, his gaze dipping to her midsection. "Are we having a baby, Kate?"

On this she could be absolutely honest. For once.

"No, we're not."

"Damn it." He fell back against the pillows and stared up at the sheers gathered together at the ceiling. "I thought for sure I was having a breakthrough."

Kate swallowed. He was remembering, but the memory was just a bit skewed. With the pregnancy lie from his ex still fresh, Kate figured it was only a matter of time before he had full recollection of the situation.

She didn't know whether to be terrified or relieved. They still hadn't slept together, so she prayed their relationship could be redeemed once the old Luc returned.

"It just seemed so real," he went on. "My hand was on your stomach, and I was so excited to be a father. I had no clue what to do, but the idea thrilled me."

Her heart swelled to near bursting at his reaction. The thought of having a baby with him made her giddy all over. But they were treading in dangerous territory. This was going to go downhill fast if she didn't do something. She might not be able to feed him his memories, but that didn't mean she couldn't find other ways to trigger him.

"How about we take the Jet Skis out for a bit?" she suggested.

His eyes drifted from the ceiling to her. "I don't want to go out right now."

Wow. She'd never known him to turn down anything on the water. Especially his Jet Ski or his boat. She needed to get him out of the house, away from the temptation of the bed, the shower…anyplace that might set the scene for seduction.

"Do you want to just go relax on the beach and do absolutely nothing?"

Though the thought of them lying next to each other wearing only swimsuits didn't seem like a great idea, now that she'd said it aloud. Granted, they'd seen each other that way before, but not with him thinking they were in love and planning holy matrimony…not to mention his promise to make love to her today.

A wide smile spread across his face. "I have an even better idea."

That naughty look was something she definitely recognized. He had a plan, and she didn't know if she should worry or just go along for the ride.

Six

Sweat poured off his head, his muscles burned and he was finally getting that rush he needed.

Kate grunted, sweat rolling off her, and he didn't recall ever seeing her look more beautiful. Of course, he didn't recall much, but right at this moment, she was positively stunning.

"I can't do this anymore," she panted, falling back against the wall.

Luc eased the sledgehammer down to rest, the wood handle falling against his leg. "We can take a break."

"I kind of meant I can't do this anymore…ever."

Luc laughed. They'd just torn out the old vanity in the main bathroom off the hallway, and the scene was a disaster. The construction workers had left the majority of their smaller tools here, so he figured he'd do something useful while he waited for his memory to return. No, he'd never done any home projects before.

He was a prince, for crying out loud. But he knew this bathroom would be gutted and replaced, so he was just blowing off some steam while helping the workers along at the same time.

"What are we going to do with all of this mess?" Kate asked as she glanced around the room.

They stood amid a pile of broken ceramic material, some huge hunks and some shards.

"Leave it," he told her. "When the guys come back to finish this, they can haul it out."

She dropped her hammer on top of the disaster and turned to stare at him. "So we're just causing destruction and closing the door on our way out?"

Luc shrugged. "I'm not really known for my renovating skills. Am I?"

Kate laughed, swiping a hand across her forehead. "No. You're royalty. I don't know of too many blue bloods who go around remodeling."

Stepping over the debris, he made his way to the door. Kate was right behind him. Extending his hand, he helped her over the rubble and out into the hallway.

"How about we take our tools to the kitchen?" he said, smiling when she rolled her eyes. "That room is hideous."

"I'd rather go to the kitchen and make some lunch, because you only had coffee for breakfast and my toast wore off about my fifth swing into that vanity countertop."

Her glistening forehead, the smudge of dirt streaked across one cheek, instantly had Luc recalling a little girl with a lopsided ponytail chasing a dog through a yard.

"You used to play with Booker," he muttered, speaking before he fully finished assessing the image. "At my family's vacation house in the US."

Kate's eyes widened. "That's right. I did. Did you have a memory?"

Rubbing his forehead, Luc cursed beneath his breath when the flash was gone. "Yeah. I've known you a long time, then."

Kate nodded, studying him. "I've known you since I was six."

"I'm a lot older than you."

A smile spread across her face. "Ten years."

"How long have we been together?"

Kate glanced away, biting her lip and focusing on anything but him.

"I know the doctor said to let me remember on my own. But I want to know."

Those doe eyes came back up to meet his gaze. "I started working for you a year ago."

Shock registered first. "You work for me?"

He tried to remember, tried to think of her in a professional atmosphere. Nothing. He'd actually rather remember her in an intimate setting, because that was what crushed him the most. They were engaged, they were obviously in love and he couldn't recall anything about the deep bond of their relationship.

"What do you do for me?" he asked. "Besides get me hot and make me want you. And how did we manage to get around the family rule about not mixing business with pleasure?"

Pink tinged her tanned face as she reached out, cupping her hand over his cheek. "I'm your assistant. I'm not telling you anything else. All right?"

Sliding his hand over hers, he squeezed it, then brought her palm to his mouth. "All right," he said, kissing her. "But I can't believe I let my fiancée work."

Her lips quirked. "Let me? Oh, honey. You've never let me do anything."

Laughing, he tugged her against him. "I have a feeling we do a lot of verbal sparring."

A lopsided grin greeted him. "You have no idea."

When he started to nuzzle the side of her neck, she eased back. "I'm sweaty and smelly, Luc. I don't think you want to bury your nose anywhere near my skin right now."

He slid his tongue along that delicate spot just below her ear. "I plan on having you sweaty later anyway, Kate."

Her body trembled. He didn't need to spell out how their day would end. Sleeping next to her last night had been sweet torture, but seeing her come apart at his touch had been so erotic, so sexy.

He couldn't wait to have her. Couldn't wait to explore her, get to know her body all over again.

"Has it always been this intense between us?" he asked, still gripping her hand and staring into those eyes any man could get lost in.

"Everything about our relationship is intense," she murmured, staring at his mouth. "I never know if I want to kiss you or strangle you."

"Kissing," he whispered against her mouth. "Always choose kissing, my *doce anjo*."

Sweet angel. Had he always called her that? When her lips parted beneath his, he knew the term was accurate. She tasted so sweet each time he kissed her. Wrapping one arm around her waist, he slid his palm over her backside. She still wore that short little sundress she'd had on all morning. She hadn't changed when they'd done the bathroom demolition, and seeing her bent over, catching a glimpse of her creamy thighs, had nearly driven him crazy.

Gathering the material beneath his hand, he cupped her bottom. "I've wanted you since last night," he muttered against her mouth. "The need for you hasn't lessened, and I may not remember our intimacy before, but something tells me I've been infatuated with you for a long time. This ache inside me isn't new."

A shaky sigh escaped her. "That's something I can't attest to. I don't know how long you've wanted me."

Luc eased back, still holding on to her backside. "Forever, Kate. I refuse to believe anything else."

Moisture gathered in her eyes. "You might end up remembering differently."

Then she stepped away, leaving him cold and confused. What did that mean? Did they not have a solid relationship, a deep love, as he'd thought?

Luc let her go. Apparently, they both had emotional demons to work through. Regardless of his temporary amnesia, he wouldn't let her go through this alone. They both needed each other, that was obvious, and even if she tried to push him away, she'd soon find out he wasn't going anywhere.

They were in this together no matter how he'd been before. She was his and he would be strong for her. He would not let this memory loss rob him of his life or his woman.

Kate threw on her suit and headed down to the beach. Luc might have been content with busting things up as a stress reliever, but she needed a good workout. There was nothing like a swim to really get the muscles burning and endorphins kicking in.

She hadn't lied when she'd told him their relationship had always been intense. And she hadn't lied when she'd said she had no clue how long he'd been infatuated with her.

But he was right about one thing. The emotions he was feeling, his actions toward her, weren't new. All that desire, that passion, had been lying dormant for some time now, and she'd wondered if it would ever break the surface. Never in her wildest dreams had she imagined it would take a major injury to further exacerbate this chemistry.

The question now was were these feelings truly directed toward her, or were they left over from his ex? A year ago he'd admitted to an attraction, but had put the brakes on it because of their professional relationship and her parents working so closely with his family. And it was then that he'd explained in great detail why members of his family never dated or got involved with an employee. The list of reasons was lengthy: reputations on the line, the employee could turn and go to the media with a fabricated story... There was too much at stake—even Luc's crown in this case—to let staff in on their personal lives. Kate didn't have a clue how Luc and his ex had been in private. She actually tried to never think of that. But now she couldn't stop herself.

Did Luc really have such strong emotions for her? If so, how had he kept it bottled up all this time?

Kate loosened the knot on her wrap, letting the sheer material fall onto the sand. Running straight into the ocean, the world at her back, she wished she could run from this whole ordeal and stop lying to Luc. She wished she could kiss him and sleep in his bed and have him know it was her and not the fake fiancée he'd conjured up.

He'd said they would be sleeping together later. Dodging that was going to be nearly impossible.

She was in desperate need of advice. She'd wanted to phone her mother earlier, but the call hadn't been able to go through. She would try again later. More than anything Kate needed her mother's guidance. Holding back from Luc was pure torture. How could she say no to the one thing she'd fantasized about for so long?

The warm water slid over her body as she sliced her arms through the gentle waves. The hot sun beat down on her back and her muscles were already screaming from the quick workout.

Kate pushed herself further, breaking the surface to take another deep breath and catch her bearings. Panting heavily, she dived back in for more. She'd not fully worked through her angst just yet.

Before she knew it, she'd gone so far up the coastline she couldn't see Luc's home anymore. She swam to the shore, trudged through the sand and sank down onto dry land. Pulling her legs up against her chest, Kate wrapped her arms around her knees and caught her breath, willing the answers to come.

One thing was clear. She and Luc needed to stay away from the house as much as possible. With just the two of them alone, there was no chaperone, nobody else to offer a buffer. At least back at the palace there was a full staff of butlers, maids, drivers, assistants to the assistants, guards, his parents, her parents, the cooks... the list was almost endless.

Perhaps an outing to the small village was in order. Anything to hold off the inevitable. The hungry look in Luc's eyes, the way he constantly kept touching her, were all indications that the moment was fast approaching. And yes, she wanted that moment to happen more

than she wanted her next breath, but she didn't want it
to be built on desperation and lies.

Pushing herself up off the sand, Kate stretched out
her muscles. She'd never been a fan of running, but she
wasn't done exorcising those demons. She headed back
toward Luc's home, passing other pristine beach houses.
Some were larger, some smaller, but they all had the
same Mediterranean charm, and their own docks, with
boats bobbing against the wood planks.

The island was a perfect getaway for a prince. Under
normal circumstances, he could hide away here without the media hounding him, without the distractions
of the internet and the outside world.

This place would be heaven on earth for any couple
wanting a romantic escape.

Too bad she was only a figment of Luc's imagination.

As Kate ran, she kept to the packed sand that the
waves had flattened. Her thigh muscles burned and
sweat poured off her as the sun beat against her back.
This felt good, liberating. She would go back to the
house and go over Luc's schedule for when they returned to Ilha Beleza. Looking at all his duties and responsibilities would surely help jog something in his
mind.

And the memories were returning. Apparently, her
dirty state earlier had shot him back to the moments
when she'd been a little girl and had gone to work
with her parents. She'd loved the Silvas' old sheepdog,
Booker. She used to play with him, roll around in the
yard with him and be completely filthy by the time
she left.

Luc's parents would just laugh, saying how they
missed having a little one around. They'd gotten Booker
when Luc was eight, so by the time he was a teen, he

wasn't so much into running through yards and spending hours playing with a dog.

Kate was all about it. When Booker had passed away, she had taken the news harder than Luc had. Of course, he'd had his women "friends" to occupy his time and keep his thoughts focused elsewhere.

Finding her discarded wrap in the sand where she'd dropped it, Kate scooped it up and quickly adjusted it around her torso. At the base of the steps leading up to Luc's home, she rested her hands on her knees and pulled in a deep gulp of air. She was going in as professional Kate. Keeping her hands and mind off Luc was the only way to proceed. Flirty, dreamy Kate had no place here. They hadn't made love yet, so she could still turn this around, and pray Luc wasn't totally furious once he remembered what her role in his life actually was.

Seven

Luc's phone bounced on the couch cushion when he tossed it aside. Useless. He recognized his parents' names, his best friend, Mikos, and Kate. Other than that, nothing.

Raking a hand down his face, Luc got to his feet and crossed to the patio doors. Kate had been gone awhile and he knew her frustrations had driven her out the door. He'd like to run from his problems, too; unfortunately, they lived inside his head. Still, he couldn't fault her for needing some time alone.

He stepped out onto the patio, his gaze immediately darting down to the dock. As he stared at the Jet Ski on one side and his boat on the other, he wondered what he'd been doing before he fell. Was he about to go out on the water so late in the evening? Was Kate coming with him? Everything before the fall was a complete blank to him. He had no idea what they'd been doing prior to his accident.

Hell, he couldn't even recall how he and Kate had started working together. And some family rule about not getting personal with staff members kept ringing in his head. He reached into his mind, knowing this was a real memory. The Silva family didn't get intimate with employees. So had Kate come to work for him after they'd become a couple? Had she been so invaluable in his life that he'd wanted her to be his right-hand woman in his professional world, as well?

The questions weren't slowing down; they were slamming into his head faster than he could comprehend them. He'd go mad if he didn't get his memory back soon, or if he kept dwelling on something that was out of his control.

Damn it. Of one thing he was certain. Losing control of anything was pure hell, and right now he'd spiraled so far he hoped and prayed he could pull back the reins on his life before this amnesia drove a wedge between him and Kate.

Luc straightened as the idea slammed into him, pushing through the uncertainty he'd been battling. All that mattered was him and Kate. This was their time away, so all he had to do was enjoy being with her. How hard could that be? A private getaway with one sexy fiancée would surely be just what he needed.

A shrill ring came from the living room. Luc ran in and found Kate's cell phone on one of the end tables. His mother's name was on the screen. Odd that she would be calling Kate.

Without giving it another thought, he answered. "Hello."

"Lucas? Darling, how are you feeling?"

His mother's worried tone came over the line. Her

familiar voice had him relieved that his mind hadn't robbed him of that connection.

"Frustrated," he admitted, sinking onto the worn accent chair. "I have a hell of a headache, but other than that I feel fine. Why did you call Kate's phone?"

"I didn't want to bother you if you weren't feeling good, or if you were resting. I spoke with Kate last night, but I needed to check on you today."

"There's no need to worry, Mom. Kate is taking good care of me and the doctor was thorough. I just need to relax, and this is the best place for me to do that."

His mother made a noise, something akin to disapproval. "Well, you call the doctor first thing if you start having other symptoms. I'm still not happy you're not home. I worry, but you're stubborn like your father, so I'm used to it."

Luc smiled, just as Kate stepped through the door. A sheen of sweat covered her. Or maybe that was water from the ocean. Regardless, she looked sexy, all wet and winded. Would his need for her ever lessen? Each time he saw her he instantly went into primal mode and wanted to carry her back to bed.

"Nothing to worry about," he said, keeping his eyes locked on Kate's. "I'm in good hands. I'll phone you later."

He ended the call and rose to his feet. Kate's eyes widened as he moved closer to where she'd stopped in the doorway.

"Were you on my phone?" she asked, tipping her head back to hold his gaze.

"My mom called to check on me. She tried your cell in case I was resting."

Kate's eyes darted around. "Um…is that all she said?"

Reaching out to stroke a fingertip along her collarbone, Luc watched the moisture disappear beneath his touch. "Yes. Why?"

"Just curious." She trembled beneath his touch as her eyes locked back onto his. "I need to go shower. Then we need to discuss your schedule and upcoming events."

Heat surged through him as he slid his mouth over hers. "Go use my shower. We can work later."

She leaned into him just slightly, then quickly pulled back. Something passed through her eyes before she glanced away. As she started to move around him, he grabbed her elbow.

"You okay?"

She offered a tight, fake smile. "Fine. Just tired from my swim and run."

The shadows beneath her eyes silently told him she hadn't slept as well as she'd claimed. He nodded, releasing her arm, and listened as she padded through the hall and into the master suite.

Waiting until he was sure she was in the shower, Luc jerked his shirt over his head and tossed it, not caring where it landed. By the time he reached his bedroom, his clothes were gone, left in a trail leading to the bedroom door.

The steady hum of the water had Luc imagining all kinds of possibilities. And all of them involved a wet, naked Kate.

When he reached the spacious, open shower, surrounded by lush plants for added privacy, he took in the entire scene. Kate with water sluicing down her curves, her wet hair clinging to her back as she tipped her face up to the rainfall showerhead. She was a vision...and she was his.

Luc crossed the room and stepped onto the wet, gritty

tile. In an instant he had his arms wrapped around her, molding her back against him.

Kate's audible gasp filled the room, and her body tensed beneath his. "Luc—"

He spun her around, cutting off anything she was about to say. He needed her, needed to get back to something normal in his life. Kate was his rock, his foundation, and he wanted to connect with her again in the most primal, natural way possible.

"Luc," she muttered against his mouth. "We shouldn't."

Her words died as he kissed his way down her neck. "We should."

That silky skin of hers was driving him insane. Kate arched into him, gripping his shoulders as if holding on.

"You're injured," she panted.

He jerked his head up to meet her gaze. "The day I can't make love to my fiancée is the day I die."

Luc hauled her up against him, an arm banded around her lower back to pull her in nice and snug, as his mouth claimed hers once again. There was a hesitancy to her response. Luc slowed his actions, not wanting her to feel she needed to protect him.

But this all-consuming need to claim her, to have her right now, had his control slipping.

"I want you, Kate," he whispered against her mouth. "Now."

Nipping at her lips, he slid his palms over her round hips, to the dip in her waist and up to her chest, which was made for a man's hands…his hands. She was perfect for him in every way. How had he gotten so lucky to have her in his life?

As he massaged her, she dropped her head back, exposing that creamy skin on her neck. Luc smoothed his tongue over her, pulling a soft moan from her lips.

After backing her up, he lifted her. "Wrap your legs around me."

Her eyes went wide. "I… Luc…"

"Now, Kate."

Just as her legs encircled his waist, he grabbed her hands and held them above her head. Sliding into her, he stilled when she gasped.

"You okay?"

Eyes closed, biting down on her lip, she nodded. Luc gripped her wrists in one hand and used his other to skim his thumb across the lip she'd been worrying with her teeth.

"Look at me," he demanded. "I want to see those eyes."

Droplets sprinkled her lashes as she blinked up at him. He moved against her, watching her reaction, wanting to see every bit of her arousal, her excitement. He might not remember their past encounters, but he damn well was going to make new memories with her, starting right now.

Kate's hips rocked with his; her body arched as he increased his speed.

"Luc," she panted. "Please…"

Gripping her waist, he trailed his mouth up her neck to her ear. "Anything," he whispered. "I'll give you anything. Just let go."

Her body tensed, shuddering all around him. As she cried out in release, Luc followed her.

Wrapping her in his arms, he couldn't help but wonder if each time they were together felt like the first time, or if this particular moment was just so powerfully intense and all-consuming. This woman had the ability to bring him to his knees in all the right ways.

So why was his beautiful fiancée—who'd just come apart in his arms—sobbing against his shoulder?

* * *

Oh, no. No, no, no.

Kate couldn't stop the tears from coming, just as she couldn't stop Luc from making love to her.

No. Not making love. They'd had sex. He didn't love her, and once his memory returned, he wouldn't even like her anymore. She'd been worried about tonight, about going to sleep. She'd truly never thought he would join her in the shower. The sex just now with Luc was unlike any encounter she'd ever had. Nothing could have prepared her for the intensity of his passion.

How had this entire situation gotten even more out of control? The reality of being with Luc had far exceeded the fantasy. And now that she had a taste of what it could be like, she wanted more.

"Kate?"

She gripped his biceps, keeping her face turned into his chest. She couldn't face him, couldn't look him in the eyes. Not after what she'd done. He would never understand.

Was this how he'd treat her if he loved her? Would he surprise her in the shower and demand so much of her body? Part of her wanted to bask in the glorious aftermath of everything intimacy should be. But she knew it couldn't last.

Luc shut off the water behind her, and in one swift move, he shifted, lifting her in his arms.

"Talk to me, baby." He stepped out of the shower and eased her down onto the cushioned bench. Grabbing a towel from the heated bar, he wrapped it around her before securing one around his waist.

Kate stared down at her unpainted nails. Focusing on her lack of manicure would not help her out of this situation. Luc gripped her hands as he crouched before her.

"Look at me."

Those words, said only moments ago under extremely different circumstances, pulled her gaze away from their joined hands and up into his dark eyes. Worry stared back at her. Didn't he know she was lying? Didn't he know he should be worried about himself?

She could come clean. She could tell him right now that she wasn't his fiancée, that she'd been dying for him to make a move on her for years. But all that sounded even more pathetic than the truth, which was that she'd gotten caught up in this spiral of lies. In an attempt to protect him, she'd deceived him. There was no turning back, and if she was honest with herself, she couldn't deny how right they'd felt together.

"Did I hurt you?" he asked.

Swiping the moisture from her cheeks, Kate shook her head. "No. You could never hurt me."

"What is it? Did you not want to make love with me?"

A vise around her heart squeezed.

She shook her head. Eventually she was going to strangle herself with this string of lies.

"I'm just overwhelmed," she admitted. "We hadn't been together before."

Luc studied her a moment before his brows rose. "You mean to tell me we hadn't made love before?"

Shame filled her. She couldn't speak, so simply nodded.

Luc muttered a slang Portuguese term that no member of the royal family should be heard saying.

"How is that possible?" he asked. "You said we've been working together for nearly a year."

"Your family has a rule about staff and royal members not being intimate. We've been professional for so long, we both just waited. Then we ended up here on this getaway and…"

She couldn't finish. She couldn't lie anymore. The emotions were too overwhelming and her body was still reeling from their passion.

Luc came to his feet, cursing enough to have her cringing. He was beating himself up over something that was 100 percent her fault.

Unable to stand the tension, the heavy weight of the guilt, she jumped to her feet. "Luc, I need to tell you—"

"No." He turned, facing her with his hands on his narrow hips. "I took advantage of you. Kate, I am so, so sorry. I had no clue. I got caught up in the moment and wanted to forget this memory loss and just be with you."

"No. This is not your fault in any way." Holding on to the knot on her towel, Kate shivered. "Let's get dressed. We need to talk."

Eight

Luc grabbed his clothes from the bedroom and went to the spare room to get dressed. Of all the plans he'd had for Kate, taking her when she wasn't mentally prepared for it sure as hell wasn't one of them.

Their history explained why she'd tensed when he'd come up behind her in the shower, explained the onslaught of tears afterward. Not to mention the way she'd stiffened against him in bed last night.

Luc cursed himself once again for losing control. He'd thought he was doing the right thing, thought he was getting them both back to where they'd been just before his ridiculous accident.

Heading back down the hallway, he spotted his clothes. Looking at them now he felt only disgust, as opposed to the excitement and anticipation he'd felt when he'd left them behind without a care.

He grabbed each article of clothing and flung them

and his towel into the laundry area. He'd worry about that mess later. Right now he had another, more important mess to clean up, and he only hoped Kate would forgive him.

Guilt literally ate at him, killing the hope he'd had of making this day less about his amnesia and more about them.

By the time she came out, she'd piled her hair atop her head and sported another one of those little sundresses that showcased her tanned shoulders and sexy legs. The legs he'd demanded she wrap around him.

Kate took a seat on the sofa and patted the cushion beside her. "Just relax. Okay?"

Relax? How could he when this entire mess had started with him forgetting every single damn thing about the woman he supposedly loved?

Wait, he *did* love her. When he looked at her and saw how amazing and patient she was with him, and damn it, how she'd let him take her in the shower, and didn't stop him, how could he not love her? When he looked at her, his heart beat a bit faster. When he touched her, his world seemed to be a better place.

He just wished he could remember actually falling in love with her, because all he could recall was this all-consuming, aching need that was only stronger now that he'd had her.

"Luc." Kate held out her hand. "Come on."

He crossed to her, took her hand and sank onto the couch beside her.

"Tell me you're okay," he started, holding her gaze. "Tell me I didn't hurt you physically or emotionally."

A soft smile spread across her face. "I already told you, I'm fine. You were perfect, Luc."

She held on to him, her eyes darting down to where their hands joined.

"Before you fell, we were fighting," she told him. "I take full responsibility for everything that's happened to you, so don't beat yourself up over the shower."

Luc squeezed her hand. "The shower was all on me. If we were fighting before my fall, then that took two, so don't place all of that blame on yourself."

Kate smiled. Her eyes lifted to his. "We could play this game all day," she told him, her smile dimming a bit. "But I need to talk to you."

"What's wrong?"

Her tone, the worry in her eyes, told him something major was keeping her on edge.

"There are so many things that you need to know, but I've been holding back because I don't want to affect your healing process."

Luc edged closer, wrapping an arm around her shoulders and pulling her to his side. Easing back against the cushions, he kept her tucked against him. "If something is worrying you, tell me. I want to be here for you. I want to be strong for you."

Kate's delicate hand rested on his thigh. She took a deep breath in, then let it out with a shudder.

"I was adopted."

Her voice was so soft, he wondered if she actually meant to say it out loud.

"Did I already know this about you?" he asked.

"No. The only people who know are my parents."

His mind started turning. Her parents worked for his parents. Memories of them in his house flashed for an instant.

"Scott and Maria, right?"

"Yes." Kate tilted her head up to meet his gaze. "You're remembering."

"Not fast enough," he muttered. "Go on."

Settling her head back against his chest, Luc wondered if it was easier for her to talk if she wasn't looking right at him.

"I was born in the States," she went on. "Georgia, to be exact. My parents adopted me when I was six. I only have vague memories of being there, but it's always held a special place in my heart."

Luc listened, wondering where she was going with this and how it all tied back into what was happening between them now.

"My parents ended up moving to Ilha Beleza to work full-time at the palace. They used to just work at the vacation home back in Georgia. Your family has one off the coast."

Closing his eyes, he saw a white house with thick pillars extended to the second story. A wraparound porch on the ground floor had hanging swings that swayed in the breeze. Booker and a young Kate running in the yard…

Yes, he remembered that house fondly.

"Since I've been your assistant, I've wanted you to visit that orphanage, the one I came from, but we've butted heads over it."

Luc jerked, forcing Kate to shift and look up at him.

"Why were we fighting over an orphanage?" he asked.

She shrugged. "I have no idea why you won't go. To be honest, I just think you don't want to, or you didn't want to take the time. You've offered to write a check, but I never can get you to go there. I just felt a visit from a real member of royalty would be something cool for those kids. They don't have much and some of them have been there awhile, because most people only want to adopt babies."

Luc glanced around the sparsely furnished room, hoping for another flash of something to enter his mind. Hoping for some minuscule image that would help him piece it all together.

"Is this why we were arguing before I fell?" he asked, focusing back on her.

"Not really. I tried bringing it up again, but you blew it off." She let go of his hand and got to her feet, pacing to the open patio doors. "We were arguing because we're both stubborn, and sometimes we do and say things before we can fully think them through."

He could see that. Without a doubt he knew he was quite a hardhead, and Kate had a stubborn streak he couldn't help but find intriguing and attractive.

"When your memory comes back, I want you to know that everything I've ever done or said has been to protect you." Her shoulders straightened as she kept her back to him and stared out the doors. "I care about you, Luc. I need you to know that above all else."

The heartfelt words, the plea in her tone, had Luc rising to his feet and crossing to her. Placing his hands on her shoulders, he kissed the top of her head.

"I know how you feel about me, Kate. You proved it to me when you let me make love to you, when you put my needs ahead of any doubts you had."

She eased back against him. "I hope you always feel that way."

The intensity of the moment had him worried they were getting swept into something so consuming, they'd never get back to the couple they used to be. Even though he didn't remember that couple, he had to assume they weren't always this intense.

"What do you say we take the boat and go into town?" he asked. "Surely there's a market or shops or restaurants to occupy our time. We need to have some fun."

She turned in his arms, a genuine smile spreading across her face. "I was going to suggest that myself. I haven't shopped in forever. I'm always working."

She cringed, as if she just realized what had come out of her mouth.

"It's okay," he told her, kissing the tip of her nose. "I'll make sure your boss gives you the rest of the day off. You deserve it."

That talk didn't go nearly the way she'd rehearsed it in her head. Coming off the euphoria of having mind-blowing sex with Luc in the shower had seriously clouded her judgment, and obviously sucked out all her common sense.

So now here she was, wearing her favorite blue halter dress, letting the wind blow her hair around her shoulders and face while Luc steered his boat to the main dock of the island's small town. Most people traveled by boat to the village, where scooters were the preferred mode of transportation. The marina was lined with crafts of various sizes and colors. As they'd made their way toward the waterfront, they'd passed by other boaters and waved. Kate really liked this area. Too bad she'd probably never be back after the mess she'd created came crashing down on her.

Through her research she knew the locals would line up along the narrow streets, set up makeshift booths and sell their goods. From what she'd seen online, she might find anything from handmade jewelry and pottery to flowers and vegetables. She was excited to see what caught her fancy, perhaps taking her mind off the fact her body was still tingling from Luc's touch.

She'd never be able to shower again—especially in that master bath—without feeling his body against hers, his breath on her shoulders. Without hearing his demanding words in her ear as he fully claimed her.

Then he'd let his guard down and opened up to her about his feelings. Slowly, she was falling in love with the man she'd been lying to, the man who was off-limits in reality. She'd opened up about her past, wanting to be as honest as she could in an area that had nothing to do with what was happening right now.

Luc secured the boat to the dock, then extended his hand to help her out. With a glance or simple touch, the man had the ability to make her stomach quiver, her heart quicken and her mind wander off into a fantasy world. Still, that was no excuse to have let the charade go this far.

There was no going back now, though. The charade may be all a farce, but her emotions were all too real.

Kate knew she should've told Luc about the false engagement when he'd hinted that he wanted to make love to her. She should've told him right that moment, but she hadn't, and now here she was on the other side of a monumental milestone they would both have to live with.

She was falling for him; there was no denying the truth to herself. What had started as physical attraction long ago had morphed into more because of his untimely incident.

How did she keep her heart protected, make sure Luc stayed safe until he remembered the truth on his own and keep hold of the man she'd come to feel a deeper bond for? There was no good way this scenario would play out. Someone was going to get hurt.

"You okay?" Luc asked, hauling her onto the dock beside him.

Pasting on a smile, Kate squeezed his hand. "Fine. Let's see what this island has to offer."

Other boats bobbed up and down in the water on either side of the long dock. Luc led her up the steps to the street. Once they reached the top, Kate gasped. It was like a mini festival, but from all she'd heard about this quaint place, the streets were always this lively.

Brightly colored umbrellas shaded each vendor. A small band played live music in an alcove of one of the ancient buildings. People were laughing, dancing, and nearly every stand had a child behind the table, working alongside an adult. Obviously, this was a family affair.

Kate tamped down that inner voice that mocked her. Her dream was to raise a family, to have a husband who loved her, to watch their babies grow. Maybe someday she'd have that opportunity. Unfortunately, with the way her life was going now, she'd be looking for a new job as opposed to a spouse.

Suddenly, one of the stands caught her eye. "Oh, Luc." She tugged on his hand. "I have to get a closer look."

She practically dragged him down the brick street to the jewelry booth. The bright colors were striking with the sun beating down on them just so. It was as if the rays were sliding beneath the umbrella shading the area. The purple amethyst, the green jade, the yellow citrine—they were all so gorgeous. Kate didn't know which piece she wanted to touch first.

"Good afternoon."

The vendor greeted her in Portuguese. Kate easily

slid into the language as she asked about the wares. Apparently, the woman was a widow and the little girl sidling up against her was her only child. They made the jewelry together and the girl was homeschooled, oftentimes doing lessons right there at the booth.

Kate opened her small clutch to pull out her money. There was no way she could walk away and not buy something from this family.

Before she could count her cash, Luc placed a hand over hers and shook his head. He asked the lady how much Kate owed for the necklace and earrings she'd chosen. Once he paid and the items were carefully wrapped in red tissue paper, they went on their way to another booth.

"You didn't have to pay," she told him. "I don't expect you to get all of the things I want, Luc."

He shrugged, taking her hand and looping it through his elbow as they strolled down the street. "I want to buy you things, Kate."

"Well, I picked these out for my mother," she said with a laugh.

Luc smiled. "I don't mind buying things for my future mother-in-law, either. Really, think nothing of it."

What had been a beautiful, relaxing moment instantly turned and smacked Kate in the face with a dose of reality. A heavy ball of dread settled in her belly. This was getting all too real. Kate's parents had been inadvertently pulled into this lie. They would never be Luc's in-laws, and once he discovered the truth, they might not even be employees of his family.

They moved to another stand, where the pottery was unique, yet simple. Kate eyed a tall, slender vase, running her hand over the smooth edge. Before she knew it, Luc had paid for it and the vendor was bagging it and wrapping it in several layers of tissue for protection.

"You don't have to buy everything I look at," she informed Luc.

"Did you like the piece?" he asked.

"I love it, but I was wondering what it would look like in your new house."

Luc kissed her softly on the lips before picking up the bag and moving away. "Our house, Kate. If you like it, then it's fine with me. I'm not much of a decorator."

"No, you prefer to demolish things."

Luc laughed. "Actually, our little project was my first experiment in destruction, but I did rather enjoy myself. I really think I'll tackle that kitchen before we leave, and give the contractors a head start."

They moved from place to place, eyeing various trinkets. Kate ended up buying a wind chime and fresh flowers while Luc was busy talking to another merchant. She wanted to liven up the dining area in the house, especially since the room was in desperate need of paint. The lavender flowers would look perfect in that new yellow vase.

Once they had all their bags, they loaded up the boat and headed home.

Home. As if this was a normal evening and they were settled in some married-couple routine. Kate shouldn't think of Luc's house as her home. She'd started getting too settled in, too comfortable with this whole lifestyle, and in the end, when her lie was exposed and his inevitable rejection sliced her in two, she would have nobody to blame but herself.

These past few hours with Luc had been amazing, but her fantasy life wouldn't last forever.

Nine

Sometime during the past hour, Kate had fully detached herself. She'd been quiet on the boat, quiet when they came into the house. She'd arranged fresh flowers in that beautiful yellow vase and placed them on the hideous dining room table without saying a word.

She'd made dinner, and the only sound he'd heard was her soft humming as she stirred the rice. Now they'd finished eating, and Luc couldn't handle the silence anymore.

He had something to say.

"Kate."

She stepped from the kitchen, wiping her hands down her dress. Luc remained standing, waited for her to cross to him.

"I know you've got a lot on your mind right now," he started. "But there's something I need to tell you."

"Wait." She held up a palm. "I need to go first. I've

been trying to figure out a way to talk to you about your amnesia."

She sighed, shaking her head. "I don't even know how to start," she muttered. "I've racked my brain, but nothing sounds right."

"The doctor said not to prompt me." Luc reached into his pocket and pulled out a small, velvet pouch. "While you're thinking about the right words, why don't you take this?"

She jerked her gaze up to his, then stared down at the present in his hand. "What is it?"

"Open it."

Her fingers shook as she took the pouch and tugged on the gathered opening. With a soft gasp, she reached in and pulled out an emerald-cut amethyst ring.

"Luc." She held the ring up, stared at it, then looked to him. "What's this for?"

"Because you don't have a ring on your finger. It hit me today, and I don't know why you don't, but I didn't want to wait and find out. I saw this and I knew you'd love it."

When she didn't say anything or put the ring on, his nerves spiked. Strange, since he'd obviously already popped the question. Unless she just didn't like it.

"If you'd rather have something else, I can take it back to the lady and exchange it. When I saw that stone, I remembered something else about you."

Her eyes widened. "You did?"

A tear slipped down her cheek as she blinked. Luc swiped it away, resting his hand on the side of her face. "I remembered your birthday is in February and that's your birthstone. I remembered you have this amethyst pendant you've worn with gowns to parties at the palace. That pendant would nestle right above your breasts. I used to be jealous of that stone."

Kate sucked in a breath as another tear fell down her face. "You say things like that to me and I feel like you've had feelings for me for longer than I ever imagined."

Taking the ring from her hand, he slid it onto her left ring finger. "There are many things I don't remember, but I know this—I've wanted you forever, Kate."

He didn't give her a chance to respond. Luc enveloped her in his arms, pulled her against him and claimed her mouth. He loved kissing her, loved feeling her lush body against his. Nothing had ever felt this perfect, as far as he could recall. And he was pretty sure if anything had ever felt this good, he'd remember.

Kate's hands pushed against his shoulders as she broke the kiss. "Wait."

She turned, coming free from his hold. With her rigid back to him, Luc's nerves ramped up a level. "Kate, what's wrong?"

"I want to tell you," she whispered. "I need to tell you, but I don't know how much I can safely say without affecting your memory."

Taking a step toward her, he cupped his hands over her shoulders. "Then don't say anything. Can't we just enjoy this moment?"

She turned in his arms, stared up at him and smiled. "I've never been happier than I am right now. I just worry what will happen once you remember everything."

His lips slid across hers. "I'm not thinking of my memory. I only want to make up for what we did this morning."

A catch in her breath had him pausing. Her eyes locked onto his.

"I want to make love to you properly, Kate."

Her body shuddered beneath his hands. "I've wanted you for so long, Luc."

Something primal ripped through him at the same time he saw a flash of Kate wearing a fitted skirt suit, bending over her desk to reach papers. He shook off the image. She'd already said she was his assistant, so that flash wasn't adding anything new to the mix.

Right now he had more pressing matters involving his beautiful fiancée.

"I want you wearing my ring, the weight of my body and nothing else."

Luc gave the halter tie on her neck a tug, stepping back just enough to have the material floating down over her bare breasts. With a quick yank, he pulled the dress and sent it swishing to the floor around her feet. Next he rid her of her silky pink panties.

With her hair tossed around her shoulders, her mouth swollen from his kisses, Luc simply stared at her, as if taking all this in for the first time.

"Perfect," he muttered, gliding his hands over her hips and around her waist. "Absolutely perfect and totally mine."

The breeze from the open patio doors enveloped them. The sunset just on the horizon created an ambience even he couldn't have bought. And everything about this moment overshadowed all that was wrong in his mind with the amnesia.

Guiding Kate backward, he led her to a chaise. When her legs bumped against the edge, Luc pressed on her shoulders, silently easing her down. Once she lay all spread out for his appreciation, he started tugging off his own clothes. The way her eyes traveled over his body, studying him, did something to his ego he couldn't explain. He found himself wanting to know what she thought when she looked at him, what she felt. All this was still new to him and he wanted to savor every single moment of their lovemaking.

"I've dreamed of this," he murmured.

Her brows quirked. "Seriously? You don't think it was a memory of something?"

Luc rested one hand on the back of the chaise, another on the cushion at her hip. As he loomed over her, his body barely brushed the tips of her breasts.

"I'm sure," he whispered. "You were on my balcony, naked, smiling. Ready for me."

A cloud of passion filled her eyes as she continued to stare up at him.

"Maybe I had that fantasy when I first looked at this place, or maybe I had that vision since we've been here." He nipped at her collarbone, gliding up her exposed throat. "Either way, you were meant to be here. With me. Only me."

Kate's body arched into his as her fingertips trailed up his biceps and rested at her shoulders. "Only you," she muttered.

Luc eased down, settling between her legs. The moment his lips touched hers, he joined them, slowly taking everything she was willing to give. This all-consuming need he had for her only grew with each passing moment. Kate was in his blood, in his heart. Was it any wonder he wanted to marry her and spend his life with her?

Kate's fingertips dug into his skin as she rested her forehead against his shoulder. Luc knew from the little pants, the soft moans, that she was on the brink of release.

He kissed her neck, working his way up to that spot

behind her ear he already knew was a trigger. Her body clenched around him as she cried out his name. Before she stopped trembling, he was falling over the edge, too, wrapped in the arms of the woman he loved, surrounded by a haze of euphoria that kept away all the ugly worries and doubts.

All that mattered was Kate and their beautiful life together.

His hand slid over her flat stomach. There was a baby, his baby, growing inside her. He hadn't thought much about being a father, but the idea warmed something within him.

Dropping to his knees, he kissed her bare stomach. "I love you already," he whispered.

Luc jerked awake, staring into the darkness. What the hell was that? A memory? Just a random dream? His heart beat so fast, so hard against the wall of his chest. That had been real. The emotions, the feel of her abdomen beneath his palm, had all been real.

Luc wasn't one to believe in coincidences. That was a memory, but how could it be? Kate wasn't pregnant. She'd said they hadn't made love before the shower, so what the hell was that dream about?

Glancing at the woman beside him, Luc rubbed a hand over his face. The sheet was twisted around her bare body, and her hair was spread over the pillow. Luc placed a hand on her midsection and closed his eyes. That dream was so real he'd actually felt it.

Surely it wasn't just a fantasy of the day he and Kate would be expecting in real life.

He fell back against his pillow, laced his hands behind his head and blinked to adjust his eyesight to the darkened room. No way could he go back to sleep now.

There was too much on his mind, too many unanswered questions.

Something involving a baby had happened to cause such a strong flashback, for the second time now. It just didn't make sense. His mind was obviously the enemy at the moment.

"Luc…"

He turned toward her, only to find her eyes were still closed. She was dreaming, too. Her hand shifted over the sheets as if seeking him out. Instantly, he took hold of her hand and clasped it against his chest. Tomorrow he would have to seek some answers. This waiting around was killing him, because tidbits of his life weren't enough. He wanted the whole damn picture and he wanted it now.

Maybe if Kate talked about herself, her personal life, that would trigger more memories for him. He was done waiting, done putting his life in this mental prison.

How could he move on with Kate when he couldn't even remember their lives before a few days ago?

Ten

She should've told him. No matter what the doctor said, she should have just told Luc that they weren't engaged. Everything else he could remember on his own, but the biggest lie of all needed to be brought out into the open.

Of course, now they'd slept together twice, and she still hadn't said a word.

The heaviness of the ring on her hand wasn't helping the guilt weighing on her heart, either. Instead of trying to make this right, she'd let every single aspect spin even more out of control.

Stepping from the bathroom, Kate tied the short, silky robe around her waist. As soon as she glanced up, she spotted Luc sitting up in bed, the stark white sheet settled low around his hips. All those tanned, toned muscles, the dark ink scrolling over one shoulder, the dark hair splattering over his pecs. The man exuded sex appeal and authority.

"You needn't have bothered with that robe if you're going to keep looking at me like that," he told her, his voice husky from sleep.

Kate leaned against the door frame to the bathroom. "Did you know you never wanted to marry?" she asked, crossing her arms over her chest.

Luc laughed, leaning back against the quilted headboard. "That's a bit off topic, but no. I didn't know that."

Swallowing, Kate pushed forward. "You had no intention of taking a wife, but Ilha Beleza has some ridiculously archaic law that states you must be married by your thirty-fifth birthday in order to succeed to the throne."

"My birthday is coming up," he muttered, as if that tidbit just hit him. Luc's brows drew together as he laced his fingers over his abdomen. "Are you saying I'm not entitled to the throne if we aren't married by then?"

This was the tricky part. "You aren't crowned until you're married."

"That's ridiculous." He laughed. "I'll change that law, first thing. What if my son doesn't want to marry? Who says you have to be married by thirty-five?"

Kate smiled. "That's exactly what you said before you fell. You were dead set on having that law rewritten."

His eyes held hers another moment, but before she could go on, he said, "I had a dream last night. It was real. I know it was a memory, but I can't figure it out."

Kate's heart beat faster in her chest. Was their time over? Was the beautiful fantasy they'd been living about to come to a crashing halt?

"What was the dream?" she asked, gripping her arms with anticipation.

"I had a dream you were pregnant. That image in my

head has hit more than once." His eyes drilled into her. "Why would I keep dreaming that, Kate?"

"Did you see me in the dream?" she asked, knowing she was treading on very shaky ground.

He shook his head. "No. I had my hands on your bare stomach and I was so happy. Nervous, but excited."

"I've never been pregnant," she told him softly. "Do you think maybe you're just thinking ahead?"

Kate glanced away, unable to look him in the eyes and see him struggle with this entire situation. Why couldn't this be real? He'd told her more than once that he loved her, but that was just what he thought he was supposed to say…wasn't it? Still, what if he was speaking from his heart? What if that fall had actually pulled out his true feelings? But even if she stood a chance with the man she'd fallen in love with, Kate had lied and deceived him. He would never forgive her.

She just wanted today, just one more night with him. She was being selfish, yes, but she couldn't let go just yet. Not when everything right at this moment was beautiful and perfect.

"Do you want children?" he asked. "I assume we've discussed this."

Kate pushed herself off the door frame and smoothed her hair back from her face. "I do want kids. It's always been my dream to have a husband who loves me and a houseful of children."

He offered her a wide, sexy smile. "We will have the most beautiful children."

Oh, when he said things like that she wanted to get swept away and believe every word. Yet again, Luc had been weaved so tightly into this web of lies she'd inadvertently created. Her heart had been in the right place. She only hoped Luc saw that once all was said and done.

"I think any child with the Silva genes would be beautiful," she countered. "Even though you're an only child, your father has a long line of exotic beauties on his side. Your mother is a natural beauty, as well."

Luc tossed his sheet aside and came to his feet. Padding across the floor wearing only a tattoo and a grin, he kept his gaze on hers.

"As much as I'd love to work on those babies, I think I'd like to do something that will help get my memory back sooner rather than later."

Kate forced her gaze up... Well, she made it to his chest and figured that was a good compromise. "What's that?"

"Maybe we should tackle that work schedule you'd mentioned." His smile kicked up higher on one side of that kissable mouth. "You know, before we got sidetracked with being naked."

Kate laughed. "Yes. Work. That's where we need to focus."

Finally. Something they could do that actually needed to be done. She could breathe a bit now.

"I'll go get my laptop," she told him. "I've got a spreadsheet there of your tentative schedule, and I have a speech written out for you that you need to look over."

As she started to walk by, he reached out, snaking an arm around her waist. "You write my speeches?"

"For the past year I have."

His eyes roamed over her face, settled on her lips, then came back up to meet her gaze. "You really are perfect for me."

Kate swallowed. "Better put some clothes on. You can't work in your birthday suit."

His laughter followed her from the room, mocking her. She wasn't perfect for him. She wanted to be. Oh, mercy, how she wanted to be. She'd give him every-thing, but this dream romance was about to come to an end. His memories were coming back a little each day. Time was not on her side.

Maybe by focusing on work, he'd start to piece more things together. Perhaps then she wouldn't have to worry about saying anything. Honestly, she didn't know what scenario would be worse, her telling him the truth or him figuring it out on his own.

Was she a coward for not wanting to tell him? Absolutely. Not only did she not want to see that hurt—and quite possibly hatred—in his eyes, she didn't want that confrontation. There were no right words to say, no good way to come out and tell him he'd been living a complete lie for these past few days.

The end result would be the same, though, no matter how he found out. He would be disgusted with her. Suddenly, losing her job, or even her parents' positions, wasn't the main problem. After this time away from their ordinary lives, she couldn't imagine life without Luc.

And every bit of this scenario made her seem fool-ish, selfish and desperate.

When had she become that woman? When had she become the woman Luc had actually been engaged to? Because Kate was no better than his lying, scheming ex.

Luc glanced over Kate's shoulder as she sat in a patio chair with her laptop on the mosaic-tiled table. They'd opted to work outside to enjoy the bright sunshine and soft ocean breeze.

Resting his hands on the back of the chair, Luc leaned in to read over the tentative spreadsheet, but he was finding it impossible to focus. Kate's floral scent kept hitting him with each passing drift of wind.

"I can move these engagements around," Kate told him, pointing to the two green lines on the screen. "Both appointments are flexible. I scheduled them like this because I thought it would save time."

"Fine. You know more about this than I do," he told her.

She shifted, peeking at him over her shoulder. "I know about scheduling, but this is your life, Luc. Give me some input here. I can add or take away time. Usually, when you don't want to stay at an event too long, I make an excuse and cut the time back."

His brows quirked. "Seriously?"

"Well, yeah. How else would you escape and still look like the charming prince?" She laughed.

"Wow, you really do everything for me." With a sigh, he straightened. "What you have works for me. You've done this for a year, so you obviously know what you're talking about."

Kate turned fully in her chair and narrowed her eyes. "That's the Luc I used to work with. You never wanted to help with the schedule. You always trusted me to make it work."

Another flash of Kate in a snug suit, black this time, filled his mind. A dark-haired woman stood next to her. Luc closed his eyes, wanting to hold on to the image, needing to see who it was. Who was this woman?

Alana.

The image was gone as fast as it entered his mind, but he had a name.

"Luc?"

He opened his eyes, meeting Kate's worried gaze. She'd come to her feet and stood directly in front of him.

"Who's Alana?" he asked.

Kate jerked as if he'd slapped her. "Do you remember her?"

"I had a flash of you and her talking, but I couldn't tell what you guys were saying. It's like a damn movie that plays in my head with no sound."

He raked a hand down his face, meeting her eyes once more. "Who is she?" he repeated.

"She was a woman you used to date."

Luc tried to remember more, but nothing came to mind. Only that the woman's name stirred emotions of anger and hurt within him.

"Were we serious?" he asked.

Kate crossed her arms and nodded. "You were."

She was really sticking to the doctor's orders and not feeding him anything more than he was asking. Damn it, he wished she'd just tell him.

Pacing across the patio, Luc came to a stop at the edge by the infinity pool and stared out at the ocean. With the world at his back, he wished he could turn away from his problems so easily.

Alana Ferella. The name slid easily into his mind as he watched the waves roll onto the shore. His heart hardened, though. What kind of relationship had they had together? Obviously, not a compatible one or he'd still be with her. Something akin to rage settled in him. She hadn't been a nice woman, that much he knew.

He didn't want to keep asking Kate about an ex-girlfriend, and most likely Alana didn't matter, anyway. He just wished he could remember more about Kate, more about the plans they'd made.

"Are we getting married soon?" he asked, turning back to face her.

She blinked a few times, as if his question had thrown

her off. Hell, it probably had. He'd just gone from quizzing her on his ex to discussing their own nuptials.

"There's no set date," she told him.

That was weird. Once they'd announced their engagement, wouldn't the proper protocol have been to set a date? "Why not?" he asked. "With my birthday approaching, the throne in question and being a member of a royal family, I'm shocked we don't have something set."

Biting on her lip, Kate shrugged. "We can discuss the details in a bit. Can we finalize this schedule first? I'd like to make some calls later, if the cell service is working, to confirm your visit. I also need to let my dad know, so security can be arranged."

She was dodging his question for a reason. Did she simply not want to discuss things because of his memory loss, or was there something more to it? She'd admitted they'd argued before his fall. Had they been arguing over the wedding? Had they been arguing over…what? Damn it.

Smacking his palm on the table hard enough to make it rattle, Luc cursed, then balled his hands into fists. Kate jumped, taking a step back.

Kate started to step forward, but he held up a hand.

"No," he ordered. "Don't say anything. There's nothing you can do unless you want to tell me everything, which goes against the doctor's orders."

The hurt look on her face had him cursing. She was just as much a victim in this as he was.

"Kate, I didn't mean to lash out at you."

She shook her head, waving a hand. "It's okay."

"No, it's not." Closing the gap between them, he pulled her into his arms. "You've been here for me, you've done so much and I'm taking out my anger and

frustrations on you when you're only trying to protect me."

Kate wrapped her arms around his waist. "I can handle it, Luc. It's partially my fault you're in this position,
anyway. If we hadn't been arguing, if I hadn't made you
so angry you went down to that wet dock, none of this
would be happening."

Luc eased back. "None of this is your fault. At least
pieces of my life are finally revealing themselves, and
I'm sure it won't be long before the rest of the puzzle
is filled in."

Kate had sacrificed so much for him. Yet he hadn't
heard her tell him once that she loved him. Luc eased
back, looking her in the eyes.

"Why are you marrying me?" he asked, stroking her
jawline with his thumbs.

Her body tensed against his as her eyes widened.
"What do you mean?"

"Do you love me?" he asked, tipping his head down
a touch to hold her gaze.

Instantly, her eyes filled. Kate's hands came up,
framed his face. "More than you'll ever know," she
whispered.

Relief coursed through him. He didn't know why, but
it was imperative to know her true feelings.

"I want to do something for you." She placed a light,
simple kiss on his lips. "Tonight I'm going to make your
favorite dinner. We're going to have a romantic evening
and there will be no talk of the amnesia, the wedding,
the work. Tonight will just be about Kate and Luc."

Wasn't that the whole point of this getaway? She
cleverly circled them back around to the purpose of
this trip. One of the many reasons he assumed he'd

fallen in love with her. She kept him grounded, kept him on track.

Tugging her closer to him, he nuzzled her neck. "Then I expect one hell of a dessert," he growled into her ear.

Eleven

She had to tell him. There was no more stalling. The anguish, the rage that was brewing deep within Luc was more than she could bear. No matter what the doctor said, she had to come clean, because Luc getting so torn up had to be more damaging than just learning the truth.

And the truth beyond this whole messed-up situation was that she loved him. She hadn't lied when he'd asked. Kate had fallen completely in love with Luc and to keep this secret another day just wasn't acceptable.

She put on her favorite strapless green dress and her gold sandals. With her hair piled atop her head, she added a pair of gold-and-amethyst earrings.

A glance down at her hand had her heart clenching. He'd given her a ring. She wore a ring from a man she loved, yet he truly had no idea who she was.

At this point, she didn't recognize herself. She'd never been a liar or a manipulator. Yet here she was, doing a bang-up job of both.

Even with the patio doors open, the house smelled amazing with their dinner of fish and veggies baking in the oven. No matter how the evening ended, Kate wanted one last perfect moment with Luc.

Her mother would be relieved that Kate was finally telling the truth. What would Luc's parents say? Would they insist she be fired? Would they dismiss her parents from their duties as well, as she'd feared all along?

No matter the ramifications, Kate had to do the right thing here.

She headed to the kitchen to check the progress of dinner. When she glanced out toward the ocean, she noticed the darkening skies. Another storm rolling in. How apropos. Hadn't this entire nightmare started with a storm? For once in her life she wasn't looking forward to the added turmoil from Mother Nature.

Luc stood on the patio with his phone. Kate had no idea who he was talking to, but whoever it was, their call would be cut off soon due to this crazy weather.

Nerves settled deep in Kate's stomach. She wanted nothing more than to go back in time and have a redo of the night Luc fell. First of all, she never would've argued with him. If he didn't want to do the orphanage visit, fine. She'd been beating her head against that proverbial wall for nearly a year and he'd never given in. Why had she assumed he'd grow a heart all of a sudden and go?

Of course, now that he was drawing a blank on certain aspects of his life, he seemed to have forgotten how cold he used to be. Kate truly wished this Luc, the one she'd spent the past few days with, the one who had made love to her as if he truly loved her, was the Luc who would emerge after all the dust settled.

The worry eating at her would not help her be strong when she most needed to be. Everything that Luc threw at her would be justified, and right now she just needed to figure out the best way to come clean, because she truly didn't want to harm him any more than she had to.

After checking the dinner, she pulled the pan from the oven. Once she had their plates made, she started to call him, but realized he was still on the phone. The electricity flickered as rumbles of thunder resounded outside. Kate quickly searched for candles, because inevitably the lights were going to go. Perfect. It seemed Mother Nature was on her side. With the lights off, Kate wouldn't have to see the hatred on Luc's face when she told him that everything he knew about her, about them, was a lie.

"Darling, did you hear what I said?"

Luc concentrated on his mother's voice, the words she was saying, but something still didn't fit.

"You said Alana contacted you because she wants to see me," he repeated slowly, still trying to process all this.

Kate had told him Alana was an ex, but why would she be contacting him if he was engaged to Kate?

"Yes," his mother confirmed. "She's called me twice and she's very adamant that she wants to see you. I'm not going to stick my nose in this—you can respond however you want—but I don't think it's a good idea."

Luc's eyes locked onto the orange horizon. This view alone was reason enough to buy this property, no matter how many upgrades he wished to have inside. But right now, his head was pounding as if memories were rushing to the surface, waiting to get out all at once.

"Why would she contact you at all?" he asked. Resting one hand on the rail, he clutched the phone with his other, struggling to hear through the static. "Alana is in my past."

"So you remember her? Good. Then you don't need me to say how ridiculous this notion is that she can just come back into our lives after the entire baby scandal…"

His mother's voice cut out, but in the midst of her talking Luc did catch the word *baby*.

He rubbed his forehead. A flash of a diamond ring, a snippet of Alana in tears saying something about a pregnancy…

"To think she could trick you into marriage simply by saying she's pregnant was absurd," his mother went on, oblivious to his inner turmoil. "The timing of you purchasing this getaway house was perfect. Alana has no idea where you are."

The timing?

Luc spun around, glancing in through the open doors. Beyond the living area was the kitchen, where Kate stood preparing dinner. Instantly, he saw it all. His mother's single, damning word *timing* had triggered an avalanche of memories.

Kate was his assistant. No doubt about that, but they weren't engaged. They were strictly employee-employer, and that had been the extent of their relationship…until just a few days ago.

He felt sick to his stomach as he reached out, seeking the edge of a wrought-iron chair. He needed support, and right now all he could call upon was an inanimate object.

"Alana has no place in this family, Lucas."

Luc swallowed, his eyes remaining locked on Kate. Obviously, he'd been played by two women in his life— two women he'd trusted and let in intimately—on so many levels.

No wonder she was always so hesitant to let him in on his past. Kate's silence probably had little to do with the doctor's warnings and everything to do with her own agenda.

How could he have been so blind? How the hell could Kate have taken advantage of his vulnerability like that? Being manipulative wasn't like her, or at least not like the Kate he'd known. What had changed? Why had she felt it necessary to lie to his face, to go along with this charade that they were engaged?

Luc closed his eyes, gritting his teeth. "Mom, I'll call you back later. The connection is bad with the weather."

The call was cut off before he could finish. This storm was going to be a big one and he didn't just mean the one brewing outside.

Luc held the phone down at his side, dropped his head and tried like hell to forget the images, the emotions that went along with the fact he'd slept with Kate. He'd had sex with his assistant. He'd thought himself in love with her, believed that he'd be marrying her, making her the next queen.

She knew full well he didn't step over the line of professional boundaries. He'd outlined that fact for her a year ago when their attraction had crept to the surface, and he'd wanted to nip it in the bud. Kate knew every single thing about him and she'd used that to her advantage. She knew of the real fiancée, the fake pregnancy, and even after he'd brought up having visions of a baby, she'd said nothing.

How far would she have let this farce go? How long was she intending to lie straight to his face? Earlier she'd claimed she loved him.

Luc's heart clenched. Love had no place in the midst of lies and deceit.

Bringing his eyes back up, he caught her gaze across the open space. She smiled, a smile that he'd once trusted, and Luc felt absolutely nothing but disgust.

He knew exactly what he had to do.

When he hadn't returned her smile, Kate worried. Again she wondered who he'd been talking to on the phone. Something or someone had upset him.

Well, whatever it was, she couldn't let that hold her back. She couldn't keep finding excuses to put this discussion off.

"Dinner is ready," she called, setting the plates on the old, scarred table.

She glanced at the bouquet she'd purchased just the other day at the street market. She and Luc had shared so many amazing memories in such a short time, but she couldn't even relish them because they were built upon the lies she'd created using the feeble excuse that it was for his benefit. No, it would be to his benefit to know exactly what was going on in his life.

Nervousness spiked through her, settling deep. Kate smoothed a hand down her knee-length halter dress and took a deep breath as she stood beside her chair and waited for him to come in. Luc entered through the patio doors, closed them, set his phone on the coffee table and crossed to her.

"Smells great," he told her, offering a wide smile.

When he leaned down to kiss her cheek, Kate closed her eyes for the briefest of moments. Getting wrapped up in this entire scenario of playing house would only hurt her more. She wished more than anything that every bit of this scene playing out were true. Wished Luc would always look at her as if he loved her, as if he wanted to spend his life with her.

"My mother called," he told her after a long moment of silence. "She asked how everything was."

Kate moved the fish around on her plate, too nervous to actually eat. "I'm sure she's worried about you."

"She cares about me. I assume anyone who cares for me would be worried."

Kate's eyes slid up to his, a knot in her throat forming when she saw him staring back at her. "Yes. You have a great many people who love you."

"And what about you, Kate?" He held her gaze another moment before looking back to his plate. "Do you love me?"

Kate set her fork down, reached over to take his hand and squeezed. "I have so much in my heart for you, Luc."

When he said nothing, they finished eating, picked up the dishes and set them on the counter.

"Leave them," Luc told her, taking her hand. "Come with me."

When he led her toward the bedroom, Kate's heart started beating harder in her chest. She couldn't let him start kissing her, undressing her or even touching more than just her hand, because she'd melt instantly and not be able to follow through with her plan to spill her guts.

She trailed into the room after him. The bed in the center of the floor mocked her. Never again would they lie there in a tangle of arms and legs.

They never should have.

"Luc." She pulled her hand from his. "We can't."

He turned, quirking a brow. "Can't what?"

Kate shook her head, glancing away. She couldn't look him in the eyes. She didn't want to see his face when she revealed the truth.

"You can't make love to me?" He stepped closer, resting his hands on her shoulders. "Or you can't continue to play the role of doting fiancée? Because I have to tell you, you did a remarkable job of lying to my face."

Kate jerked her head up, meeting his cold, hard stare. All breath whooshed out of her lungs as fear gripped her heart like a vise.

"Apparently my real fiancée has been trying to get in touch with me," he went on, dropping his hands and stepping back as if he couldn't stand to touch Kate anymore. "After I heard my mother say that, the pieces started clicking into place."

Kate wrapped her arms around her waist. "You remember everything?"

"I know you're my assistant and you lied, manipulated and schemed to get into my bed." Luc laughed, the sound mocking. "Now I know why we never slept together before."

The pain in his voice sliced her heart open. Words died in her throat. Any defense she had was moot at this point.

"How far would you have gone, Kate? Would you have walked down the aisle and pretended to love me forever?"

She did love him. She'd chosen the absolute worst way to show him, but she truly did love the man. Kate pressed her lips together and remained still, waiting for the continuation of her punishment.

"Would you have gone so far as to have my kids?"

He took a step forward, but Kate squared her shoulders. She wasn't afraid of him and she wasn't going to turn and run, no matter how much she wanted to. Right now, he was entitled to lash out at her, and she had to take it.

"How could you do this to me?" His voice was low,

calm, cold. "Now I know why you cried after we had sex in the shower. Apparently, the guilt got to you, but only for a short time, because you were quick to get back in my bed."

Kate squeezed her arms tighter, as if to keep his hurtful words from seeping in. She glanced away, out the glass doors toward the sun, which had all but set.

"Look at me," he demanded. "You don't get to drift away. You started this and you're damn well going to face reality and give me the answers I want. Are you even going to say anything?"

Kate shook her head. "Anything I say won't change the fact that I lied to you, and you won't believe any defense I have."

Luc threw his arms out. "What was your motivation, Kate? Did you think I'd fall in love with you? Did you think you'd play with my mind for a bit?"

"No," she whispered through the tears clogging her throat. "Hurting you was the last thing I wanted to do."

"Oh, you didn't hurt me," he retorted, his face reddening. "I can't be hurt by someone I don't love. Didn't you know that? I'm furious I ever trusted you."

Kate nodded. "When we made love—"

"We didn't make love," he spat. Luc took a step closer, so close she could see the whiskey-colored flecks in his eyes. "We had sex. Meaningless sex that never should've happened."

Kate looked into his eyes, hoping to see a flicker of that emotion she'd seen during their days together, or when they'd been intimate. But all that stared back at her was hatred. Anything he thought he'd felt days ago, even hours ago, was false. The old Luc was back and harsher than ever.

"I'll call for someone to come pick me up," she told

him. "I'll be at the cottage until then. Anything I have here I can send for later."

Kate walked out of the room, surprised he didn't call her back so he could finish her off.

Mercifully, he let her go. She couldn't cry in front of him, didn't want him to think she was using tears as a defense. Her tears were a product of her own selfishness. She'd lived it up for a few days, had had the man she loved in her arms and had even worn his ring.

Kate stepped out onto the patio and glanced down at the gem on her finger. Thunder rolled, lightning streaked in the not so distant sky as fat drops of rain pelted her.

"Kate," Luc called from behind her.

She froze.

"What the hell are you doing, just standing in the storm?"

Kate turned, blinking the rain out of her eyes. At this point she couldn't honestly tell what was rain and what were tears.

"Do you care?" she asked.

"I'm angry, but I don't want to see anyone struck by lightning."

Luc stood in the doorway, his broad frame filling the open space. The lights behind him flickered and then everything went black, save for the candles she'd lit on the dining room table and the fat pillar on the coffee table.

Cursing under his breath, Luc stepped back. "Get in here."

Slowly, Kate crossed the wet patio, hugging her midsection against the cool drops. She brushed by him, shivering from the brief contact and cringing the second he stepped back and broke the touch.

"I just—"

"I'll be in my room." He cut her off with a wave of his hand as if she was nothing more than a nuisance. "Don't take this as a sign that I care. You can stay in here until the storm passes, and that's all."

Luc went to the dining room table, picked up a candle and walked away, leaving her shivering in the darkened living room. The pillar on the coffee table flickered, but she couldn't see much beyond the sofa. Kate sank down, pulling her feet up onto the cushion, hugging her knees to her chest.

Closing her eyes, she dropped her head forward and sighed. For the first time in her life she prayed the storm would stop. She had to get to her cottage, pack her things and call for someone to come and get her.

The hurt that had settled into this house was more than she could handle, and she didn't want to be here when Luc came out of his room. She didn't want to see that anger, that wounded look in his eyes again, knowing she'd put it there.

Whatever they'd had, be it their professional relationship or this fake engagement, she'd ruined any chance of ever having Luc in her life again. She'd taken what didn't belong to her, and she had no choice now but to live with the consequences.

Twelve

Luc must be insane. That was the only explanation for why he found himself crossing the path between the main house and the cottage so early in the morning. He hadn't slept all night. Every moment since his fall kept playing out in his mind like a movie, only he couldn't stop this one.

Kate's rigidity when he would initially touch her, her hesitancy to make love to him, why she was so adamant about him not buying her things at the market. The signs were there, but he'd assumed she was his fiancée, and she'd never said any differently. She'd had time, plenty of time, to tell him the truth. Even if the doctor hadn't given the order to not feed him any information, Luc was pretty sure she still would've kept up the charade.

Now that he'd had time to think, he'd fully processed how deeply her betrayal had sliced him. How could someone get so far into his life, work with him every single day, and manage to take advantage of him like that? Had he been that easy to manipulate? More important, how far would she have been willing to take that twisted game she'd played?

He wanted answers and he wanted them five minutes ago. He wasn't waiting another second to find out what the hell she'd been thinking to even contemplate getting away with such a potentially life-altering, monumental lie.

The anger raging inside him didn't stem just from her deception, but from the fact he'd fallen for her; making her betrayal even worse, Kate knew the emotional state he was in, just coming off a major breakup. Not only that, she knew he didn't date, much less sleep, with staff. How could she claim to care about him and then betray him in the next breath?

Even now that he knew everything, he still cared. He still ached for her, because with his old memories, he also had fresh ones. Memories he'd made with Kate, now tarnished by lies.

As Luc stepped into a clearing of lush plants, he glanced down to the dock. He froze when he spotted Kate standing by the water, two suitcases at her feet. She was not leaving without telling him why the hell she'd done this to him. She didn't get to escape that easily.

Marching toward the steps leading down to the beach, Luc had no clue what he'd say to her. She had plenty of explaining to do, but there was so much inside his mind, so much he wanted to say, he didn't even know where to start. He figured once he opened his mouth, things would start pouring out, most likely hurtful things. He couldn't care about her feelings just yet… if ever.

Kate jerked around as he approached. The dark circles beneath her eyes, the red rims, indicated she'd slept about as well as he had. The storm had lasted most of the night and he truly had no clue when she'd ended up leaving the main house. He'd closed the bedroom door, wanting to shut her out. Unfortunately, his bedroom was filled with visions of Kate.

The shower, the bed, her pair of flip-flops by the closet door, her robe draped across the foot of the bed. She was everywhere, and she'd wedged herself so intimately into his life, as no other woman had.

She'd had so much control over the situation and she'd used that power to consume him. Now he had to figure out how the hell to get out from under her spell, because even seeing her right now, with all his bubbling rage, he found his body still responded to her.

Damn it. How could he still want her? Anything that had happened between them was dead to him. He couldn't think back on those times, because just like this "engagement," they meant nothing.

Her eyes widened as he came to stand within inches of her. "I'm waiting for a boat. My father is sending one of the guards to pick me up."

"Why?" Luc asked, clenching his fists at his sides. "Before you leave, tell me why you lied to me."

Her head tipped slightly as she studied him. "Would it matter?"

Strands of her long, dark hair had slipped loose from her knot and were dancing about her shoulders. She had on another of those little strapless sundresses, this one black. Appropriately matching the color of his mood.

"Maybe not, but I deserve to know why you would betray my trust and think it was okay."

Dark eyes held his. Part of him wanted to admire her

for not backing away, not playing the victim or defending herself. The other part wished she'd defend herself and say something, so they could argue about it and get everything out in the open. He needed a good outlet, someone to yell at, and the perfect target stood directly in front of him.

"I was shocked at first that you thought I was your fiancée," she told him, her pink tongue darting out to lick her lips. She shoved a wayward strand of hair behind her ear and shrugged. "Then I wanted to see what the doctor would say before I told you otherwise. He said not to give you any information, so I didn't. I didn't want to lie to you, Luc. I was in a tough spot and everything blew out of my control before I knew what was happening. I tried to keep my distance, but once we had sex, I wanted more. I took what I shouldn't have. Nothing I can say can change that fact, but I am sorry I hurt you."

Luc propped his hands on his hips, waiting to hear more, but she remained silent and continued to hold his gaze. "There has to be another reason, a deeper motivation than you simply being afraid to tell me."

Kate's eyes darted away as she turned her back to him and focused on the water again. Not a boat in sight. He still had time to get answers from her before she left.

"My reasons are irrelevant."

He almost didn't hear her whispered answer over the ocean breeze. With her back to him, Luc wasn't sure what was worse, looking her in the eyes or looking at that exposed, creamy neck he could practically taste. He would never taste that skin again.

He cursed beneath his breath, raked a hand down his face and sighed. "What were you trying to gain?" he demanded. "I'm giving you the opportunity to say something here, Kate. Tell me why I shouldn't fire you, why I shouldn't remove you from every aspect of my life."

The low hum of a motor jerked his attention in the direction of the royal yacht moving toward them. Kate said nothing as she turned, picking up her suitcases.

Here he was gearing up for a good fight, and she couldn't even afford him that? Did she feel nothing at all? How had he misread her all these years?

If she wasn't going to talk now, then fine. He wasn't done with her, but if she needed to go, he'd let her. She could stew and worry back in Ilha Beleza. Luc actually wanted her uncomfortable, contemplating his next move. She deserved to be miserable, and he had to steel himself against any remorse.

His mother had always taught him to respect women, which he did, but right now that didn't mean he had to make her life all rainbows and sunshine, either.

"Go back to the palace," he told her, hating how she refused to look at him. "I'll be home in a few days and we'll add on to that schedule we finalized the other night."

Kate threw him a glance over her shoulder. "What?"

Luc stepped around her, blocking her view of the incoming boat. He waited until her eyes locked onto his. "You're not quitting. You're going to be with me until I know what game you're playing. And don't try to get sneaky once you're back. I have eyes and ears everywhere."

Her chin tipped up in defiance...a quality he'd once admired when she was speaking with the media or other pushy individuals. "I think it's best if I resign."

Luc gripped her shoulders, cursing himself for having a weakness where she was concerned, considering all she'd done. "I don't care what you think is best.

You're mine until I say otherwise. You started this game, Kate. You're going to see it through to the end."

Pushing away from her, he stalked toward the main house. Not once did he consider glancing back. He was finished looking over his shoulder to see if anyone was stabbing him in the back or betraying him. From here on out, he was regaining control, and he was damn well going to come out on top.

Luc stared at the area he used to call his kitchen. If this royalty thing didn't work out, he was seriously getting a job with a contractor. Demolishing things was an excellent outlet for his anger.

Wiping his forearm across his forehead, he sank down onto a dining room chair and surveyed his destruction. The cabinets were torn out; the countertop lay beneath the rubble. He'd pulled the fridge out enough that he could get to the food, but other than that, he'd completely torn up the space.

Kate had been gone a week. Two weeks had passed since he'd arrived here, and he was heading home tomorrow. In these past seven days alone, he'd had more than enough time to reflect on everything, and he still had no clue what he was going to do once he saw her again.

He'd had to sleep in the guest room on a lumpy old mattress because he couldn't lie in his master suite without smelling her, seeing her…feeling her at his side. The shower he'd so loved when the renovations started was now tainted, because all he could see was Kate's wet body as he claimed her with the false knowledge they were a real couple. They'd been damn good together, but he would never, ever admit that to her or anybody else.

Luc's cell chimed. He thought about ignoring it, but figured he'd at least see who wanted to talk to him.

Crossing the open room, he glanced at his phone on the coffee table. Mikos, his best friend.

Considering he had called Mikos three days ago and spilled his guts like some whiny high school girl with sad love songs playing in the background, Luc assumed his friend was calling to check on him.

"Hey, man," he answered with a sigh.

"You still sound like hell."

Luc laughed, sinking onto the sofa, resting his elbow on the arm. "Yeah, well, I feel like it. What's up?"

"Just checking in."

"Shouldn't you be planning the wedding of the century?" Luc asked, feeling a slight pang of envy.

Envy? Why the hell would he be envious? Sure, he needed to be married because of the throne, but he didn't want to be tied to one woman. No, Mikos had found the perfect woman for him, and Luc was happy for both of them.

There was no perfect woman for Luc. Hadn't he proved that by getting too close to two very convincing liars?

"The wedding is planned down to the last petal and place card," Mikos stated. "Are you still in?"

Luc was supposed to stand up with Mikos, right next to Mikos's brother, Stefan. An honor Luc wasn't letting Kate's untimely backstabbing steal from him.

"I'm in. I'm not letting my disaster ruin your day."

"Have you talked to Kate?"

Luc closed his eyes. Even hearing her name elicited a mixture of feelings, a myriad of emotions. Beyond the hurt, the anger and the bitterness there was still that underlying fact that he wanted the hell out of her. How twisted was that?

"No. I'm heading back tomorrow," Luc answered.

"What are you going to do?"

"I have no clue, man."

Mikos sighed. "Want my advice?"

"You're going to give it anyway, so why ask?"

"I am," Mikos agreed with a laugh. "Figure out why she lied. You told me once you had a thing for her. Maybe she was acting on her own feelings and taking a cue from yours before the accident."

"Are you defending her actions?" The last thing Luc wanted to hear was a justifiable cause. Damn it, he wanted to be angry, wanted to place all the blame on her.

"Hell, no. I'm saying love is a strong emotion."

"You're too blinded by this wedding," Luc replied. "Kate doesn't love me. You don't lie and scheme with those you love, no matter the circumstances."

"I did to Darcy," Mikos reminded him. "She had no idea who I was, and I was totally in love with her. I nearly lost her, but she forgave me. You know how things can get mixed up, Luc."

Luc recalled that time when Mikos's nanny had first been hired. She'd had no clue Mikos was a widowed prince. The two had fallen in love before Mikos could fully explain the truth.

"Our situations are completely different," Luc muttered. "I'm not forgiving her. No matter what."

"Just make sure you really think this through before you go off on her once you get home," Mikos warned. "What she did was wrong, no doubt about it. But she's not like Alana. I know that's something you'll never forget or get over, but Alana had an ulterior motive from the start. You've known Kate for years and she's never once done you wrong."

Luc finished the call, unable to think of anything else but the truth Mikos had laid out before him. No, Kate had never deceived him in any way before. She'd been the best assistant he'd ever had. To be honest, the only reason he hadn't pursued her before was because of their working relationship and possible repercussions to his ascension to the throne. With the mess he'd gotten himself into lately, it would be a miracle if the press didn't rip his family's reputation to shreds if the truth came out.

Once he returned to Ilha Beleza, he and Kate would have a one-on-one chat, now that they'd both had time to absorb all that had happened. They needed to talk. He couldn't keep her around if he didn't trust her. And that was the problem. When it came to his professional life, he trusted no one else.

Unfortunately, when it came to his personal life, he didn't trust her one bit…but that didn't stop him from wanting her. Even this week apart hadn't dimmed his attraction toward her. Which begged the question: What the hell was going to happen once he got home? And would he be able to control himself?

Thirteen

His desk was exactly how he always kept it—neat, tidy and organized, with his schedule in hard copies just as he wanted it. He knew there would also be emails on his computer with the same information.

Kate had kept up her end of the bargain and continued working just as if she hadn't torn their entire lives to shreds. He didn't know whether to be relieved or angry that she was still here, still within reaching distance... not that he was going to reach out to her. He had more pride than that.

Luc flipped through the papers, even though he'd looked through his email earlier and knew what he had coming up. Mikos's wedding was only two weeks away, and other than that, there were a handful of meetings and social events at which he was expected to make an appearance. He'd been knocked down so many times in the past few months he didn't know if he had the energy to put forth for anyone outside his immediate family and staff. He was so exhausted, spent and depleted from trying to perform damage control on his personal life, there was no way he could keep up with his royal obligations, too.

Thankfully, from the looks of his schedule, Kate had helped him dodge any media interviews over the next few months. For that he was grateful, but not enough to seek her out and thank her. He wasn't ready to thank her for anything…and he might never be.

"Oh, sweetheart. You're back."

Luc glanced toward the high, arched doorway as his mother breezed in. The woman possessed more elegance and grace than anyone he'd ever known. With her polished style and loving grin, she made the perfect queen, but her reign was soon coming to an end. Well, it would be if he managed to find a way to secure his title before his birthday, and without a wife.

Luc crossed the room and relished her embrace. Even though he'd always been close with his parents, he didn't have it in him to discuss all the ways he was struggling right now.

"How are you?" she asked, pulling back to assess him. Clutching his arms, she studied his face. "No more symptoms? You remember everything now?"

Luc nodded. "I'm perfectly fine."

She held on to him another moment, then broke the contact. "We need to talk."

He crossed his arms as his mother shut the double doors, giving them complete privacy.

"Have you seen Kate since you've been back?" she asked.

Luc shook his head. "No."

"Darling, she told me what happened." His mother

reached out, took one of his hands in hers and squeezed. "I'm sure she left out some details, but I know you believed she was your fiancée, and she went along with it."

Luc gritted his teeth. Seriously? Kate went to his mom?

"I wished I'd learned this from you," she went on. "I can't imagine how angry you must be, and I know you're feeling betrayed—"

"Don't defend her," Luc growled. "I'm not near that point."

"I'm not defending her actions." His mother smiled, tipping her head. "I just want you to really think about how you're going to handle this. Kate is a wonderful woman and I've always been so fond of her. I know we have a rule about remaining distant from employees, but she and her parents have been around so long, they're like family."

His feelings for Kate were far from family-like, and he sure as hell hadn't been feeling brotherly in that shower.

"I will admit I'm surprised you didn't fire her," his mother added. "She's good for you, Luc. She's the best assistant you've ever had. I'm proud of you for not blowing up."

"It was tempting."

Temptation. The word seemed to go hand in hand with Kate's name.

"I still don't know what to do, but for now, she's going to be working for me like always. I don't have time to find a new assistant, and I sure as hell don't want to have to get to know someone new. I've got enough of a mess to deal with."

"We do need to figure out what's going to happen on your birthday." His mother pursed her lips, as if in deep thought. "Your father would change the law if he could, but the truth is, we never dreamed…"

Luc laughed, the sound void of all humor. "I know. You never thought a child of yours would still be single at thirty-five. It's okay to say it."

She squeezed his arm. "We'll figure something out. We have to."

Luc nodded, unable to speak past the lump of worry in his throat. Failure was not an option. Ever. He was the next leader, for crying out loud. Why couldn't he figure out a way around this ridiculous issue?

"I'll let you get settled back in, then." His mother reached up, kissed him on the cheek. "Glad you're back home and safe. And I'm glad you didn't fire Kate. She means more to this family than you may realize."

What did that mean? Did his mother actually think he and Kate…

No. That was ridiculous. As torn as he was, he couldn't entertain the idea that Kate could remain in his life as anything other than his assistant…and even that role was still up in the air. He'd have to worry about that later. At this point, time was against him, and finding another assistant before finding a wife—or before the coronation—was impossible.

Once he was alone again, Luc turned and went to his desk. Bracing his palms on its glossy top, he leaned forward and closed his eyes. He would do a great job ruling this country, as his father had before him. Luc just needed a chance to prove he could do so without a wife.

The echo of soft footsteps hit him and he knew instantly who would be behind him. He didn't turn, though. He wasn't quite ready to take in the sight of Kate with all her beauty and sexiness.

The click of the heels stopped, Luc's heart beat faster

than he liked. Damn it, he hadn't even turned to look at her, hadn't said a word, yet she had already sent his body into overdrive.

"I'll come back."

Her soft words washed over him as he turned to face her.

"No." He spoke to her retreating back, and she froze in the doorway. "Come in and close the door."

She stood still so long, he thought for sure she wasn't going to stay. After a moment, she stepped back, closed the door and whipped around to face him.

Luc hadn't thought it possible, but he still found her breathtakingly gorgeous and arousing. Seeing Kate in a dark blue suit, with a fitted jacket that hugged her waist and accentuated her breasts, and her snug skirt made it hard for him to form words right now. As her heels clicked across the floor, his eyes were drawn to her open-toed, animal-print pumps. Damn, she looked like a woman who was ready to be stripped and laid out on his desk.

What was worse, now that he'd had her wrapped all around him, he knew exactly how amazing they were together. Why was he paying a penance in all this? He was the victim.

She stopped well out of his reach, clasped her hands in front of her and met his gaze. "I didn't know you were back," she said. "I was just coming in to make sure your computer was ready to go when you needed it."

Luc tore his gaze from her painted red lips and glanced at his desk. He hadn't even noticed the new computer. Hell, he hadn't even asked for one. Once again, she stayed on top of things and kept his life running smoothly.

"Where's my old one?" he asked.

"All of the palace computers have been upgraded, and they put yours in while you were gone. I made sure the security on yours was set up the same as your old one, and I also made sure your old files were transferred. Everything is on there under the same names, just how they always were."

When he glanced back at her, there wasn't a hint of any emotion on her face. Not a twinge of a smile, no dark circles under her eyes to indicate she'd been losing sleep. Absolutely nothing.

Which pissed him off even more.

"Is this how it's going to be?" he asked, gritting his teeth. "With you pretending you didn't change the dynamics between us?"

Kate blinked, pulled in a deep breath and shook her head. "I don't know what you want from me. I can't erase what happened, yet you still want me to work for you, so I'm doing what I can under the circumstances. I can't tell you what you want to know, because—"

She spun around. Luc waited for her to finish, but she kept her back to him as silence settled heavily between them. There was no easy way, no secret formula for them to get beyond this. He wasn't all that convinced they could move on, despite what his mother and Mikos had said during their pep talks.

"Because why?" he pressed, when she remained quiet. "Why can't you tell me your reasons? I'm ready to hear it. I *need* to hear it, Kate."

Still nothing. Luc stepped forward, closing the space between them. "Damn it, I deserve more than your silence. You can't hide like this. You don't get that right. Tell me what prompted you to not only lie, but keep up the charade and play me so perfectly that you ended up in my bed."

"Don't," she whispered. "Don't make me say it."

Luc grabbed her arm, spun her around and forced himself to hold her watery gaze. "I refuse to let you out of this scot-free."

Squaring her shoulders, tipping her chin up and swiping a hand beneath her eye as one lone tear streaked out, Kate nodded. "Fine. You want to know why I did it? Why I lied to you so easily? Besides the doctor's orders of not saying anything more, besides the fact that the deception just got out of control, I knew it was the only time in my life you'd ever look at me like you cared for me. Like you actually wanted me. I knew it was wrong. I never justified my actions, and I won't defend them, because there's no way to make any of it okay. But don't make me tell you more. I can't, Luc."

Her voice cracked on his name. Luc kept his hand on her arm as he took a half step closer, nearly towering over her. "You can," he murmured. "Tell me the rest. Now."

He was so torn between arousal and anger. He'd always heard there was a fine line between hatred and passion. No truer words were ever spoken.

"I fell in love with you," she whispered, her eyes locking onto his. "Is that what you wanted to hear? Do you hate me so much that humiliating me is the only way to make yourself get past the anger? Well, now you know. I've bared my soul to you, Luc. You know about my adoption, which few people do. You know my secret fantasies—you're the only one in that category— and that I'm in love with a man who'd rather belittle me than ever forgive me, let alone love me back. My fault, I know, but that doesn't stop the hurt."

A viselike grip squeezed his heart at her declaration. Why did he feel anything akin to sympathy toward her? She'd done every bit of this to herself, pulling him along for the ride.

"You don't love me." He dropped his hand and stepped back. "You don't lie to someone and manipulate them, taking advantage of their weaknesses, when you love them."

"I never lied to you before this and I won't lie to you again," she vowed, crossing her arms over her chest. "So when I tell you I love you, I'm being honest. I know my word means nothing to you, and I know I went about everything the wrong way. There is no excuse for my behavior, so I'm not going to stand here and try to make one."

Luc watched as she pulled herself together, patting her damp cheeks, smoothing her hair behind her shoulders and standing tall.

Even through all this, she remained strong. He wanted to hate her, because that would be so much easier than to stand here and be torn in two. She'd betrayed the trust they had built, yet at the same time she had tried to keep her distance. He'd been the one to pursue the intimacy. He could look at this situation from so many angles, but none of them gave him the answer or made things any easier.

"You have every right to fire me—I deserve it. But if you insist on keeping me, I think it's best if we keep our relationship professional and try to move on. That means no rehashing the mistakes I made. I can't have you throwing them in my face."

The longer she spoke, the stronger her voice got. The woman who'd emotionally professed her love for him just moments earlier had transformed back into the businesslike assistant he'd always known. Who was the real Kate?

Was she the loving, passionate woman back at the beach house? Was she the take-charge assistant, or was she the conniving woman who'd ruthlessly insinuated herself into his life when he'd been weak?

"I agree that from here on out, we'll keep our relationship strictly professional."

Luc prayed like hell he was telling the truth. He needed to keep his head on straight, focus on securing the title and not think about how much he'd fallen for his assistant.

Well, that plan to keep things professional was about to get blown apart.

Kate closed her eyes, gripped the stick and willed the results to be different.

Peeking through one eyelid, she still saw the two pink lines glaring back at her. If they had been on a billboard or neon sign they couldn't have been any more eye-catching… She couldn't look anywhere else.

And no matter how long she stared at it, the results were still going to be the same. Positive.

Something between a moan and a cry escaped her as she came to her feet. Staring at herself in the vanity mirror, Kate didn't know what she expected to see. She didn't look any different, but in the past three minutes the course of her entire life had been altered.

Now what should she do? She was pregnant with Luc's baby and the man practically loathed her, unless she was writing a speech for him or running interference for some engagement he didn't want to attend.

There was no getting around this. She'd been on the pill since she was a teen, to keep her cycle regular, but they hadn't used a condom the times they'd been intimate, and birth control wasn't fail-safe…obviously.

There was only one answer. She'd promised Luc she'd never lie to him again, and she certainly wasn't going to start off by keeping this baby a secret.

Laying the test stick on the back of the vanity, Kate washed her hands and stepped out of the restroom. She wanted to find Luc now. This couldn't wait, because the nerves in her stomach were threatening to overtake her. She had to find him.

At this point in the day, she honestly had no idea what he was doing, but she did know he was working from home. If she stopped to think, she could figure out his schedule—she had created it. But her mind wasn't in work mode right now and she couldn't process anything other than the fact she was having a baby with a man she loved…a man who could hardly look at her. She was on the verge of freaking out.

Her lies had not only killed the trust Luc had for her, now the whirlwind of secrets had formed a new life…literally.

Kate's hand slid over her stomach as she made her way out of her office and into the wide hallway. She smiled as she passed one of the maids, but her smile faded the second she reached Luc's office door. In just moments, both their lives and the future of this country would be changed forever.

She was carrying an heir.

Kate rested her forehead against the smooth wood and closed her eyes. The sooner she told Luc, the sooner they could start figuring out what to do. Summoning all the strength she possessed, she tapped on his office door, cursing her shaking hands. She heard familiar voices on the other side. Apparently, he was having a private meeting with his parents. Still, this couldn't wait.

Yes, they were the king and queen. Yes, Kate was being rude by interrupting. But she didn't care.

Fisting her hand, she knocked louder and longer, until the door jerked open to an angry-looking Luc. His jaw clenched, his lips thinned, and once he saw her, his eyes narrowed.

"Kate? We're in the middle of something."

Pushing by him, she offered a shaky smile to his parents, who sat with their eyes locked on her. "I'm sorry, but this can't wait."

Ana Silva rose to her feet and crossed the room. Kate swallowed as her heart started beating faster. She was going to be sick. The overwhelming urge to pass out or throw up all over the Persian rug had nothing to do with the pregnancy.

"Darling, you're trembling," Ana said. "Come, sit down."

"We're in the middle of something," Luc repeated.

Luc's father stood, gesturing toward the chair he'd just vacated. "Here, Kate."

Luc muttered a string of Portuguese slang.

"I'm sorry," Kate muttered. "I didn't mean to cause a scene. I just need a few minutes with Luc."

His parents exchanged a look and Kate noticed Luc standing off to the side, arms crossed, jaw still clenched. He wasn't happy. Too bad she was about to drop another bomb on his life. Would he be even angrier at her? Most likely, but hiding the pregnancy wasn't an option.

Kate closed her eyes as she rested her elbows on her knees and dropped her head into her hands. Luc's parents muttered something to him and moments later Kate heard the office door click shut.

"What the hell is this all about?" Luc demanded.

Kate pushed her hair away from her face as she looked up. He was leaning against the edge of his desk, ankles crossed, palms resting on either side of his slim hips. Wearing dark designer jeans and a fitted black T-shirt, he didn't look like a member of the royal family, but he still exuded power. It was the stare, the unyielding body language, that told her she needed to get on with her speech…one she hadn't rehearsed at all.

"I…" Kate shook her head, came to her feet. No way could she remain still; her body was too shaky, too wound up to stay seated.

"Just say it."

Luc's harsh words cut through her. Kate stopped pacing, turned and gazed at him. "I'm pregnant."

He stared at her for several moments without saying a word. Then suddenly, he burst out laughing, and straightened.

"Nice try, Kate." His expression sobered. "That's already been used on me."

"What?"

His words took a moment to sink in. He didn't believe her. Of course he wouldn't. Why should he? He'd been played for a fool by his ex-fiancée, who tried the pregnancy trap, and Kate had also lied to him.

"Luc, I'm not lying," she reiterated. "I have the test in my office bathroom. I need to call Dr. Couchot to confirm with a blood test, though."

Something dark clouded Luc's eyes. "You did this on purpose."

Fury rose to the surface, pushing through the nerves. No matter how much she loved him, no matter how much she wished he would see her as a woman worthy of his love and trust, Kate refused to stand here and be degraded and blamed for something they'd both taken part in.

"I think it was you who came to me," she retorted,

crossing her arms over her chest. "You think I wanted a child with a man who doesn't love me? I made a mistake by lying to you, but I'm not pathetic and I'm not trying to trap you. I promised I would always be honest with you, and I just found out about this myself ten minutes ago. So lose the ego. I don't want to snag you that much."

Kate turned to go and managed to get across the room with her hand on the doorknob before Luc grabbed her arm and spun her back around. Leaning flat against the door, trapped between the wood and Luc's hard body, she stared up into those eyes that could make a woman forget all her problems…almost. Even the great Prince Lucas Silva wasn't that powerful.

"You think you can drop that bomb and then just walk out?" he demanded. "We're not done here."

"We both need to process this before we say anything we might regret." Though they'd already said plenty to cause damaging scars. "I just need… I need to think this through, Luc."

His eyes widened. "What's there to think through? You're having my child. I will be part of his or her life."

A sliver of relief coursed through her. "I would never deny you the chance to be with your child."

Tears welled up, the familiar burn in her throat formed and Kate cursed herself. She absolutely hated crying, hated the predicament she was in, but hated even more that she was pulling in an innocent child.

"I'm scared," she whispered, closing her eyes.

She jerked when Luc's hand slid over her cheek. Focusing back on him, she saw something in his eyes she hadn't expected…fear. Obviously, she wasn't the only one with insecurities.

"No matter what happened prior to this moment,

I won't leave you alone with a baby." He dropped his hand, but didn't step back. "Our baby."

When he stood so close, smelling so amazingly familiar and feeling so sexy against her, Kate couldn't think straight. She wished she didn't still want him, wished she'd never lied to him to begin with. And she truly wished something as beautiful as creating a life with the man she loved hadn't been tainted because of her lies.

"I don't want our baby to suffer from my actions," she told him. "I want to be able to work with you on this, and I know the timing—"

She cut herself off with a sad laugh. "Sorry. There would be no good timing," she corrected. "I just meant with the throne, your birthday and all of that on your mind, I didn't mean to add to your stress, but you needed to know."

When he said nothing, Kate carefully turned. There was no way to avoid rubbing up against him, because he'd barely moved since he'd trapped her against the door.

Luc's hands came up to cup her shoulders as he moved in behind her.

"Who are you, Kate?" he whispered.

Her head dropped against the wood as she tried to ignore all of the ways her body responded to his. Tried and failed miserably.

"Are you the efficient assistant? The woman who stands up for me to the public? Are you the woman who lied to me for selfish reasons? Or are you the woman who claims to love me and who's now carrying my child?"

Drawing in a shaky breath, Kate glanced over her shoulder just enough to catch his gaze. "I'm all of them."

"Part of me hates you for what you did." Luc's eyes darted down to her lips. "I wish I still didn't want you so damn much."

Breath caught in Kate's throat as Luc pushed away and stalked back to his desk. He kept his back to her, as if that revelation had cost him dearly. She had no doubt he hadn't meant to let that slip, and as much as she wanted to revel in his obvious discomfort over the fact that he wanted her, Kate had to put this baby first, above all else.

Even the fact that her own heart was still beating for only one man.

Fourteen

He hadn't planned on taking Kate to Greece for his best friend's wedding, but once she had opened her heart to him and bared her soul, Luc wasn't able to deny the fact that he still wanted her.

Plans were taking root in his mind and he was going to have to take action. Perhaps he could have Kate, the crown and his child without ever putting his heart on the line where she was concerned. Surely she'd stay for the sake of their child. Why not make it official, so he could keep the title that was rightfully his?

But if he wanted to sway her into marriage, he needed to start convincing her, or she'd never say yes.

No, he hadn't forgiven her for lying, but she was pregnant, confirmed by Dr. Couchot, and Luc knew the child was his. The plan forming in his mind was anything but nice, but he couldn't back down. Too much was at stake.

Luc glanced across the aisle to where Kate had reclined her seat and was curled onto her side, with her hand beneath her cheek. She'd been exhausted when they'd left that morning, and he'd nearly told her to stay behind, but he knew she was just as stubborn as him and wouldn't listen. Either the baby was making her more tired than usual or she wasn't sleeping because of the stress. Knowing her, it was probably both.

He'd cursed himself every which way after she'd left his office a few days ago. He'd hated how his heart had flipped when she'd whispered her fears. Damn it, he didn't want his heart to be affected by this woman. There was no space in his life for such things. He had a title to secure, and now he had an heir to think about. Kate couldn't fall under the category of things he cared about, because if he allowed that, then she would have the upper hand. Wanting her physically was difficult enough to have to deal with each time she was near.

His mind kept wandering back to how right it had felt when they'd been playing house. He'd gladly dismissed his family's rule about fraternizing with staff. He would have done anything for her. He'd never felt so connected to a woman in all his life.

Kate embodied sex appeal, that was a given. It had been what had drawn him to her when she'd first come to work for him. He vaguely recalled the little girl, and later on the teen, who used to hang around the palace with her parents.

Then when the time came that he'd needed an assistant and Kate had been recommended, he'd jumped at the chance, because her family knew his so well and he knew she'd be a trustworthy candidate. Plus her references and academics had been superb.

Yet somehow, over the course of a professional relationship that had started out with an attraction, and involved his messy engagement to another woman, Luc's life had spiraled spectacularly out of control.

The irony that he'd gone from a fiancée with a fake pregnancy to a poser fiancée with a real pregnancy was not lost on him. He was a walking tabloid and fodder for the press. Thankfully, Kate was in charge of press releases, and no doubt she'd come up with something amazingly brilliant once they were ready to go public.

Kate stirred in her sleep, letting out a soft moan. The simple sound hit his gut with a swift punch of lust he couldn't ignore. He'd heard those moans in his ear as she'd wrapped her body around his. He'd felt the whisper of breath on his skin that accompanied her sighs.

But no matter how compatible they were in the bedroom, no matter how much he still ached for her on a level he'd never admit aloud, Luc wouldn't, couldn't, allow himself to be pulled into whatever spell Kate had over him.

Even if he would let his guard down and shove the royal rule aside and see a staff member personally, Kate had killed any chance of him ever trusting her fully. So she could sit across from him and make all the noises she wanted; he was ignoring them.

Too bad his body hadn't received that memo, because certain parts of him couldn't forget the intimacy they'd shared.

Luc needed to focus on the brilliant plot he'd started forming. Would she be angry when he approached her with the solution? Yes. Did he care? No. He was plenty angry still, but he wanted her, wanted the crown and refused to allow his heart to become vulnerable again.

The phone near Luc's seat rang and the pilot informed him they'd be landing within a half hour. Once

Luc hung up, he crossed the space and sank down in the plush white leather chair next to Kate. He hated waking her up. Not that he was worried about disturbing her sleep; he was more concerned with the fact he'd have to touch her, have to see her blinking back to reality as she sat there, looking all rumpled and sexy.

As if she was ever *not* appealing. But he couldn't be blinded by lust and sexual chemistry. He didn't need a bed partner, no matter what his body told him. Making love with her was how he'd gotten entangled in this web to begin with.

"Kate."

He purposely said her name loudly, so she'd wake without him having to lay a hand on her. She let out a soft snore and Luc gritted his teeth and called her name again.

Still nothing.

Who was he kidding? It didn't matter if he touched her or not. He wanted her, his body responded to her as it had to no other woman and she was carrying his child. As if he needed another reason to be physically pulled toward her. Knowing she was carrying his child was beyond sexy. There was something so primal about knowing Kate sat there with their baby safely inside her body.

Even when Alana had said she was expecting, Luc hadn't felt this much of a tug on his heart. He'd had an instant protective instinct toward the child, but he'd never felt a bond with Alana.

Damn it, he couldn't afford a tug on his heart or some invisible bond. Kate wasn't trustworthy. Regardless, he didn't need her trust for his plan to work. He didn't need anything from her, because he wouldn't take no for an answer.

Marrying Kate was the only solution. As much as he hated to give in to his country's archaic rule, it was the only way to come out of this situation on top. Some marriages were based on far less than sexual chemistry and they worked just fine.

The fact remained that he still wanted her something fierce. He wanted her with an intensity that scared him, but he had to risk his heart, his sanity, in order to get what he wanted.

Luc reached around, pulled on her seat belt and fastened it with a click. Just as he was about to move away and fasten his own, Kate jerked awake. Sleepy eyes locked onto his and he realized his mistake. He'd leaned in too close, so close he was only inches from her face, and his hand hovered over her abdomen.

"What are you doing?" she asked, her voice husky from sleep.

"Preparing you for landing."

Why hadn't he eased back, and why was he staring at her lips?

"You can't look at me like that, Luc," she whispered. "You don't even like me."

Something clenched in his gut. Something harsher, more intense than lust.

He was a damn *tolo*. Fool. That was the only explanation for having these reactions after what she'd done to him. He needed to focus on the plan, the throne, the baby. Everything else—including his lustful feelings—would have to be put aside.

"I don't trust you," he countered. "There's a difference."

Those heavy lids shielded her dark eyes for a moment as she stared down to where his hands lay on her stomach.

"I didn't trap you," she whispered as her eyes drifted back up to his. "No matter what you think of me, I'd never do that to you or an innocent child."

Luc swallowed as her hand settled over his. There was so much emotion in her eyes, so much he was too afraid to identify, because if he did, he'd start feeling more for her, and he refused to be played like a *fantouche*, a puppet, for a third time.

Pride and ego fueled his decisions. Power and control ran a close second. And all those things combined would get him everything he'd ever wanted…everything he was entitled to.

Luc shifted to sit up, but didn't remove his hand, and for some asinine reason he didn't break eye contact, either. Obviously, he was a glutton for punishment.

"I want you to move into the palace."

Of course, he had bigger plans, but he had to ease her into this. She wasn't the only one skilled at manipulation.

"I'm not sure that's a good idea."

She removed her hand from his, a silent plea for him to move, so he pulled back. The first slight dip in the plane's decent reminded Luc he hadn't fastened his seat belt because he'd been worried for her. He quickly buckled it, then turned his attention back to Kate.

"Why not?" he asked. "Moving into the palace is the ideal solution. We'll be sharing responsibilities. I know we'll hire a nanny, but I plan on being a hands-on dad."

Kate shoved her hair away from her face. A thin sleep mark ran down her cheek. It made her seem so vulnerable, and it was all he could do not to touch her again. "What will happen when you want to actually marry someone? Are you going to explain to your bride that your baby mama is living there, too?"

Luc laughed. "That's a pretty crass way to put it."

Kate shrugged, lacing her fingers together as she glanced out the window. "I'm not sugarcoating this situation and neither should you."

Luc didn't say anything else. He would sway her with his actions, not his words. She would come to see that living with him, ultimately marrying him, would be the best way to approach their predicament. And when they married, she would be sleeping in his bed again. He'd make sure of it.

Now he just needed to get his hormones under control, because he was physically aching for her. Being near her now that he'd had her was pure hell. The woman was made for him. Nobody had ever matched him in the bedroom—or shower—the way she did.

Yet Kate was so much more than a sex partner. He'd discovered an emptiness in him now that they were back to keeping things professional. No matter the circumstances surrounding the false engagement, Luc couldn't help but think back and realize those days spent on the island were some of the happiest of his life.

Kate had been to many royal events over the past year as an official employee of the Silva family. Before that, she'd seen enough to know that royalty never did anything halfway, especially when it came to weddings.

The ceremony uniting Darcy and Mikos Alexander had taken place earlier in the day, and now only the couple's closest family and guests, of which there appeared to be several hundred, remained for the reception.

No expense had been spared for the event taking place both in the ballroom and out in the courtyard at the palace on Galini Isle, off the coast of Greece. Every stationary item was draped with something crystal, shimmering or sheer.

As she watched the bride and groom dance, Kate couldn't help but smile. Mikos had lost his first wife suddenly, leaving him to care for their infant daughter alone. Needing a break, he'd gone to Los Angeles to get away and think. He'd hired Darcy to be his daughter's nanny, and before long the two had fallen in love...even though Mikos had slightly deceived Darcy, because she'd had no idea he was royalty. Of course, none of that had made it to the press, but Kate knew the whole story from Luc.

Luc and Mikos had been best friends forever. Kate was quite familiar with Mikos and his brother, Stefan, who was also in attendance, with his stunning wife, Victoria.

Even if the crystal chandeliers, flawless ice sculptures, millions of clear twinkling lights and yards upon yards of sheer draping hadn't screamed elegance and beauty, the gorgeous people milling about certainly would have.

This was definitely one of those times she was thankful her mother was the royal seamstress. By the time Luc had sprung the trip on her, Kate hadn't had time to go shopping. So her mom had taken an old gown and made enough modifications to transform it into something lovely and totally unique. What had once been a simple, fitted silver dress was now unrecognizable. The sleeves had been removed and the top had been cut into a sweetheart neckline to give the allure of sexiness with a slight show of cleavage. Her mother had then had the brilliant idea of taking strands of clear beads and sewing them so they would drape across Kate's arms, as if her straps had fallen and settled just above her biceps.

Kate actually felt beautiful in this dress, and judging from the way Luc had stared at her without saying a word when he'd come to get her for the wedding, she had to assume he thought she looked nice, as well.

She still couldn't get the image out of her mind of him waking her for the landing. He'd been so close, staring at her as if he wanted to touch her, kiss her. Their chemistry wasn't in question, that was obvious, but he clearly battled whether or not to act on it.

Maybe their time apart would have him coming around, to see that she truly wasn't aiming for the crown. She sure as hell wasn't Alana.

Nervously glancing around the room, Kate toyed with the amethyst pendant that hung just above her breasts. She hadn't worn the ring Luc had bought her; that would've just felt wrong. She'd actually placed it in his desk drawer days ago, though she had no clue if he'd found it.

Since Luc had started his best-man duties, she'd pretty much been on her own. That was fine, actually. The more she was around Luc, the harder she was finding it to face the reality that while she was having his baby, he'd never see her as more than a speech writer who happened to be giving him an heir.

Once the evening wound down, perhaps they could talk. She held out hope that he would remember the woman she was before his accident, not the liar she'd turned into for a few short days.

"Champagne, ma'am?"

The waiter, balancing a tray full of flutes of the bubbly drink, smiled at her. Kate shook her head.

"No, thank you."

As soon as he moved on another man approached her. He'd been only a few feet away and she'd seen him a few times during the evening. The tall stranger with tanned skin and black hair was hard to miss, especially when she'd caught him eyeing her more than once. He'd been smiling her way for a while, and now he was closing the gap between them.

"You turned down champagne and you're not dancing," he said in lieu of hello. "One would think you're not having a good time."

Kate smiled, trying to place his accent. Not Greek. Mikos had friends and acquaintances all over the world, so who knew where he was from?

"I'm having a great time," she told him. "It's so beautiful, I'm just taking in all the scenery."

"I've been taking in the scenery, too."

His eyes held hers, and the implication was not lost on her. At one time that line may have worked on her, but she felt absolutely no tingling or giddiness in her stomach when this man approached, blatantly hitting on her. Good thing, because she was certain she didn't have the strength to be tied up with more than one man.

"Would you care to dance?"

Kate glanced around. She hadn't seen Luc for a while, and more than likely he was schmoozing with people he rarely got to see. Besides, it wasn't as if he had a claim on her. He'd pretty much brought her here for one of two reasons: as a lame plan B or to keep an eye on her. Either way, he'd ignored her most of the evening, and she was entitled to some fun, too.

"I'd love to."

Kate slid her hand through the stranger's arm and held on to the crook of his elbow as he led her to the dance floor. When he found an opening, he spun her around until she was in his arms. Kate purposely kept her body from lining up against his as she placed her hand on his shoulder and curled her fingers around his outstretched hand.

"I'm Kate, by the way."

A smile kicked up at the corner of his mouth. "I'm Lars."

"Pleasure to meet you," she said as he turned her in a wide circle. "You're a great dancer."

"I'm actually a professional ballroom dancer." He laughed as he led her into a slower dance when the song changed. "Stick with me tonight and we'll be the envy of all the other couples."

Kate couldn't help but laugh at his blatant ego. "I should tell you, I'm taken."

Well, she wasn't exactly taken, but she was having another man's child, and she was in love with said man, even though he didn't return the feelings. So she felt it necessary to let Lars know he stood no chance with her.

He leaned in closer to whisper into her ear. "Yet he's not here and I am." When he leaned back, his smile remained in place. "Don't worry. I just wanted to dance with the most stunning woman in the room."

"I think that honor goes to the bride," Kate corrected.

Darcy had looked magnificent in a fitted ivory dress with an elegant lace overlay, complete with a lace train that would make any princess envious. Darcy had looked like a character from a fairy-tale romance, and her Prince Charming at the end of the aisle had had nothing but love on his face for his bride.

Would Kate ever find that? Would she ever find a man who looked at her as though there was nothing greater in the world than the fact she lived in it?

"Uh-oh. I'm going to start questioning my skills if you keep frowning."

Kate shook the thoughts away. "Your dance skills

are perfect, though I'm sure you already knew that. I think the jet lag is getting to me."

Not to mention the pregnancy…which she and Luc still hadn't discussed announcing. So for now, she was keeping it to herself. Granted, not many people knew who she was, but the same could not be said for Luc.

Lars opened his mouth to say something, but his eyes darted over Kate's shoulder as he came to a stop.

"It's time to go, Kate."

Turning, she saw Luc standing less than a foot away.

"I'm dancing right now," she commented, not letting go of her partner's hand. "I can find my way back. You go on."

Luc pasted on a deadly smile and glanced at Lars. "I'm sure he will understand. Won't you, Lars?"

The other man merely nodded and stepped back, but not before kissing Kate's hand. "It was truly my pleasure."

Then he disappeared in the crowd of dancers, most likely heading to find another partner. Kate jerked around, clenching her teeth.

"Watch what you say," Luc warned as he took her arm and led her away. "I've got plenty to tell you, too, so save it until we're alone."

"What makes you think I'm going anywhere with you?" she said through gritted teeth. "You can't tell me who to spend time with."

Luc's fingers tightened around her arm as he leaned in closer to her side. "Oh, we're going to be alone, and I'm going to explain to you exactly why that little scene will never happen again."

Fifteen

Luc was seething. He hated like hell that his emotions had overridden common sense, but the second he'd seen Kate dancing with Lars, all rational thoughts had vanished.

The palace was big enough to house the special guests of the bride and groom, so Luc was glad he didn't have to drag Kate too far before he lit into her.

He'd purposely avoided her as much as he could because of her body-hugging dress. That damn gown nearly had him babbling like some horny teen, but he'd somehow managed to keep his tongue in his mouth when he first saw her. Luc knew if he'd stayed too close to Kate this evening, there would be no way to hide his obvious attraction.

And he couldn't let the attraction show, because Kate might try to use that…for what? Wasn't he set on using her?

Only now that he'd seen her in the arms of another man, the game had just changed. Luc wanted her. Right now.

He reached the second floor and headed down the hall to his suite. He had no clue if Kate was deliberately toying with him, but she had him tied in knots he'd never be able to untangle thanks to that little stunt with Lars…a man Luc despised.

"I want to go to my room," she demanded, yanking from his hold as soon as he stopped in front of a set of double doors. "I'm not going in there with you."

Resting his hand on the knob, Luc threw a smirk over his shoulder. "You are."

Kate's eyes narrowed. "No, my room is down the hall."

Before he realized his intentions, he'd pulled her around, wedging her body between his and the door. "Your room is right here until I'm done with you."

"Well, I'm already done talking. You were completely rude down there. You can't just—"

His mouth covered hers. If she was done talking, then he'd find better use for that mouth and ignore all the damn red flags waving around in his mind. He didn't care about all the reasons this was wrong, didn't care that moments ago she'd been in another man's arms. Right now she was in *his* arms, and he was taking full advantage of that lush, curvy body.

Kate's hands came up to his shoulders to push at him, but Luc settled his palms on her hips and pressed against her. Suddenly, her fingertips were curling into his tuxedo jacket.

The feel of her rounded hips beneath her killer dress was just as potent as this steamy kiss. Kate tipped her head slightly, but the silent invitation was all he needed to trace a path with his tongue down the column of her throat.

"Luc," she panted in a whisper. "We're in the hallway."

Gripping her hips, Luc rested his forehead against her collarbone. "You make me crazy, Kate. Out of my mind crazy."

Reaching around her, he opened the door. As soon as they were inside, he closed it, flicked the lock and leaned back against it.

"Did you bring me to your suite to talk or to have sex?" she asked, her arms folded across her beautifully displayed chest. "Because I know what you said, but that episode in the hall has me confused."

Luc remained where he was as he raked a hand down his face. "Lars isn't a good idea." He ignored her narrowed gaze. "Seeing you in his arms... He's a player, Kate."

She held Luc's eyes for a moment before she burst out laughing. "You're kidding me. You interrupt my dance, you manhandle me out of the ballroom and up the steps, and then you attempt to make out with me in the hallway because you're jealous? And you're calling someone else a player?"

"First of all, I'm not jealous." Wow, that almost sounded convincing. "Second, I never manhandled you, and third, you were completely on board with what was going on in the hallway. You moaned."

Kate rolled her eyes and turned to stalk across the open suite. "I did not moan."

Luc didn't know which view was better, the front of Kate's gown with the glimpse of her breasts or the back, where he could fully focus on the perfection of her shape. She stood at the desk, her hands resting on it, her head dropped forward.

"I don't know what you want from me." Her voice was so low he had to move closer to hear. "I won't allow you to pull me all these directions because of your out-of-control emotions, Luc. You know how strongly I feel for you, and yet you continue to torture me."

He was counting on those feelings to get him what he wanted. As much as he hated to admit it, he needed Kate in every way.

Before Luc realized it, he'd completely closed the distance between them. Sliding his hands around her waist, he pressed his palms against her still-flat stomach and jerked her body against his.

"You think you don't torture me?" he asked, his lips brushing the side of her ear. She shivered against him. "You think seeing you dressed like this, moving your body against another man's, isn't pure hell?"

"Why do you care?"

"Because just the thought of you turns me inside out. Because knowing how sexy you are wearing only a smile that I put on your lips turns me on faster than anything."

Luc eased her around and framed her face with his hands. "Because I'm so torn up over what to do about you, all I can think of is getting you out of this damn dress and seeing if this chemistry is real or if it only existed when I thought we were engaged."

Kate's breath caught in her throat as she stared back at him. "I can't sleep with you as an experiment, Luc. I love you." Her voice cracked and her eyes filled with tears. "I'm not hiding how I feel. I can't. But I also can't be used on a whim, whenever you get an itch you need to scratch."

"You're more than an itch."

"What am I?" she whispered.

Luc couldn't put a label to this madness that had become his life. He'd planned on seduction, but he hadn't planned on the jealousy that had speared through him moments ago. Kate was his.

"You're the woman I'm about to put on this desk and strip until she's wearing nothing but that pendant. You're the woman who is going to forget everything else but what's happening right here, right now."

"Sex won't solve anything."

"No, but it will take the edge off for both of us."

Luc leaned closer, rubbing his lips across hers, so slowly. He reached around, found the zipper and eased it down. When the material parted in the back, he splayed his hand across her bare skin, relishing the way she trembled against him.

"Tell me you don't want this," he murmured against her mouth. "Tell me you don't want to see what happens right now between us, and you can walk out that door before we get too far to turn back."

Luc started to peel her dress away from her body. He stepped back just enough for the gown to ease down and puddle at her feet, leaving her standing in a strapless bra and matching panties, and that purple stone that rested against her flawless skin. Trailing his fingertips over the swell of her breasts, Luc smiled when she arched against his touch.

"Say the word, Kate, and I'll stop."

Her eyes closed as she dipped her head back. "You don't play fair."

"Oh, baby, I haven't even begun to play."

She was going to put a stop to this…then Luc had to go and say those words dripping in seduction while he tempted her with just the tips of his fingers. The man was potent. He knew exactly what to do to get her aroused, to get her wanting more.

Why was she letting this happen? He had no intention of professing his love. He wouldn't even give her a straight answer earlier when she'd asked who she was to him.

Yet here she stood, in her heels, her underwear and goose bumps from his touch.

How could she deny him? How could she deny herself? All she wanted was this man, and here he was. If she had even a glimmer of a chance to get him to see how good they were together, she'd take it. Her heart couldn't break any more...could it?

Luc's mouth followed the trail of his fingertips along the tops of her breasts, just over the lacy bra cups. "I'll take your silence as a go-ahead."

Kate slid her fingers into his inky-black hair as she looked down at him. "I can't say no to you."

"I didn't intend to let you."

He crushed her body to his as his mouth claimed hers. Kate shoved his tux jacket off and to the floor. Without breaking contact, she started unbuttoning his shirt. The need to feel his skin next to hers was all-consuming.

Luc wrapped his hands around her waist and lifted her onto the desk. He jerked his shirt off, sending the rest of the buttons popping and scattering across the hardwood floor. The sight of that bare chest, the familiar tattoo and a smattering of chest hair had her heart beating in double time and her body aching.

He stepped between her thighs, encircled her torso with his arms and jerked her to the edge.

"Wrap your legs around me."

His husky demand had her obeying in an instant.

What was it about this man that could have her throwing all common sense aside and practically bowing to his every wish?

Love. That's all it boiled down to. If she didn't love him, if she hadn't been in love with him for some time, she never would've allowed herself to be put in this vulnerable position.

Luc managed to work off her bra and panties with a quick, clever snap and torn material. The fact he was so eager sent warmth spreading through her. She'd made him this reckless, this out of control.

And that right there told her she had the upper hand.

Squeezing her legs tighter against his narrow hips, Kate gripped his head and pulled him down to her mouth. Instantly, he opened, groaning against her. His hands seemed to be everywhere at once. How else could she explain all the shivers, the rippling, the tingling?

"Lean back," he muttered against her lips.

Kate leaned back on the smooth desk, resting her weight on her elbows. When his eyes locked onto hers, the moment he joined them, Kate couldn't help the burn in her throat, the instant tears pricking her eyes. Even though their bond may have started off with a lie, it didn't diminish the fact she loved him. He cared for her more than he let on, too, or they wouldn't be here right now.

Kate shoved aside all worry, all thoughts, and reveled in the moment. Luc was here, with her. He was making love to her in a slow, passionate way that was polar opposite to the frantic way he'd stripped them both moments ago. Did she dare hope he wanted more from her?

Luc leaned over her, kissed her softly and rested his forehead against hers. With Luc's hands gripping her waist, she held on to his shoulders and kept her gaze on him.

Within moments, her body climbed, tightened. Luc muttered something she didn't quite understand. Between the Portuguese and the low whisper, his words were lost. But then his own body stiffened against hers as he squeezed his eyes shut.

Once the tremors ceased, Luc picked her up and carried her to his bed, draped in gold-and-white sheers. He laid her down and slid in beside her, pulling her body against his.

"Sleep." His hands immediately went to her stomach. "Rest for our baby."

Kate closed her eyes, wondering if this blossom of hope in her chest would still be there come morning. Wondering if the man she'd fallen in love with was actually starting to love her back.

Sixteen

Nausea hit her hard. Kate prayed that if she just lay still the queasiness would pass. Until now, she'd had no symptoms of pregnancy, save for the missed period and being tired. Those things she could handle.

As for the man who had put her in this situation in the first place, well, that was another story.

Kate tried to focus on the fact she'd spent the night in Luc's bed, this time with him fully aware of who she was and why she was there. Surely that meant something. Surely they'd crossed some major barrier and things would only get better from here.

Kate wasn't naive, but she was hopeful. She had to be.

But the bed next to her was empty, cool. She sat up, clutching the sheet to her chest. That abrupt movement had her stomach roiling. Bad idea. She closed her eyes and waited for the dizziness to pass before she risked scanning the oversize bedroom for Luc.

He stood near the floor-to-ceiling window, sipping a cup of coffee. His bare back, with bronze skin and dark ink, stared back at her. She didn't want this to be awkward, but she had no idea what to say, how to act. She'd selfishly given in to her desires last night, not thinking of consequences. Well, she had thought of them, but she'd chosen to weigh heavily on the side of optimism.

Her legs shifted beneath the warm satin sheets. Luc glanced over his shoulder at the sound, then focused his attention back on the sunrise. She had to admit the orange sky glowing with radiant beauty was a sight to behold, but was he not going to say anything?

Please, please don't let this be awkward.

Kate eased back against the headboard and tucked the sheet beneath her arms to stay fully covered. Not that he hadn't seen all of her multiple times, but she was getting a vibe that this wasn't going to be a good morning, and the last thing she wanted to do was go into battle fully naked.

"I've been trying to figure out what the hell to do here."

His words sliced right through the beauty of the morning, killing any hope she'd built. His tone wasn't promising. If anything, it was angry, confused.

"I watched you sleep," he went on, still not looking at her. Damn it, why wouldn't he turn around? "I even tried to rest, but there are so many thoughts going around in my mind that I don't even know where to start or what's real."

"Everything that happened in this room last night was real." If nothing else, she wanted, needed, him to realize that. "Did you only bring me here for sex, Luc?"

Speaking her fear aloud had her heart cracking. She

wanted to be strong, she truly did, but there was only so much a woman could take.

"I wanted you." Luc turned to face her, but made no move to cross the room. "I've fought this urge since you came to work for me. I got engaged to another woman knowing full well I wanted you physically. Even after that engagement ended, I still had this ache for you, even though I knew I couldn't act on it."

Kate clutched the sheet as he went on.

"I wasn't in a good spot when we were at the beach house," he continued. "I was an emotional wreck, and I never should've had you come with me, not when I knew just how much I wanted you."

Her eyes darted back to his. "You were angry with me," she reminded him. "Before the accident, you kissed me—"

"I kissed you because I couldn't keep fighting the attraction. I kissed you out of anger toward myself, and then I was even angrier. I was rough with you, so I stomped off like a child."

And then he'd been injured and forgotten everything.

Kate licked her dry lips. "I don't know what to say."

"Honestly, I don't, either." Luc slowly walked toward the bed, coming to stand at the end of it and holding her gaze. "There's part of me that wants to be able to trust you again, but you hurt me, Kate. I never thought that was possible. And that's what had me up all night."

Kate cringed at his harsh words. What could she say? He was right.

"I thought we were going to move past that," she stated, praying the possibility even existed. "You said we'd move on, that we'd have a professional relationship."

Luc's arms stretched wide as he eyed the bed. "Is

this professional? I sure as hell don't feel like your boss right now, Kate. You're having my child, the next heir to the throne after me."

"And is that all I am, then? The mother to the next heir?" She needed more. Even after her lies, she deserved to know. "Are you using my feelings against me? You know how I feel, and you got so jealous last night. Was that all to stroke your ego or to puff your chest out because you're in control?"

Luc propped his hands on his narrow hips as he stared down at her. He'd put on his black tuxedo pants, but hadn't buttoned them. It was hard to sit here and discuss all of this with him half-dressed and her wearing a sheet, but Kate had her pride, and she refused to give in to her body's needs. She didn't need Luc; she wanted him. Yes, it hurt to know he didn't feel the same, but she wasn't going to beg…ever.

His silence was deafening. Kate shook her hair away from her face. The nausea hadn't lessened; if anything, she felt worse. She placed a hand beside her hip on the bed, closed her eyes and took a deep breath.

"Kate?"

The mattress dipped beside her. When Luc grabbed her hand, she pulled back. "No." She met his worried gaze. "I'm not playing the pregnancy card for your sympathy and attention. You don't get to pick and choose when it's convenient to show affection."

"You're pale. Are you all right?"

If only he would have cared first thing this morning instead of starting this day with voicing his doubts and crushing her hopes.

"I'm dizzy. It's to be expected." She shifted, scooting a bit farther away from him. "I'm not going to be pulled in different directions depending on your moods, either. You either want me, on a personal level and not just for sex, or you don't. If my dancing with some guy bothers you, then maybe you need to reevaluate your feelings. But don't come to me again unless you're sure I'm more than just a warm body to you."

Slowly, Luc came to his feet and nodded. "I plan on having you, Kate. I plan on marrying you, actually. You'll become my wife before my birthday. I'll secure the title and you'll get to live out whatever fantasy you had when you wanted to play the engaged couple."

"What?" Shock replaced her nausea instantly. "I'm not marrying you just so you can get a title. I want to marry for love."

Luc's eyes narrowed. "You say you love me, so why not marry me?"

"Because you don't love me. I won't be used as a pawn in your royal quest."

Air whooshed from her lungs. She'd never thought herself naive, but that's exactly what she was. She should've gone into this with eyes wide-open and seen his motivations for what they were…lust and greed. Any love between them was absolutely one-sided, and she had no one to blame but herself…yet again.

She should've seen this coming, should've known nothing would ever get in the way of the great Luc Silva and his crown. The man she'd grown to love from the island was just as fake as their engagement. Then, he'd been warm, open. Now he was all business.

"I'm going back to the palace as soon as I get my stuff together," she told him. "I'll have the pilot come back whenever you want to leave, but I won't be flying with you. I also won't be working for you. I'll finish out my duties for the next couple of weeks, but after that, I'm done."

"As my wife, I wouldn't expect you to work for me."

Kate clenched her teeth, praying she didn't burst into angry tears. "I won't be your wife."

Luc shoved his hands in his pockets, hesitated, then made his way to the door. "Don't make any hasty decisions. I'll leave you to get your dress back on."

Then he was gone, leaving only the deafening sound of the door clicking shut as she sat there in the rumpled sheets.

That was it? Luc may have walked out of this conversation, but he wasn't going to back down on this ridiculous notion of them getting married. Kate needed to prepare herself, because this fight was just getting started.

She tossed back the sheet and was thankful she wasn't dizzy when she got to her feet. At least she had one thing going for her this morning.

Of course, now she had to put on her dress from last night and do the walk of shame down the wide, long hallway to her own suite, to change and pack. Which was fine, because she wasn't staying any longer. If he planned on using her, using her feelings against her in some ploy to get ahead, then maybe he wasn't the man she loved at all. Maybe she'd been living a lie this entire time…

There was no way she could continue working for Luc indefinitely. No way she could look at him every single day and know she was good enough for sex, but not good enough to build a life with if the throne wasn't at stake. They'd made a baby and he still was only looking out for his title. Well, she sure as hell wasn't sticking around to see him parade his possible future wives in and out of his life.

Kate had been a fool to think their intimacy had

changed Luc's mind. The struggle of seeing him every day, knowing he didn't return her love, would be just too hurtful.

When she returned to the palace, she would call her parents and make plans. She would finish up the projects she and Luc had begun, and then she needed to get away. She needed to focus on what was truly important in her life.

Luc brought the sledgehammer up and swung it through the partial non-load-bearing wall. Busting this drywall to expand the living space with the kitchen wasn't even remotely helping to quell his frustration and anger. All he was doing was working up a good sweat and a bit of nostalgia from when he and Kate had torn into the bathroom.

When Luc had gotten back to the palace, he'd taken his boat—sans guards, much to Kate's father's disapproval—and headed to his beach house. Luc knew the workers would be done for the day, and since the house was only an hour from the palace, he needed time to think, to reflect on what an insufferable jerk he'd been in that bedroom three days ago.

His intention had been to get Kate to agree to marry him. He hadn't cared about her feelings. But the way she'd sat there, all rumpled in a mess of satin sheets, as she'd stared up at him with hurt in her eyes, had seriously gotten to him. He hadn't expected to feel anything beyond want and need for her. Yet it was hard to ignore the constant lump of guilt that kept creeping up when he thought of how he'd broken her so fast, with so few words.

Luc eased the sledgehammer down on the rubble and wiped his arm across his forehead. His mother would probably die if she saw he had blisters on his hands from manual labor, but he needed the outlet. Unfortunately, it wasn't doing the job.

And it didn't help that Kate was everywhere in this house. The empty yellow vase on the scarred dining table mocked him. He couldn't even look at the damn shower in his master suite. The balcony, the chaise in the living room, the bed, the beach… The memories flooded his mind. She'd touched literally every surface here.

Just as she'd touched every part of him.

Luc reached behind his neck and yanked his T-shirt over his head. His cell vibrated in his pocket and he thought about ignoring it, but with Kate being pregnant, he had to be on full alert.

Pulling the cell out, he glanced at the screen. Swallowing a curse, he let out a sigh and answered.

"Yes?"

"You rushed out of here and didn't take a guard?"

His mother's question didn't require an answer, because she already knew. "I needed to be alone."

"That's not smart. You can't be taking off like this, Lucas. You know your birthday is less than two months away. You need to be home so we can figure out what we're going to do."

Luc raked a hand over his damp face and stared out at the sun, which was starting to dip toward the horizon.

"I just needed a few days to myself."

"Is this about Kate? Darling, I know she hurt you, but that poor girl is miserable. I didn't want to say anything, but since the wedding she's been looking pale and drained."

Luc straightened. "Is she sick?"

"I'd guess she's pregnant."

Silence filled the line and Luc's heart sank. They hadn't said a word to anybody, and the pain in his mother's tone came through loud and clear.

"We haven't told anyone," Luc stated in a low voice, suddenly feeling like a kid again for lying to his mother. "She just found out before the wedding, and we had a bit of a fight. Is she okay?"

"A fight?" Of course his mom honed in on that and not his question. "Lucas, the woman is carrying your child and you argue with her? No wonder she looks exhausted. She's been working like a dog since she got back. That's why I wanted to know why you left the palace so suddenly."

Luc gripped the phone. "It's best if I'm not there right now."

"I think you two need to talk. If you're worried about the no-fraternizing rule, I think we can make an exception for Kate. Maybe she's the answer to—"

"I've already thought of that," he interrupted, cutting her off. "Kate doesn't want to marry me."

"Why don't you come home," his mother stated. "We can't solve any problems with you brooding alone."

He glanced at the mess he'd made. It wasn't as if he knew what to do next, but the contractors had done an amazing job of renovating the bathroom he and Kate had torn into. They'd come to finish the kitchen once Luc gave the go-ahead after this wall was gone.

"I'm leaving now," he told his mother. "Tell Kate I want to see her."

"I'll see what I can do, but she may have left for the day."

If she'd left, he'd go to her place. She didn't live too far from the palace, and if he had any say, she'd be inside that palace by the time their baby came.

Anything else was unacceptable.

Having her that last time had changed something in him, and nearly changed his marriage plan. That's why he'd been up all night, second-guessing his motives. He'd thought he could check out emotionally, but he felt too much—guilt, desire...more.

He'd hurt her in ways he'd never, ever imagined he could. Yet she still did her job. She'd still come with him to the wedding. She still supported him.

And he loved her. His feelings were as simple and as complicated as that. He loved Kate with everything he had and he'd messed up—man, had he messed up.

Luc needed to tell her how he felt. More important, he needed to show her. Saying the words was easy; proving to Kate how much she meant to him would be the hurdle. But he hadn't gone through all of this to give up now. Kate was his and he damn well wasn't going to let her go.

Seventeen

It had been nearly a week since he'd last talked to Kate, and he was going out of his mind.

He'd come back to his office and found a letter of resignation on his desk. She'd left a message through her mother that she was fine and the baby was fine, but she wanted to be on her own for a bit.

A bit was longer than he could stand.

He'd lived without this woman for too long and refused to live that way another second.

His birthday was fast approaching, but even the looming date hadn't entered his mind. For the past few days all that had played over and over was how stupid he'd been, how heartless and crass he'd been with his words, his actions. No wonder Kate wanted to leave, to steer clear of him. She loved him and he'd proposed to her with the pretense that he was doing so only to climb higher on the royal ladder.

He hadn't needed much time after their last night together to realize walking away had been a mistake. Letting her believe he wanted her only for the crown was wrong.

Luc wanted Kate because she made him whole.

It had taken him some time to get the information on her whereabouts from her parents, and to have the construction crew finish some of the renovations on his beach home. He'd pulled some strings to get her here, but he wanted this to be perfect when he finally revealed the house and his true feelings. Nothing but the best for Kate from here on out.

He'd taken that extra time to find out more about the woman he loved. And he hoped the surprise he'd planned would help her understand just how much he wanted her in his life.

Luc stood in the living room watching the water, waiting for that familiar boat to dock. He'd recruited the help of Kate's parents. Of course, in order to do that, he'd had to pull out all the stops and really grovel to them. If everything worked out the way he'd hoped, every ego-bursting, pride-crushing moment would be worth it.

When the boat finally came into view, Luc's nerves really kicked into gear. He might have planned every bit of this evening, but Kate ultimately held all the power and control.

Her father helped her up onto the dock, leaned forward for a hug and watched as Kate mounted the steps. Luc moved to the doorway and waved as the man began to pull the boat away from the berth.

By the time Kate got to the top of the steps, Luc's heart was beating faster than ever. She lifted her head, pushing her windblown hair away from her face. The second her eyes locked onto his, Luc felt that familiar punch to his gut. The punch that said if she turned him down he would be absolutely crushed and broken.

"I was hoping you wouldn't put up a fight," he told her, remaining in the doorway.

"I was tempted to jump overboard a couple of times, but I knew my dad would only go in after me." She clasped her hands together and remained still. "What am I doing here, Luc, and why am I being held hostage?"

"You're not a hostage," he countered.

She glanced over her shoulder before looking back. "My father left with the boat and the only other one here is yours. By my accounts, I'm here with no way out except with your permission."

"Come inside."

Her brow quirked as she crossed her arms over her chest…a chest that was more voluptuous than when he'd seen her last.

"Please," he added, when she didn't move. "Please come inside so we can talk."

Finally, she moved forward, and Luc let her pass him and enter first. The familiar, floral scent teased his senses and mocked him. He'd lain awake at night imagining that scent, pretending she was by his side.

"Oh, Luc."

Her gasp was enough to have him smiling. "Looks a little different, doesn't it?"

He watched her survey the newly designed, open floor plan. Thick columns stood as support beams, but they didn't take away from the romantic ambience, they merely added to it. He'd left the back wall of patio doors open, to put the Mediterranean on full display.

"It's gorgeous," she exclaimed, running her hand along the marble-topped table behind the sofa. "This was all done so fast."

"I wanted it done before I invited you back." He remained in the doorway, but kept his eyes on her as she walked through the living area and kitchen. "I even helped the contractors and learned how to do more than tear things down."

She stopped by the old dining table and her eyes landed on the yellow vase, then darted across the room to him.

"I couldn't get rid of either of those," he told her. "We shared too many meals at that table, and even though it's not new, it reminds me of you. Every time I see that vase I think of how excited you were that day at the market."

She picked up the vase, running her hands around it. For a moment Luc worried she might launch it at his head, but she finally set it down and turned back to face him. With her arms crossed over her midsection, she let out a sigh.

"What do you want, Luc?"

Her eyes held his. Now that they were face-to-face, he couldn't deny the force that hovered between them.

"Are you feeling okay?" he asked, taking slow, cautious steps toward her. "Everything all right with our baby?"

"We're both doing great," she informed him. "And you could've texted or called or replied to the emails I sent."

"You sent final work emails through your father."

She nodded. "That's because I quit, remember? I've outlined your next year of engagements. I'm assuming you came up with a way to secure your title? Is that why you can bother with me now?"

"No. I didn't secure the title."

Kate gasped. "Your birthday is only weeks away."

"I'm aware of that." He stood directly in front of her, so close she had to tip her head up to look him in the eyes. "That's why you're here."

Her lips thinned as she narrowed her gaze at him. "You've got to be kidding me. You brought me here to use me? You still think I'm going to swoon, fall at your feet and marry you so you can get a shiny new crown?"

Just as she started to push past him, Luc grabbed her arm and halted her escape. "No. I think you're going to listen to me and look in my eyes when I tell you how much I love you."

Those dark eyes held his, but he saw no emotion there.

"Did you hear me?"

"I hear you just fine," she said through clenched teeth. "How convenient that you love me right before you're set to lose it all if you don't have a wife."

He turned to face her fully as he gripped both her bare shoulders. "You and these damn sexy strapless dresses," he muttered, stroking her skin with his thumbs. "Cause me to forget the powerful speech I was about to make. I'm pretty proud, considering it's the first one I've had to write for myself."

"I don't want to hear your speech and I don't want you touching me."

Luc smiled. "Then why is the pulse at the base of your neck pounding as fast as my heart? You may lie to yourself, Kate, but your body is telling me the truth."

Her eyes widened. "Oh, no. You brought me here for sex? You think I'll fall back into bed with you and then, in the throes of passion, agree to a marriage?"

Luc laughed, then kissed her full on the mouth before easing back. "Your imagination is running away with you and I'm royally screwing this up."

"That's the only thing that's getting screwed tonight."

His heart was so full, he couldn't help but keep smiling. "I've missed that smart mouth."

Kate didn't say a word, didn't move and didn't make any attempt to touch him.

"Tell me I didn't mess things up so badly that I've lost you forever."

"You never fully had me," she told him. "I wanted everything with you, but went about it the wrong way. Then you decided to use my love and try to force me into marriage. That's no foundation to build a relationship on."

"We both messed up," he agreed. "I never meant to hurt you, but I was so confused. I wanted to trust my feelings, but how could I when I couldn't even trust you? I thought if you wanted me so badly, you'd marry me and I'd get the title. I didn't realize you truly had no ulterior motive."

"I understand why you couldn't trust me." She reached up, wrapped her hands around his wrists and pulled his hands off her shoulders. "What I can't understand is why you used my feelings against me, why you made love to me at Mikos's wedding and then acted like you had no clue where to slot me in your life."

Luc shoved his hands in his pockets. She didn't want to be touched, and right now he was dying to have her in his arms. This was going to be trickier than he'd thought, but he wasn't giving up. She'd come, she was talking to him and that had to mean a lot.

"I have something to show you."

He walked to the desk tucked in the corner of the room and grabbed the email he'd printed out. When he handed it to her, she didn't take it.

"Please?"

Kate slid the paper from his grasp. Luc watched her face as she read. When her eyes filled with tears, her hand came up to cover her quivering chin and her lips, Luc knew she wasn't completely lost to him.

She clutched the letter to her chest. "You went to the orphanage?"

"I did." And he'd loved every minute of it. "I met Carly and Thomas. I was told they were friends of yours."

Kate nodded, the jerky movement causing a tear to spill. "I love those two so much. They are such sweet kids, but most people want to adopt new babies. The twins are nine, but they have such big hearts and they say they want the babies to go to new homes. Still, I know they long for a set of parents to love them."

"I was told it's hard, too, because most people are only looking to adopt one," he added.

"I try to get there to visit them as often as I can," she said, swiping at her eyes. "I call them if I get too busy working and can't make it."

"They're at the orphanage you were living in as a baby." Luc cupped her damp face. "And that's why they are so important to you. I can completely see why you wanted me to go visit. Those little kids thought talking to a real prince was so neat. I didn't talk much about the royalty side of my life with Carly and Thomas, but we did discuss Portuguese culture, and they were so fascinated."

"I can't believe you went and didn't tell me," she exclaimed.

"Actually, we just missed each other. When I arrived, I was told you had left the day before."

Kate's eyes widened. "I wish I'd known."

"Why, Kate? Would you have stayed there? Would you have waited for me?"

She shook her head. "I—I don't know."

"I want to start over with you." That sounded so

lame he laughed. "I've been miserable without you and I went to that orphanage not because you kept asking me to, but because I wanted to know more about you. I wanted to know more about the woman I had fallen in love with. I love you, Kate. I want a life with you, a life just like the one we had when we were all alone here."

Kate closed her eyes as her body fell into his. Her forehead rested against his chest. "You don't mean all of that," she whispered. "Because if you even think I can just try this out, or be with you because of some tradition, you're wrong."

When she lifted her head, Luc smoothed her hair away from her damp cheeks. "I don't want to try it, Kate. I want to do it. My calling you here has nothing to do with the throne, my birthday or the baby. I mean, I want to build a family with you, but I'm not using the baby to do so. I want you for you. The days we spent here were some of the best of my life. I want more days like that, and nobody else will do. You're it for me, Kate."

When her mouth parted in another gasp, he kissed her. Luc nipped at her lips and nearly cried when she responded and opened for him.

The gentle, tender kiss had that sliver of hope in his chest practically exploding now.

"I missed you," he murmured against her lips. "I missed holding you, I missed watching you cook, I missed seeing you smile, and even arguing with you over stupid things like my schedule. I missed seeing you wearing my ring."

Her brows drew in as Luc pulled the amethyst ring from his pocket.

"Você vai casar comigo?" he asked.

Will you marry me?

"Not because of the throne, not because of anything else but us," he quickly said, before she got the wrong idea of his intentions. "I can feel utter fullness and love only with you, Kate. You're the only one who can make me complete."

Without waiting for her reply, he slid the ring onto her finger and gripped her hand in his. "This is where the ring belongs, until I can get you a diamond or whatever you want."

Kate stared down at her hand and said nothing. She studied the ring, even toyed with it before she smiled up at him. "I don't want another ring. I want this one. It's exactly what I would have chosen, and I don't need anything more."

"Does this mean you'll marry me?" he asked.

Kate threw her arms around his neck, buried her face against his skin and squeezed him tight. "I'll marry you, Luc. I'll raise babies with you and grow old with you."

Luc crushed her body to his and let out the first good breath he'd had since she stepped into his house. No, their house.

Kate jerked back. "Wait. We need to marry soon. Your birthday—"

"It will be fine. My father may have rigged the law a tad to buy us a few extra weeks. I want to give you the wedding you deserve."

"I don't want a huge, highly publicized wedding. Is that okay?"

Luc framed her face, sliding his thumb across her full bottom lip. "Perfectly fine with me. But right now I'd rather have you in my shower, where I can properly show you how much I've missed you."

"I do love that shower of yours."

He kissed her smile. "After I make love to you, we

can discuss the wedding. Oh, and the fact I'd like to adopt Carly and Thomas. I wanted to talk to you first. With the new baby and all I wasn't sure—"

Kate's mouth cut him off as she rained kisses all over his lips, his chin, his cheeks. "Yes, yes, yes. I'd love to have them with me. I love those two so much. I just felt such a connection the first time I saw them."

"I did, too, honey." Luc picked her up and headed toward the master suite. "We'll discuss that later, too."

"You can't carry me," she cried. "I've gained weight."

His eyes dipped to her chest. "I've noticed, and I'm certainly not complaining."

She slapped his shoulder. "That's so typical of a man, to say that when bigger boobs are involved."

"There better never be another man eyeing your boobs," he scolded. "That's my job."

Kate's head fell against his shoulder as she laced her fingers together behind his neck. "Always, Luc. You're the only man for me."

* * * * *

If you loved this royal hero from
Jules Bennett
pick up her other royal novels

BEHIND PALACE DOORS
WHAT THE PRINCE WANTS

**Don't miss Sarah Morgan's
next Puffin Island story**

Some Kind of Wonderful

Brittany Forrest has stayed away from Puffin Island
since her relationship with Zach Flynn went bad.
They were married for ten days and only just
managed not to kill each other by the
end of the honeymoon.

But, when a broken arm means she must return,
Brittany moves back to her Puffin Island home.
Only to discover that Zac is there as well.

Will a summer together help two lovers reunite or
will their stormy relationship crash on to the
rocks of Puffin Island?

Some Kind of Wonderful
COMING JULY 2015
Pre-order your copy today

0315/MB507

Join our *EXCLUSIVE* eBook club

FROM JUST £1.99 A MONTH!

Never miss a book again with our hassle-free eBook subscription.

★ Pick how many titles you want from each series with our flexible subscription

★ Your titles are delivered to your device on the first of every month

★ Zero risk, zero obligation!

There really is nothing standing in the way of you and your favourite books!

Start your eBook subscription today at www.millsandboon.co.uk/subscribe

MILLS & BOON®

Desire™

PASSIONATE AND DRAMATIC LOVE STORIES

A sneak peek at next month's titles...

In stores from 17th July 2015:

- **Second Chance with the Billionaire** – Janice Maynard
  and **The Princess and the Player** – Kat Cantrell

- **Demanding His Brother's Heirs** – Michelle Celmer
  and **Having Her Boss's Baby** – Maureen Child

- **A Royal Baby Surprise** – Cat Schield
  and **That Night with the CEO** – Karen Booth

Available at WHSmith, Tesco, Asda, Eason, Amazon and Apple

Just can't wait?
Buy our books online a month before they hit the shops!
visit www.millsandboon.co.uk

These books are also available in eBook format!